John Williams was born in Cardiff in 1961. He wrote a punk fanzine and played in bands before moving to London and becoming a journalist, writing for everyone from *The Face* to the *Financial Times*. Following *Into the Badlands*, his book *Bloody Valentine*, about the Lynette White murder case in the Cardiff docks, provoked a libel action from the police. His novels include the London-set *Faithless*, and *The Cardiff Trilogy*. He now lives in Cardiff with his family.

Back to the badlands
Crime writing in the USA

John Williams

A complete catalogue record for this book can
be obtained from the British Library on request

First published in 2007 by Serpent's Tail,
4 Blackstock Mews, London N4 2BT
website: www.serpentstail.com

ISBN: 1 85242 921 6
ISBN-13: 978 1 85242 921 8

Designed and typeset at Neuadd Bwll, Llanwrtyd Wells

Printed in Great Britain by Mackays of Chatham, plc

10 9 8 7 6 5 4 3 2

Contents

Acknowledgements

FROM THE FIRST time round I would like to thank: Sandhya Ellis for her friendship and support throughout; Nick Kimberley, Chris Render, Kevin Allerton, Pete Webb, Paul Hammond and Liz Young for sharing their knowledge and insight; my various editors, including Sheryl Garratt, Dylan Jones, Kimberley Leston, Nick Logan and Sean O'Hagan for helping me make a living out of writing; everyone whose hospitality I enjoyed while travelling around the States, particularly Marcia Pilliciotti in Detroit, Lee Esbenshade in Los Angeles and Sarah Edkins in New York; my agent Anne McDermid and my editor Ian Paten for the work they put into this; the writers themselves for giving me their time; my parents for their belief and support; and my wife Charlotte Greig for everything.

Second time around I would like to offer additional thanks to my agent Abner Stein, my editor and publisher Pete Ayrton and the rest of the crew at Serpent's Tail, and to everyone I met on the road this time out, in particular Tracy Quan and Sarah Weinman in New York, Terrill Lankford in Los Angeles and Jesse Sublett in Austin.

Finally, I would like to mourn the fact that no less than four of the people mentioned in my acknowledgments for *Into the Badlands* are no longer with us. Mike Hart, Pete Webb, Liz Young and Kimberley Leston: all gone, not forgotten.

For Charlotte, then and now

Introductory note

THIS BOOK IS in two parts. The first part consists of an abridged version of my original book on American crime fiction, *Into The Badlands*, published in 1991. The second part consists of new material written in 2005/6.

Introduction to the first edition: 1989

I WROTE THIS book because I wanted to go to America. I wrote about crime writers because it is largely down to them that I wanted to go to America. It seems to me that crime writers are the best chroniclers of American society as it is today, and yet they are routinely ignored or patronised by the arbiters of literature – not just in patrician Britain, but in the US too. Europeans propagate the myth that America has no culture, and Americans tend to believe them. Those Americans that can afford to are forever coming to Europe in search of culture: suggest to the average New Yorker that there might be culture to be had in Texas, and they'll laugh out loud. So onward they'll proceed to visit the great museums of Europe, paying tribute to a culture in its death throes, and leaving it up to crazy people from Europe and Japan to identify *le film noir*, to worship Charlie Parker, to reprint the novels of Jim Thompson, and to make the pilgrimages to the many birthplaces of American music, whether Sun Records studios in Memphis or the cajun dance halls of Louisiana. American culture is seen as not measuring up to the great traditions of European culture, its newness viewed as déclassé rather than vital; and it is constantly undervalued for the reason, ultimately, that it is not dead.

The one area of cultural activity in which American innovation is grudgingly recognised – with the very debatable exception of cinema – is popular music. And it's through music that I came to crime fiction. In the early 1980s, in the aftermath of punk, I was working in a record shop and, like a lot of other people, I started listening to the rootsier forms of American popular music: soul, country, gospel, doo-wop, cajun. All of which seemed to have in common a directness of approach and a depth of feeling that were absent from the vast majority of rock music, which I began to see as shallow, merely clever, emotionally withheld. Meanwhile, during my early twenties, I fancied myself something of a reader; this meant that I would consume, at a rate of approximately one every three months, a book by the novelist of the moment: Salman Rushdie, Milan Kundera… global Booker Prize types. I would read about these books, faithfully buy them, but only ever get about halfway through, admiring their wit and elegance and being too embarrassed to admit boredom.

Then came Elmore. For once, when I went into the bookshop across the road from where I worked, I asked for some advice, and the assistant placed an imported Elmore Leonard paperback in front of me. And there it was: the America of Stax and Motown, George Jones and Grover Washington Jr, present in fiction as it simply is not in the work of the major American moderns – Updike or Tyler or Bellow, all of whom seem possessed by the idea that it is the duty of an American writer to render the American experience into English literature.

Even when American literary figures are concerned with the working population they tend either to dwell on the past – Doctorow, Kennedy, Alice Walker even – or to write about 'ordinary people' as if they were zoological specimens under a microscope – Raymond Carver, Richard Ford, et al. In contrast, the best American crime writers display an involvement with their characters: they are not simply writing about people, they have a close relationship with them, born, if nothing else, out of the demands of writing for a mass audience, not a literary one. Out of which comes the fact that they are, by and large, more politically engaged than the mainstream; crime, after all, demands a political response.

Which also may contribute to its neglect; political and popular culture – from Mayakovsky to Billie Holiday – tends to be appreciated only in retrospect. Once again this is particularly clear in the instance of popular music. Old soul or country artists, Otis Redding or Patsy Cline, are deemed to be 'legends' while new artists are ignored. Likewise Hammett and Chandler are considered greats, while contemporary writers such as James Crumley or James Ellroy are by and large ignored. And this seems symptomatic of a wider ill: there is something particularly depressing in the spectacle of the US beginning to fetishise its recent past. It's a sign that this is no longer a culture at least united in one dream of advancement. The have-nots are still making something new, the hip-hop culture of the streets. The haves are looking back fondly at the '50s, the time, not coincidentally, before civil rights, before Vietnam, a mythical Ronald Reagan time of white picket fences, Jimmy Stewart and the *Dick Van Dyke Show*. Out of the tensions these discrepancies provoke comes crime on a new scale. And as a corollary, the necessity for any writing about America today to deal with such crime.

One thing led to another. I read Elmore Leonard's *Stick* faster than I'd read a book in years. I read whatever else of Leonard's I could find, discovered or was introduced to other contemporary writers – George V. Higgins, James Crumley, Ross Thomas, Charles Willeford; discovered also – once again in common with a lot of other people – the forgotten noir writers of the '30s, '40s, '50s, even '60s: Jim Thompson, David Goodis, Horace McCoy, Charles Williams; discovered originals like Chester Himes or Patricia Highsmith. I started writing about these books, and got published because too few other people were paying attention.

And, back to where I started, I wrote this book because

reading Elmore Leonard made me want to go to Miami Beach, reading James Crumley made me want to go to Montana, reading Sara Paretsky made me want to go to Chicago. And so on. Not that they portrayed these places as necessarily lovely, but because they portrayed them always as alive. And I wanted to write a book that would convey something of why I liked these writers. I knew what I didn't want such a book to be – a work of apologist literary criticism ('actually some of these crime writer types are nearly as good as real writers...'), an absurdly patronising tack, as if novelists are not all engaged in the identical business of making fictions. As far as casting literary bouquets goes, it'll do for me to say that a good writer is one you want to read.

What follows is not literary criticism. I may point out bad books that a writer has produced, but in general it'll have to be taken as read that these are writers I admire. Instead what I have attempted to do is give some idea of their America. It has become the cliché in reviewing these books to commend them for their sense of place. I figured that if James Ellroy gives you a good sense of Los Angeles, and Tony Hillerman of Navajo country, then maybe if you put a selection of writers together, they'll give you a sense of America...So I decided to find out.

What follows is the result of that finding out: two months spent circling America with the aid of a flight pass and a series of rental cars, radios tuned into soul and country stations, staying in what seemed like one endless motel room, equipped always with the same TV set showing the same out-of-focus cable channels, fuelled on the best breakfasts and the worst beers I've ever encountered, talking to crime writers along the way.

Introduction to the second edition: 2006

AND SIXTEEN YEARS later I went back. The original book, *Into the Badlands*, had been out of print for a decade and now and again people would ask me about doing a new edition. Finally enough time had passed for this to seem like an interesting project. The question was how to go about it. Should I go back and revisit all the original writers? I considered doing that, and then decided against it on the grounds that, apart from anything else, two of them were dead (George V. Higgins and Eugene Izzi), and one (Joseph Koenig) had more or less vanished.

So, if I wasn't going to literally go back to where I'd been before, what was I going to do? I thought about focusing on the emerging generation of US crime writers – people like Jason Starr, A. N. Smith and Dave Zeltserman – but something in me baulked at the prospect of writing about novelists newer to the game than I am myself. Then I realised that there were actually a bunch of writers who I had, for one reason or another, missed out on talking to last time around, or who had emerged in the years immediately after the first book came out.

The original *Into the Badlands* was essentially a portrait of a generation of writers, the post-Vietnam generation if you like, and I decided to complete that portrait by adding some previously missing faces. So I drew up a wish list of ten or so writers I wanted to talk to, cross-referenced that with a list of places I wanted to go to and hadn't visited last time, and came up with a final list of five. Five writers and five places. George Pelecanos, Vicki Hendricks, Kem Nunn, Kinky Friedman and Daniel Woodrell. From Hollywood Beach to Huntington Beach, from the nation's capital to its forgotten Ozark heartland.

Thanks to the Internet, which hadn't been invented last time around, organising the trip this time was a cinch. So here it is, the product of a month spent circling America on a series of new-fangled low-cost airlines and the same old-style rental cars, listening to country and hip-hop stations, staying in what still seemed to be the same identical endless motel room, but this time I drank some great beer and ate some lousy breakfasts. Go figure, as they didn't say back in 1989.

Part one

1989

1   Miami: the city that coke built

THE CAB DRIVER didn't want to go to South Beach. 'This car don't speak Spanish', is how he put it. That's the way the day was shaping up. The hotel I'd booked had never heard of me or my reservation when I called up from Miami/Fort Lauderdale Airport either. Having no idea where else to go, though, I persuaded the guy that seeing as we were already in his cab, and halfway there, he might as well keep going and take me to whatever street had the most hotels – at least test his theory that South Beach was not where I wanted to be. So at this point talkative, six-foot, sandy-haired Burt stops telling me about the time he spent in London when he was in the forces and confines himself to grimly pointing out salubrious North Beach hotels that would provoke any decent tourist to exchange a couple a hundred dollars for a room. 'I hope y'all like Spanish people', he says darkly, and slumps into resignation, barely cheered by the meter's upward progress.

Miami Beach turns out to be a long thin island reclaimed from the sea and running north south in parallel to the city itself, like a densely populated offshore reef protecting the city from the ocean. It's connected to the city proper by a series of causeways. The main drag is called Collins Avenue, the one link between toney North Beach with its country clubs and private housing estates and the sleazy South Beach, sometime Crime Capital of the USA.

North Beach, round about Bal Harbour, is mostly boring, the kind of place where Frank and Dean and Sammy and Liza may show for a winter engagement at the Fontainebleu Hilton; not so much a family resort as a place for rich people to keep warm in winter. The hotels, with the exception of the old guard like the spectacularly swanky Fontainebleu, are mostly bland modern, as are North Beach's latest developments, the endless condos, well-guarded apartment blocks thrown up by Miami's building boom.

South Beach really starts when you get down to Collins Park at Collins and 22nd Street. We stop at a hotel a couple of blocks farther down. I go in, leaving the door open, and ask for a room, talk to a bearded guy in shorts who says he's full but try another hotel a block back. I go back to the car and tell Burt. Who gets immediately, and bizarrely, mad. Jumps out of the car and accosts the guy. 'How come you're full! This guy's come all the way from England! What do you mean you're full, asshole!'...About to explode, he gets back in the car. I attempt to explain that I want to try a hotel one block behind us. Burt refuses to grasp this and shoots off in the wrong direction. I tell him to turn around, my voice rising to a kind of nervous near-shriek. Reluctantly he hangs a right and circles back a couple of blocks, belatedly delivering us at hotel number two. This time I jump out and, my mistake, shut the door behind me. It takes less that a minute to run in and secure a room, which is fortunate as, when I come back out on the street, the cab is starting to edge along the kerb with my worldly goods securely inside. I run up to the car and pull the door open, gabbling, 'Yeah, great, I've got a room, how much do I owe you, thanks, bye.' Burt refuses to be rushed, opens the trunk, pulls out the bags and looks disgustedly at the Latinate cast of the guy running the hotel; then he gets back in the car and burns rubber. Welcome to Miami Beach.

This of course is too good to be true. Arrive in Florida and the first person you meet is the prototype Florida psychopath.

Sitting down in the hotel room, I'm laughing at the absurdity of it; Burt fits just too perfectly the blueprint for a bland, blond killer that Elmore Leonard came up with in his first Florida thriler, *Gold Coast*, developed in books like *Stick* and *La Brava*, and which Charles Willeford picked up and ran with in his Miami cop novels.

Back at the hotel, I've had time to shower, admire the deco chest of drawers and shudder at the discomfort of the bed. I've switched to my 'Hey, I've seen *Miami Vice*' outfit – shorts, loafers, no socks – and it's time to take a stroll round the neighbourhood. From ground level and in daylight what Miami Beach does not look like is anywhere's crime capital. Simply, South Beach is beautiful. I knew to expect some art deco hotels, but here are twenty blocks of '30s deco dream hotels. A few are refurbished in *Miami Vice* pastels, but most are faded, immaculate in wind-blown ice-cream colours – peach, pistachio and strawberry. Mine has been recently repainted, awaiting the Beach's return as a yuppie tourist centre, following the Deco District's new-found status as a Heritage Zone. It even has the fountain out front working again. The hotel is on 21st Street, half a block west of Collins Avenue. On the corner of Collins there's Wolfies, one of the last of the great American Jewish delis (x million muffins sold since 1947); on the other corner, and every bit as much the fading monument, is the Gaiety Burlesque theatre, now a forlorn husk showing porno movies to crowds ever dwindling since the arrival of the VCR. One screen shows an all-male programme, the other a male/female programme. Keep going a little farther over Collins on 21st and I pass the Beirut café, local surf-punk hangout, before arriving on the Beach at the same split second as a police jeep tears down 21st behind me, mounts the pavement and heads, tyres screaming and dust billowing, on to the beach.

The jeep pulls up 400 yards down the beach, next to a small cluster of people. Words are exchanged and the jeep tears off again, heading farther down the beach. Wondering what next, I walk on to the beach only to discover that it isn't really a beach at all; what it resembles is concrete covered in a kind of rock dust. Certainly you don't want to walk on it in bare feet, unless you want them cut to ribbons. It's strange, I'm standing in the midst of twenty miles of what looks like prime beach, next to a major city, and, on a hot sunny day, it's virtually deserted with scarcely anyone at all in the water. On the basis that the locals probably know something I don't, I decide to forgo swimming for the moment and head back to Collins to find something to eat.

Walking down Collins is as surreal a stroll as I've made. First off, there's the abundance of deco hotels, all with rows of chairs laid out on the front verandah for the retirees to sit and watch the world ebb away from them. These represent the toughest strain of old folks, the ones who survived having the Marielitos boarded alongside them in the hotels when the city couldn't think of anything else to do with them – a decision akin to billeting a group of hungry wolves in a sheep pen. These old people have seen Miami Beach descend from being a retirement-age reward for blue-collar northern Jews to a crime capital, and are now seeing it move tentatively towards a kind of regeneration that may, like as not, reward them for their steadfastness by evicting them in the name of escalating property values.

Now, mid-afternoon in May, things are quiet. Collins Avenue has an amiable mix of population: Latin, Jewish, Anglo, a few blacks. The shops and restaurants are mostly low-income, Woolworths and Burger King, drab haberdashers and fifty-cent novelty shops. There's a bunch of Cuban *cantinas* offering subsistence-level eating, *arroz con pollo*, black-eyed beans and plantains, and while there aren't many bars, there are a lot of liquor stores where you can stand and have a drink before you take the six-pack home. Strangely there's almost a complete absence of any of the normal seaside stores – nowhere selling Miami souvenirs, hot dogs or rubber rings. Parallel to Collins, a block east, is Ocean Drive, running along the beach. Here I pick up a Cuban tuna sandwich before settling down at a beach-front bar with a windswept, end-of-season feeling. There's a Cuban guy cooking chicken on a barbeque, trying to conjure up the spirit of summer, and another guy with a beard, a halfway biker type, hammering out seventies rock classics on an electric guitar. After a couple of Eagles numbers he tries to placate his predominantly Latin audience by playing 'La Bamba' at some length, and quite unbothered by the discrepancy between the song's Mexican origins and his audience's Cuban roots. The barmaid claps anyway and I get offered some free chicken barbeque. By now the wind is starting to chill, so I head back to the hotel in time to see the street people start to emerge from their daytime resting places. The corner by the burlesque theatre and the liquor store is getting seedy as thin, wired folk congregate, each starting to figure out where they're going to get the money that'll get them what they need for another night. As mean streets go, though, it's more pathetic, even absurd (given the setting and the number of oblivious retirees strolling by doing their shopping), than threatening.

Sitting in the hotel again I turn on the TV just in time to catch a show called *America's Most Wanted*. This features dramatised reconstructions of a selection of crimes whose perpetrators are currently at large. First up are a couple straight out of the movie *Badlands*, a blonde teen called May and her low-life boyfriend Jason leaving a trail of havoc across South Carolina. After the ads it's the 'Prime Time Burglar', a guy, described as 'black' and little else, who likes to burgle people's houses in the middle of the evening while they watch TV or eat dinner. To illustrate this there's a piece of footage lifted from a French farce of a generic black guy walking around the background of a dinner party stealing things until someone notices, at which point he runs away. A rent-a-shrink is then dragged on-screen to opine that the Prime Time Burglar is 'attracted to danger'.

Reeling with amazement at this disclosure, I pick up the *Miami Herald*. The local news section shows that Miami still has its fair share of urban mayhem. Among the stories currently running are the contract killing of a black guy in West Perrine, a man named Lee Lawrence who ran a corner grocery store and had the nerve to speak out against local drug dealers. A Melvin Garcia shot his prospective son-in-law essentially for being an asshole, and tried to claim he thought he was a burglar. Another guy, Frank Stramaglia, part-owner of Vito's Trucking & Excavating Co., a firm involved in building expressways in Florida, was found in a hot tub in a Detroit motel, his body pumped with twenty times the lethal dosage of cocaine. More prosaically a ton of marijuana was found on an Air Jamaica jet at Miami Airport, and a fifty-two-year-old high-school athletic director was arrested for supplying half a kilo of coke. And senior citizens in Royal Country mobile home park are organising a crime patrol following the theft of two pink flamingos from Jerry Rivero and a statue of the Virgin Mary from Rolando Scott.

All of which is the kind of thing you'd expect if you've been reading Florida crime fiction over the past ten years or so. Leaving aside the vast body of writing by John D. Macdonald, author of the Travis McGee novels, the modern Florida crime novel started in 1977 with Douglas Fairbairn's *Street 8* and began to gain greater currency when Elmore Leonard broke through to mass popularity with his series of novels set in Florida. Leonard was the man who brought Miami crime to a wider audience. His first Florida novel, *Gold Coast*, dealt with the people who don't call themselves the Mafia, the kind of people who the Frank Stramaglia that my *Miami Herald* told me was found dead in the hot tub doubtless had no connection to. It was with his third Florida novel, *Stick*, however, that Leonard assembled the combination that caught the public imagination – Miami, Marielitos, movies and drugs.

At one point in *Stick* one of the bad guys, a Vietnam vet turned big-time coke dealer, is thinking of making a semi-legit investment in the movie business, a B-movie producer is in town hustling investors for a script about two slick Miami cops, two undercover guys caught up in the glamour and danger of the drug trade; he wants to call it *Shuck and Jive*. In the book no one goes for it. In real life a man called Michael Mann must have read the same script as, within a year of *Stick* coming out, *Miami Vice* was on screen, and a city started to remake itself in the image of a TV show. Suddenly the Coconut Grove boutiques started selling unstructured Gianni Versace suits to drug dealers whose idea of style had been Al Pacino in *Scarface* – white suits and black shirts with big collars – six months earlier.

Going out at night in Miami Beach, *Miami Vice* is literally inescapable. Walking down Collins in the evening I have to start sidestepping seriously thin people with nothing in their eyes heading up towards 21st Street and temporary salvation. Down on 14th Street I see a regular-looking neighbourhood bar called the Deuce. Inside the Deuce it is such a regular bar as to approach self-parody, like finding an average pub and entering the Queen Vic or the Rovers Return. The Deuce has a pool table, a TV showing the basketball game, 1950s neon bar signs and a big figure-eight bar crowded with cheery regulars exchanging wisecracks with the two tough, sassy women bartenders. It's like the whole place has conspired to construct a *tableau vivant* of what makes America great (or at least what made *Cheers* great). The feeling of being in an advert for American beer is so strong that it comes as something of a surprise to be asked to pay for the

drinks and more of a surprise to discover that this is the kind of
real bar that charges around double what most real bars charge,
which in turn prompts you to notice that most of your fellow
drinkers are perhaps a little less blue-collar than they seem;
the baseball caps are a little too new, the T-shirts too freshly
laundered – in fact the place seems to be full of junior execs
who think they're Burt Reynolds on weekends. Leaving, I catch
sight of a newspaper clipping on the wall, extolling the Deuce's
virtues and going on to mention that it's regularly used as a set
for *Miami Vice*, whose production team installed the neat neon
signs in order to give it more of that 'real bar' feeling.

Having absorbed this, I walk back along Collins. The next
cross-street is cordoned off and drenched in spotlights. I edge
towards it, wondering whether this is the scene of a police shoot-
out. Turns out they're shooting *Miami Vice*. This will be the last
series and the locals are about to be deprived of a useful income.
Sitting at a bar a little while later, I'm told by Karen, the waitress
in the Wet Paint Café, that virtually everyone on the Beach has
worked as an extra or had their shop or bar or hotel used as
a location. The Wet Paint Café is no exception; it's a kind of
upmarket bohemian hangout in the distinctly unreal Lincoln
Road Mall, a failed '50s shopping centre deserted for years and
now attempting a regeneration as an artists' community, the
shopfronts being converted into studio spaces. Lincoln Road
Mall has some way to go though; at ten o'clock it's closed down
– apart from the Wet Paint – and the only people in there are
myself, Karen and a guy named Ed. Ed is a thin Latin-looking
guy sitting slumped over the bar wearing dark glasses. I'm the
only other person sitting at the bar but he hardly seems to
register me. Hey! Time for some field research: 'Well, sir, what's
it like being a Miami Beach cokehead?' – that kind of stuff. Karen
introduces us. Ed seems to be a nice guy who DJ's around the
local clubs; twenty minutes later he lets slip the reason for his

apparent terminal hipsterdom – he's blind from diabetes, has moved to Miami from New York because the climate's easier on him and DJ's because he can't paint any more. Feeling like a fool, I promise I'll come and hear him play records the next night. He tells me to head to Ocean Drive below 14th if I want a little more nightlife.

So I do, and find a strip of refurbished deco on one side, palm trees and beach on the other; perfect territory for cruising in your convertible. Latin jazz drifts out of the hotel bars, urban dance from car stereos, reggae and punk from the clubs, but beneath the noise it's a quiet night.

Next morning I go to see about renting a car. Apparently there won't be one available till this evening, so I'm going to have to take the bus to visit Carl Hiaasen. Carl Hiaasen, aside from writing novels, has a day job as star columnist on the *Miami Herald*, so it's to the *Herald* offices in downtown Miami that I'm headed. The bus from Miami Beach takes us over a causeway across Biscayne Bay into Miami itself. Sitting on the bus I read a Miami weekly magazine that promises to expose 'the brotherhood of crack'. In best 'I've been there and I want a Pulitzer' factional style this attempts to paint a picture of life as it is lived on Miami Beach's worst crack-dealing street. This is apparently 21st Street at Collins, i.e. the one on which I'm staying. What emerges from comparing this attempted dramatisation of the situation with the comparatively low-key experience of actually walking down what I am now tempted to call Crack Street is an underlining of the sheer boredom of the drug world at this level – guys nodded out on park benches, guys standing on the corner doing ten-dollar deals all day long. Crack's a fast-food drug and the society it engenders is similarly minimal; there's none of the endless chatter about what great shit this is that goes with a dope deal; you just hand five bucks per rock out of your car window, the guy gives you the rocks and you drive off. Later you come back. And again, and so on, until you don't have a car any more, and then you buy your rock in the crack house, an abandoned hotel down the street. Calling this a brotherhood is about as appropriate as calling people who eat in McDonald's a brotherhood. As drugs go, its demonstrable effects are about as community-oriented as a neutron bomb.

The bus is a great equaliser in the States. You can understand why the back of the bus was such a pillar of Jim Crow as this Miami bus careers across the causeway – a whole rainbow coalition of folks are thrown into each other and it can easily damage people's stereotypes to watch the homeboys giving up their seats to the little old white ladies. Ken Kesey said you're either on the bus or you're off the bus – in Miami if you're on the bus you know it's because words like growth and regeneration were never meant to have to do with the likes of you. Public transport is strictly for the have-nots.

Downtown Miami is completely alienating, the centre of a place that doesn't have a centre, just a financial zone. The bus drops me off in an urban jungle of endless discount hi-fi stores and shoe shops. After thirty minutes of trying to find some basic amenities – a phone, a post office, a record store – but finding nothing except more shoes and hi-fi, I give up and try to find a bar. There are no bars to be seen. I don't know what time it is so I go to Woolworths and buy a four-dollar watch. The strap breaks as I leave the store. I'm getting near-hysterical as I ask a newspaper seller where I can find a bar. Simple, he says, and directs me between a couple of stores into what looks like an office block, 'just follow the signs to the bar'. The bar, La Cucuracha or some such, is in the basement and has a miniature lake and an aquarium and a *nuit americaine* atmosphere. It also has a phone so I call Carl Hiaasen and he tells me to come on over.

Sitting in the *Herald*'s lobby I pick up a copy of the paper and there on the front of the local news section is Carl Hiaasen's column – today it's a disgusted assault on the practice of lawyers touting for business. Carl Hiaasen hit the bestseller lists a couple of years back with a book called *Tourist Season*, a furious assault on virtually every aspect of the Florida establishment in the shape of a black comedy. It starts with the head of the chamber of commerce being washed up on Miami Beach in a trunk, wearing a Hawaiian shirt, minus his legs beneath the knee and with a rubber alligator blocking his windpipe. This is merely the first salvo in a campaign of surreal terrorism being waged against the Florida tourist industry. The terrorists include a Cuban bomber called Jesus Bernal, a man who has been thrown out of every far-right anti-communist group for incompetence, a Seminole Indian bingo millionaire named Tommy Tigertail, a black ex-football player turned anarchist in Carrera frames called Viceroy Wilson, a demented newspaper columnist called Skip Wiley and a saltwater crocodile. Further stunts include dive-bombing a cruise liner with designer carrier bags which turn out to be filled with live snakes. Tracking down the terrorists is a newspaper man turned private investigator called Brian Keyes, in his thirties but irredeemably boyish. Not unlike the tousle-haired photo that adorns Carl Hiaasen's book jackets.

The Carl Hiaasen who greets me as I come out of the lift on the fourth floor of the *Miami Herald*, however, looks as if he is in the process of transmuting from nice boyish Brian Keyes into drawn, demented Skip Wiley, the gonzo journalist gone too far. He's dressed soberly enough in a corduroy jacket and tie, but, compared to his photographs, he looks drawn and there is a distinct touch of wildness around his eyes. We cross the news offices of the *Herald* (which are irresistibly reminiscent of the amiable chaos familiar from *Lou Grant*, right down to the proliferation of characters in bow ties) and enter an office overlooking Biscayne Bay that Hiaasen has commandeered for us to talk in. Hiaasen needs no encouragement to talk. He is angry, going on furious, at the state of Miami and Florida. 'Some mornings I sit in the traffic and I think the best thing that could happen would be for a force-five hurricane to blow through here and make us start all over again – nothing would better remind people of where we came from…God didn't want condos on the beaches and some day he's going to tear the shit out of this place. That would be fine with me, separate out the people who really love this place,' he says, starting out in Skip Wiley, by-any-means-necessary fashion.

Then he reverts to the mild-mannered Brian Keyes pesona to talk about the human impact of Florida's growth over the last twenty to thirty years. 'My grandfather was a lawyer, my other grandfather was a doctor and I grew up in West Broward County at a time when it was very rural, very undeveloped, when I could get on my bike and in a couple of blocks there'd be animals, you'd catch snakes and birds. There wasn't anything else to do, there was no city to go to to see a play or a movie. My dad had an acre of land; that doesn't sound like much, but, in South Florida now, that's like an estate because now instead of one house they put eight houses on it. So all the dumb things you do when you're a kid, camping, fishing, I have hardly been able to show my son. I live about three doors down from where I grew up and all those places are gone. There are five shopping malls on a strip of highway where all there was before was pastureland and canals and lakes. As a result, to give my son any sense of the outdoors I have to go farther and farther west, or actually go out west to Colorado or Montana. I used to fish in little canals and creeks for bass; he has to go to a golf course and sneak on and cast into the man-made lakes. That's what hits home.'

Hiaasen is a newspaperman through and through. There's clearly nowhere, with the possible exception of fishing on Biscayne Bay, that he'd rather be than in a newsroom. His novels make him more than enough to live on but he's committed to writing the column: 'You know, when I wrote *Tourist Season* I wasn't writing a column, halfway through my editor called me up and asked me to write one. What's scary is the feeling that I'm turning into one of my characters!' Writing the column gives him the sense of having some kind of say in the way things are done: 'Little victories, I've done a couple of things…my job is to hold the corruption up to the light and, if the people decide that's how they want their state run, then that's their decision, but at least they should know what's going on.'

The newspaper business also gives him the raw material for his novels. 'I have a kind of mental Rolodex. I file away characters I meet and episodes I read about. In real life my job's here as a journalist, then I go home at night and instead of using this one quote in a column I can invent a character based on someone I met in the street or someone who called me up and I can spin off a whole line of a novel that way. It's fun, you get to work a whole lot out of your system, and the best part is I can get to write a happy ending. I don't get to do that much as a journalist. When I write a novel the bad guys get what they deserve and the good guy gets the girl, or the good girl gets the guy.'

Before writing *Tourist Season* Hiaasen co-authored three novels with another *Herald* journalist, William Montalbano. These are more conventional thrillers set amid the Miami drug trade, a subject that occupied much of his time as an investigative reporter in the early '80s (Elmore Leonard later told me that it was investigative pieces by Hiaasen in the *Herald*'s *Tropics* magazine that provided much of his own background for tackling the subject). As for the drug trade in Miami now, Hiaasen is fairly fatalistic.

'Is this the drug capital of America? Of course it is, because it's the entry point for most of the drugs. It's not that it's an evil city, it's just geographic, it's the big American city nearest the places where they manufacture the drugs. Also the huge Latin population makes it possible for bad guys from Colombia and Bolivia and other places to converse and do their business in their native language. They're not going to be in Helsinki trying to do a cocaine deal, they wouldn't connect, but in Miami you can be on the street an hour and you can sell your cocaine. Crack has added a whole new dimension. Cocaine has gone through several phases in this country; back in the '30s it was a society toot, then in the '70s everyone was snorting the stuff, and then you got freebasing among the rich and famous, people started blowing up and a lot of middle-class people started going off cocaine. Now you've got crack, which goes right into the ghetto and is in my view a more dangerous drug than heroin. It's cheaper, more accessible, you can blow it or smoke it and it's created an enormous new cycle of crime. Cocaine users, being largely middle class, were not typically thieves and killers, just people who got high; they may have had a psychological addiction and it may have wrecked their lives but they were not out on the streets killing over it. It's scary as hell but it's not unique to Miami. Some of what's written about Miami is a little fanciful, a rub-off from *Miami Vice*, but every day in the paper there's something that makes you go, "Holy Shit! I can't believe I still live down here."'

What infuriates him, though, is the craven attitude of the administration, who are interested only in maintaining Miami's public image. This reached a high point when riots broke out in the black ghetto of Overtown in January '89, just as the city was preparing to host the Superbowl. 'You literally heard people saying, "What a terrible time for a race riot." Like, when is a good time? In the dead of summer? Screw the Superbowl, we're talking about human lives!'

The hypocrisy of Miami's 'see no evil, hear no evil, speak no evil' policy was summed up for Hiaasen by a typical little

Miami news item: 'Our Chamber of Commerce is continually telling people what a safe place it is. Well, the former chief of the Chamber of Commerce, his house is burgled and an Uzi machine gun is stolen out of a bedroom where he kept it for "personal protection". Like "it's perfectly safe, here, but yeah, I do own an Uzi". These are the people who are lecturing us about overstating crime! I don't own a gun!'

Ultimately, too, all these problems go hand in hand. The growth that is destroying the Florida Hiaasen loves is fuelled by the vast sums of money generated by the drug trade: 'A lot of real estate is bought and sold with drug money, not just lately but since '74/'75. You look at that skyline.' He waves out of the window at downtown Miami's futuristic skyline rising out of Biscayne Bay. 'Very impressive, lot of empty office space up there, but the banks are full up with money, so they've got to loan it out, which creates this cycle as they loan it out for construction. Even if there's no demand the developer is going to make his money anyway and leave, and what have you got? Another shopping mall, another cheesy condo development you don't need, all because you've got to lay off the money someplace. To me, that's the most unsavoury aspect of it because it feeds the growth and all the other problems. I couldn't tell you precisely how much coke money is sitting in Miami now. I'm sure there's a ton of it in New York and in LA too. But I did a piece on where the Medellin cartel invests; we detailed apartments, shopping centres…Look out the window – you see the condo with the blue awnings? The building's owned by them and was seized by US marshals after we wrote about it. It's a hell of an investment, right on the water in Miami. People I know who lived there said the service was great – you had a plumbing problem, boy they'd fix it! – but these are drug dealers, they're spreading misery. But the County Commission does not want to pass a law requiring people who come before the zoning board to reveal their names

– the County Commision think it will *deter investment*. You're goddam right it will. No one is going to come up here and say, "Yeah, I'm a cocaine dealer from Medellin and I'd like to invest in that tomato ranch out west, do you mind?" It's just greed, and the price you pay is you have drug dealers who love it here, this is their playground, the place where they buy their cars – you can't buy the kind of Mercedes you want in Bogotá. That's what happens when you hang out the welcome mat, and in the ghettos of Washington, Chicago and LA they're paying the price for this greed – the greed which Florida has always been about.'

Since *Tourist Season*, Hiaasen has written two more novels; first was *Double Whammy*, another black comedy, set this time in the world of pro bass fishing. More out-and-out funny than *Tourist Season*, particularly in a hilariously gruesome sequence involving the irrevocable attachment of a pit bull terrier to a bad guy's arm, it uses similar characters – newspapermen and berserk conservationists – and again arises out of Hiaasen's Florida background. 'Where I came to that was from growing up down here fishing when it was a bucolic, friendly sport. Now it's big money. It's very much a corrupted pleasure for me. In the book this crooked developer/TV evangelist builds this development which is totally phoney, he digs a bunch of lakes so he can put that name in the title, and of course it's built on a landfill and the fish that are put in there all start dying. Well, if you picked up the *Miami Herald* a couple of weeks ago, you would have read that the largemouth bass, which is, believe it or not, our state fish, the most popular game fish in Florida – well, from northern Florida to the tip of the Everglades – all the tests that are being done on these fish are finding dangerously high levels of mercury. So the state is now warning people not to eat any largemouth bass caught in the Everglades. They don't know the source, it's probably agriculture, pesticides. You're in a bad state when the state government has to announce – come look at our state fish, but don't catch it, don't eat it.'

Corruption is also at the root of *Skin Tight*, an ultra-black comedy involving a lethal plastic surgeon and the death by liposuction of a talk-show host. Hiaasen comments, 'It doesn't stress the environmental themes so much, it's more about corruption, the corruption of everything, a black comedy of Florida as a refuge for scoundrels. In this book the main scoundrel is an inept plastic surgeon who has failed at every other specialty. The great thing about the States is once you get a medical degree you can practise in any damn thing you want, you don't have to be good at it, you don't have to know the first thing about brain surgery, you'll probably find a place to practise. He hires a hitman to kill one of his enemies; everyone is corrupt, including the hitman. The hero, the victim of all this, lives out in Stiltsville in Biscayne Bay, an extraordinary place – these houses rising on pilings out of Biscayne Bay, there's not even a dozen of them left. Storms have taken most of them down. It's a very romantic place and at the same time incongruous because you've got this tropical setting and then you turn around and there's the Miami skyline. And here I am writing about a guy living out there and having a killer come out to the stilt house, and I pick up the paper and sure enough there's a story about some couple out fishing in Stiltsville with their kid, minding their own business, when two guys come up in a boat, both armed, they hop out of the boat, put a nine-millimetre to the husband's head, rob them in broad daylight and roar off. Then, typically stupid criminals, they go drinking in the marina bar. So then, when the couple limps in after their day of terror, a fight has broken out between one of the robbers and a patron at the bar. They immediately recognise the bad guy and everyone gets arrested. But it's just such an obscenity – you're out for a day on the water and some geek with a nine-millimetre hops in your boat.'

By now Hiaasen is looking edgy, clearly wanting to get back to writing tomorrow's column, trying for another small satiric victory against the bland, the pompous, the corrupt and the vicious. As we're leaving he tells me that if he were choosing a state symbol he'd go for a 'gator: 'That's a really primordial beast that has somehow survived, and to me it's a symbol of nature, a reminder that, given half a chance, it'll fight back and bite your ass off.' So ends an audience with Carl Hiaasen, an eminently courteous, all-American (he's at great pains to tell you his views 'don't make me a communist') madman – Brian Keyes and Skip Wiley still just about managing to cohabit in the one body.

2   Southern Louisiana: tell it like it is

WITHIN THREE HOURS of arriving at New Orleans Airport I'm walking down Bourbon Street. Bourbon Street is a kind of Dixieland Carnaby Street, offering a titillating whiff of debauchery for tourists from the Midwest. For five or six blocks the three main businesses are bars, novelty T-shirt shops and strip clubs. Tourists are expected to file an itinerary along the lines of get drunk, buy a stupid T-shirt, get even more drunk and go to a strip show.

I do my best. Drinking can be done either indoors at inflated prices or alfresco from paper 'go-cups' filled with either beer or a sickly local concoction called a Hurricane, which is alleged to be a N'Awlins (as tourists are ordered to refer to New Orleans, to make us feel in the swing of things or something) Tradition and appears to be made from dark rum and sugar, both in lethal proportions. On spotting an Oirish-style pub, however, I experience a sudden yen for a glass of Guinness, so in I go to enjoy an over-priced and indifferently kept sip of stout while listening to a band dressed in Nashville cowboy outfits declare that they'll play the wild rover no more, and generally express their longing to return to Erin's green shore.

A little of this goes a long way at this remove from Tipperary and soon I'm back on the street savouring the strains of 'When The Saints Go Marching In' piping out from the novelty shops. I can't work up much enthusiasm for the souvenirs, which are tacky in a disappointingly half-hearted kind of way. Stroll farther along Bourbon and I'm enticed into another bar by its relatively downbeat appearance and the sounds of R&B percolating on to the street. Inside, though, it's much like the rest of Bourbon: the waitress hits you up for your two-drink minimum within seconds and the R&B group prove to be a bunch of young black guys trying not to yawn as they wade through a selection of the kind of '60s soul numbers likely to appeal to white college kids who think the Blues Brothers invented funk. Clearly they know their audience; they have only to hit the intro to 'Sitting On The Dock Of The Bay' for all the collegiate couples to start smooching ferociously. The one black girl in the audience then goes up to the bass player to make a request, he grins and briefly the band comes alive as they career through the big black pop hit of the moment, Bobby Brown's 'My Prerogative'.

Considerably fortified by the rapid ingestion of my two-drink minimum I head back on to Bourbon Street and look for a rat's nest of vice. Soon enough I'm standing outside a place offering 'Live! Male and female! Topless and bottomless!' So in I go to a dark room with a bar at one end and a small raised stage surrounded by rows of seating. The seating is mostly taken up by whooping student types equally divided between the sexes. Towards the back are seated a number of middle-aged couples who look to be on a Kiwani Club outing from Des Moines. The waiter relays my drinks order to the biker-clad barman and suddenly it's show time. First up is a shortish muscular guy in a jockstrap who proceeds to cavort about, swing round the pole set into the centre of the stage, clench his buttocks and grind his crotch into the faces of the women sat adjacent to the stage, in the apparent hope of provoking lust-crazed females to stuff dollars into his jockstrap. These basic manoeuvres are then repeated for some considerable time to the accompaniment of much giggling and cat-calling from the women in the audience, encouraging the performer to remove his remaining clothing.

This, however, he declines to do, and his place is taken by a skinny woman with a California wavy perm wearing a pair of rather worn white knickers and a baggy T-shirt. When she performs the first of the many handstands that are the mainstay of her performance – and add a saddening little-girl-showing-off quality to the act – the T-shirt falls off to reveal a boyish torso. Essentially her act is the same as her predecessor's except that it's the men in the audience who get her crotch rotated in their faces. She seems in a worse temper, though; when marks like me refuse to stuff her knickers with loot her hard mouth gets harder. And who could blame her?

As the act finishes I head out back to the toilet, where I am confronted with a wall dispenser offering a product called Brisk that promises 'to increase alertness and aid highway driving', while assuring me that it is 'no more dangerous than caffeine'. No *more* dangerous, huh, I muse, while inserting the appropriate coinage and waiting for the ersatz speed to fall into my hand. The machine calmly takes the money and gives nothing away. When a poorly aimed karate kick fails to set matters right I head, chastened, back into the club. As I pass the stage a man approaches to offer me the chance to see 'a real show' somewhere out back. At which point I, as they say, make my excuses and leave.

Next morning, following what passes in the States for a Continental breakfast, I decide to take a stroll along Magazine Street, which stretches from the Central Business District, just west of the French Quarter, for several miles through the elegant Garden District to end up at Audubon Park, home of the Zoo, in which Nastassia Kinski transforms herself into a panther in the course of Paul Schrader's *Cat People*.

Magazine Street, in the morning sunshine, where it runs through the Lower Garden District, is just about perfect. It has old wooden houses with wrought-iron decorative work, it has porches with people sitting on rocking chairs, and yet it is not gentrified or prettied up for the tourists. It is clearly a somewhat down-at-heel neighbourhood, but it is also beautiful and, on seeing a couple of 'To Let' signs, I think that I could very happily live here. What is amazing is that, as with the Deco District of Miami, there is just so much beauty and that it is just *there*, has not yet been reconstructed as a theme park.

Keep walking and I come to a clump of shops. There's a sign saying 'Records', which lures me into a record store that looks like it has been kept in a time capsule since 1963. It's a huge and chaotic shrine to the music that came out of the South in the '50s and '60s – country, soul and blues from all over; cajun and zydeco from the Louisiana swamplands and, above all, the music from the New Orleans melting pot; from Fats Domino to the Neville Brothers, via Smiley Lewis, Ernie K-Doe, Irma Thomas, the Dixie Cups, Lee Dorsey, Allen Toussaint and the Meters. The stock of albums is remarkable, but the selection of singles phenomenal; original pressings of virtually every great New Orleans record are piled up all over. Unfortunately the pricing policy, unlike the decor, has kept firmly up with the times. The place is run by a wiry white guy in his fifties who succinctly sums up the difference between retailing and collecting when he tells a regular customer, a black guy who's come in for the new Neville Brothers album, that 'your trouble is you have a passion for this stuff. I don't. I don't take all this home with me!'

And so the morning wears on; '60s records and '50s paperbacks are acquired, antique shops are gawped at, the neighbourhood turns entirely black for a while and I pay a disappointing visit to Soul Train Fashions, which is just a rather poorly stocked version of any white high-street discount clothing store, and eventually, exhausted, I wind up in a bar half full of ageing rednecks where the jukebox alternates Hank Williams with Aaron Neville's aching New Orleans classic 'Tell It Like It Is' and I eat a Po' Boy Sandwich, something like a regular French bread sandwich only much, much bigger.

After lunch I decide to catch a bus back to the French Quarter, see what it has to offer outside of Bourbon Street. Which turns out to be a lot, almost too much. There is something overheated about the French Quarter. It is startlingly elegant, long narrow streets of houses with overhanging wrought-iron balconies, and it is so much of a piece, so distinctly atmospheric as to approach the overblown. It is no accident that the most popular writer working in New Orleans at the moment should be Anne Rice, whose modern vampire novels represent Louisiana generally, and the French Quarter particularly, as less a place than a narcotic, an essence of sickly sensuality.

Certainly the French Quarter is an appropriate enough place in which to set an occult novel. After the obligatory and wonderful coffee and *beignets* at the Café Du Monde on Jackson Square, I head up Dumaine Street to the Voodoo Museum, where a startlingly Gothic young woman with an alabaster face and a black dress that, severe from the front, proves to be backless to the waist when seen from behind ushers me through to the rooms where they keep the altar and the snake.

The history of voodoo is the hidden history of New Orleans. Its existence stems from New Orleans' unique historical role as the landing point for the slave traders. Much of the trade's terrible effectiveness came from the systematic way in which the slaves were stripped of their culture; those from the same tribe were split up so that groups of slaves would have no common language except that of their masters, and they would be deprived of their musical instruments, particularly their drums. So New Orleans, where the slaves waited to be sold, served as the one American repository of African culture. Until 1830 the slaves were allowed to play drums in Congo Square on Sundays, and it was this tradition of African rhythm which informed a black cornettist named Buddy Bolden when he took over the leadership of Charlie Galloway's band during the 1890s and helped to create something that came to be called jazz.

African religion also persisted. In New Orleans, as in Haiti and other French West Indies slave communities, it merged with Catholicism to form a mutant religion known as voodoo (from the word *vodun* meaning God in the language of the Fon tribes of Dahomey). The Voodoo Museum sports a working voodoo altar, which gives some idea of how this mix panned out. The emphasis of worship shifts from one God indivisible to a focus on the company of saints. On the altar sits a whole array of saints, heroes and villains both. Surrounding them is a selection of the kind of offerings not generally found at the Harvest Festival. Voodoo followers figure that their saints are less interested in ears of corn than in the same little luxuries of life that their earthly followers covet. So the altar is laden with cigarettes and alcohol, dollar bills and candies – carnal offerings.

Looking at the voodoo artefacts mounted on the wall of the next room, I fail to pay attention to to the glass case that I'm leaning over. This is just as well as, when I step back, I notice that it is largely taken up by a boa constrictor. The sight of a large snake successfully puts the hex on me, so I retire to the outer room to examine the selection of voodoo herbal remedies and take a pinch of gris-gris dust for luck.

Next stop is a neighbourhood bar where I drink Dixie beers and check the music listings to find out where to go tonight. Best bet looks to be Charmaine Neville – cousin to the Brothers – at a place called Snug Harbor, east of the quarter. Before that I decide to head up to Chez Hélène, a soul-food restaurant north of the quarter. I take a cab up there and, once we head past North Rampart Street, the quarter's northern edge, it becomes clear that while New Orleans may be the Rainbow City, very visibly integrated, in its poorest areas the faces you see are still overwhelmingly black, and the streets aren't Creole quaint but poverty plain.

It's round here that Congo Square used to be, and round here also that New Orleans experimented with legalised prostitution, in what was known as Storyville. The conjunction of the two is at the root of the perfectly American process by which its great indigenous art – jazz – should have been nurtured in the parlours of brothels. Both Congo Square and Storyville are now long gone, replaced, respectively, by a moderately dangerous park, named after Louis Armstrong, and a housing project.

The cab turns into the depressed length of N. Robertson Street to bring me to Chez Hélène. Along the way the stoned immaculate cab driver commends my choice: 'Good restaurant, man, good restaurant.' He shakes his head, and suggests I try the fried chicken: 'Best fried chicken you'll ever eat, man,' he says, and laughs incredulously. Then he cautions me to take another taxi when I leave. 'Bad neighbourhood,' he drawls, back to shaking his head, 'bad neighbourhood.'

Inside Chez Hélène I pass through a bar, piled high with cardboard boxes, and enter the dining room. This is down-home simple: red-and-white checked tablecloths, a jukebox in the corner, and the walls covered with news clippings and stories about Chez Hélène and its chef, Austin Leslie. Turns out that Chez Hélène has lately been used as the model for a TV sitcom, set in a soul-food restaurant and called *Frank's Place*. They've apparently built a replica of the place as the set. Thankfully neither the food nor the prices appear to have been affected by this success. I blow out on Oysters Rockefeller and soft shell crab and fried chicken, served with potato salad, okra and fries and some fairly transcendent stuffed peppers. By the time the fresh-baked corn bread arrives I am sufficiently stuffed as to have to remain motionless for some considerable while, which gives me a chance to contemplate my fellow diners. The clientele is an amiable mix of blue-collar locals, mostly black but some white also, and smarter types, again both black and white. The smarter types are all discreetly asked by the genial proprietress, as she brings them the bill, whether they would like her to order a cab. As I wait for my cab to show, I speculate as to the possible connection between the humour of a restaurant and the kind of food it serves; surely the cheeriness prevalent in a place like Chez Hélène must be related to the fact that a condition of entry is that you're prepared to acquire the girth of a Solomon Burke. Anyway, by the time I leave I'm glad to be getting a cab to Snug Harbor, less because of any danger on the street than simply through not being able to walk.

And so, round about midnight, I find myself in Snug Harbor, drinking whisky sours and listening to Charmaine Neville take flight in her second set. The first half of the show has been solid enough entertainment in the New Orleans groove, featuring some fine piano playing from Amasa Miller, but in the second show she sings whatever the crowd request. Which, in front of a knowledgeable home crowd, makes for considerable entertainment. The highlight is when someone from the audience hands her a set of lyrics to an old blues, an invitation to 'Meet me with your black drawers on, not your pink ones or yellow ones or brown ones, honey, meet me with your black drawers on' – an appropriate enough tune for a city in which gradations of skin colour have long been of enormous significance, New Orleans being the birthplace of such racial micro-definitions as quadroon (a woman with one quarter black blood), octoroon, etc. Whatever, Charmaine, a slim black woman with Indian cheekbones, sings the grown woman's dirty blues with unusual assurance.

Morning finds me at a car rental place out near the Louisiana Superdome. What I get is a Ford Coronary or somesuch which shakes like hell as soon as it hits fifty miles an hour on IS 10 heading up to Baton Rouge. I'm on my way west into cajun country looking to hear some music and see a little of the rural South. I've been given the names of two places to check out: Fred's Lounge in Mamou, which apparently sports a remarkable daytime cajun music session and Slim's Y-Ki-Ki Lounge in Opelousas, a zydeco hot-spot. (The difference between cajun and zydeco might be described in terms of cajun being more shot through with country music and zydeco more blues, but the essential difference is of the straighforward southern kind – white people play cajun, blacks play zydeco).

The route I'm taking follows the Mississippi as far as Baton Rouge before heading west to Opelousas. It ought to be a pleasant scenic journey, and if I'd taken the minor roads maybe it would have been, but, as it is, it's like pretty much any trunk route to anywhere. It also takes rather longer than I had expected. I thought driving in America would be done with enormous speed and recklessness. Instead everyone drives eminently sensibly and keeps religiously to the speed limit – 55 mph, except on some of the interstates when it is raised to a whopping 65 mph. So there's plenty of time for idle contemplation of the 'Honk If You Love Jesus' stickers on the backs of the cars and pick-ups in front, and trying to find some cajun music on the radio. The radio however, seems designed to pick up nothing beamed from more than fifty yards away, and it's a blessing when at last a country music station cuts through the static.

So, listening to Baillie And The Boys singing the marvellously guilt-tripping 'She Deserves You' ('If she wants a man/who'll take a gold ring off his hand/and turn around and tell you he'll be true/then she deserves you'), I leave Baton Rouge and cross a rust-red bridge over the Mississippi. Another hour or so and I'm in Opelousas.

There is not a lot shaking in Opelousas. There's a motel on the main street that looks OK, so I pull in and almost collide with a black wedding party who are gathered taking photos in the car park. Otherwise the place is deserted and it takes considerable sleuth skills to find someone prepared to check me in. Once that has been achieved and I've watched a piece of a bass-fishing show on the TV, thus confirming that Carl Hiaasen has only to use documentary realism to achieve most of his comic effects, I decide to take a quick stroll down main-street Opelousas. After taking in the local black barbers-cum-insurance sales office and the bookstore which maintains a ratio of approx forty per cent bibles and religious material to thirty per cent cookbooks to thirty per cent Dick Francis/Clive Cussler, etc., and attracting a fair degree of curiosity from the local teens, I head back to the motel to pick up the car and make for Mamou.

Forty minutes later I've wound down a lot of country roads and still haven't reached Mamou. My petrol gauge is reading empty and the afternoon is definitely drawing in. And I'm just waiting for the car to stop moving and the funny guy with the chain saw and the face that looks like it's made of leather to come by and take me to meet his family. Or, to put it another way, it's getting mighty backwoodsy round here. This not being a movie, however, and the car not being packed with wholesome teenagers, instead a sign saying Mamou appears and after that a gas station. So I pull in, fill up and ask the attendant whether he knows where Fred's Lounge is. He nods and looks me up and down and says you just turn left. So I just turn left and soon enough what must qualify as downtown Mamou comes into view. Far from being a hot spot of cajun revelry, though, it seems to consist of a closed-down hotel and a closed-down beauty parlour, plus, on further scrutiny, across the road a building with 'Fred's Lounge – The Home Of Cajun Music' written in faded paint on the side. On closer inspection Fred's Lounge turns out to be at least shut, if not closed down too. So I pick the least intimidating of the two bars that do seem to be more or less open and go in to find out what's happened. Ask a few questions: 'Cajun music gone out of fashion round here or what?' That kind of thing. The bar is dark and cavernous with a huge dance floor. Nobody's on the dance floor. Nobody's anywhere much, except for three old guys sat at the bar and a barmaid who is currently about ten yards away across the dance floor, feeding the jukebox.

A country-and-western version of 'Tell It Like It Is' starts playing and the barmaid walks back to the bar. I'm offered a choice between Bud or Bud Light so I take a Bud, and ponder on the question of why, almost uniquely, in America beer brewed for domestic consumption is infinitely less pleasant than licensed versions brewed abroad. Then I ask what's happened to Fred's Lounge. After the old guys have indulged in a little staring at me as if I have just dropped in from Mars, the barmaid gently explains that, as all right-thinking people should already know, the session at Fred's Lounge runs only on Saturday mornings from 7 till 12 a.m., and I certainly should have been there because it was quite a time. Quite a time. However, she says, there's a church fête going on just up the road and there's meant to be some zydeco music on, why don't I try that? Which seems like a good idea, so I choke down the Bud and head on up to the fête.

The fête's in full swing and at first sight it's a cute-as-can-be piece of traditional Americana; there are rides and swings and candy floss and hamburgers cooking on the open griddle, laughing children and teenagers holding hands, oh and all sorts. Closer inspection reveals that tradition certainly does run deep at this event. Mamou's population seems to include quite a number of black folks, but integrated it is clearly not. All the black people keep together and so do all the whites; none of them seem to be talking to each other and, when you look at the queues for the rides, well, maybe it's just coincidence that all the white kids get on first and then the black kids. Mamou seems to be a place where folks know their place.

What my place might be seems to be a question attracting a little attention. No sooner have I orientated myself, found out where the band are setting up and where they sell the beer – Bud or, Jeez, am I spoilt for choice, Bud Light – than a guy who looks like he's been sent from central casting walks over to me and introduces himself as the sheriff. I could have guessed; what else would a white guy in his fifties with a beer gut, red face, cigar in his mouth and a can of Bud in his hand be but the goshdarned sheriff? 'So,' he says in the distinctly Southern tone of voice that could be defined as menacing friendly, 'where y'all from?' I tell him I'm from London, England, giving my accent as much plumminess as it can stand, and this seems to placate him a little. 'Well, what brings y'all to Mamou?' I tell him I've come to hear the music. 'Ole Boissec, huh,' he says, waving at the stage, where several elderly black men in frighteningly authentic sharecropper gear are tuning up. 'Yep, those nigras like to play for the church, sure are God-fearing folks, play real good once they've had a few drinks, you know,' he finishes, inviting me to chuckle with him at the childlike ways of good nigras. Instead I shuffle about a bit and he walks away in moderate disgust and a cloud of cigar smoke. The band, led by one of zydeco's seminal figures, Boissec Andoine, start playing. The noise they make is so spectacularly unpleasant and hard to listen to that it's hard to believe that they're not doing it deliberately.

Whatever, within a minute or so another gent with red face, beer gut, cigar and Bud looms up, tells me he's the parish assessor, presumably a local euphemism meaning 'hombre with big nose'. And it is as he too launches into the friendly-as-a-rattlesnake spiel about where I'm from and what I'm doing that the penny starts to drop. Nightfall is coming on apace and funny-looking strangers with an interest in nigra music are superfluous to local requirements. Welcome outstayed, I leave.

Back in Opelousas it's around seven o'clock and I decide to call in at Slim's Y-Ki-Ki. This proves to be on the edge of the town, a big barn-like building with a low ceiling. Inside it's empty this early in this evening, apart from the guy behind the bar, a big, muscular, light-skinned guy who looks a little like Aaron Neville. Turns out he's Slim. He too wonders where I'm from, and on hearing the answer nods and says yeah, he had some folks from round there before, California, he thought. I suspect something of a country put-on and move over to play the jukebox while trying to drink my beer – selected from another choice-that-is-no-choice, this time between Miller and Miller Lite. Slim advises me to come back around ten for the music; Boozoo Chavis is going to be on tonight.

Back at the hotel I collapse on the bed for a while before waking up around 10.30 feeling terrible. I try to revive myself with a shot of Early Times Bourbon, but that doesn't work so I head out in search of food. Food in Opelousas seems to consist of fast-food fried chicken or fried chicken fast-food style or, indeed, fast-fried chicken food. I end up sitting in the car attempting to force down a box of Kentucky Fried quite as unpleasant as that available on Shepherd's Bush Green at 4 a.m, which I had previously and naively assumed to represent some kind of nadir in the art of the fried chicken.

On reaching Slim's Y-Ki-Ki, though, such complaints are forgotten. Outside, the neighbourhood is jammed with pickups and a selection of ageing American motors, it being axiomatic that American blacks have greater faith in the American auto industry than anyone else. Maybe because they are the ones whose jobs on the line are on the line. Inside, the place is jammed with maybe six-hundred or so adults of all ages, almost exclusively black and one and all having a Saturday night country good time. The blondes all look like Etta James and the men range from big guys in Stetsons with the forearms that come only with thirty years or more manual labour to young guys in baseball caps, who look a touch more citified. The whole place is moving as one to the music; timeless zydeco – Boozoo pumping out the melodies on accordion and singing in French patois, a bass player with the biggest hands you ever saw, shaking the floors with riffs he could, and on occasion would, play one-handed. Half the floor space is taken up by tables strewn with the quarter-bottles of bourbon or rum and bottles of Coke that are the bar's stock in trade. Nobody sits at the tables too much of the time; the rest of the floor is given up to dancing. And dance people do, formally in pairs by invitation as in country dances the world over. And while in Mamou I had managed to incur the displeasure of the white folks simply by looking as if I had come from out of town, in Slim's Y-Ki-Ki, in a part of the country where the Klan still ride, I received nothing but friendliness.

Later at the motel, in a state of considerable elation, I turn on the TV. There's nothing much on but MTV. Just as I'm falling asleep on comes Madonna with the video for 'Like A Prayer'. In the course of this, Madonna rescues and, more or less, makes love to a Christ figure. Which Christ figure is a young black man with short dreadlocks in danger of crucifixion by a bunch of fat white-racist types. And which apparition here in the heart of God-fearing country seems so implausible as to be a dream (that it is not a dream is soon enough confirmed by the decision of Pepsi-Cola to cancel their advertising contract with Madonna following the outrage the video inspired in the Bible Belt).

Further levels of coincidence are soon added when I call up the Louisiana writer I'm due to be interviewing, James Lee Burke, and he suggests that I visit him on Sunday morning after mass.

James Lee Burke lives out in the suburbs in a nice house in a nice tree-lined street. His late-teenage-ish daughter Pamela opens the door and then James Lee Burke himself appears. He's a medium-built fiftyish guy with sandy hair, welcomes me with country courtliness and ushers me into the kitchen. He asks me whether I'd like a cold drink; juice, soda, Coke, maybe a beer. I say maybe a beer sounds fine, so he roots around in the fridge and produces a beer for me and a Diet Coke for himself.

At this point it might be worth mentioning that James Lee Burke has lately, nearly thirty years after he wrote his first novel, come to prominence with a series of books featuring a cajun cop from New Iberia, Louisiana, called Dave Robicheaux, who is among other things crowding fifty, a practising Catholic and an alcoholic, albeit one who has mostly succeeded in giving up drinking. Already some intriguing parallels between writer and hero seem to be appearing. Still and all, just because a man drinks a Diet Coke in preference to a beer doesn't mean he's a reformed alcoholic.

Before I can find myself asking intrusive questions about his drinking habits, however, Burke's wife Pearl comes down to meet me. She's originally from China, has been married to Burke for close on thirty years and, like her husband, she seems quietly happy in a way that comes only, I suspect, from having been through a fair share of hard times. As James Lee Burke tells me, 'We had some real hard times but my wife Pearl and my children

Jimmy, Andre, Pamela and Alafair have been the greatest; really hung in there. We lived in a garage once, Okie motels, spent a year in a trailer, we bounced all over the country. It's worked out OK but it's a long haul. What a guy has to remember, it's like Kenny Rogers said, it's all peaks and valleys. I've been very successful lately but I could be out of print in five years.'

Through the hard times Burke was always writing, just not making a living from it, and so economic necessity has been the mother of a rich and varied CV: 'I was a social worker on skid row in Los Angeles, I worked on the pipeline, I was a land surveyor for a couple of firms in Colorado, I was a newspaperman, I worked for the State of Louisiana Employment Service, I've been a truck driver, worked for the US Fire Service, taught at five colleges, and I've been unemployed a lot too.'

We chat for a while about the new house that Burke's recent success has bought them. In a few months they'll be moving to a farm at the head of a canyon above Missoula, Montana. A dream home: 'when good people die they go to western Montana,' says James Lee Burke. Then he says he likes to take a walk around this time of day and why don't we talk as we walk. So we set off to stroll for a few miles through pure American dreamland. It is all so pleasant as to be surreal. Burke, a man who seems as genuinely sweet-natured as any I've met, simply enjoys it. As he talks he keeps breaking off to say 'How ya doing, podna' to passers-by or to comment on cute dogs and beautiful cats. One family's dog is so taken with Burke's charm as to keep us company for a while, and all is so serene that it's difficult to believe that there's a world out there where people kill each other for the most sordid and arbitrary of motives.

So we start talking about Burke's early life. It turns out that he does indeed share the same Louisiana roots as Dave Robicheaux: 'I grew up down South in Texas and Louisiana. My family is from New Iberia in Louisiana. I went to school at the University of South-West Louisiana in Lafayette, and later at the University of Missouri. I go back to Louisiana quite a bit. I grew up for a while down on the Gulf Coast. Though I consider Louisiana my home, I was actually born in Texas. My father worked for a Houston pipeline company, he was a natural gas engineer, my mother comes from a little town called Yoakum, Texas, she still lives in Houston today, though we're fixing to move her up to Montana. The Burke family were always either attorneys, schoolteachers or writers. And guess who's got all the money! My first cousin is Andre Dubus, who I think is maybe the best short-story writer in America, certainly in the top three or four. He's a great writer and his sister is Elizabeth Dubus, or Beth Dubus, she lives in Baton Rouge, and she's had quite a success with her novels set in historical Louisiana. Andre Dubus's son, Andre Dubus Jr, has just published his first collection of stories. My father was something of a historian. Writing kind of runs in the family; I think it's Irish loquaciousness.'

Writing may always have been in the Burke family but James Lee scarcely looked as if he was going to follow in the family tradition: 'I was a very poor student in high school, I think I graduated in the bottom quarter of my class, I didn't study and I cut classes, that sort of thing. I graduated so dumb I could hardly write my name. In college I had an elderly teacher by the name of Mrs Lyle Williams, boy, she was tough, made me rewrite all my papers. I owe her an enormous debt. At the same time my cousin Andre, who is four months older than I, was writing some very fine stories. He entered the Louisiana College writing contest, it was 1954, and he won first place. Andre and I were always a bit competitive, so I thought, I'm going to try that, so I wrote some stories during my freshman year. I entered one in the contest, a Western set in the nineteenth century in Texas, and I got an honourable mention. That was really something for me, I was this guy who was so dumb in high school that I could probably identify the men's room, you know, by the sign, that was about it. I published that story in the college writing magazine, I was nineteen years old. And that's all I've ever wanted to do since. And that's been thirty-five years.'

Burke's career started out like a rocket: 'I finished my first novel, *Half of Paradise*, two weeks after my twenty-fourth birthday and I published it with Houghton Mifflin. It took me two or three years to find a publisher, but I felt very proud. I got a six-column review in the *New York Times*, best review I ever had, and I thought that was normal. Of course, I thought I was in the door then, but I had a lot to learn. I wrote two more books after that which are still unpublished. My fourth novel, *To the Bright and Shining Sun*, was accepted by Scribner's and again I thought big success was imminent and again discovered I had a way to go. Then I published another novel, *Lay Down My Sword and Shield*, with Thomas Y Crowell. I was thirty-four, I had three novels published, I thought I was cooking with Butane, throwing elevens and sevens every time.'

At this point, in the early to mid '70s, he started work on a book called *The Lost Get-back Boogie*. This pre-figured the Robicheaux books, dealt with his favourite territories of southern Louisiana and Montana, and once more focused critical attention upon him. Only trouble was it took about thirteen years to do it: 'It was really a struggle. The *Lost Get-back Boogie* had been under submission in New York for nine years, it had been rejected by fifty-two New York publishers. I finished it about '73, I spent twenty-five months writing it and I revised it four times. Then, in 1985, LSU Press published a collection of short stories called *The Convict* and, man, that put me back in business. After that, in '86, they published *The Lost Get-back Boogie*, and, boy, in terms of critical reception, I'd never published anything as successful, it just kicked open all kinds of doors. I have a movie contract on it now. It was purchased then by Henry Holt in New York, now Little, Brown want to give it another lease of life. And before, in the '70s, people didn't just reject it, they flung it at me with a catapult. I think that says something about the times – it's a male novel that deals with the environment. Now we're in the '90s and that's what it's going to be about – the environment.'

The Lost Get-back Boogie, set in the early '60s, starts with a country musician called Iry Paret getting out of jail in Angola, Louisiana, where he's been serving time for killing a man in a bar-room brawl. Back home in New Iberia his father's dying and his siblings sicken him, so Iry ends up taking his dobro up to Montana, to get away from it all. Instead he runs into a whole mess of trouble. The old prison buddy he's staying with likes to mix booze and acid, and his buddy's farmer dad is engaged in a small war with a lumber mill that's polluting the valley. It's a tough novel, more in the Thomas McGuane Western idiom than a crime novel, but it is also desperately bleak. Its theme is essentially that a man's gotta do what a man's gotta do, but it'll like as not not do him any good.

James Lee Burke puts the publishers' lack of interest down to the fact that it is very much a male novel, set in a distinctly male world, which chimed badly with the political fashions in publishing at the time: 'During the 1970s it was real tough for male writers. The country was involved in national self-recrimination, it was a time when, I don't know, minority literature came into its own. Which was great because black writers had long been denied their place, but after the fascination with black writing had passed in the late '60s then Indian writing came into fashion, then feminist writing, and that's all fine, but you have to wait, to hang in there till the wheel comes around. And I think that ironically the same social forces that elected Ronald Reagan are responsible for the return of interest in male fiction. Because Reagan represents, in a cosmetic way, a superficial set of male values – jackboots, riding pants, red hunting vest – all that stuff that makes everybody's genitalia begin to hum! The country wanted to feel good and they had this fella willing to stand up there and tell them everything was all right, a kind of innocuous man in jackboots, a John Wayne without the tattoos. What's dangerous about these kinds of people is that they vicariously revise their lives through the suffering of others. And when countries follow them down the road in some sort of national misadventure it's usually a calamity.'

Burke's love for Louisiana music permeates much of his writing. Country-picking Iry Paret, for instance, shares a name with the early cajun star Iry Lajeune, whose version of 'Jole Blon' (or 'Jolie Blonde') is repeatedly listened to by Dave Robicheaux. I asked him how far back his interest went: 'I play guitar a little bit, I grew up listening to country music, rhythm and blues. I've known some real good players – Hogman Matthew Maxie, you ever hear him? He was a twelve-string guitarist, he was kind of legendary where I come from. I knew a lot of country musicians. I went to high school with a couple of guys who became big stuff: Tommy Sands, big rock'n'roller back in the '50s, Tommy Overstreet, who still is a big star in Nashville. Down South music is a kind of way of life. I remember in 1954 I went to see Big Mama Thornton. When I was growing up the big R&B singers were people like Jimmy Reed – they used to say, "Bring him on out here, yes indeed, Mr Jimmy Reed, the hippy-dippy from Mississippi." He was great. Fats Domino, of course, Big Joe Turner, Ruth Brown, Gatemouth Brown…I used to go to the Dance Palladium where Smiley Lewis played. Lloyd Price was real good, great R&B, sometimes it was called race music, then rock'n'roll came along – Bill Haley and the white guys who were good guys but sanitised. Much of the objection to early rock'n'roll was racial. I remember in 1956 the state of Alabama banned rock'n'roll from the airwaves; fear was so pervasive down South then.'

'When I was a kid and you went to a rhythm-and-blues concert, white people had to sit up on the balcony. Everything was segregated, and in those kinds of instances it was to the detriment of the white people; that's the great irony of it, ultimately its victimisation included whites as well as people of colour. I remember one time in New Orleans, about 1960, another guy and I were looking for this great jazz joint, called the Jazz Room, it was a great place to hear progressive bands, black progressive bands. We'd been in there before but when we got in there was plywood nailed all across half the bar, this plywood wall. I said, what's going on here, where's the band? The guy said it's on the other side of the wall, man. The white people had segregated themselves away from the music, the other side was all black and the blacks had the band. The whites are sitting there listening to Conway Twitty on the jukebox. Which indicates how intelligent an attitude segregation was! That's the advantage a Southern writer has – you grow up in a mixed culture that is deeply neurotic and you never run out of story material, brother,' finishes Burke, spluttering with laughter.

Just around the time he finally made it back into print in the mid '80s Burke had started work on his first out-and-out crime novel, *The Neon Rain*. 'I wrote it because I couldn't get back into print. I thought maybe if I wrote within a genre and tried to write a literary novel within a genre I'd really accomplish something. It was the first time I had written a crime novel. Some of my other books had elements of it, but I had never read mystery novels, I didn't know much about them apart from the work of Charles Willeford, my old compadre from Miami. Charles and I worked together for nine years and were friends for twenty. Charles gave me a lot of encouragement with *The Neon Rain*, he was a real good critic. Then bingo, I couldn't believe it, my agent sent it off and I had three companies bid on it. And since then the success of that book and the two that followed has been enormous. I was just dumbfounded.'

The Neon Rain, set mostly in New Orleans with a complex plot linking up the CIA with Latin American drug dealers and the Contras (all this written well before the Irangate revelations), introduced the concerns that continue throughout the series, concerns that immediately separated Burke from the pack – concerns of personal and national redemption. The personal side is centred on Robicheaux's struggle with his demons, his fight to stay sober; the national side is centred on the corruption of American foreign policy with regard to Central America. And for Burke the character of the one is inextricable from the moral issues provoked by the other: 'He's my favourite character, I think he represents everything I admire in people. He's kind, he has courage, he's intelligent, in many ways he's a moral man living in an amoral world. We must remember that in recent times the United States has been involved in some very nasty things and that fact will not go away. There are too many good people who are unconcerned about the slaughter of peasants in Central America, there's a lot of blood on people's heads in this country – the murder of people in Guatemala or El Salvador with US weapons is not an abstraction, not a matter of interpretation. These atrocities have gone on for a long time and I think they are a direct consequence of the policies of Ronald Reagan. I've said this in interviews several times and those words never show up. There's a lot of factual material in *Neon Rain* that hardly anyone picked up on.

'For example, I mention an atrocity that occurred in a small village in Guatemala, the murder of Father Stan Rother, a missionary, and sixteen or so Indians, all killed with US automatic weapons as a warning. That's a true story. I thought there'd be some interest in the book's political content. There's an enormous act of denial with regard to this country's policies. And to my mind this is the greatest country in the world. I believe Americans are people who have enormous social conscience and goodwill, but we've closed our eyes to some very bad things. Dave Robicheaux is a man who has to pay a lot of dues, has to make a lot of hard choices. Also he's a man who has fought the booze for years, and these books are meant to be as much about one man's struggle with his demons as they are books about criminals.'

The same unholy conjunction of government and organised crime comes to haunt Robicheaux in the second of the series, Burke's favourite to date, *Heaven's Prisoners*, set this time in the Louisiana bayous, in the course of which Robicheaux rescues a little Nicaraguan girl from the wreckage of a plane that had contained her family and a radical American priest.

In this novel too Robicheaux is laden with enough bad fortune to destroy several lesser men. Bad luck would appear to be his middle name. In *The Neon Rain* he is pumped up with alcohol and tipped off a third-storey building in a car, when not being almost drowned in a bathtub by ex-Mossad torturers. In *Heaven's Prisoners* a terrible act of violence is visited accidentally on his wife Annie rather than on him, the intended victim. So when in the third book, *Black Cherry Blues*, Dave is fitted up on a murder charge, it seems inevitable that he should draw the meanest judge on the circuit. In *The Neon Rain* someone tells Dave, as he teeters on the brink of being thrown off the New Orleans police force and sinking back into the booze, that this is his dark night of the soul. So far this seems a good enough description of the series as a whole, and the religious reference is fully appropriate – Burke is deeply concerned with upholding Christian morality in a society in which such values are commonly hijacked by criminal charlatans. Robicheaux is perhaps the most explicitly moral agent in contemporary crime fiction.

'I think a lot of crime writing is superficial because it doesn't treat the problem of evil within us. I have a hard time taking it seriously without that. It's the fundamental theological question, how do we reconcile a benevolent God with the presence of evil in the world. I think any novel that treats evil has to address that problem. Every thinking person has to. I believe in God and I believe in a merciful God and I think it's a hard question. When you deal with evil in a book your responsibilities as a writer are not decreased, they are increased. How do you explain pathological behaviour? Do people elect to be evil, are they environmentally shaped? My feeling is probably that people who are genuinely evil elect to be so. I've come to believe that. Most people who do evil things are not intrinsically evil, they're buffoons. As Dave Robicheaux says, take a visit to any county jail, the guys you meet there have banana peels for fingers, and if you turned them all loose it wouldn't make much difference. The guys really doing the damage, the people polluting the environment, the people in the munitions industry, the people who are responsible for the systematic exploitation of the third world – they're not doing time. But these are the guys I think we ought to be worried about. Forget about the two-bit boosters and the penny ante crooks.'

Black Cherry Blues has Burke returning to the territory of *The Lost Get-back Boogie*. In *The Lost Get-back Boogie* Iry Paret, on parole in Louisiana, heads for Montana; in *Black Cherry Blues* Dave Robicheaux, on bail in Louisiana, heads for Montana. And while Robicheaux is not a musician like Paret, he is drawn to Montana by the reappearance in his life of a faded rock'n'roll singer called Dixie Lee Pugh, a character who owes something to Jerry Lee Lewis and, for all I know, Tommy Sands. Both books too take their titles from song lyrics Burke has created for his characters. The differences are in tone: *The Lost Get-back Boogie* is packd with calamity and is, in many ways, a bleak and bitter book. *Black Cherry Blues*, despite having a hero who makes Job look like Pee Wee Herman, is a book shot through with a belief that redemption is at hand, that things will get better.

By now our walk has returned us to Burke's house. He and Pearl have decided to take me out for a real heart-of-America lunch. Off we head to a steakhouse, where I eat a pound or so of fine red-blooded American cow meat and we all visit the salad bar, which is laden with enough food – most of it related to anything one might reasonably describe as salad in only the most tenuous of ways – to feed most of a small-size country. Burke is sticking to salad – he's on a diet, worried that success might be making him fat.

To further combat this eventuality, when we return to the house Burke invites me to finish off the interview while he does some weight training. This is somewhat disconcerting, and the questions and answers become a little sporadic until he puts down the weights to tell me about his new book. 'It will be called *A Morning for Flamingos* and I think it's a smasher of a book. It deals with fear and it deals with black magic in southern Louisiana. It has a number of black characters and also people who would refer to themselves as Creoles, part black, Indian and French, who'd be offended if you called them black – it's an American characteristic that we revise our identities and our point of view linguistically.'

Burke's own memories of the black and Creole people he grew up around are nothing but warm: 'I remember all the people of colour I knew; their kindness and the trust I had in them because you could confide in them in a way you could not to white adults. White adults would drop the dime on you, the people of colour would cover up for you. When we were kids a white person would tell you what you were doing wrong, a black person would say, "You boys going to drink that beer, you'd best do it behind my barn where's nobody can see you,'" he says, breaking into nostalgic laughter.

He acknowledges, however, that such happy memories of the South are no antidote to the continuing poison of racism, rather just an illustration of the fact that to paint the history of race relations in the South *simply* in terms of the appalling racism is to ignore another part of the story – the real closeness between the races that persisted in the rural South while the notionally liberal North constructed its giant ghettos. And now Burke feels that it is hard to be optimistic about the racial situation anywhere in America: 'White people of conscience looked the other way and allowed the worst people in our society to have their way, the demagogues and the Klansmen. We kept the black people poor and fearful and oppressed and now we have to face the consequences of that. What's happening with the gangs in south central Los Angeles is just a preview of what's to come.'

James Lee Burke has things to attend to, so I head off to drive around a little and bask in the park for a while. I return chez Burke in the evening, and we head off to the movies to see the film of Bobbie Ann Mason's *In Country*. Which is a reasonable enough tale of alienated Vietnam vets in a small Southern town twenty years on from what was the forgotten war and has lately become the rewritten war. It's a film marred though, by a silly, sentimental ending, which, as Burke points out, attempts to offer an instant redemption that is inconceivable in the circumstances.

Later still, back in James Lee Burke's kitchen, Pearl has disappeared upstairs and he finally reveals the reasons for the change of tone between a book like *The Lost Get-back Boogie* and his current work – the perhaps unfashionable virtues of faith and sobriety: 'I feel I was given a second chance. I had problems with alcohol for years. I've had twelve years' sobriety now and it's made all the difference. Through my thirties I just became more and more bitter in my view of things, more and more jaundiced, virtually nihilistic. In my prose there was very little in the way of light. I'm not knocking that point of view but I don't feel that way today. I don't keep score any more. But I do like to think that these books might help somebody else.'

As to how Burke does feel today, the last words he had to say on the character of Dave Robicheaux reflect clearly on his creator: 'The amount of compassion and empathy in a person's life is directly in proportion to the amount of suffering he endures. One has everything to do with the other, I've never met anybody who has not suffered who is a compassionate person. Anyone who's ever hitch-hiked down South knows that the people who pick you up are the working-class whites and the Negroes; the middle-class folks don't stop.'

I am fairly confident that James Lee Burke would stop.

3 · Los Angeles: looking for the big nowhere

LOS ANGELES IS a place it's almost compulsory to dislike. Expressing a fondness for it is tantamount to saying, 'I'm going to make it in the movies', 'I'm addicted to cocaine' or 'I like to watch drive-by killings'. The twin images are Beverly Hills boredom or ghetto gunfire. The other thing you hear, and which is more like it, is that there's nothing there – a bunch of suburbs in search of a city, a gigantic freeway interchange, etc.

Certainly it's a hard place to grasp. A friend of a friend met me at the airport and drove me across most of LA to her flat in east Hollywood, where I'd be staying while I was in LA. The strangest sight along the way was the oil-rigs next to the freeway – oil-rigs, cars and smog, the one feeding the others – that's LA. And a little unfair; the smog is not what it was, everyone drives unleaded now. Then we cut through crowded Koreatown, which looks like any busy twentieth-century cityscape, and arrive at a quiet street just a block off Sunset Boulevard on the borders of Hollywood and Silverlake.

Sunset Boulevard is inevitably anticlimactic, neither glamorous nor even spectacularly seedy. Instead it's seedy in a drab and dusty kind of way. All that's on it around here are a couple of supermarkets – LA, I quickly discover, is a city in which giant supermarkets are the familiar reference points; ask where some place is and you'll be told 'on Sunset, next to Von's', or 'on Hollywood, near Ron's'. Best time to visit them is around 4 a.m., when the weird go shopping. Otherwise all this end of Sunset has to recommend it is a hot-shoe motel offering waterbeds and adult movies in every room, a couple of twenty-four-hour porno stores and a diner or two, plus the usual complement of gas stations, drive-through McDonald's and Korean fruit stalls that every American thoroughfare possesses these days.

After sitting and drinking herb tea with my hosts – hey, this is California – I try to explain what I'm doing in LA. I've come to talk to a guy called Gar Haywood, who writes PI novels set in south central LA, the ghetto home of the gang warfare, and to look for James Ellroy's LA – this is a guy who writes books set in LA over the past forty years which are filled with homicidal madness. Oh, right, how interesting, they say, and I have a sense of the perversity of what I'm doing, here in the quiet flat of nice leftish, post-hippy types, a smoke-free zone. In a place of intended harmony I've come looking for sickness and violence, will be disappointed if that's not what I find.

That's James Ellroy's mission. After a series of thrillers set in contemporary LA he's now embarked on an epic series of LA life in the '40s and '50s, novels designed to rip apart the cosy nostalgia that surrounds '50s America. 'The '50s to me is darkness, hidden history, perversion behind most doors waiting to creep out,' says Ellroy. 'The '50s to most people is kitsch and Mickey Mouse watches and all this intolerable stuff...'

My first couple of days in LA give no handle on the place, though I do nothing but travel around it. Anyway it's a fool's errand looking for James Ellroy's LA – it's like trying to find his childhood, it simply isn't there any more. Ellroy, perhaps more than any of America's crime writers, is fascinated by the extremes of crime, the grotesque, the savage and the mad. And more than any other writer he is identified with his work. Ellroy has required a reputation for strangeness; American crime writers are generally a fairly clubbable bunch, eager to say nice things about their fellow writers. Someone like Tony Hillerman is known and loved by all; when Sara Paretsky in Chicago says she's heard Tony's a lovely man I laugh, having heard the same thing from so many mouths. Mention James Ellroy, anywhere except New York, though, and there is a general coolness; barbed compliments suggest that this is a man a little too big for his boots. He has long proclaimed his desire to be 'the best writer of crime fiction, ever' and is generally dismissive of other writers. He is also reputed to be a little too close to the madness of his books.

And Ellroy has been happy enough to exploit this reputation for all it's worth. The first time I met James Ellroy I had barely had time to take stock of this, before he was telling me about his mother's murder and the grimness of his childhood. This first time he was playing the angles. An inordinately tall man with glasses, a receding hairline and an Ivy League outfit, with gold buttons still cased in dry cleaner's tinfoil, he delivered what was clearly and unashamedly the James Ellroy rap, a journalist-friendly life story taking in events like his mother's murder and his own life of petty crime, culminating in salvation through brutal fiction writing. If the professionalism with which this was delivered undercut the message to some degree, at the same time its very offhandedness combined with the fact that he delivered it while staring relentlessly at the breasts of the woman sat next to me had a certain chill of its own.

'I was born in Los Angeles in 1948. My father was a womaniser, a minor hero in the First World War. He was briefly Rita Hayworth's business manager in the late '40s. He would jump on any woman that moved, he was a raconteur, a bon vivant. My mother was a registered nurse, they were divorced when I was six. I was an only child.

'I grew up very tall. I was a very early reader. My father taught me to read when I was three and a half. It was the only evidence of precocity that I ever evinced. I couldn't tie my shoes too well. I couldn't tell the time till I was eight or nine, but, boy, could I read. Hence I escaped into books at an early age. My parents were divorced when I was six and I went to live with my mother, saw my father on weekends. June of 1958 my mother was murdered; a man picked her up in a bar, strangled her, did not rape her, dumped her body in the bushes outside Arroyo High School in El Monte, a sleazy, very lower-middle class, white-trash and Mexican neighbourhood in East Los Angeles.

'I went to live with my father. My reading then took on a distinct focus – crime books, anything to do with crime. I was much closer to my father than my mother, hence it wasn't quite the bereavement one would normally think. My father was much better to me. My mother wasn't an abusive woman, I simply loved my father more. I was very curious. I wanted to know *why*. Sex fascinated me at an early age. At forty it continues to: aberrant sexual behaviour is a real fascination, even though I was, at that time, pre-pubescent. During that summer I lived with my father in a dingy small apartment at the edge of a rich neighbourhood in Los Angeles, and I took to breaking into places – this was the '50s and people didn't lock their doors. I would go in, prowl around and steal some trinkets, make myself a sandwich out of the refrigerator. I enjoyed being in other people's houses. So…

'…So I grew up bookish and strange and tall and frightened and volatile and…And for my eleventh birthday, 1959, my father bought me a book called *The Badge* by Jack Webb, which was a stupefyingly right-wing paean to the Los Angeles Police Department, and it contained, among other things, a haunting ten-page summary of the Black Dahlia murder case, and I became obsessed, because it was all the horror of my mother's death plus a lot more. It was a much more explicit crime, a brutal, awful sex crime and it, like my mother's killing, was unsolved. I became sexually obsessed with the Black Dahlia victim, Elizabeth Short. I had fantasies of going back to 1947 and saving her and, uh, enjoying sexual adventures with her. I speculated in my mind and with a friend I made at that time, Randy Rice, endlessly. Who killed the Dahlia? How did she come to die? And on and on and on.

'Well, my father was old. He was fifty when I was born and he got sick fast. I sort of went crazy. I was kicked out of high school, I drank and used drugs, I joined the army and faked a nervous breakdown to get out. I was seventeen and came back to Los Angeles and caught the '60s dope revolution in full flow. So for the next twelve years I drank a lot of cheap wine, smoked a lot of marijuana, took a lot of pills, slept in parks, broke into houses, stole things, shoplifted, uh, went to jail a lot. Not for any great length of time, I was only arrested for misdemeanours, thirty days here, thirty days there, ten days, twenty days, drunk, drunk, drunk, drunk. I slept in parks, I was homeless before it was in vogue and I almost died from a series of booze-related maladies, and in early 1977 I got sober and realised 'no more booze, no more drugs or you will die'.

'Throughout this time I'd been reading many, many, many crime novels. I loved it, it was my *raison d'être*. I read and I read and I read and harboured dreams of being a great novelist. So… I got sober in August '77 and I stayed off the booze for a year and a half, and for a couple of years I worked as a golf caddy and got an idea for a crime novel.'

A footnote to the story. I ran down a copy of Jack Webb's *The Badge* and here is the description of the murder that burned itself on to Ellroy's brain.

'The Dahlia had been roped and spread-eagled and then hour after hour, for possibly two or three days, slowly tortured with the little knife thrusts that hurt terribly but couldn't kill. She had made the rope burns on her wrists and ankles as she writhed in agony. Finally in hot rage or *coup de grâce*, there had come the slash across the face from ear to ear, and the Dahlia had choked to death on her own blood. But the killer had not done with her body. Afterwards, he (or she) drained the system of blood, scrubbed the body clean and even shampooed the hair. Then it was neatly cut in two and deposited at 39th and Norton.'

God knows what kind of a gift that was to the fantasy life of the tall and strange young Ellroy – tales from the morgue, the pornography of an authoritarian time.

It took Ellroy seven books to get famous. He'd got sober in '77 and the first novel, *Brown's Requiem*, came out in '81. Seven years later *The Black Dahlia* made it into the *New York Times* bestseller lists. In between he's written three novels featuring an LA cop called Lloyd Hopkins, a book called *Clandestine*, which uses his mother's murder as a starting point, and a book called Silent Terror, a novel in the shape of an autobiography of a serial killer with a discomfiting amount of Ellroy's own background.

This is the problem with Ellroy: there is a temptation, which he has done little to discourage, to view him as another Jack Henry Abbott (the convicted murderer who wrote an autobiography, *In The Belly of the Beast* while in prison, which led Norman Mailer, among others, to campaign for his freedom, on receipt of which he promptly killed again), a man who has been to the abyss and lived to tell, a tame psycho. What is muddied is whether Ellroy is interpreting his past or his nightmares, or whether he is consumed by them. His first novel, *Brown's Requiem*, has a central character, an ex-cop turned repo man and occasional PI named Fritz Brown, who has more than a little in common with Ellroy. A tall ex-alcoholic with a love of classical music and a distaste for counter-culture types, he has a best friend named Walter who likes to talk about the Black Dahlia, just like Ellroy and his buddy Randy Rice: 'Walter was a sort of spin-off from Randy Rice, though Randy didn't kill himself. He's a guy I grew up with, we got drunk together, got sober together, did all kinds of crazy stuff. He's got light blue eyes so light it looks like he sends them out to be bleached. He's a book scout now, lives in Venice Beach.'

Much of the book is set in the surprisingly low-life world of the LA golf caddie, again a throwback to Ellroy's lost years. 'I used to know a caddie who later drank himself to death. He got me a job as a caddie in a country club. It was great, tax-free cash every day, which encourages behaviour such as alcoholism, drug addiction, compulsive gambling…absolutely no responsibilities, good cash flow. I loved it.'

This time, the second time I meet James Ellroy, he's in Ivy League casual mode – button-down shirt, loafers and Levi's just barely long enough for his legs, faded and fraying at the bottoms. On this occasion, as on the first, I won't have much time with Ellroy, he's hot right now and seriously busy. Though it doesn't seem to matter; Ellroy is the reverse of the normal interviewee – the longer you spend with him the less there seems to be to say; he has mastered the art of the interview as publicity and seems largely unwilling to allow it to move off into uncharted regions that might reveal anything more than what he wants revealed. His answers are either off pat, or general to the point of evasiveness.

He has a new book out, *The Big Nowhere*, far more ambitious than anything he has previously tried, and he's keen to impress me with the extent to which he's a serious writer, not some psycho who writes slasher novels. He wants at least to be seen as some psycho who writes Dostoyevskian slasher novels. He's intent on pulling back from his carefully constructed persona, talks about how marriage has changed him ('I got married in December, you know…we've got a dog now'). He claims to have found a new maturity. 'I think *The Black Dahlia* was my last book as a young man. I was thirty-nine when it came out. I think *The Big Nowhere* is my first book as a mature man.' He goes on to poke fun at the 'I've been there' schtick: 'I think there are people who've written great novels, who've had checkered pasts, who've experienced the darkness first hand. And then there are people like myself who are now morally appalled at the way they once lived and now get a vicarious kick out of reliving that and taking it much farther. Yeah, I was a drunk, yeah, I slept in parks, yeah, I rolled a drunk maybe two times in my life and did maybe eight months of county jail time, but I like writing about pervert killers who wear wolverine teeth, you know...'

Oh yeah, wolverine teeth – now which Dostoyevsky novel was it in which the plot hinged on plastic surgery and the use of wolverine teeth? Like, excuse me, but you're telling me you want to be up there with the big names, and yet – in 1988 – you have the unmitigated gall to serve up a novel where the denouement involves the bad guy changing his appearance via plastic surgery! Ellroy's writing is jammed with contradictions; *The Big Nowhere* is more serious than previous books, has an extraordinary scope but it is also full of hack cartoonery, horror-comic stuff. The gore is increasingly the least interesting aspect of Ellroy's work; what grips is the sweep of his recreation of '50s LA.

As he was born in 1948 I wonder what he remembers of that time. 'I remember it in many different ways, I remember it inchoately, right on the edge of memory. Also, and as with a lot of writers, I don't know what is actually my memory and what is memory I've created out of my imagination. I remember Micky Cohen – celebrated '50s LA gangster who makes an appearance in *The Big Nowhere* – I remember meeting Mickey Cohen in a barber shop on Fairfax Avenue, he had a bulldog named Mickey Cohen Jr. I remember LA back then as a time when men cut deals, travelled in packs and cut deals, talked about women openly and blatantly, and ate steak a lot and went to the fights a lot. And frankly I miss that time. Writing about the '50s is very much a way of reclaiming my past, though it's not my literal past, it's one I'm re-creating out of my imagination.'

Prior to *The Black Dahlia* Ellroy had used contemporary LA as the backdrop for his series of novels featuring Lloyd Hopkins: 'What I wanted was to create my antidote to the world-weary, beer-drinking, woman-yearning, predictable private eye. You know, the private eye icon/hero who has become such a ritual, such a cliché. He hates authority, he has such a distinct past, he'd really like to be with a woman but no woman would go with him because of the violent lifestyle he leads. He gets weepy over lost dogs and little kids, he hates authority, he hates big money. He has a witty riposte and an astute sociological observation for every situation that comes his way. I think that the character that Raymond Chandler created and which has spawned so many imitators is essentially bullshit. So I wanted an antidote to that. I wanted a real, repressed, violent, right-wing, though not particularly right-wing ideologically, LA cop. I wanted a man who is obsessed with order because he has no order in his own life. I wanted a man with more than his share of hypocrisy, full of ambiguities and contradictions. Heroes don't interest me in the least and I don't think Hopkins is a hero. I think he's efficacious in that he puts evil people away and I love and respect him for that, but the price, of course, is great.'

I wonder whether he intends writing again about contemporary LA: 'I may set other novels in LA in the present. But not in the foreseeable future. There's a great deal I don't know about LA today. When I grew up it was a white man's town, now it's largely oriental and Latin and there are entire pockets where they don't speak English at all. My old neighbourhood is now Koreatown. I've gotten away from LA, I've lived there in the past to such an extent that LA now eludes me. I come back to LA and I want to eat in places that used to be there. I want to stay in the mindset of LA in the past.'

Ellroy has to go; his agent has someone for him to lunch with. He gives me his number in Connecticut, the American dream home the books have bought him; 'Let's keep in touch'. And he's gone. Meanwhile I keep looking for LA. Word has it that Melrose is the hip place to be these days, where the chic go shopping. Deployment of the not entirely accurately named Rapid Transport System (i.e. a rather slow bus) lands me on the Melrose strip, and it does indeed have the requisite complement of boutiques, eateries, record, book and sunglasses emporia that mark it out as a happening youth zone. But it is depressingly like anywhere, a sunny version of London's King's Road, for instance. Most alarmingly its dominant theme is retro: 1950s America. There are mock-1950s diners, American classic clothing stores and places selling tarted-up 1950s kitsch at alarming prices, and I have a strong sense that this is symbolic of a huge failure of nerve. Fetishising your recent past used to be the preserve of faded European nations; the American dream has always been of a better future. This mass flight to get back to the future, to an imaginary 1950s wonderland, is perhaps the most depressing legacy of the Reagan 'let's feel good about America' ethos. At least Ellroy's work offers a savage and salutary reminder that this sanitised version of the 1950s conceals a much darker reality.

Melrose, then, sure as hell isn't Ellroy country. Undaunted, though, I head back over to the eastern end of Hollywood and take a walk west up Sunset Boulevard. Things don't look up too fast: for miles it insists on looking like the outskirts of any place – not the suburbs, just the motley developments that cling to the main drag out of town. For about a mile past LaBrea there isn't even a place to eat. Finally there's a Jewish deli which turns out to be run by Koreans but serves up a passable tuna on rye. Sitting down, I listen to a woman trying to impress a bloke who doesn't need impressing.

Farther on down the road I at last encounter something. Something is in the shape of Rock World, a glorified instrument shop with the handprints of heavy metal drummers embedded into the marble-ette pavement outside. Inside are a bevy of guys with blond corkscrew perms and leather trousers. Neat.

Finally I'm getting close to the Sunset Strip section of Sunset Boulevard. This is signalled by the appearance on my left of a shop selling rock'n'roll cowboy boots and on my right by the shadow of the Chateau Marmont, a hotel popular with rock'n'roll stars of the hotel-room trashing-era. It is of course 'legendary' – legendary being a specialised rock'n'roll term meaning 'vaguely connected with Jim Morrison' (incidentally, one exception to Ellroy's blanket hatred of the counter-culture – Ellroy's own title for his serial killer novel *Silent Terror* was *Killer on the Road*, a take from Morrison's 'Riders On The Storm'). The Strip itself looks like the fag end of the King's Road – second-division designer stores and pot-plant-festooned brasseries. It seems like a stopping place on your way up to Beverly Hills or a place to go for the bored offspring of those who already live in Beverly Hills.

A fast Dos Equis and back on the bus to Hollywood Boulevard. Past Mann's Chinese Theatre, the classic cod-oriental movie palace currently showing *Dead Calm*, a movie made from a fine book by Charles Williams, a great crime writer of the '50s and '60s who killed himself in the mid '70s. Past Frederick's of Hollywood, a deco institution decked out in purple and pink, the place where countless travelling salespeople have come to buy crotchless undies and baby-doll nighties for their loved ones. On Hollywood Boulevard there are stars on the pavement, each one dedicated to a Hollywood legend – allowing for a definition of legend loose enough to include the likes of Leif Garrett.

Coming up to the junction of Hollywood and Vine, the one-time key corner of the movie world, there's a bunch of street vendors, a few places selling genuine English new wave gear, even real Doc Martens for LA skinheads. And there's a cluster of sex shops.

The sex trade has long been a stand-by for thriller writers looking for a nexus of evil. A rash of novels – Robert Campbell's *In La La Land We Trust*, for example – suggest that you need only walk into a sex shop to be asked which variety of snuff movie tickles your fancy – 'Would sir be interested in a strangulated Latina or perhaps something a little harder, a brace of dismembered pre-teens mebbe?' The truth is thankfully less lurid. Inside the delightfully named Le Sex Shoppe about the first thing you see is a bunch of disclaimers – ALL MODELS OVER 18/NO ACTS OF VIOLENCE/ALL CONSENTING ADULTS. Next thing you see is a range of luridly packaged videos and then a vast array of magazines whose titles seem designed to discover every possible permutation of the following words – sexy, cum, lesbian, orgy, whoppers, anal, wet, fantasy, blonde, big, black, tits, hot, oral, ass, suck and oriental. Often in the most implausible combinations (anal lesbians??). Noticeably absent, though, are words like torture, pain, Alsatian or snuff. Another side of the shop is devoted to the same again except delete lesbian and tits and replace with dude, gay, honcho, cowboy and meat. In between, though, is the really strange stuff. This is a rack of contact magazines and newspapers. Magazines like *Cocoa'n'Creme* for interracial swingers, which is made up of polaroids of black and white individuals and couples in explicit poses attached to brief résumés of sexual peccadilloes and contact addresses.

Which invites speculation on two counts; first as to whether placing such advertisements is conceivably safe in the homeland of the serial sex killer. Maybe, as with British football hooligans who disdain to attack fans actually dressed in the colours of an opposing team (preferring to wait for the greater challenge of identifying opposing hooligans who will be spotted by more arcane details – the brand name of their footwear or whatever), they are seen as simply too easy, soft targets, clay pigeons. Second, on the sex shop as an underground index of what used to be called the race question. As with most areas of American life there is the evidence of segregation in porn, slick white magazines for white folks and slightly old-fashioned-looking, cheaply produced, black porno for black folks. Then, in among the white folks mags, you have a selection of titles catering to one of America's most potent and thus most repressed fantasies – the black man with the white woman. As ever, as must be, in this fantasy the black man has a huge dick and the girl is blonde. But in the porno version, unlike in *Birth Of A Nation*, the white girl isn't screaming rape, she's loving it. That this fantasy should, still, be saleable to an audience, presumably, of white men seems to point to some sexual equivalent of *in vino veritas*. Certainly a country in which white couples place ads in magazines for 'well-hung black men' to come round and fuck the wife while the husband videos the event is not one in which the race question might be said to have been answered.

Not that, in LA, there's much danger of suspecting that it has been. Riding the bus back to where I'm staying, I watch a man and his mom get on. Mom is a middle-aged black woman, defiantly respectable, sits down with a huge purse balanced on her knees. Son is altogether funkier, wears a burnoose and torn sneakers hanging off his feet. He sits down next to me and gives me his hard-luck story, an epic that starts in the Detroit ghetto, moves to Vietnam, takes in an ankle fucked up in an industrial accident in Florida, and leads via Detroit once more to the streets of LA. At the end he asks me to lend him two dollars. I do, wondering all the while why I care whether the story is true; obviously it's true enough in spirit, and surely it must be more interesting to embroider a story you're going to have to keep repeating all day long. Maybe he should write a novel, I think, wondering what the hell I'm doing – a tourist not simply confronted incidentally by other people's misery on holiday but actually seeking out that misery, soliciting stories of violence. Maybe he will write a book himself; he took enough interest in the book I was reading, Anne Rice's *Interview with a Vampire* – 'Hey, you're lucky to have that book, man, my family told me about that book, that's a hard book to find, man.' Then he goes over to Mom, gives her the money. She smiles at me, puts it in her purse.

Were the man in the burnoose to write a novel he'd have few enough precedents. Even in crime fiction authors tend to have had at least some advantages in life. Even Ellroy had a starting point above zero from which his life fell to pieces. The names of black American crime writers you can count on one hand – Chester Himes, Clifford Mason, Donald Goines and the man I'm going to meet next, Gar Anthony Haywood. And even of these, only Goines really came from the streets (Himes spent a long period in prison after a short and incompetent career as a jewel thief but came from a relatively middle-class background). As such, too, Goines's life followed his art to the extent that he wound up dead at thirty-eight, shot repeatedly in the head by two white men, perhaps drug business associates. The killers were never found. Goines's two daughters, who saw him killed, were too young to be much help as witnesses. At his funeral he was placed in his coffin with copies of two of his paperback originals, *Daddy Cool* and *Never Die Alone*. Some time during the funeral the copy of *Daddy Cool* was stolen. Which is about as grim as funny stories get. And too appropriate.

Gar Haywood, however, proves to be hardly in the Goines mould, when he shows up next morning at the place where I'm staying. He's a tall, lightly bearded, light-skinned guy wearing jeans, a leather jacket and an LA Lakers T-shirt.

We decide to go get some breakfast. Haywood has stopped off on his way to work. He's a roving computer troubleshooter for a firm called Control Data, and his van is parked outside. He clears away a pile of *Sports Illustrated*s and we drive down Sunset into Silverlake, stopping at a place called Millie's that takes the truism about all LA waiters being resting actors a step farther. In the case of Millie's the whole place seems to be a resting sitcom; premises, staff and customers all appear to be in a state of perpetual audition, waiting for a peckish producer to drop in and suddenly exclaim, 'Hey, you guys are funnier than Alice's Restaurant any day. Let's rebuild this place on the Universal lot, you're all hired.' Wisecracks fly somewhat faster than the service, which is a little trying at nine in the morning, but still, once the eggs and coffee kick in, we get down to talking.

Haywood is thirty-three. His first novel, a private-eye tale called *Fear of the Dark*, set in the giant ghetto of south central LA and infused with a good deal of cynical political awareness, has just come out. His father, Jack Haywood, is an architect and, when Gar was six, was one of the first blacks to move into the middle-class suburb of Walden Hill: 'We moved there in '63. It was a predominantly Jewish area at the time, so I was there for the evolution of the community from an all-Jewish one to an all-black one. That was quite an eye-opening experience, to see most of your friends migrate out of the neighbourhood.'

So Haywood grew up in black suburbia, part of a social world largely ignored by whites, who tend to see black communities as inevitably deprived ghettos, turning a blind eye to the fact that segregation in American life does not operate only at the bottom of the economic ladder. Blacks who achieve middle-class status have black middle-class suburbs to live in behind their very own white picket fences, black colleges to send their kids to, *Ebony* and *EM* to read instead of *Harpers* and *GQ*, a kind of separate-but-equalish-up-to-a-point-and-given-the-breaks policy.

Haywood went to a mostly black high school, upscale enough to be clear of the gang rivalries that make school an urban battlefield for most black Angeleno kids; 'all the colour lines I had to deal with were racially drawn, black and white not red and blue' as he puts it. At school he was a comic-book obsessive, writing his own comics with a couple of friends. From his father, meanwhile, he acquired both a fondness for sci-fi and a dauntingly high set of expectations: 'My father's expectations were always pretty great. He's one of those guys, no matter what you accomplish, rather than applaud you for it his approach is to say, "That's great, but if you had done this much more then…" I often think that one day I'll bring home the Pulitzer Prize and he'll say, "Only one, huh, you should have tried, you could have got two." That's the kind of guy he is. His expectations for my writing were, like, if I was any good I'd be published by the time I was twenty-two. I recall a conversation when I was about twenty-two, twenty-three, I showed him something I'd written and he said, "Yeah, this is OK, but let me show you some good writing." and he showed me *The Andromeda Strain* and said, "This is what you could be doing if you really put your mind to it." And the fact of the matter is that given my age and background there was no way I was about to write *The Andromeda Strain*, not just the subject matter but that quality of writing.'

Unsurprisingly intimidated by this pressure to succeed, Haywood drifted for a while after school. He toyed with becoming an architect in his father's footsteps, attended a series of junior colleges and finally, at twenty-one, started working for Control Data. Now he's married, to Lynette, they have two small daughters and live out in the San Fernando Valley in Sherman Oaks, a pleasant, and mixed, middle-class community. He has clearly internalised his father's drive, however. Where many people would feel pleased to have continued writing while establishing a money earning career and starting a family, then having a first novel published at thirty-two, Haywood sees himself as a dawdler: 'I always felt I should have developed quicker than I did.'

Through his twenties he was writing sci-fi: 'I read a lot of Larry Niven. My biggest influence as far as motivating me to write was Robert E. Howard and the Conan books – they were really really good I think. Failed sci-fi stories were what I concentrated on up till the last five or six years.' At which time his reading tastes were moving away from sci-fi: 'By my mid-twenties I was reading a lot of mysteries. Everyone starts with Chandler and I guess I did too. I got into John D. MacDonald. Science fiction was growing more and more technical, getting into hard science, and I wasn't qualified to do that. One of the reasons I moved towards mystery writing is that there are very few rules. You set a guy down in a situation and how he reacts is how he reacts.'

So Haywood switched from a kind of writing as far removed from everyday reality as possible to one that is positively mired in it; from writing as escapism to following the familiar advice to 'write about what you know'. What Haywood knew was LA. The first time he left southern California he was twenty-five and Control Data flew him to Minneapolis for a training course. Writing about what you know is, of course, a highly selective process. Haywood has chosen to write about the streets of south central rather than, say, a family drama of black suburbia, though he is concerned to stress his distance from those mean streets. Talking about south central he jokes, 'I cruise the neighbourhood, you know, eighty or ninety miles an hour.' This is the reverse of most crime writers, who are desperately keen to impress on you just how streetwise they are and, at worst, end up coming over as the kind of people who desperately try to think of black acquaintances they can invite to their barbeques to impress their friends on the university staff. Haywood has far too much of a sense that there but for fortune he would be to want to play the part of an Uzi-toting, Tyson-cropped, urban guerrilla novelist. Not for him the Ellroy route of giving the people what they want.

And, in fact, Haywood is connected to south central far more directly than any white liberal novelist trying to dress up sociological theses as crime fiction: 'I scouted some locations, others I made up. I don't want anyone to say, "That's my bar he's talking about." I may have moved the odd gas station but I know the neighbourhood pretty well. I've never actually lived there, but I have friends there, some members of my family live there. I've spent enough time to know what it's like. This might sound very shallow but I think the fact of the matter is that being black you feel kindred with other black people. So even though I've never experienced genuine poverty I think in some way I can relate to it. The factors that are holding black people down in the ghetto are the same pressures that apply to all of us. All you're talking about is a difference in degrees. I don't feel that I had to fabricate any of the emotion.'

Fear of the Dark's protagonist also reverses the familiar relation of the crime writer and his/her fiction. The private eye is conventionally some kind of wish-fulfilment alter ego for an author, younger, stronger, better looking, sexually irresistible, etc. Haywood's Aaron Gunner is older, shorter, balder and generally unhealthier than his creator, and his love life is disastrous: 'I wanted to create a black PI in LA who was not going to come off as John Shaft, who was not going to be a typical soul brother. And I knew that somewhere along the line he was going to quit. That was one thing I was determined about. We've seen enough heroes who just deflect everything that comes their way – I wanted someone who was capable of saying, "Hey, this is getting very heavy, I don't know if I can cut this, let me quit now, while I'm ahead".'

Gunner is an army veteran and failed cop, just barely making it as south central's lone freelance operative, constantly under pressure from his cousin Del to take a proper job as an electrician. He's a man whose energies are taken up with keeping his head above water. 'I'm as apolitical as a guy can get,' he tells Verna Gail, the woman who shows up to ask him to investigate the murder of her brother, Buddy, a black nationalist militant. It's money not political commitment which drags Gunner into the middle of what looks like an approaching race war between the black nationalist group, the Brothers of Volition, and the forces of reaction being whipped up by a right-wing congressional candidate. By the end of the novel Gunner is still in the middle and finding it a mighty lonely place to be. But by now he is not in the middle simply through apathy, but through consciously believing that, for all its disappointments, the integrationist tradition of the civil rights movement offers the only real chance, that fantasies of war on whitey may be satisfying, even necessary, as daydreams, but could only be suicidal given the realities of power in corporate America.

Other writers, Ellroy among them, disparage the private eye as a protagonist, arguing that cops are infinitely more believable. For Haywood though, to make his character a cop would be to embroil him in such overwhelming contradictions as to prevent him functioning. The desirability of law and order may be a given for most crime writers; for a black writer, however, it must be open to question: 'Law and order is definitely more of a grey area for black people, especially the underprivileged, than for the rest of us. You can't expect the cop on the beat to change the system, you can't expect the homicide detective to change the system. The changes that have to be made to make law and order mean something in this city have to come from a lot farther up.'

Even as a PI Gunner is distinctly unconvinced as to the value of his work ('he didn't have to spend many nights in motel parking lots, waiting for one client or another's stray spouse to cut an incriminating pose for his Polaroid, to understand what he had become and where he was headed'), and the law is only a support in the absence of anything better. 'He was living in an age in which conviction to causes was out of vogue and apathy was often confused with open-mindedness. The only line that remained indelible between men was the law. Corruption was blurring that line more every day…but the illusion of just men waging war against the forces of darkness was still intact in the realm of law enforcement, and for Gunner the lost lamb, an illusion seemed good enough.'

It's a difficult illusion to maintain at a time when the US administration seems to have a crudely literal interpretation of what kinds of peoples constitute 'forces of darkness'. As Haywood observes: 'Somewhere in the last four to five years I became aware of the shift in American politics since Reagan came into office. The greatest damage that he has done is to repopularise the approach to American capitalism that says as a businessman you have a God-given right to call your own shots. Meaning that in the interests of free enterprise you can go ahead and discriminate as you see fit. Whatever is most profitable, this is what we endorse as an administration, that's the Reagan line. It was suddenly OK to come out of the closet and call a black man a nigger if you wanted to, have the freedom you used to have in the good old days – Happy Days. All your blemishes and pimples – it was OK to have them back out in the open.'

The rebirth of black militant groups, like the book's Brothers of Volition, seems to Haywood to be the inevitable consequence of the changed political climate: 'I was sitting there thinking, where are we going? There's a lot of pressure on black Americans to get the movement back in gear. In the last few years it seems we've let the battle go. We felt we'd got all the rights we wanted and it's OK to put the picket signs down and enjoy our lives, and the fact is that we've allowed right-wing politicians to reverse the process. Now we're reliving history; the same forces that produced the Black Panthers are coming to the fore again. Americans have been lulled to sleep as far as the civil rights movement is concerned. In the '60s we had no illusion as to everything being all right – we knew it wasn't – but now black people have had a little taste of what it's like to get a job without being discriminated against, they've moved into a neighbourhood they might not have been able to before. And these people are going to be harder to get excited. So I think it's still some years ahead before we reach that point of frustration again where we have enough self-awareness to see that we've got to go back to work, pick up the picket signs – and the guns – and whatever and go back to work.'

For the moment, though, the quotidian reality of life in south central is not dominated by thoughts of militancy but simply by concerns of staying alive in the midst of a terrifying escalation of black-on-black violence. This is gangland; the territory that is fought over by the Crips and the Bloods. Here young black males are faced with a choice that is no choice. Whether to stay out of the gangs and be fair game to all, or to seek the protection afforded by joining one gang while accepting the increased possibility of being shot by the other.

The gangs aren't new. They were around in the '40s when LA exploded into racial violence during the Zoot Suit Riots, so called because of the fondness of young black and Hispanic gang members for the hugely over-sized 'zoot' suits as worn by the likes of the bandleader Cab Calloway. What has changed is that the gangs are now heavily armed and are in control, at street level, of the hugely popular crack industry. It's a story familiar from a heap of hand-wringing magazine articles and the movie *Colors* – ten-year-old kids earning a fortune as lookouts for the dealers, addicted mothers bearing addicted babies, random drive-by killings.

For his new novel, *Not Long for This World*, Gar Haywood has turned his attention to the gangs, looking to go beyond the dominant commonsense perception that deprivation plus some kind of black pathology equals madness and violence: 'I think the gangs exemplify how easily black problems and black concerns are written off by the general public. I think if you were to take a poll of the Los Angeles people who read an article about one of these killings you'd find about eighty per cent saying these people are nuts, they're sick, they should be put in a camp and gassed – I'm not just talking about white people, I mean black people, everyone. That's just the general attitude.

'But it's a lot deeper than that. If they are crazy there's a whole lot of things to blame for that. And essentially I wrote the book because I realised I had this hang-up that I couldn't relate to these kids who are aiming Uzis out of a moving car and firing into a crowd. I can't relate to that and my first reaction was "this is insane". But I think what we're losing track of from the beginning is that the majority of these kids think it's all a game, they have no concept of the value of human life because of the kind of life they've had to lead. We're talking about kids that from day one have had no hope of anything, they have totally lost all faith in their own future. They are surrounded by people who don't have anything, never had anything and are convinced they never will have anything, so how do you motivate these people to care for themselves? Your concept of life and my concept of life are going to differ totally from that of someone who lives in that environment. Their idea of life is hell on earth, being forced to dodge bullets going to and from school, coming home to see your mom doing crack and your father deal whatever. What is the value of that and what are you doing when you kill this sixteen-year-old kid because he's wearing the wrong colours except sparing him a few more years of this?

'These are the kinds of things I wanted to explore. I wanted Gunner to take the attitude from day one that was my original attitude – these kids are crazy. So when the case first comes along for Gunner to work in the interests of a gang leader who is accused of killing an anti-gang figure, he doesn't want anything to do with it. Gunner's sense of frustration and self-hatred and whatever is far greater than mine because he has to live in south central. I don't, I live in Sherman Oaks. I might have to drive through it once in a while, he sees it daily. Like he says in the book, "I don't have to read about it. If I want to see a shooting all I have to do is go to the nearest mall and sit around in the parking lot for a few hours." So what I'm trying to do is take Gunner from point A of not wanting anything to do with it to point B where he realises that these kids are lost from day one. The title *Not Long for This World* comes from a preacher describing these kids. They're born not long for this world. These kids come into this world with a life expectancy of zero and it doesn't go up from there. Maybe I'm painting an overly bleak picture but I don't think so.'

Politicians like to deliver little homilies to the kids – put down the guns, get educated so one day you can work for minimum wage at McDonald's. For the kids themselves, Haywood points out, such talk is a tired comedy routine: 'I have a friend who lives in that neighbourhood, he's educated, got a job, most articulate guy I know. And people will point to him and say, "Why can't you all be like this guy, pick yourselves up by your bootstraps, ignore the gangs, just say no." You got to understand that there aren't many people like that born every day. There are certain tools that this guy had from birth, not everyone has them. For each one who has the strength and determination there's another kid who doesn't, and first time he comes under a burst of shotgun fire he thinks, "That's enough, I'm going to attach myself to a gang." That's not an offensive manoeuvre, that's a defensive manoeuvre, like if I'm going to get shot at I could use a little help! These kids are not angels, none of us are. And a lot of them are lost, you can't just pat them on the back and say, "We love you, chile, let's get our act together." But you can't ignore their environment and their economic outlook.'

So what does Haywood hope to achieve by writing about this all? 'In the end the biggest uplift for me is in that Gunner has come from point A to point B. Next time he reads about two kids killing each other he's not going to write it off as a couple of nuts, he's going to have a little more awareness. And that's where it all begins. We as a society have to realise that these lives do have value, that we're throwing away potential there, otherwise it's never going to change.'

Haywood is by no means exclusively interested in writing for a black audience. He recognises that the mass audience is white, and on one level would simply like to add a believable black PI to the crime fiction canon. Reaching a black readership is, however, important to him, and here he feels frustrated by the same forces that are the bedrock of his subject matter – ghetto economics. 'One thing that upsets me is you won't find my book in any of the bookstore chains. They tell me that's not unique to my book and that may be true, but the fact of the matter is that the black readership on the south side don't have mom-and-pop bookstores to go to down the street. If it's not in the one Crown Bookstore within a sixty-mile radius they're not going to find it; if it's not at the mall, where they gonna go? So I don't think that many black readers have had access to it.'

The interview is winding up now and we start talking about this and that – the role of crime fiction as social commentary, something Haywood passionately believes ('the problem is that crime fiction is viewed as pseudo literature. I think we have to move away from the idea that because a novel has a dead body in it, it can't say anything about the world we live in'); the fondness of publishers and reviewers for pigeon-holing novels ('they always want to call my book *gritty*. Like before they've read it they're saying "Hey this is about a black PI in south central LA. Hm, gotta be gritty!"'). Haywood says his next novel won't be a private-eye book but something in the ultra-realist style of Elmore Leonard, the one white writer whose black characters Haywood feels ring true. And then, having consumed more coffee that the Surgeon General would advise, we leave.

During our talk on his research for *Not Long for This World*, Haywood mentions the lack of any modern reference work on the gangs. As it happens I've been given the number of a man called Mike Davis, who is engaged on more or less that project. Later in the morning I call Davis up and he suggests taking a trip that night to what he describes as 'the last blues club left in south central'; we'll meet at his place this evening.

Beforehand I read an article Davis has written about the gangs. Called 'Los Angeles: Civil Liberties between the Hammer and the Rock', it details the awful lack of a considered response to the gang violence. Mostly there is repression; the hard line police chief, Daryl Gates, has launched Operation Hammer, in which more black youths were arrested in one weekend than at any time since the Watts riots of 1965. The city attorney, James Hahn, has invoked all manner of arcane laws in an attempt to rescind the civil liberties of gang members. This is seen as both going too far and not far enough. The charge of not far enough can be heard, surprisingly enough, from black groups who see the gangs and drug dealers (referred to by the novelist

Ishmael Reed as 'crack fascists') as destroying the fabric of an
already economically embattled community. Thus the former
Black Panther Minister of Propaganda, Harry Edwards, calls for
crack-dealing teenagers to be imprisoned indefinitely. Too far
in that the notoriously racist LAPD is not the ideal organisation
to be let loose on the black community, if you're concerned that
only the bad guys should be arrested. As it is there have been
incidents such as LAPD officers shooting innocent teenagers
on sight. On one occasion a supposed crack house was stormed
and its inhabitant shot dead. Unfortunate that the inhabitant
should have been an eighty-one-year-old retired construction
worker. No problem for the LAPD; despite the complete
absence of drugs on the scene they put out a statement saying
that the gangs are paying the elderly to use their houses. This
is no less than you would expect from Chief Gates, a man who
explained a rash of deaths among young blacks, resulting from
choke holds put on them by police, by telling the world that
black people's arteries fail to open as fast as they do on normal
people.' Ah.

Meanwhile liberals and the left have not even the
beginnings of an alternative law-and-order strategy. The
eminently concerned leftist types I'm staying with are all
heavily politically involved in Latin American politics, helping
refugees, campaigning against US involvement in El Salvador
and Nicaragua, but mention south central and they just shake
their heads and say, 'Oh, God, it's terrible.'

Finding Mike Davis's place is something of an adventure in
itself. After negotiating a series of LA freeways – an operation
which, at night, is something like being part of a giant video
game with the disadvantage that when you crash you crash – I
wind my way up a hill and the road turns into a kind of country
lane. Eventually I find the address; my directions tell me to
go through the door at the side of the house and round to the

back. The door, however, is locked. So I figure, time to ask the neighbours, check I've got the right place. Out in the lane some guys with torches are working on a car. As I approach they walk into the house opposite. I follow them, passing the car, which looks like it's auditioning for a part in *Mad Max Goes to Hell* and looks in need of resurrection rather than repair. Through the window of the house I see two guys who look as if Charles Manson would have thought twice before letting them meet his family. The room is empty apart from a vast quantity of dime-store religious icons – Day-Glo madonnas and 3D-effect pictures of Jesus. Maybe the guys're looking to invoke the miracle of the dead automobile. Anyway, I'm already so irritated by not being able to get where I'm going that rationality is not playing too great a part in my thought processes, so I bang on the door and ask whether I can use their phone. The first guy laughs, then the second guy laughs, the first guy splutters, 'We don't have a phone, hur, hur, they took it away, ha, ha,' and the second guy manages to get a grip on himself. 'Maybe we'll get one for the *car*, hur, har, hur, har.'

I quit while I'm ahead and they're still laughing and try next door. The entrance to next door is round the back. I knock and the door is opened by a young woman wearing a bath towel who was evidently expecting some person else. I explain what I'm doing, talking very fast, and she suggests I drive back a few miles and use a payphone. Which I do, and Mike Davis says, 'Oh yeah, I thought everyone knew how to unlock those kinds of doors. Well, everyone from California does anyhow. It'll be open when you get back.' It is, and I meet Davis and a couple of friends drinking wine and discussing gang warfare. The friends are a woman from some Midwestern, I think, university, who is also researching a book on gangs and Davis's next-door neighbour, a Latin guy who's a social worker in east LA. It's a strange conversation I've walked in on; they're all talking about gang leaders as other people talk about baseball stars – 'Hey, one time I interviewed this guy in San Quentin, killed twenty or thirty dudes before they put him away, now he can quote whole pages of Frantz Fanon'; 'Yeah, well, have you heard about this guy in Cleveland – he's in for like ninety-nine life sentences and he's still running the drug trade from his cell. Jesus, I'm hoping to talk to him.' Academics as armchair gangbangers.

The other two take one car and Mike comes with me to direct me and chat a little. Back on the freeways we angle across the downtown district heading south till an off-ramp deposits us on Central Avenue. Central is still the main thoroughfare of south central LA, but forty years ago, when West Coast jazz and blues were riding high, it rivalled 125th Street in Harlem as the main street of black America. Mike points out a few surviving landmarks, notably the Dunbar Hotel, now being restored, one tiny suggestion of resurgence. Just around here, Mike reminds me, is where Chandler set the beginning of *Farewell My Lovely*; this is the street on which Moose Malloy went searching for his Velma, looking, as Chandler put it, 'about as inconspicuous as a tarantula on a slice of angel food'. Compared to most of LA it can't have changed much since Chandler's day; nothing new has been built, the old has just got older.

Moose Malloy went looking for Velma in what Chandler's white characters refer to as 'a dinge joint', and Central used to be full of places where one could go looking for a good time of one variety or another. Now it's windswept and empty, cold enough to keep even the crack heads indoors. As we get down to 52nd Street the road surface is already starting to deteriorate, not to the undercarriage-destroying extent prevalent farther south in Watts or Compton but enough to warm up your suspension and provide one more indication as to where the ghettos figure in the priority stakes when it comes to public funding. We pull up on Central, just past 52nd, one of precious few cars parked on this once busy road. As I'm locking the doors the wind carries the sound of a series of loud popping noises. It takes a couple of seconds to register – oh, that's gunfire. It's not the bang-bang of the movies, just an indistinct, muffled exhalation.

It's odd how fear works. Had someone said, 'If you go to south central there will definitely be people shooting in your vicinity' the prospect would have terrified me. Actually being there, however, my frame of reference changes – what is significant is that this shooting is at least a block away and not directed at me. Precisely where I am there is no shooting, so why should I be scared? Which is not to say I wasn't in a hurry to get inside Babe & Ricky's Inn, our nightspot of choice.

The inside of Babe & Ricky's Inn is a pop video director's wet dream. Instant back to the '50s. First thing you encounter is a giant floor-standing fan, that's on your left, then there's a long bar on the right; farther along on the left, opposite the middle of the bar, there's a small stage; keep walking and the place opens out into a pool room with a jukebox and doors to the outside toilets. On the wall near the fan there is a 1989 calendar depicting great kings and queens of Africa, a hangover from pre-civil rights Marcus Garvey-style black nationalism. The only visible impact the last thirty years have made on the clientele is in the styling of the three-piece suits worn by most of the men here; these mostly look to be as recent as the early '70s superfly era. So here we are in this place where everyone else is black, the average age around fifty, the men in suits and hats, the women in sporty dresses reserved for Sunday after church, in the last place to go in a neighbourhood that has gone to hell. And all we receive is friendliness.

Mike has been here before, is greeted effusively by the woman behind the bar, who runs the place. He introduces his friends. We are not exactly inconspicuous and soon most of the customers pass by our bar stools, say hello, wonder how a

guy from England likes it here. Then the band start up, playing
jump blues like it's still 1952 and Little Richard, Elvis Presley,
John Coltrane and Grover Wasington and all the rest of them
had never happened. After the first set the band stroll over
to say hello. They're all veterans of the LA black music scene,
most of the time they make their living playing to tourists and
white college kids at the clubs out along the beach. But Sunday
nights they come home to Babe & Ricky's and play for their
own. The bandleader is a guy called Ray Brooks, toured with
Chuck Berry for a while in the '50s and '60s. He tells me he
was in London once. 'I just stopped over at the airport, man, it
was grey and raining and Floyd Patterson was there, he'd just
been fighting that Swedish guy, I think, yeah. All I remember
'bout London was playing poker in that airport lounge with
Floyd and a few of the guys.' So we talk about boxing for a
while. Sugar Ray Robinson has just died and Mike reckons he
was the all-time greatest. Me and Ray put forward the claims
of Marvelous Marvin Hagler, Ray and Mike run down Rocky
Marciano – 'overrated, he only fought kids and old men' – and
then Mike starts telling us about the time he saw Archie Moore,
the man who fought on well into his forties, at which age he was
still able to give the young Cassius Clay a fair fight, when we're
interrupted by the arrival of the comic.

The comic is a black woman of indeterminate age wearing a
little red dress and a glamour wig, and she tells jokes that aren't
funny about being black and poor in south central LA and
reading the *National Enquirer*. She's trying to model her style
on a hip lifestyle comic, finding fun in the little details of your
life you have in common with your audience. Unfortunately
this is difficult when your audience's major desire is to forget
the little details of their lives. So you are left with a comic who
would like to be funny but has nothing to laugh about. Finally
she takes refuge in sex jokes, but still there is too much real

bitterness for humour; hers is a feminism informed by the politics of desperation. It's a relief when the band comes back on, this time with a singer, Eddie Cleanhead Vinson lookalike Delmar Jackson. This set the band move into Bobby Bland territory, soul-flecked blues, slow to mid tempo, and soon the floor is filled with couples slow-dancing. And for a moment everything is all right.

Mike's girlfriend has shown up, she's been working as a waitress and she's tired. So the Davis party leaves. I stay for the end of the set, drink one more Corona, say goodbye to one and all – 'Come back soon, y'hear'; well, I certainly hope so – and walk out to the car. A woman is walking down the street, wearing nothing but a nightgown. Mike has told me this is a common occurrence – 'they call them strawberries', he says. These are women whose drug habits are hurting sufficiently for them to appear on the street at any time of night, looking to earn the price of a couple more rocks in the back of some guy's car.

Which is as stark an example as you like of the effect of drugs on the dignity of a community. Efforts have been made by the likes of Chief Gates to suggest that the degree of the drug problem is to do with some kind of black pathology, a supposed lack of stable family structures and suchlike. To this end anecdotes of doubtful authenticity involving crack welfare mothers with Uzis and suchlike are quoted. All of which, as Gar Haywood pointed out to me earlier, is a large ration of shit. 'We're looking at crimes of economics more than anything else. I mean, there's no doubt – you can't sell crack on every corner and it not have a negative effect on the community. If you told the LAPD, hands off Westwood, leave it to the crack dealers, you'd have the same situation in Westwood. But they're not going to allow that, because those people in Westwood are not expendable, they have value to the economic well-being of the state of California. The people in Watts, in Compton, are unemployed to begin with so what are you losing if you make junkies out of them. So crack has a great deal to do with it. People keep saying war on drugs, war on drugs, we haven't seen a war on drugs, a little bit here, a little bit there maybe. That's not a war. You've got to bring out the tanks, bring out the guns, go to work on it.'

Ruminating on this last, and on what it points up – that the majority of writers of crime fiction, too, are more interested in the denizens of the Westwoods of this world than the Watts; that the democracy of the form is still very much a relative democracy; that a James Ellroy may be some way closer to the street than a John Updike, but is still scarcely hanging with the brothers – I get in the car and look for a freeway to take me back to Hollywood.

4   Missoula, Montana: Saturday night at Charlie's bar

SITTING AT THE bar of the Top Hat on Front Street, I make another attempt at calling James Crumley, and for the fifth time I get his answering service, who will once again certainly give him the message as soon as he calls in. It has not been a good day. Most of it has been spent in airports or aeroplanes, including an enchanting stopover in Salt Lake City, where you can't get a drink except with food, which means that the bar does cracking business with a peculiarly repellent line of cookies, which apparently conform to the Mormon definition of food. My big mistake was actually eating one of these cookies rather than just piling them up on my plate after the fashion of my fellow drinkers, who had clearly passed this way before.

Arriving in Missoula, I was welcomed by a wave of unforced friendliness and the news that my credit card was 'maxed out' and thus rendered me unfit to rent a car. After considerable faffing about the remarkably helpful car rental folks manage to fix me up with the local branch of Rent-a-Wreck, who are actually willing to accept cash.

An hour later I've checked into a motel on East Broadway, driven around Missoula's new western suburbs, and inadvertently consumed a Big Mac, in between whiles attempting to call Crumley. Towards six o'clock I wind up back in the old town centre, walk around a little and decide to rest up a while in the Top Hat, a big dark bar, with a stage at the back and pool tables in the centre. It's quiet and it's dark and after a couple of Dos Equis I've summoned up enough bonhomie to start talking to the laid-back longhair barman. I explain I'm here to see James Crumley and he says, 'Oh God, Crumley! He was here just a couple of hours ago. Have you tried him at home?' Well, yes that's just what I've been doing. 'OK,' says the barman, 'let's try Charlie's.' He picks up the phone and gets what is clearly another bar on the line and asks has Crumley been in. The word comes back that Crumley has indeed been in, has just left and is thought to be heading homewards. Another call to his home is picked up by the answering service. The barman says tell them you're in the Top Hat. So I do. And barely has enough time to order another drink elapsed before the phone rings and it's Crumley to say come on over, Frank'll tell you where I live. So Frank draws me a map, which, while somewhat short on street names and long on directions of the 'turn left by the big tree' variety, still proves serviceable enough.

Crumley is easily cast as the Hemingway of the detective novel. He's a big bearded bear-like man who loves to drink and raise hell and talk about literature. He writes books about troubled macho men, adrift in a world where simple values, a desire for decency, can get you killed; books in which the hero is doomed always to lose the girl in the last chapter, desperately romantic novels of the private eye as the last denizen of the old west; novels in which Missoula, renamed Meriwether, stands as the last simple place left.

Crumley has written only four novels in twenty years. The first, *One to Count Cadence*, came out in 1969 and is rooted in Crumley's time in the army in the early days of the Vietnam War. The three succeeding novels, appearing at intervals of five years or so, *The Wrong Case*, *The Last Good Kiss* and *Dancing*

Bear, are all private-eye novels of a sort. All are based around the north-west USA.

This tough-guy romanticism peaked with *The Last Good Kiss*, in which Texan Vietnam vet C.W. Sughrue, part-time PI and part-time bartender, searches the north-west states for a woman named Betty Sue Flowers. The book opens, however, with Sughrue running down an alcoholic middle-aged novelist named Abraham Trahearne, a self-consciously Hemingwayesque bull of a man. Trahearne leads Sughrue though a liver-critical interstate bar crawl: 'We covered the west, touring the bars, seeing the sights. The Chugwater Hotel down in Wyoming, the Mayflower in Cheyenne, the Stockman's in Rawlins, a barbed-wire collection in the Sacjawea Hotel Bar in Three Forks, Montana, rocks in Fossil, Oregon, drunken Mormons all over northern Utah and southern Idaho – circling, wandering in an aimless drift. Twice I hired private planes to get ahead of the old man, and twice he failed to show up until after I had left. I liked his taste in bars but I was in and out of so many that they began to seem like the same endless bar.'

Chasing Crumley around the bars of Missoula is hardly in the same league, but when I succeed in following Frank's map to Crumley's place there's a distinct sense of relief that attaches to finding him in, drinking a can of Pabst Blue Riband and talking down the phone to someone who would appear to have a) just got married and b) quit using cocaine, both admissions provoking gales of laughter from Crumley. He puts down the phone and welcomes me in, *mi casa es su casa*-style, fetches some more cans of Pabst from the refrigerator and introduces his two boys, aged around four and six, the product of his now defunct fourth marriage. They're watching cable TV and do their best to look interested in the visitor for at least fifteen seconds. A couple more Pabsts and supplies are looking low so

Crumley calls up a neighbour to come over and watch the kids while we go out for supplies.

The neighbour turns out to be a young man on a motorbike named Steve, a student out at the university. He's brought over a story he's working on. We leave him to it and head over to Charlie's. Where I get introduced to a bunch of people including a man named Denis MacMillan, who looks like one of the Flying Burrito Brothers circa *Gilded Palace Of Sin* – somewhere between country hippie and riverboat gambler – and turns out to be the publisher Denis MacMillan, the man responsible for one of the most interesting small presses currently extant in the States, specialising in neglected works by crime writers like Charles Willeford and Jim Thompson, and recently responsible for putting out a collection of Crumley's short stories, simply entitled *Whores*. We discuss the possibility of shooting some pool but by now it's time to leave and put Crumley's kids to bed. On the way out we pick up a crate of beer. 'Just put it on my slate,' says Crumley, and the woman behind the bar smiles the resigned smile of someone used to dealing with writers whose income comprises irregular large cheques leavened with long stretches of scuffling.

After all, everyone in Missoula seems to be a writer. The guy in the Top Hat told me his brother had a book out. Crumley's telling me about a great book written by a local cop, James Lee Burke will be moving up here for good soon, there's a major creative writing programme out at the university and then there's the likes of William Kittredge, Jon Jackson, Richard Ford and Thomas McGuane all living within hailing distance.

Back at Crumley's place, he disentangles the kids from the TV, gets into a little horseplay and puts them to bed. Meanwhile I sit around talking to Steve and listening to Jimmy Buffett sing 'Margaritaville' on the tape player. Crumley comes back into the living room and starts talking about how he finally doesn't care whether people call him a crime or a mystery writer. 'I used to be ashamed of it,' he says. 'There's a feeling you get in academic circles that it's a lesser form. But I look at Elmore Leonard, I look at Ross Thomas, why should I be ashamed to stand alongside these guys? Great fucking writers!' We're all happy enough to drink to that and the evening starts to blur. Crumley's firing on all cylinders. People from Charlie's start drifting by. Denis MacMillan comes by with a pile of his books for me, for which I'm incoherently grateful. We send out for sandwiches in an effort to moderate the booze, but they take a couple of hours to arrive, by which time it's far too little, too late.

Last thing I remember is digging through Crumley's tape collection and finding a David Allan Coe collection. Coe is one of country music's major mavericks. He certainly did some time in Ohio State Prison in the '60s, he claims he killed a man while he was there, others doubt it, but the fact he makes the claim gives you some idea of what you're dealing with. After he got out he built a career as the troubadour of the outlaw biker gang, selling albums of deliberate obscenity through the small ads columns of *Easy Rider*s. Meanwhile he was also writing straight country songs and hawking them around Nashville. One of these, 'Would You Lay With Me In a Field Of Stone', was a country number one for Tanya Tucker in 1973, and is as lovely and tender a song as country music has produced. Since then Coe has carved out a career which veers between extremes of braggadocio and self-pity, shot through with moments of something like beauty. His ethos is outlaw country through and through. One of his mid '80s albums features songs dedicated to no less than four ex-wives. I put the tape on and Crumley reacts the way you do when an old friend turned reprobate drunk shows up on your porch and you're half cut yourself. Like, oh Jesus, here we go!

Next morning I'm woken up by some bastard banging on

the door at what must be about six o'clock. Wrapping myself in a sheet, I drag myself to the door to encounter a grinning Crumley, looking disgustingly healthy in a sweatshirt and jeans. He tells me it's eleven o'clock, he's taking the kids for breakfast and aren't I coming along. Slowly my eyes start to focus and I notice that the kids are waving at me from the back of the jeep. Half an hour, I plead, and go throw some cold water at my face.

Forty minutes or so later we're in a booth at the Tropicana, a vaguely hippified place near the railroad tracks, the part of Missoula where you turn in any direction and see an Edward Hopper vista. Crumley's jammed on to a bench with his kids, they're both burrowing into him, and he tells me he's taking them back to their mother in a couple of hours. She's looking to find a job out of state, which Crumley is all in favour of, inasmuch as it'll relieve him of a crippling burden of alimony, but which turn of events is also desolating him and the children both. Watching then clambering all over him, in the mood of morbid sentimentality that acute hangovers provoke in me, is almost too much to take, so I speedily order up the giant Tex-Mex-style breakfast, a mammoth plate of chilli, hash browns, sausages, tomatoes and an omelette, which has a sufficiently cathartic effect on my nervous system to put aside sentiment for the moment.

After breakfast we head back to Crumley's for a warm-up beer and to meet Bob Reid. Bob's a detective with the Missoula Police Department and, this being Missoula, he has of course written a book. He's got a copy with him for me. It's a paperback original called Big Sky Blues and, reading it on the plane to Chicago, it turns out that the quote on the back has it about right – 'perhaps the finest police novel I've ever read…wonderful writing, fine characters'. The author of the quote is James Crumley, of course. Missoula writers looking after their own.

Bob Reid is a clean-cut guy in jeans, looks a little like a sporty teacher and, to coin a phrase, not old enough to be the father of teenage kids. Bob tells me he works violent crime; it's 'more interesting' than the other kind. He just drifted into the police about eight years previously, needing, apart from anything else, the money to support his family during Reagan's first years. He took a while to fit in. He'd been writing before, 'kind of subversive stuff, I guess'. Like Ray Bartell in *Big Sky Blues*, Bob seems like a huntin', fishin' and poetry-readin' kind of guy, so after a while his colleagues figured that two out of three ain't bad. Further suspicion was generated when they found out he'd written a book. But *Big Sky Blues* is no Serpico-style tale of one honest cop fighting the bad guys off and on the force with only his trusty Magnum to protect him. Rather it is a genuinely sensitive attempt to get to grips with what being a police detective is, and, from that, what masculinity is and how decency can operate in an unjust and unfair society. It's not a book in favour of the police or opposed to the police, it's simply a book about the police written by a real writer who is also a policeman. And now his colleagues are coming up to him quietly: 'Bob, let me tell you about the time...'

By now it's time for Crumley to get the kids ready to go to their mother's. He suggests I call back around late afternoon, there's something going on at Charlie's. I decide to take my hangover out into the big-sky countryside and, just for reference purposes, ask Crumley whether he can recommend a nice drive with perhaps a good bar at the end of it. He tells me that the Lumberjack, out past Lollo on the Idaho road, is the place for me. Bob says, 'Oh yeah, uh, you mean the place where the bikers hang out? Well...it should be OK this time of day.' What the hell, I say, enjoying the sensation of invulnerability that goes with having recently and voluntarily destroyed millions of your own brain cells. So it's goodbye to Bob, Crumley stomps off to see to the kids, and I head off in the Chevy.

Out through south west Missoula, with its shopping mall and McDonald's, past the timber yards on the way to Lollo, through Lollo itself, less a place than two bars and a truckstop, miss the turn-off, double back and climb for a while up the side of the valley, before turning on to a dirt track for a mile or so and seeing a building built entirely from giant logs laid horizontally on top of each other – that's the Lumberjack.

And after a brisk stroll among some very tall trees, a babbling brook and the remnants of the winter's snow, designed to convince myself of my love of nature and devotion to the cult of the body, it's time to venture into the Lumberjack for a little rest and recuperation, hopefully non-inclusive of a skull-busting from crazed bikers. Inside there's absolutely no sign of any bikers, crazed or otherwise. Instead there's a collection of notably rowdy young people playing pool, drinking beer and singing along to party records on the jukebox, all of which young people, as it happens, are female. I park myself at the bar, which, like my seat and the vast majority of the place's furnishings, is constructed out of huge logs.

Nursing a beer, I start to suffer intensely from the strain of listening to Chris Montez's 'Let's Dance' followed by Danny and the Juniors' 'At The Hop', followed by The Contours' 'Do You Love Me', all with whooping accompaniment from the pool crew, so I gingerly make my way to the jukebox and put on my quarter's worth – Rodney Crowell's miserable-going-on-maudlin country ballad 'After All This Time'. The intrusion of this note of beer-sodden gloom doesn't go down too well with the gels. Angry muttering starts up as they try to figure out which killjoy was responsible for putting this on. They're just about to get it right when some other stranger in town walks up to the bar and rings the big old bell hanging there. 'Do you know what you just did?' enquires the woman behind the bar gently. 'Because what you just did was announce you're going

to buy a round for the whole bar.' And sure enough there is a
faded note next to the bell explaining this quaint local custom.
The resultant debate as to whether the sucker should pay up
distracts attention from my questionable musical taste and I
decide it's time to get back, leaving just as the first strains of my
second selection, the Shirelles singing 'Baby It's You', waft from
the jukebox. Shame.

Back to Crumley's and he's not there. So, figuring that when
in Missoula…I head on to Charlie's and sure enough Crumley is
holding court at the front of the bar. He's still on a high and falls
on me as his nearest and dearest. The place is packed already.
Turns out this is the occasion of J. Rummel's birthday. J. Rummel
is Missoula's resident artist; one of his pieces hangs behind the
bar at Charlie's, another is on Crumley's wall. He's fifty today
and is holding court at the back of the bar, another big bearded
man running to fat in jeans, cowboy boots and a Stetson. The
atmosphere in Charlie's suggests a kind of gathering of the clans,
following the literal big chill that's gripped Missoula for the past
months. The wind-chill factor had brought the temperature
down on occasion to minus 100, everyone's been too cold to go
out. Denis MacMillan says he's had enough and will move to
Hawaii before next winter. Now everyone's jumping at the first
chance to get out and party without risking frostbite setting in
on the way home. The place is full of authentic '60s survivors.

History is being rewritten so fast these days that it's easy
to believe that the kind of people you see on *thirtysomething*
are '60s survivors, radicals turned yuppies; in fact they're '70s
survivors, people who caught the fag-end of the hippie thing,
people who maybe saw *Woodstock* when it showed up on TV, but
whose formative musical memories are later, Joni Mitchell and
the Eagles. The '70s generation never sold out, they had nothing
to sell; liking the Eagles and then working in advertising hardly
indicates a loss of faith, simply a tendency to go with the flow.

The fortysomethings in Charlie's, celebrating J. Rummel's fiftieth, have signally failed to go with the flow; these are people who used to like the Grateful Dead or Country Joe, now they'll listen to Hank Williams or Patsy Cline, people who've mostly been divorced at least once and still come to Charlie's to drink and flirt. It's easier for the men who have, at forty, a range of flattering adjectives available – rugged, lived in, experienced, worldly – enough to let them try to charm the pants off stray college girls looking for adventure. For the women in Charlie's it looks like murder; at forty you've been married to every damn man you can stand in the place, and so you say what the hell and you try to act as the guys act but you know that sooner than later people are going to tell you you're an embarrassment.

Still, at seven o'clock the joint is jumping. As I push my way through the throng, looking for the toilets, Denis MacMillan calls me from the bar, wants to buy me a tequila, so I fall in with him and his drinking buddies for a while. The drinking buddies include an old guy who says he came over here from Ireland to work in the mines, but is too drunk to remember when, and a guy with an unnerving stare says his name is Jim and he's a painter, also he's the short-order cook at the place we had breakfast. He saw me with Crumley and would like to know what I'm doing here. I tell him I'm a writer and he enquires as to what the fucking hell writers think they know about anything and why they fucking think anyone should pay them for it. I equivocate a little and he debates whether or not to hit me. Fortunately he realises that in the state of drunkenness he's achieved he is more liable to fall over than connect, so he settles for giving me his life story instead. Turn's out he's half Indian, which maybe explains his remarkable cheekbones, and has no money, which maybe explains his antipathy to people who do. By now Denis, wearing a superfine Western shirt that turns out to be an early Ralph Lauren, has bought us all further tequilas and beer chasers and my second evening in Missoula starts to blur like the first.

Crumley disappeared at some point to go and have dinner with his new girlfriend – 'a feminist,' he says, 'she keeps me in line'. Denis tells me that Crumley only has two states, 'in love or hurt in love'. A western swing band starts up and soon the whole place is dancing, apart from those of us welded to the bar, J. Rummel gets up to sing some Hank Williams songs; there's a commotion when an Angel on a Harley drives right through the bar as a mark of respect to Rummel. By the time I leave the men are all singing and the women crying into their beer.

Next morning, after another kill-or-cure breakfast and the discovery that even Missoula has a Sunday paper it takes two hands to lift, I decide it's time to try to get some kind of formal interview done with Crumley. So around one o'clock I go and bang on his door. After a minute or so I hear a grunt and then Crumley staggers up to the door, half dressed and looking decidedly rough. 'How are you doing?' I say, somewhat unnecessarily. Crumley groans and says, 'You know, you can have too much fun.' He's going back to bed and suggests we meet up in the evening, try and do the interview then. So I decide to visit Denis MacMillan. I get around to his house only to find nobody home. As I'm wondering what to do next, a figure with longish fair hair, wearing a white suit and walking a large dog, hoves to. Lo, it's Denis. He invites me in and says he'll make himself something to eat, then we'll go for a ride in the Cadillac he bought from Crumley, maybe drive out down Bitterroot Valley, call in on Jon Jackson, another Montana crime writer.

While Denis is getting busy in the kitchen, he plays me some videotapes of his friend Charles Willeford, being interviewed on Miami public service TV. Willeford is great, looking like a caricature of a gin-soaked old soldier; bald headed, with a huge, bristling moustache, courteous to interviewers who clearly know next to nothing about him, but possessed of a ferociously dry sense of humour. Denis is clearly much saddened by Willeford's death the previous year, and tells me with some frustration that Willeford's widow, Betsey, is putting a stop to the exceptionally well-presented series of reissues that he, Denis, is putting out, apparently having acquired a somewhat inflated idea of the commercial potential of her husband's catalogue. By now Denis is ready to go, so after giving me a quick guided tour of his awesome book collection, he leads me out to the car.

Which is a Cadillac Fleetwoood limousine, which may not be as large as a house, but the back seat alone is bigger than certain hotel rooms I've stayed in. It does approximately zero miles to the gallon but it drives like a dream once we hit the open road, out past Lollo. The Bitterroot Valley is extraordinary, a green I've only seen before in pictures of China. Then we turn on to small country roads heading to Jon Jackson's place. Jackson wrote two books in the late '70s, *The Diehard* and *The Blind Pig*, both fine urban thrillers featuring a Detroit cop named Mulheisen. Since then it's been hard times for Jackson; his first wife died, he was drinking heavily, couldn't get another novel published. Now maybe things are looking up. He's remarried, quit drinking, Denis reissued *The Blind Pig*, and he's reportedly hard at work in his garden shed. Not today he isn't though; when we arrive at Jackson's place both shed and house are locked up.

Such is life. We head back down the valley, and seeing as it's now late afternoon we stop off at one of Lollo's bars, the Traveller's Rest or somesuch. There's a bunch of bikes outside. When we go in it turns out that one of them belongs to Steve, Crumley's babysitter of the other night. He's deep in conversation with a moderately serious-looking biker named Mel, who gives us the hard-stare treatment until Denis's Southern charm wins him over. Apparently he and Steve met by the side of the road, where Mel was having something of a bust-up with his old lady, the upshot of which was that Mel and Steve went racing along the road to Idaho, and the old lady got left in the middle of nowhere, trying to thumb a ride home. Which she appeared to have succeeded in doing by the time Mel and Steve came back to see whether, as Mel put it, 'she'd learned her lesson'. Mel's clearly enjoying impressing Steve with what a bad motherfucker he is, tells us that he's serving some kind of apprenticeship before joining the local chapter of motorbike desperadoes. Then he tells us about some real bad guys he knows, survivalists living up in the Idaho hills.

Frightening people, he says, which is about right. The North-West's deserved reputation as the last unspoilt place left has appealed not only to migratory writers but also to that section of American society which combines belief in such things as the literal truth of the Old Testament with a conviction that nuclear war is both inevitable and survivable. Which combination of beliefs leads people to arm themselves to the teeth and head for the hills, there to form post-Manson communities that have a tendency to start killing anyone who comes near them and eventually each other. What is worrying is the prospect of these various communes starting to organise together. This weekend the local papers are full of news about a neo-Nazi skinhead get-together in Idaho. The general consensus seems to have been that it's a hyped-up non-event. But there is certainly some scary shit stirring in the beautiful North-West.

Back in Missoula Crumley is partially revived but obviously down. We head off to Charlie's but conversation is hard work. I make the mistake of asking what's happening with the script Crumley has written for *Judge Dredd, the Movie*. Last time I'd met Crumley, this actually looked like getting made. Crumley had written it, like several previous scripts, with his friend, the director Tim Hunter, and he felt that here at last was a project so copper-bottomed commercial that it had to be made. He should have known better, maybe; he's now been working on and off in Hollywood for twenty years. Each one of his books has been bought for the movies, yet none of his screenplays has been made or his books filmed, despite Joe Gores telling me that Crumley and Hunter's screeplay for *Dancing Bear* was one of the very best he'd ever read. The trouble this time seems to be that the people with the money had fixated on Schwarzenegger as the man to be Judge Dredd, a part in which you would never see the actor's face anyway, and it turns out that Arnie is booked up to somewhere round the year 2000 and much as he might like to can't do it...Talking about the screenwriting now, Crumley is distinctly wearied: 'It's too much work for too little return. When you finish a screenplay, you've put a year's hard work into it and more often than not all you've got is the cheque. It's a survivable experience but not a very pleasant one.'

We adjourn to a nearby Italian resturant to see whether food will liven the conversation up. It doesn't. Even the Chianti fails to help, and shortly we abandon the attempt at an interview till first thing the following morning. At which Crumley suddenly brightens and tells me about the time a German film crew came to interview him, but were never able to pin him down at all. On this ominous note he goes back home to get some sleep. Showing rather less good sense I head back to Charlie's, meet up with Denis, and in the course of the next several hours play some pool, adjourn to a place called the 8 Ball where we can play snooker till it closes, return to Charlie's for several nightcaps and round the evening off back at Denis's, tearing the side door off the Chevy somewhere along the way.

So at 9 a.m. the next morning it's a rested, if still subdued, Crumley who has distinctly the advantage as I attempt to conduct an interview.

James Crumley is not an easy man to interview. The turning on of a tape-recorder has a tendency to send him into instant

English professor mode; the simplest query will receive an answer of considerable abstraction, both formal and rambling. This stems in particular from the entirely reasonable desire that his work should be seen as work and not as autobiography. It's a fear particularly well-grounded for Crumley. More perhaps than with any other crime writer apart from Hammett, Crumley's readers want to believe that this is a man who walks it like he talks it. Crumley's heroes are so much the dream apotheoses of every '6os survivor, so simply romantic. Sughrue in *The Last Good Kiss* is the perfect hard-boiled hero for the fortysomething Vietnam generation:

> Home? Home is my apartment on the east side of Hell-Roaring Creek, three rooms where I have to open the closets and drawers to be sure I'm in the right place. Home? Try a motel bar at eleven o'clock on a Sunday night, my silence shared by a pretty barmaid who thinks I'm a creep and some asshole in a plastic jacket who thinks I'm his buddy. (*The Last Good Kiss*)

And, of course, what makes Crumley so keen to distance himself from his characters is precisely a sense that perhaps he isn't that far away from them. It's undeniably tempting, the Hemingway idea of the man behind the books being his ultimate creation. In Charlie's a couple of nights before, Crumley was revelling in it. Now he's weary, wrung out from the effort of being the public James Crumley: 'I guess I'm the last writer in Missoula still to spend some time hanging out, to have a home bar. But even I feel like drifting away from that now.'

After talking for a while about writing in fairly general terms, Crumley suddenly shifts up, or perhaps down, a gear, snaps out of literary interview mode and starts talking about the vicissitudes of a writer's life: 'I've been broke almost all the time.

Everybody thinks I'm this successful Hollywood screenwriter now, but that's not even true. Most of it goes on the enormous expense I have for alimony and child support – two thousand dollars a month is a tremendous sum for me. It's one of life's little ironies that as soon as I get into a position where I'm going to be financially secure for the first time in my life, that doesn't even last a moment…that marriage broke up two weeks before I had to go and work on the script for *Dancing Bear*…

'…I'm a much different person now. I've lived alone for four years and I'm much more careful about, you know, who I fall in love with, and what living arrangements I have. I have more energy and have survived more things than most people, and because of that I've done too many things without thinking of the consequences. I've now learned the consequences, to say the least. So I'm no longer engaged in domestic disasters. It might make me a better writer, it might make me a worse writer, it might make it impossible for me to write, but, whatever, I'm fairly content with my life. I've lived in this house longer than any house since I got out of high school. This is the longest I've gotten to live in Missoula at one stretch. I always come back here, but always before I've gotten broke and had to go away.'

Not that being broke has simply been part of Crumley's adult life. Given his background his career is practically the American Dream in action. Like C.W. Sughrue's, Crumley's origins are in Texas dirt poverty of a kind few contemporary American writers have experienced. 'Oh, yeah,' says Crumley, only half joking, 'the only writer in America who is as down-home as me is Harry Crews. I grew up out in the country in south Texas. My only sibling was ten years younger than me. My father worked in the oilfields, my mother was a waitress. I was lucky, during the war, to live in New Mexico so I grew up with Mexican Americans and I didn't have that Texas prejudice when I moved back there. I grew up wearing chickenfeed shirts to school and the only reason I had shoes was because my mother always insisted I wear shoes. I'd hide them under the cattleguard before I'd catch the bus and I'd go to school barefoot. We were country people. My mother wouldn't go to church, she sort of insisted I belong to a church and she would take me to Sunday school, and then she would come and pick me up, but she wouldn't go into the church because she felt that people might make fun of her. This was in a town where the richest people who belonged to the Baptist church made three thousand dollars, maybe! Her father was in prison, my father never finished high school...'

It would be a mistake, too, to see this poverty as in some way romantic. As Crumley observes: 'South Texas has certainly lots of charm, but it was never a place I was very happy. It's a place I was always uncomfortable about going back to. Over the last few years I've felt somewhat more comfortable. The part of south Texas I grew up in is different from Texas and different from Mexico. When I was growing up there my home town was sixty-five per cent Chicano yet it was ruled by the Anglos, I found it to be a really repressive and uncomfortable place. Also the wind blows all the time and it's unbearably hot in the summertime...It took me coming to terms with south Texas, finding things that I honestly like, to write about it.'

Crumley got out of south Texas by the classic route, working hard and going to college: 'I got a scholarship to Georgia Tech when I got out of high school. At the time, in the '50s, engineering was going to be the big thing, and I did well in physics. Plus south Texas is tremendously anti-intellectual, nobody reads much, so reading gets to be a secret habit like masturbation. Nobody ever told me what to read, I taught myself, so I had a very odd education, I didn't read the books that influenced me until I was in my mid-twenties. So I went off to be an engineer, but I didn't like Georgia much and I clearly didn't want to be an engineer, and after a year I hitch-hiked back to Texas and joined the army.

'I had a good time in the army but I didn't do well. I was always in trouble. I had the chance to spend a year and a half in the Philippines, ten days in Hong Kong, saw some parts of the country I wouldn't have seen otherwise. I also got busted twice, spent some time in the stockade. I hit a cook one night, he was being snotty to me, army cooks are traditionally snots. I knocked the snot out of this guy. Then I got busted again when I was playing baseball with the base team and we were smuggling cigarettes and Dewar's White Label Scotch and stuff like that to sell on the black market. The major who sat at my court martial had moved his entire household full of new appliances from the States, had the army move them for him, had showed a month early to be sure he couldn't have a house on base, got a house off-base. One night when he was conveniently drunk at the officers' club, the entire contents of the house and a new Cadillac were stolen. He made about thirty thousand dollars on that deal, the most I ever made was about three hundred. I didn't feel that the black market was a major crime as long as you weren't dealing with medical supplies or weapons. There was a basic problem in the Philippines – we had things they wanted and they were figuring out ways to get them.'

It was only after coming out of the army that Crumley started to make some moves towards becoming a writer: 'I didn't know what was going to happen to me till I was twenty-two, twenty-three and I started writing a story. In the real, autobiographical story my father put a sledgehammer through the top of a mud pump in the oilfield, but as I was writing, and I remember the moment exactly, in the story the father picks up the sledgehammer and instead of hitting the mud pump he hits the son in the head. Didn't kill him but made him into the kind of son his mother actually wanted. Now, my father had only spanked me twice, he'd never hit me or anything, this was nothing out of my past, but it was then I realised "Jeez, you can write about stuff that didn't happen." It was then that I realised I was a writer and not some kid looking for…dust.'

After leaving college Crumley worked for a while before, aged twenty-five, sending a story to the University of Iowa and being accepted on to the justly celebrated writers' workshop there. Among the writers teaching there were Kurt Vonnegut and the great Chicago novelist Nelson Algren; 'he never taught me but I played poker with him a time or two', says Crumley. More directly influential on his writing, though, was the presence of R. V. Cassill, a prolific writer of pulp novels for the likes of Gold Medal Books and a seminal critic, one of the very few American critics to realise at the time the value of '50s pulp writers like Jim Thompson and David Goodis. It was Cassill who introduced Crumley to the greats of American crime writing and to the idea that they might be taken seriously.

At Iowa Crumley began writing his first novel, *One to Count Cadence*, a book that drew on his army experience, and which stands up now as a remarkably mature and considered novel about the realities of war. It alienated critics at the time, however, by refusing to propagandise for either left or right. It did well enough, though, for a first novel; it sold to paperback and was bought for the movies, suddenly and temporarily shifting Crumley into an unexpected tax bracket. But its aftermath left Crumley with enough problems of one kind or another for it to take six and a half years for the next book to appear. Crumley chuckles sardonically going on bitterly when I ask him what took so long.

'That might have had something to do with three different teaching jobs, two divorces, the adoption of my three older children and, back of the row, eight hundred pages of a novel called *The Muddy Fork*, which I later destroyed. A lot of it was education. I wrote that first novel without really knowing what I was doing. You never get to do that again. Once I knew what I was doing then it became more difficult. I think some of it, too, had to do with the reaction I had from reviewers. As with most first novels it was soundly ignored. Those who did take time to review it, with a few notable exceptions, took sides – it came out while the war was still going on, it wasn't anti-war enough to suit the left and it wasn't pro-war enough to suit the right. It was ambiguous, which was maybe necessary. I'm not sure what it would be like if I wrote it now; it might be somewhat more anti-war, anti-military; more compassionate of the Vietnamese people and also less forgiving of them. A lot of people hated that book when it came out. I had put everything I had into that book and it looked like it might sell some copies, it sold to the movies…then all of that fell apart. The producer ended up not paying me a third of the money. That caused me a great deal of trouble, cost me a house, a couple of cars, and sent me back to teaching.'

The key problem in Crumley's career, though, seems to have been the pressure of literature, the desire to do something truly epic and great, a desire strong enough to lead him to burn far more work than he has ever published, and a desire that must have made him hell to live with. The complexity of Crumley's domestic arrangements at this time make it amazing that he ever wrote anything at all: 'My first marriage broke up two days after I finished the first book. I married again a year or so after that. It broke up four years later, and then I was living with a woman in Colorado when I was writing *The Wrong Case* and then that broke up. By the time *The Wrong Case* came out I was married a third time. As happens when you're young, you don't understand the emotional energy that goes into things like that. It seems like it might be civilised but it takes more time than you realise. It made it difficult to write. I finished *Cadence* here, moved to Arkansas, moved back here, moved to Colorado, moved to Seattle, moved back to Colorado and moved to Texas before *The Wrong Case* came out.'

The Wrong Case was Crumley's first detective novel. It was intended as a one-off, a way to cure his writer's block and make some money at the same time. 'It was something I started when I realised I was going to quit teaching at Colorado. It seemed quite quick and easy to do.' It introduced into Crumley's fiction both the town of Missoula, disguised as Meriwether, and the character of broken-down private eye Milo Milodragovitch, the alcoholic scion of one of the town's founding families. Milo will be rich when he reaches the age of fifty-two, that's when he comes into his father's legacy. Meanwhile he's been scraping a living doing divorce work and destroying his self-respect. But, as *The Wrong Case* opens, the divorce laws have been liberalised and he's contemplating ruin from the vantage point of the bottom of a bottle. Milo is a man much taken advantage of; in both books he appears in, *The Wrong Case* and *Dancing Bear*, he is set up to be the patsy, never sees the big picture till the end. But his progress is an effective illustration of the maxim that you can't con an honest man, even if he is behind the game by enough coke and booze to stop a regiment.

Milo is also the character closest to Crumley's heart: 'He comes from the good side of my unconscious; at the worst moments of my life I think, 'I can't be a horrible person because I invented Milo.' He takes care of things, he takes care of all the drunks in the town, he's kind of a saint. None of Milo's background is mine. but I'm sure it's somehow connected metaphorically, in the search for the lost father. When we came back from the war my father was off working all the time in the oilfield and I never saw much of him. He was a very quiet, gentle man, and my mother was a very forceful, violent woman, so I got an atypical American upbringing. I'm sure the things I write about Milo and his father, or Sughrue and his father, come out of my feeling when my father died thirteen years ago. But,' he hastens to add, 'none of the experiences are mine, I'm a writer not an autobiographer.'

I comment on the disparity between Milo's social origins and Crumley's, to which he replies: 'The rich and the poor have more in common than the middle class. That's one of the funny things in the *Kinsey Report*. About the only people who were engaging in oral sex, or at least admitting it, were the highest-income groups and the lowest. My friends say that Milo's the character that reminds them most of me. Whether in his good-heartedness or his self-destruction I don't ask!'

The Wrong Case wasn't a one-off. Both the novels Crumley has written since have been crime novels, more or less, but it has only been lately that he has stopped regarding them as a waste of his potential. The book he's currently working on is another version of *The Muddy Fork*, one that will have some kind of crime format. 'I'm trying to do a new book, an even less traditional detective novel than anything else I've done. It's more of a family novel, in the Faulkner sense rather than the domestic sense, narrated by the Sughrue character.'

This latest version of the south Texas novel Crumley has been trying to write since the early '70s stems from his discovery of an attempt he made at writing it in thriller form in the late '70s, right after *The Last Good Kiss*: 'I discovered the opening fifty odd pages by accident, didn't even know I had it, because I had burned or thrown away most things. On re-reading it I discovered I couldn't see why I stopped, so I went back to it. I suppose, at the time, because of a certain feeling that you get sometimes in academic circles that detective novels are a lesser form, I felt like I was giving this novel short shrift by using it as a detective novel. I no longer feel that way. I no longer not only do not have the notion that the serious novel is more important than the detective novel, I can't remember why I ever had that notion. Must have been crazed, ignorant or stupid to have fallen prey to the cheapest kind of intellectual snobbery.'

Now Crumley has come round to the view that the detective novel has a particular usefulness in dissecting modern-day America: 'You can do what you want in a detective novel as long as it's entertaining and interesting. I've never been much interested in traditional crime, solving a mystery. It's a nice literary conceit, but most crimes are solved because somebody rolls over, somebody grasses. It's like the courtroom novel; most things never reach the courtroom, way less than a third of crimes are ever solved and, of those that are, more than half are plea-bargained.

'The real criminal thing that happens in *The Wrong Case* is simply a personal failure. In *The Last Good Kiss* I think the real crime is a sort of literary arrogance on the part of the Trahearne character. Then there are other kinds of crimes in *Dancing Bear*; the dispersal of toxic waste across an entire countryside, for instance. There are other things; international arms-dealer cartels, the sort of casualness with which greed seems to rule things out there, but I've been out of politics too long to feel qualified...'

Qualified or not, Crumley is always keen to talk politics, and his books, while scarcely overt revolutionary texts, have politics as a continual sub-text. Crumley, like his characters and like the people he hangs out with, is a man who was changed for ever by the political upheavals of the '60s, and, while he may be disillusioned, he is certainly no born-again Republican. Crumley's '60s did not begin with the hippy period either, but came out of the militancy of the civil rights period and the attraction of the proto-hippy beat lifestyle centred around San Francisco in the late '50s, which Crumley came into contact with while waiting to be shipped out to the Philippines. 'I was in San Francisco waiting to go overseas in 1958. Had I had a little more control over my life I would have stayed there when I came back from the Philippines. But I had to go back to Texas for six months. Then I got engaged to a woman there, went to college there, played football for the college as a linebacker...Also there was a kind of prejudice against California, full of kooks and nuts and freaks. So while the '60s were going on I had long hair and I did a lot of drugs, but I didn't identify with the movement in any great way. In my most political days when I was in the SDS [Students for a Democratic Society], what I liked best about it was that middle-class kids discovered how the police had been treating blacks and Chicanos and poor people all the time. Suddenly middle-class white kids from Evanston, Illinois, were getting their heads busted. I think it changed the way America looks at itself. It was a good time, it was a revolution that failed but made some significant changes.'

As the '60s wore on, though, the pitch of Crumley's political involvement slackened. 'I was ready for revolution at the point of a gun then I realised I didn't want to kill anybody. It took the edge off my politics and I backed away somewhere in the early '70s. I stayed active in the Vietnam veterans against the war. I donate money for environmental things, I try to save what's left of the West. Mostly it's money and time whereas in the '60s it was passion. I'm not sure which is better. Once you discover that you're not going to blow shit up....'

And a degree of scepticism as to the usefulness of much of the '60s idealism crept in, a suspicion that much of it boiled down to rhetoric and posturing, summed up today by the way in which Kennedy is revered as a secular saint, while Lyndon Johnson is firmly consigned to the dustbin of history by both left and right: 'I never much admired public figures. By the time Kennedy was president I knew enough about history to know he came from the most corrupt political machine anywhere in the world and I knew what kind of guy he was. He thought he was untouchable, he could fuck any woman he wanted to, nobody would say anything about it. I don't think he had any ideals at all. Lyndon Johnson was someone who grew up in the same town my parents did. I liked Lyndon's programmes and ideas but he was the kind of guy who would sell you a pair of socks and there'd only be one sock in the package. But every now and then I try and remind myself that we got Lyndon Johnson not to run again and what we really did was to elect Nixon. Being right is not always the best thing there is, being thoughtful and kind is more important than being right.'

The interview is winding up now. As ever it degenerates into both of us coming out with political commonplaces and the kind of literary conversation that tends to run along the lines of 'Have you read so-and-so?', 'No', 'Oh, well, they're good'. Then Crumley tells me that he's recently read a thriller put out by a feminist publishing house and he's looking to pick up an option on it and, together with his girlfriend, work it up into a script, see whether he has better luck getting someone else's book made. By now he's cheered up somewhat, and feels like summing things up. 'It's nice now, I'm forty-nine, to feel it's OK to be an outsider. All through my youth I always wanted to belong. I was a juvenile delinquent, a football player, I was on the student council, I was on the yearbook staff, I was in the army, I went to a good college on a scholarship. I went back to college on a football scholarship, I played everything but quarterback, mostly I was a linebacker. I grew up learning to run into people at high speeds.'

On which note we walk outside to inspect the damage I'd done to the rental car the night before. Which provokes, one more time, the James Crumley laugh.

5   Detroit: where the weak are killed and eaten

AT THE MOTOR City airport I pick up the best and the cheapest car yet, a maroon Buick with a mock-mahogany dash, and swing on to the Edsel Ford Expressway, heading for downtown. I have not been looking forward to this leg of the trip. You tell people you're going to Detroit and the first thing most of them say is 'why?' Driving in, I'm envisaging something like the nightmare New York that John Carpenter created for his film *Escape from New York*; a place of decay and violence.

On my left there's a sign to Inkster – the town that Ford built outside the city limits when he bowed to the economic necessity to hire black people to work on his production lines. He wasn't having no nigras living in the nice model housing developments he was building for his white workforce, however, so he built a shanty-town version for the blacks and called it, with redneck humour, Inkster. Now it's subsumed into the Detroit sprawl, but it lives in my heart as the place that gave the world the girl group with the best name of all – the Marvelettes. Tuning my radio, at five in the afternoon, I encounter the usual selection of smarmy drive-time jocks playing the Top 40, when suddenly I'm struck by the sound of the blues shout of Johnny Taylor. The record finishes and I find out I'm listening to the AM radio sound of Inkster, Michigan, and it's deep soul and down-home blues all the way; Johnny Taylor gives way to Bobby 'Blue' Bland gives way to Miss Lynn White from Memphis and there is not a trace of anything even remotely urban contemporary. The strange thing is that up here, about as far north I've been, is the first time I've heard a station like this.

Mark and Alan in Chicago called up a friend of theirs in Detroit, a woman named Marcia. So I've got a place to stay which, I suspect, is a blessing. My guidebook more or less gives up when it comes to places to stay in Detroit, confining itself to the menacing observation that 'accommodations are usually either cheap or safe; if you choose cheap be sure to arrive in daylight and be willing to forgo nightlife'. Which didn't sound like a whole lot of fun, even allowing for the guidebook habit of painting everything about fifty per cent worse than real life.

Marcia's address is on Atkinson Street which looks on the map to be a litle way north of downtown Detroit. So I get off the expressway at the Woodward Avenue exit, head up north and get my first view of Detroit street life. Woodward looks like the main street of a ghost city. To the left there are the great deco hulks of the industrial palaces: the General Motors building and the Fisher building. Everywhere there are churches, there's a Woolworths on the corner of Grand with a few harassed black and Hispanic folks waiting for a bus alongside, but there is simply not enough life on the street to justify its scale.

Atkinson is off to the left a mile or so up the road, and once again as soon as you get off the main road you are instantly in a totally residential neighbourhood. The houses look great, large detached places with big gardens front and back, but seeming a little down at heel, and the cars parked outside are mostly big old gas-guzzling American motors. I find Marcia's house, park and bang on the door, which is opened by a tall young woman dressed in black who looks to be both in a hurry and surprised to see me. The situation is resolved by the appearance of a third party who says, 'Hi, I'm Marcia, you must be John, this is Heidi, my daughter, I'm afraid she's got to run.'

Marcia, Detroit Italian and possessed of a startling

enthusiasm for life and art, sits me down in her kitchen, produces some fine local brewery beer and starts telling me about the neighbourhood. This was the prime real estate in Detroit in the old days, the housing built by or for car company executives. Then came white flight to the suburbs and by the mid '70s the area was almost entirely black. Which meant – this of course being God's own country, where each man is equal under the sun – that the cost of housing shot through the floor and kept on falling. Which is how Marcia, a single mother with virtually no money, managed to buy herself what they call round here a mansion – a detached inner-city house with a grand central staircase, servants' quarters and quite as many bedrooms as you would want to shake a stick at.

The place is a bohemian dream home of the sort that is virtually extinct in every other major Western city, taken over by the gentrifiers years ago. The moral presumably being that yuppies don't mind living in a converted abattoir or something but they're a bit sniffy about the next-door neighbours. Marcia, on the other hand has no alarm system, has lived here for fifteen years and never been burgled. So there you go, living proof that it's not the colour of the people in it which makes a neighbourhood safe or unsafe. An all-black neighbourhood like this one is going to be peaceful enough because its surroundings are green and pleasant, the scale is human and people know each other. Put people in some conglomeration of twenty-storey rat-traps and it's hardly surprising it's dangerous.

Later in the evening Marcia decides to take me for a drive around downtown Detroit. We head back south down Woodward, more deserted than ever at ten o'clock. Past the expressway, on the left, there's a burst of activity; limo-lock surrounds the Art Institute, some black-tie opening. On the other side of the road there's the derelict-looking bulk of the Gaiety Burlesque Theater, a landmark familiar from Elmore

Leonard's Detroit thrillers. Detroit not having a whole heap of cultural icons at the moment, a certain degree of civic pride seems to have attached itself to Leonard. His books are well displayed everywhere and Marcia tells me how well she thinks his latest paperback, *Freaky Deaky*, fixes a time and a place in the city.

A little farther down the road is the Fox Theater, a reminder of Detroit's cultural heyday. This is where the great Motown revues would take place, where once a week you had the chance of seeing the likes of the Supremes, the Miracles, Martha and the Vandellas and Little Stevie Wonder all on the one bill and all for 75 cents. Recently the Fox Theatre has been restored to its original deco opulence. It's attracting crowds in from the suburbs and is being touted as a sign that Detroit is coming back from the brink – i.e. becoming a suitable place for middle-class whites to stroll about of an evening.

For the moment, though, Detroit central after dark is left to the blacks and the bohemians. We swing east towards the warehouse district over near the big meat market, to visit some friends of Marcia's. As we're looking for a place to park, we see Detroit's current black music stars Inner City loading their gear into a van. Then we go visit the chaotic art-strewn warehouse of Marcia's friend, who's a painter, but scrapes a living doing portrait photography, weddings and bar mitzvahs not excluded. Being there is like stepping a little way back in time, to an era of bohemianism of a sort that has simply become financially non-viable in most major cities, a bohemian culture in which lack of commercial success does not make you a non-person.

On our way back we stop off at the Union Street bar, an oasis of life on Woodward not far from the Wayne State University campus. It's a pleasant old-fashioned saloon and, sitting at the bar, we discover Marcia's lodger, an English guy called Malcolm, who is part of an avant-garde theatre company who have based themselves in Detroit largely because the living is cheap enough for non-commercial artists to survive, and tough enough to prevent complacency. Malcolm is shattered from driving the company's van back from a performance in Minnesota, and soon enough we all head back to sleep.

Next day it's time for some serious sightseeing. First up is the Motown museum. Down Woodward, take a right at the Woolworths on Grand, and head west for a mile or so to a neighbourhood of ordinary two-storey wood-frame houses. Number 2648 still has the big window with the HITSVILLE USA sign that it's had since 1960, when it read like a piece of wild bravado, along the lines of proclaiming that you serve the best pizza in America. Now, sadly, it seems rather more like a lament. Motown is now wholly owned by MCA and has for years, anyway, been indistinguishable in its output from the black music divisions of any major record label, maybe a little less innovative than most. Inside, a couple of oldish women in old-style wigs are deep in debate and don't notice me for a while. When my presence is finally registered they ask me to wait a moment and employ the intercom in an attempt to find someone to show me round. A couple of minutes later a spectacularly pomaded individual who gives the appearance of having been raised from birth in the fabled Motown charm school (which he reveals operated out of a nondescript red-brick building over the road) welcomes me to the Motown Museum and proceeds to deliver a spiel on the greatness of Motown, which, considering that his audience consisted of one person paying $3.50 for the pleasure, was a model of professionalism.

It is also some way out of keeping with the tackiness that otherwise characterises the Motown Museum. After the introductory spiel a junior member of the Gordy clan, possessed of an unfortunate speech impediment, ushers me into a room to watch a video, badly recorded from the TV, of

Detroit's mayor, the high-profile Coleman Young, unveiling a Motown plaque in the rain. Then Mr Pomade returns to usher me through the original Motown studio, which has an appealing *Mary Celeste* quality, and upstairs into the historical display section – which consists almost entirely of a bunch of album covers tacked more or less randomly on to the walls. He continues the spiel until his girlfriend appears, at which event he breaks off in mid-flow, suggests I might like to explore a little by myself, and retreats into another room to canoodle a little. I stare at the album covers a while and then spot a glass case in the corner containing Michael Jackson's glove. Next to this is a clipping relating that when Michael was last in Detroit he came to the museum and then donated the proceeds of his concert that night – $120,000 or so – towards extending the collection. Presumably Michael knows tacky when he sees tacky. Where the money has gone, however, is hard to divine. Certainly not on a bunch of old album covers and a newspaper cutting in which 'Punk rock group the Clash tour the Motown Museum', which is unaccountably set under glass on top of Berry Gordy's old desk. As memorials go the Motown Museum doesn't fit too well, but still I acquire Motown frisbees, T-shirts, mugs, caps and drinks coasters to delight the folks back home.

Next stop is some way north, in a down-at-heel black neighbourhood, off McNichols Road. Here, in a nondescript white-painted warehouse, is the headquarters of a rather less publicised black business empire – Skippy's. Skippy's is a retail, wholesale and mail-order operation specialising in all the little necessities for the practice of voodoo or santeria – a for-real magic store. Inside it's white-painted and brightly lit; the products are laid out supermarket-style. Not that there are a lot of supermarkets with a rack of rabbits' eyes on sale, or selections of ingredients for a mojo, or bats' hearts. Slightly less menacing is an array of bottles full of viscous liquid in a selection of spectacularly artificial hues, including the loudest orange I've encountered. On closer examination the labels proclaim the bottles to be efficacious in sorting out your problems, whether of money, health or love. All of them are billed as 'Skippy's Indian Spirit House Blessing – Triple Fast Action Spiritual – Bath & Floor Wash'. Small print suggests a 'Bath Ritual: Fill bath with warm water, pour in half bottle. Read 23rd Psalm. Concentrate on your desires'. What it doesn't mention is whether you should actually get into the bath, which, having smelt the lethal liquid in the bottles, would appear to be a piece of tactful ambivalence perhaps suggested by Skippy's lawyers. The facing shelves contain the same bottles but with the labels this time in Spanish. Then, as my attention is caught by the display of bottles of pimp oil (to perfume your pimpmobile, y'unnerstand), someone emerges from a back room and leaves the door half open. Peering through, I can see into the Skippy factory. Big vats of the alarming liquids are being tapped into bottles; identical bottles stand waiting to discover whether they are going to be used to drive away evil, promote romance or bring financial reward.

Financial benefit is the attraction of much of the merchandise. Sticks of Sweet Smell of Success incense nestle alongside a selection of dream books – pamphlets which explain that certain kinds of dream correspond to certain numbers which you should therefore select when gambling on them. The numbers racket is clearly alive and well in Detroit. As I purchase my selection of dubious potions the orange-haired black woman on the till slips a piece of paper into my bag. On it is Skippy's lucky number for today. Back in the car, listening to the Inkster blues station, it strikes me that Detroit is really the last great Southern town. Here amid the industrial decay of the city that first offered well-paid work for blacks, back around the time of the First World War, is where voodoo and deep soul persist, not in the shopping malls of the New South.

From here I just drive around for a while, looking for a place to eat. Head out to east Detroit, taking the expressway as far as Cadieux, find myself in a suburban industrial zone and head back towards downtown along Warren Avenue. As you get closer to the centre the area gets seedier, the road surface deteriorates and the faces are gradually all black. There are a few record shops and barber shops straight out of 1972 *Superfly* times, with names like Soul to Soul, but little life on a grey midweek lunchtime. Turn on to Gratiot and soon enough I'm downtown. Left on to Beaubien where the police HQ is and left again on to Monroe, and park. A couple of blocks of Monroe are known as Greektown, for the unsurprising reason that they've got a lot of Greek restaurants on them. I pick up a sandwich and wander into Trapper's Alley, a cutesy shopping mall which is much the same as any other apart from a nice line in T-shirts emblazoned with the slogan 'Detroit – where the weak are killed and eaten'.

Next stop is a few blocks away on East Adams, the offices of the city-funded *City Arts* magazine. I want to pick up a back number with a piece on Donald Goines. *City Arts* is edited by John Sinclair, sometime manager of the legendary Detroit rock band the MC5. The MC5 had one great song, which is fondly remembered by Skip, the ageing counter-culture bomber in Elmore Leonard's *Freaky Deaky*. Skip requests the number from a smarmy guitarist playing romantic tunes for the dinner dates in a downtown restaurant; it's called 'Kick Out The Jams, Motherfuckers'. Sinclair was also responsible for founding the White Panthers, more of an idea than an army perhaps, but still enough to make Sinclair distinctly *persona non grata* with the FBI who were more than satisfied to see him spend much of the '70s in jail after a highly dubious dope bust. Sinclair's not in the office at the moment, so I pick up the magazine and head off to spend the afternoon following the thread of Elmore Leonard's Detroit.

Leonard lives out in a suburb called Birmingham, around fifteen miles north of downtown, straight out along Woodward. Much of the action in his Detroit-set novels is set along this Woodward axis, particularly in swank golf-course country around Bloomfield Hills, in Highland Park seediness, or in the ghetto bohemian neighbourhood known as the Cass Corridor.

The Cass Corridor starts just north of downtown and runs parallel to Woodward, a block or so to the west, up to Wayne State University. In *The Switch*, written in the late '70s, a black hustler named Ordell Robbie describes it like this: 'A fine example of neo-ghetto… you can see it's not quite your classic ghetto yet, not quite ratty or rotten enough, but it's coming.' Actually, like much of what I've seen of Detroit it doesn't seem to have deteriorated much from that time, but neither has it improved, it just seems kind of stuck. There are still shopfronts being used by hippy sculptors, just as described in Leonard's *Unknown Man Number 89*, still a lot of heavily fortified corner stores where they'll happily let you buy liquor with your welfare food stamps, as specifically forbidden by the federal government, and there are still whores wandering in and out of severely low-life bars. I stroll around a bit and follow a trail of half-dead records and books into what looks like a derelict basement but turns out to be second-hand bookstore on the point of collapse. When I wander out again I'm three dollars lighter but up a first edition of Nelson Algren's great novel of heroin addiction, *The Man With the Golden Arm*.

Back in the car and keep going north on Woodward, past Atkinson, where I'm staying, and, after a desolate mile or so dotted with churches and crack houses, the street population increases as I get to Highland Park, mostly Arab and black and dotted with storefront mosques, porno parlours that look as if they've seen better days, and motels that offer a special deal – $12 all day. All day?? Just over Six Mile Road and to the left is Palmer Park, with its golf course, while, on the right-hand side of Woodward, there are a selection of places with names like the Sassy Cat, Lucky Lips or Tender Trap; topless restaurants offering businessmen's lunches. It's in one of these that Harry Michell, the tough-guy hero of Leonard's first Detroit thriller, *52 Pick-Up*, meets the wrong girl: 'We stopped at four of them. Nice sunny afternoon we're doing the topless tour. The last place, she's sitting at the bar. Ross sees her, pats her on the ass thinking she's one of the go-goers, and tries to move in.'

After Palmer Park the neighbourhood starts to creep upscale. By the time I get to Nine Mile Road it's all funeral parlours, used-car lots and an unaccountable number of rare book dealers. By now Woodward has opened up into a big multi-lane highway. Apparently this used to be a favourite spot for road racing; hot-rods and muscle cars would congregate from miles around.

Birmingham starts at around Fourteen Mile Road and is a mall-defined kind of place; banks and CD stores line Woodward, while hair replacement clinics nestle discreetly in the side roads. The record store I walk into is full of the kind of music Elmore's characters tend to listen to, sophisticated '70s jazz-funk – Grover Washington, Roy Ayers, Joe Farrell, music for slick black hustlers and bored suburban housewives. Away from the main drag Birmingham is a pleasant suburban district, well off but not flash. Flash is provided a mile or two farther down the road in Bloomfield Hills, with its country clubs and lakes and high-status golf clubs, like the one in which Mickey, heroine of *The Switch*, spends her time being bored out of her mind, until the day that Ordell Robbie and his friend Louis kidnap her and take her back to a house off Highland Park, see how much her husband wants her back (answer, as it happens, not much).

Drinking coffee in a Denny's on my way back down Woodward, it strikes me that the ideal way to interview Elmore Leonard would be in the course of a slow crawl along this thoroughfare. Unfortunately this isn't going to be. Leonard is too busy and, maybe, too dignified, and I'm going to have to make do with a conversation in an anonymous hotel lounge, one of a series promoting his new novel.

Also, most of his Detroit writing was done in the '70s when he was somewhat less successful than today; his marriage was breaking up and he was, not incidentally, an alcoholic. All of which factors no doubt contributed to the novels of that period having a rather more street-level feel to them. Particularly this is the case with *Unknown Man Number 89*, a pivotal novel that came out in 1977, around the time Leonard was giving up drinking, which features a partially reformed alcoholic named Jack Ryan who makes a living by finding people who don't want to be found. Mostly people who owe other people money. At one point in the book Ryan is looking for a guy. He finds the guy's wife in a low-life bar on Cass, she's blind drunk on white wine, at two o'clock in the afternoon: Ryan says to her:

'You want to get there, what're you fooling around with wine for?'

She didn't answer him.

'I used to drink mostly Bourbon, over crushed ice, fill up a lowball glass. I also drank beer, wine, gin, vodka, Cuba Libres, Diet-Rite and scotch, and rye with red pop, but I preferred Bourbon, Early Times. I knew a guy who drank only Fresca and chartreuse. I took a sip one time, I said to him, "Jesus, this is the worst drink I ever tasted in my life." He said, "I know it is. It's so bad you can't drink very many of them." A real alcoholic, though, can drink anything, right?…What time you start in the morning?'

Without looking at him the girl said, 'Fuck off.'

All of which is clearly not a million miles from Leonard's own experience at the time, as he records in an essay written for a book called *The Courage to Change*, a collection of essays by alcoholics about their experiences of quitting drinking:

> I never reached the point of a couple of fifths a day. Not until the very end did I drink before noon. Noon was always that magic time when it became all right. Sunday morning I used to hold out and then come back from Mass and have a big bowl of chili and a couple of ice-cold beers. Hangovers never bothered me because all I had to do was drink a few ice-cold beers or a real hot, spicy bloody mary and I was back. I would drink a bottle of red wine and I'd be off. The next day it might be something else. Scotch or anything, though usually the next day I would disguise it. I would put scotch in something that you never put scotch in – Vernors ginger ale or something like that. I was great at trying to disguise the booze from myself. If I'd put that in a story, nobody would believe it.
>
> (Elmore Leonard quoted in *The Courage To Change* by Dennis Wholey)

In the mid '70s Elmore Leonard was in deep shit. He was a screenwriter whose films weren't getting made, a novelist who wasn't selling. He was separated from his wife of twenty years and living in a hotel. And drinking. Now Elmore Leonard, successful and sober, is sitting in a hotel lounge, finishing lunch with his second wife, Joan, whom he married in 1979 and who he credits with getting him off the booze and on to where he is today. Elmore Leonard is a small, neat man, with a trim beard and a careful way of looking at you. He doesn't miss much; if he played poker they'd call him 'Doc' and you would be ill advised to compete.

Joan, a smart, friendly blonde in late middle age like Elmore, and tired of hearing the familiar questions and answers, disappears offstage. I ask Elmore how he started writing: 'I used to tell stories when I was in grade school, we'd go to a movie and later on they would ask me to tell the movie to them. I wrote a play when I was in the fifth grade – a World War One play; this was after reading parts of *All Quiet on the Western Front*. We put the play on in the classroom using rows of desks as the trenches. After that I didn't write anything till college. I was in the services from '43 to '46 then I went to the University of Detroit and entered a short story contest; 1949 I got married and got a job in an ad agency. By 1951 I had started to write Westerns, without enough background, without having done enough research, without even having read very many Westerns. I liked Western movies and there was a very good market for the stories in the '50s, a lot of pulp magazines with the good ones paying two cents a word. In the '50s I sold thirty short stories and wrote five books. Two of the short stories were sold to Hollywood. *The Tall T* came out with Randolph Scott and *3.10 to Yuma* with Glenn Ford and Van Heflin.'

Elmore Leonard's Westerns are not typical. They provide a simple, clear backdrop for his Hemingway-inspired tough tales of decent men pushed too far, of outsiders fighting back. In those McCarthy years the Western was as good an area as any in which to uphold human dignity against bigotry and oppression. You can see that kind of opposition in films like *Bad Day at Black Rock* and you can see it in Leonard's *Hombre* or *Lawless River*. These were not simply *Bonanza*-style stories of good cowboys and bad Indians. 'I wanted to give them a sense of realism. People said my Westerns were too grim, didn't have enough blue sky in them, no romance.'

For all the considerable success of his Westerns, writing wasn't bringing in enough to support his growing family. So through the '50s he stayed at the ad agency, writing ads for Chevrolet. In 1961 he packed that in and went freelance. 'From '61 to late '65 I didn't write at all because I was too busy earning a living doing freelance work scriptwriting movies for *Encyclopaedia Britannica*. After *Hombre* sold to Fox in '66 I had enough money for about six months so I got back to writing and I've been doing it ever since.'

The market for Westerns, though, had been drying up since the late '50s with the proliferation of cowboy TV shows. So Leonard made his first book after the break a thriller called *The Big Bounce*. Rejected by several publishers as too grim, this short, sharp saga of migrant workers taking a little direct action in the pursuit of money was eventually put out by Gold Medal, the great pulp crime publishers of the '50s and '60s. The next decade is the most confusing part of Elmore Leonard's career. He succeeded in making a good living writing, mostly from Hollywood, and produced some great books, but had yet to settle into a pattern. He wrote some more Westerns, *Valdez Is Coming*, which made a fine film, and *Forty Lashes Less One*, which broke firmly with tradition by having as its heroes an Indian and a black man. He wrote a historical screwball comedy called *The Moonshine War* which made a terrible film; and he wrote thrillers like *Mr Majestyk*, filmed as a Charles Bronson vehicle, and *The Hunted*, an oddity set in Israel.

In 1974 he wrote *52 Pick-Up*, which was his first thriller to be set in Detroit, his home town. Like his Westerns it's the story of a worm turning, a regular joe taking on the bad guys. It is marred, though, by a sadistic, faintly misogynist edge to the plot. In the next novel, *Swag*, he got it right. Fast, tough and funny, this is the story of two guys, Frank and Stick, who, having made a thorough study of the options, decide that the way to better living is via armed robbery. From *Swag* onwards Elmore Leonard has simply written the best villains ever. His particular strength is the way people talk, the speech rhythms of Detroit's black and white low life: 'When I audition my characters at the start of a book they have to be able to talk or they don't get in. I use a lot of black characters because I can hear them and they use patterns of speech that I like.'

The book didn't sell, though, and meanwhile Leonard's home life was falling apart. 'We always drank. Every single night, we would get into arguments with me drunk and her part of the way, with me saying vicious things, which I couldn't believe the next day' (*The Courage to Change*). Which is where we came in.

The arrival of Joan in his life had an immediate effect on his writing. His next novel, *The Switch*, features his first really strong, autonomous female character. 'Joan has helped me tremendously with my women, to let them stand up and become part of the story. What I had to learn was to treat the woman as a person.'

Next came a move to a new publisher, Arbor House, who had faith in him, and, alongside further Detroit novels, Leonard started writing books set in Miami. 'I'd been going to Miami every year since 1950. I was drawn to writing about it because of the great contrast in the kinds of people that live in Florida from very rich in Palm Beach to Cubans in Miami.'

Stick, a follow-on from *Swag* set in Florida, was the first of his books to make it really big. It was subsequently filmed (very badly) by Burt Reynolds. The next one, *LaBrava*, was bought by Dustin Hoffman, but was never actually filmed. Then came *Glitz*, which was a major bestseller and is soon to be a TV blockbuster mini-series, which bodes less than well.

Elmore, however, is sanguine about the quality of the films made of his work.

'It really doesn't bother me that much because I know the problems. I know going in that you'll be dealing with a lot of people who don't know anything about story, nothing about casting apart from "let's get the guy who was in a successful picture before" – their ideas are all about what worked in another picture. They don't have any story sense at all. But for about twenty years this has supported my novel writing and I'm very optimistic about each film. All along the way I'll think, "This could be a good picture, who knows?" and I'll do what the director says even though I think he's wrong. Generally it turns out I was right, but I don't regret it.'

After *Glitz* came *Bandits*, fresh out here in paperback. '*Bandits* came about when a film producer said, "How would you like to write the script of a big caper movie: several old pros get together for one last heist" and I said, "Sure, but I want to write it as a book first and I want to set it in New Orleans." Then, planning the book, I had to think of something for these guys to steal, so I read in the paper about money being collected privately for the Contras. And I thought that this money could be sitting in one place and these guys could find out about it, so I introduced the ex-nun who enlists them and told them what was going on down in Nicaragua. But I've been asked if I wrote that book to get my political views across. I didn't. It was only something for these guys to steal. Of course you do get politically involved when you have to explain what's going on and you have to show some passion for one side or the other... and of course it's going to be for the former nun against the Contras.'

Bandits seems perhaps a little over-researched and occasionally uncertain in tone. For the next book, *Freaky Deaky*, Elmore returned to Detroit and wrote a much funnier book on a much smaller scale. I ask whether this was a deliberate reaction to

Bandits. '*Bandits* may have wandered a little more than I had planned and, because I make it up as I go along, maybe it took a little longer to decide what was going to happen. A lot of surprising things happen while I'm writing. A minor character, Franklin De Dios, just pushed himself into the story. Certainly *Freaky Deaky* is more compressed and *Killshot* is even more so.'

Freaky Deaky is the story of two former '60s radicals turning to crime. I wonder what Elmore had been up to in the '60s. 'I remember that time. I didn't participate in any demonstrations. I saw *Woodstock* when it came out and I saw it again a couple more times when I was writing the book. I was beyond the age where I was going to participate. So it was research, *Rolling Stone* magazine, articles on the weather underground, what they were into. I used my researcher, who did go to the George Wallace rally in Detroit where everyone stood up and said, "*Sieg Heil* y'all!"'

Elmore Leonard's practice of using a researcher on his recent books has provoked a degree of unfavourable comment, so I ask him what his researcher actually does. 'My researcher, Greg Sutter, works for me part time. He works with computers mostly so he can go into a library and pull the material and bring it to me. When he begins I'm never sure what I'm looking for. For *Stick* I asked for material on the investment world, women in business, the boatlift, what is the main prison in Havana and so on. For *LaBrava* I was trying to find out what Harry Truman's living room looked like, where his wife was living with secret service men guarding her. So I called up a retired secret service man and asked him if he knew where I could get this information and he said there's a guy in Little Rock who had been the duty officer. So I called the guy and he said I'd have to get clearance from Washington. I said I don't want to know about the surveillance, what colour's the carpet? And he said, "You'll have to go through Washington." So I called a guy named

Gerald Petievitch and he said call him back and tell him I'll vouch for you. So the guy says, "I don't know Gerry Petievitch's phone voice. Could be anybody." So I told my researcher about the situation. Next day he came back with a picture of the room and a description and I said, "How did you find that out?" He said, "I called the house." He's a researcher!'

One constant of Leonard's writing is his attention to the music his characters listen to. The Detroit villains of the earlier books favour the kind of black jazz that now gets marketed as rare groove – Roy Ayers, Herbie Mann and suchlike. Then again, a Southern boy like Ernest 'Stick' Stickley will show a preference for Waylon Jennings or Loretta Lynn. Elmore's own taste leans towards the former: 'I listen mostly to jazz – in the car I set the radio to a black jazz station and whatever comes on is fine, Herbie Hancock, George Benson, though he's getting more into rock. Recently I took all my kids to Joe Cocker, I always liked him, I like the contrast of him and his band, he looks like he's just come home from work. The way I work the music into the novels is that I like to use what's current. I'll turn the TV on, get MTV, very often whatever's on I'll use. I did get to meet Iggy Pop and talk to him, because I referred to him several times in *Freaky Deaky*. I asked him what it was like, what he was trying to do, was he trying to fly over the audience? [referring here to Iggy's legendary Detroit performances with the Stooges]. He said: "No, I just wanted to *hover* over them!"'

Time's up and the successful, sober, born-again, though entirely unpreachy Mr Leonard leaves for photographs and a radio interview.

That evening Marcia says let's go to the movies so we head up to a cinemall in Birmingham, meet up with a couple of Marcia's friends, two young artist-type guys, one black, one white, and watch *Sex, Lies and Videotape*, everyone but me seeing it for the second time. Afterwards we discuss where to go for a drink and the consensus arrived at is that the ideal place would be a transvestite bar on Woodward called the Backstage.

The Backstage is way back down Woodward, opposite Palmer Park and just at the end of the strip of topless bars. It turns out, however, not to be the kind of dive I'm expecting. Instead it's a swish bar and restaurant packed at midnight with a mixture of what used to be known as theatrical types and a number of middle-aged black couples happy to have a pleasant place to eat in this otherwise seedy neighbourhood. Talk at our table turns to whether Spike Lee's *Do the Right Thing* is a better movie than *Sex, Lies and Videotape*. On the one hand it is clearly a political argument – a choice between yuppie introspection or a warning from the ghetto of the fire next time – and sure enough the black guy goes for *Do the Right Thing*, the white guy for *Sex, Lies*, but what on the other hand is revealing is that there is not much in it. In a city as racially riven as Detroit it is still possible for black and white folks to go see both movies, and here in the Backstage, in a bad neighbourhood in America's most deprived city, the clientele is the most mixed I will find anywhere on my travels.

Part two

2005

6   Washington, DC: chili dogs in the chocolate city

'IT'S THE NATION's capital, it's Washington, DC.' I've got this line from a Gil Scott Heron song going through my head. I'm sure the rest of the song is a smart and sarky portrayal of the Chocolate City's legion of social ills, but sadly all I can remember, as the plane dips in to land at Dulles Airport, is the clinching tag line, which, taken on its own, is a spot on the inane side.

Its emptiness is kind of appropriate though, it strikes me, as I make my way through the airport to the coach that will take me to the metro station that will take me to my hotel, as it mirrors my own profound lack of knowledge about America's capital, Washington, DC.

OK, this is what I know. It's where the big state buildings are, the White House, the Capitol, etc. Apart from that it's mostly black and poor. There's also an area called Georgetown where diplomats and politicians, people who appear in spy novels, live. What I don't have is much of a sense of how all these places fit together.

I also know Washington, DC, through the crime novels of George Pelecanos, the guy I'm here to interview. There's no question: Pelecanos's DC is a vivid, 3-D kind of a place; big on diners, bars and strip clubs, full of life and danger. I can imagine George Pelecanos's DC pretty well. I just can't make it marry up with the actual images of Washington I have, the manicured lawns of the White House, the Capitol and the Mall, the end-of-movie set-piece places.

So I'm kind of curious, when I make it out of the metro at the Capitol Hill stop, as to what I'm going to find. Well, first thing I find is that I really am on Capitol Hill; there's big white buildings, armed cops and tourists milling around, all sweltering in the September heat. My hotel is a couple of blocks east down a leafy road, full of elegant brownstones that doubtless house lawyers and lobbyists.

The hotel itself, or at least its lobby, is packed with what would appear to be the archetypal Midwestern conventioneers, people so straight that they're almost self-parodic. So packed is the hotel, in fact, that the staff, while acknowledging that I do indeed have a reservation, are very dubious as to whether that does in fact entitle me to a room. After much humming and hahing they decide that there will probably be a room available some unspecified time later, and maybe I'd like to leave my bags in the meantime.

Fine by me, as my immediate priority is to go out and find something to eat. A quick scan of my immediate neighbourhood doesn't reveal anything particularly promising, so I decide to avail myself of one of George Pelecanos's recommendations and head back to the metro station.

George Pelecanos is the crime novelist who's made DC his own. When I wrote the original *Into the Badlands*, I'd been keen to have a chapter on the city, it being the nation's capital and all, but I hadn't found a writer to hang it on. The great, and now sadly late, Ross Thomas had written at least one very fine Washington novel, *Briarpatch*, but to call him a Washington novelist would have been stretching a point a little far, and anyway he was living in Malibu at the time.

In fact, around about the same time I was writing my book, Pelecanos must have been writing his first, *A Firing Offense*. This was a novel which seemed to announce the arrival of a new generation of crime novelists, not so much post-Vietnam as post-punk, even in some cases a little postmodern (actually, in some cases, a lot postmodern – witness the new generation's avatar, Quentin Tarantino, a man responsible for more bad crime novels than anyone since Robert B. Parker).

The postmodernism in Pelecanos's work thankfully confines itself to a constant barrage of references to films, books and music. In every other way these are traditional hard-boiled crime novels whose twin strengths are recognisable street level characters and recognisable street-level milieux.

Pelecanos's writing career began with the Nick Stefanos books, three contemporary private eye novels. They're a young man's books, full of sex, drugs and rock'n'roll. He followed up with the mature work, his DC quartet of novels offering an alternative history of the city over the past half-century, and arguably still his defining work. Next came the Strange and Quinn series of contemporary DC crime novels, and lately there's been a move into stand-alone crime novels, including the epic story of the city's descent into racial conflict in the late sixties, *Hard Revolution*. What the books have in common is that they're all part of a long love letter to the city of DC.

· So, before setting out on this trip, and in the interests of matching up his DC with the one in the guidebooks, I asked Pelecanos by e-mail to provide me with a few tips as to where to find this city of his. I'm planning on trying a few of them out this afternoon, prior to meeting up with Mr Pelecanos in the morning.

Now I have to say, I'm not sure I totally understand George Pelecanos. Our e-mail exchanges leading up to this visit have been intermittently baffling. One e-mail will rather sternly warn me against imagining I could visit him on a Sunday morning as he will of course be taking his wife, kids and aged mother to church, the next one suggests an all-black strip club on the east side as one of the city's not-to-be-missed attractions. I've been starting to wonder whether he's winding me up.

Oh well, now's the time to find out. George Pelecanos's number-one must-see tip is a place called Ben's Chili Bowl on U Street, in a neighbourhood called Shaw. Ben's Chili Bowl apparently offers 'the best soul jukebox in town, not to mention the best chilli dogs in the world', while U Street was the main street of black DC in the old days (the old days being any time before the riots of 1968, which changed the city irrevocably).

Twenty minutes or so on Washington's very smart metro and I resurface in an area so spick and span and equipped with Footlockers and Starbucks that I can't help but double-check that I'm in the right place. Black parts of American cities do not, in my experience, look this prosperous, or at least they only do if they're not really black neighbourhoods any more but gentrified white neighbourhoods that nod slightly to their black heritage as an extra selling point for bohemian types. But this area, Shaw, doesn't seem like that. It just seems like a buzzy businesslike area that's mostly populated by black people.

Which is, of course, how things should be, but is not exactly the norm in America – or at least, hasn't been in many places I've been – and, to be honest, its very calm and functionality make me a little uneasy. Can I relax the level of vigilance I would habitually maintain, if I was in southside Chicago, say, or would that simply be naive?

Well, I'm not going to be relaxing at all unless I get something to eat, so I'm just checking the address, trying to figure out where Ben's Chili Bowl might be, when I see that answer staring me in the face. It's right opposite me on U Street with a sign saying Ben's Chili Bowl in three-foot-high letters.

Cross the road and head inside and I'm in a classic '50s American diner, the sort of place that a million shopping malls and waterfront developments try and fail to copy. There are tables to the left and a counter to the right. I take a seat at the counter and watch an array of chefs and counter staff tending to hot dogs and chilli and probably some other stuff, burgers and so forth, but what kind of person would go into Ben's Chili Bowl and not order a chilli dog? Not me, that's for sure.

I'm hardly in a position to judge whether George P is right in proclaiming them the best chilli dogs in the world but they're the certainly the best I've ever had, and, just to check, I order lunch all over again, right after I've finished the first lot off. Then, sated to the point of being barely able to move, I decide to check out whether the jukebox likewise lives up to its billing. It's certainly very fine, with an exemplary mixture of new and old R&B. Best of all, from my point of view, is the hefty amount of Maze to be found.

Maze? Well if you have to ask you certainly weren't on the London jazz-funk scene in the early 1980s, and that's for sure. Basically Maze were a soul band whose heyday came at a time – the late '70s to mid '80s – when the conventional wisdom was that soul was dead. In the USA they were enormously popular with black audiences, and almost entirely unknown to white audiences, despite being a multiracial combo with a very accessible Earth Wind and Fire meets Marvin Gaye kind of vibe.

In the UK they were almost entirely unknown to everyone except the jazz-funk crowd, to whom they were basically the Beatles. They came over to play in London in the early '80s and were stunned to find a multiracial capacity crowd who knew every word of their songs and generally went nuts. There are a couple of their songs – 'Joy and Pain' and 'Golden Time Of Day' in particular – that are among the most life-affirming pieces of music I know, but I'm also aware that for most people I know their music comes over as intolerably smooth.

Smooth is a bit of problem for culture vultures. We tend to prize the rough every time. Frank Sinatra is allowed to be smooth and that's about it. This however is essentially because we – as in people like me – are spoiled and decadent. In places like Ben's Chili Bowl, with its clientele of generally black working people with both blue and white collars, smooth is still good, sophisticated is still good. It's about aspiration and about building a better world where we can all live together as one and all that cheesy stuff. That's what Maze are about, and if you've any interest in soul music you should check them out.

Anyway, sermon over, the point is that Maze are a group DC has taken to its heart. And while a lot of African-American communities tend to be voracious in their appetite for new artists, and quick to tire of those who've fallen out of fashion, DC, by contrast, respects those acts that continue to deliver the sound that made them great in the first place. As a result it has its own black music stars like Chuck Brown who've been local legends for decades without hardly ever playing out of the city, and its venues have a long history of hosting the real greats from black music history.

Most of whom appear to have eaten at Ben's Chili Bowl. According to its website they include everyone from Duke Ellington to Miles Davis. My confidence in this information ebbs a little, however, when I notice that among the legends listed is none other than the Empress of the Blues herself, Bessie Smith. For a moment I really was impressed, then I stopped to consider that Ben's opened in 1958 and Bessie died in 1937. Anyway, of more relevance to people who like quality American food may be the endorsement of Bill Clinton, a man who, one can't help suspecting, knows his chilli dogs.

Back out on U Street, DC's respect for musical tradition is immediately evident. U Street has a heritage trail marked out for visitors to follow with regular information boards pointing out sights of interest. Now these kinds of heritage trail are quite a common sight these days, but, again, not normally in African-

American neighbourhoods, and not with the same sense of relevance that this one has. I stop outside a theatre where Sarah Vaughan used to sing, and it's still used for jazz, and I get the sense for once that people actually do care, and know who Sarah Vaughan was, and that this is a city in which respect for tradition is real.

Just to back it up, on the other side of the road there's a Duke Ellington mural – Sir Duke was a long time local resident – then, on the next corner, there's the African-American Civil War Museum. Keep going a little farther and hang a left and there's the Howard University campus. Howard is an all-black university founded in 1867 in the immediate aftermath of the Civil War, and it has played an enormous role in American public life since.

Its alumni include Thurgood Marshall, the legal architect of the civil rights movement. It's where Lyndon Johnson came to announce key civil rights legislation in 1965. It's the alma mater of a host of notable African-American politicians, from Andrew Young to David Dinkins. On the arts side it taught both Roberta Flack and Donny Hathaway. If there's a spiritual home of the black middle class, it's Howard University. Tellingly enough, among its more recent old boys is none other than Sean Puffy Combs, the music and menswear marketing phenomenon.

From here I wander back west, and while on closer inspection there are plenty of signs of gentrification – newly renovated brownstones, shops selling things no one actually needs and so forth – there isn't the sense you too often get that it's simply a matter of rich white people taking over nice but run-down inner-city housing from poor black people; rather there's a feeling of a community rising up and attracting some newcomers along the way. At least, that how it seemed to me, one sunny afternoon in September.

West of Shaw I take a bit of an uphill turn through leafy, faintly

Mediterranean, streets until I arrive in Adams Morgan, an area I've heard referred to as the Greenwich Village of Washington. Which, I suppose, is a way of saying that it's something of a melting pot.

Where Shaw is still essentially culturally African-American, Adams Morgan is essentially multi-cultural. There's a definite Hispanic flavour, but also African-American, Ethiopian, West Indian and white boho. There are bars and clubs and record stores where you can buy hardcore punk and alt country along with go-go and funk, and every other building has the image of Bob Marley somewhere on display.

It's the kind of place that is scarcely ever written about without the word funky being applied to it. And it's very nice, but compared to the freshness, and sense of a unique tradition, apparent in Shaw, this feels a lot like every other multi-ethnic boho zone I've ever been in. Which is fine and cool but less, um, interesting, I suppose.

Head south-west from Adams Morgan and I emerge on to Connecticut Avenue heading for Dupont Circle. And I'm in another world again. This world, oddly enough, looks rather Mediterranean as well, but Mediterranean like an expensive shopping street in Madrid or Athens – slightly deracinated. Maybe it's something to do with all the embassies around here. One thing it does have, though, is a fine bookshop, Kramerbooks, with a really excellent innovation that more bookstores should consider – its own bar with a bewildering range of beer options.

And having walked around a fair percentage of DC by now, I fall upon it with Assyrian-on-wolf levels of enthusiasm, put my feet up and a pint of something dark and micro-brewed down my neck, and pick up a George Pelecanos novel from the shelves.

It's *The Sweet Forever*, the third book in his DC quartet, set in the late 1980s, a year or two before I wrote the original

Badlands, just as the city was ravaged by drug wars. It starts, oddly enough, right on U Street, just a block or so from Ben's Chili Bowl. The hero, Marcus Clay, a black businessman with a small chain of record stores, has just opened up his newest store there. At the time the book's set this is seen as an act of philanthropic folly, as U Street is terminally run down and is being taken over by the drug trade. Now, I suspect, it would look like a shrewd investment. Things have clearly changed, and for the better at that.

It gives me pause to think. In recent years, both in Europe and the US, I've been noticing plenty of bohemian areas getting richer, but I suppose I've tended to suspect that the rich have been getting richer, while the poor are getting poorer. Otherwise my left-liberal world-view might have to accept that capitalism is working, even here in George W. Bush's USA, which would be a shock to the system.

It's something to think on, though, as I prepare for the next day's tour of the DC badlands with Mr Pelecanos – the question of whether the mean streets are just a little less mean than they used to be. Another beer and I head back to the hotel, where, after a protracted wrangle, I persuade them that they may have a room for me after all, and by that time my plans to check out the DC nightlife have shrunk down to a weary decision to find the closest viable place for a burger and beer, ideally in the company of sports TV, before hitting the hay very firmly indeed.

The answer to my prayers comes in the shape of the Tune Inn, a real old-school American beers, burgers and sports establishment round the back of the Capitol, with a cute tired waitress who digs out a pair of glasses every time she has to check something on the menu, just as I do. I watch a little baseball in there, a little soccer in the yuppie bar next door, and a little tennis on my hotel TV as I fall asleep.

Next morning I head downstairs to meet Pelecanos. I've got

half an hour to kill so wander into the breakfast room for a cup of coffee and a look at my complementary *USA Today*. The breakfast room is full of the cartoon Midwesterners from the day before, all talking about their assorted lobbying activities. I wonder what on earth people this straight looking could be lobbying for; something grain-related, most probably.

Outside on the sidewalk, however, I find the answer – there's a bus gradually filling up with Midwesterners and on the side of it there's a billboard with a spectacularly bloody picture of an aborted fetus on it. Hey, I've just been sharing a breakfast room with the right-to-life crew. I try to persuade myself that maybe they hadn't seemed so innocuous after all, but obvious foaming-mouthed bigots. But no, it's no good, they're either very mild-mannered flaming bigots, or just people of deep if rather blinkered Christian conviction.

Before I can speculate any further, George Pelecanos pulls up to the kerb. George Pelecanos is a fit-looking guy in his late forties. Last time I saw him he was sporting a rock'n'roll goatee, but since then he's clearly decided it's time to stop hanging on to outlaw cool, at least on the surface. Instead he looks like what he is: a busy and successful novelist, screenwriter and producer, with an Infiniti G 35 to prove it.

'You had breakfast?' he asks, and I say. 'Not exactly,' and he says, 'Good, I'll take you somewhere really DC.'

So I get into the Infiniti and George starts driving, and soul music obscurities start playing on the sound system, and we do a little catching up. I've met George only a couple of times before, once at a crime festival in London, the other time at a book launch, but I was instrumental in George getting a publishing deal in the UK. Right when I started working as a freelance editor, the writer and DJ Charlie Gillett told me I had to read *A Firing Offense*, and I read it and liked it and eventually things fell into place. So there's stuff to talk about as we head north past the Civic Centre and into Shaw, before coming to a stop a few blocks north of U Street, and east of Howard University, at a place called the Florida Avenue Grill.

No doubt it's something to do with being the son and grandson of diner owners, but George Pelecanos clearly knows his classic American food establishments. Like Ben's Chili Bowl, the Florida Avenue Grill follows the classic diner layout – lunch counter and kitchen on one side, tables on the other side – but while Ben's keeps pretty much to its speciality, the Florida Avenue Grill is more your full-service American diner with a soul-food base.

Taking George's advice, I go for the Derek Strange special, eggs and half-smoke and grits. It's a combo ordered by the detective in each one of the three novels he stars in. The only difference being that for fictional purposes the Florida Avenue Grill has become the last Greek-run diner in town, rather than the solidly African-American establishment it is.

The actual Florida Avenue Grill is clearly a popular place. Its walls are festooned with photos of pretty much every black DC celebrity you can imagine. There's Natalie Cole and there's, wow, there's Kashif, the much underrated godfather of electronic funk, from back in the '80s. There's any number of sportsmen and women and plenty of people in uniform. And of course there's a picture of DC's most controversial black celebrity, the sometime mayor, Mr Marion Barry.

Barry became mayor of DC back in the '80s, when the notion of major cities having black mayors was a lot less common than it has since become. Add in the fact that Barry was a loud-mouthed populist and it isn't surprising that the press gave him a terribly hard time. Then again, Barry didn't exactly help himself by getting arrested after being caught on film smoking crack cocaine in a hotel room with a prostitute.

This event provoked one of Barry's many celebrated public utterances of the kind you're slightly surprised to hear coming from the mouth of an elected public official, in this case the pithy 'Bitch set me up'. Another self-explanatory classic following a brush with the law runs as follows: 'First, it was not a strip bar, it was an erotic club. And second, what can I say? I'm a night owl.'

It's hard not to warm to a guy capable of such spectacular insouciance. Likewise another celebrated quote: 'If you take out the killings, Washington actually has a very, very low crime rate.' And this one is actually not half as dumb as it initially sounds. The fact is that, even at its lowest ebb back in the 1980s, Washington, DC, was not overall a dangerous city. It became one only if you were engaged in the drug trade. Otherwise your chances of being killed in DC were about the same as in Copenhagen.

And the victims of the drug trade were, after all, overwhelmingly poor and black, living in parts of DC that the kind of people who liked to mock Marion Barry's supposed idiocy never went near. Thus the public humiliation of Barry suited the media well: it was much easier to laugh at the crackhead mayor than try and do something about the crack epidemic that was threatening to wipe out DC at the time, or to try to understand, let alone sympathise, with the lives of those caught up in it.

This is at the heart of the task George Pelecanos has set himself. If his work has a single subject it's that of the racial divide. Almost all the crime in his novels is underpinned by this divide. And in every American city there's always that line, a railroad or street that marks the boundary between where the white people live and where the black people live. And on one side of the line the drug trade causes havoc. On the other side of the line people are reassured that the war on drugs is a sure-fire winner.

As we eat George talks about the personal importance the issue of race has for him: 'Racism is our national disease. I have a personal stake in seeing it cured. My sons are mixed race and my daughter is Latina. I love my children, of course, and like any father want a better world for them than the one we live in now. I want racism to go away. And I can honestly say that when I look at my children I don't see their skin colour, except to remark on its beauty.

'Still, when I walk the streets at night and a young black man is headed my way, I assume things, and often these assumptions are negative. What I'm saying is, I'm an American and a product of my generation, and as much as I hate this thing inside me, I too have prejudices that will probably never go away. I'm sick just like anybody else, and it bothers me. People who say they don't "see colour" are either liars or delusional, or both. Liberals are the worst because they are always talking about other people's problem with racism and ignoring their own. They think that by putting a nice bumper sticker on their car or sending Happy Kwanza cards or by giving their white daughter a black baby doll they are doing something…that they are doing enough. And they are doing nothing. They are doing jack shit. The crazy thing is, I have no answers. But I do raise a lot of questions. That's my job as a writer, in my opinion.'

In the interests of illustrating these points George leads the way out of the Florida Grill and back into the Infiniti for a tour of some of the neighbourhoods that too often get written off as no-go areas. Heading north from Florida Avenue up Georgia Avenue, the main street of black DC, there's soon an obvious decline in the prosperity levels. It's a familiar ghetto mix of shut-down businesses and barely-hanging-in-there businesses. Liquor stores and the occasional barber shop are prominent among those hanging on. Signs are mostly badly hand painted; no multinational food corp stumps up for neon signs in these parts.

After a while George points out the block where Derek Strange has his office. It's in one of the more functional-looking commercial strips. This area is called Petworth and, if you look closely, you can see the signs that this is a neighbourhood struggling to make its way back up, albeit from a pretty serious down. Just around from Derek Strange's imaginary office there's even an unlikely-sounding but real, and distinctly chic, Polish café called Y Domku.

Petworth is the neighbourhood plenty of Pelecanos's black characters live in. It's had a bad reputation for drug dealing for years, and George points out the apartment blocks that still function as drug-dealing hubs, but again there's a definite sign of improvement away from the main drag, and the streets are lined with well-maintained homes. And, as Y Domku suggests, white people, or at least adventurous young white people, are starting to move in.

From Petworth we head north and west over to Mount Pleasant, the area George lived in when he was young. He shows me his grandparents' house, a roomy-looking place in a leafy neighbourhood. Then we head back south into Shaw to see the lunch counter George's grandfather used to run. It's a shop now, run by Ethiopians, as many of DC's mini-markets seem to be (in fact Ethiopians are the coming entrepreneurs across DC, a definite contrast from their fortunes in Britain).

From there we head east out to the green expanse of Rock Creek Park, as immortalised in song by the Blackbyrds, and down south to East Potomac Park, where we stop to walk for a while in the late morning sunshine and talk a little about George's background in Washington, DC.

'I was born in Columbia Hospital for women, in 1957. My early years I lived in Mount Pleasant in north-west, my grandparents' house, we all lived together. The rest of my life I've lived in Silver Spring, Maryland.

'My dad was working for my grandfather when I was young at that carry-out shop on Fourteenth Street, and then he bought his own place in 1965, on Nineteenth south of Dupont Circle, a lunch counter with twenty-seven seats. My mom was what they used to call a secretary, and now call an administrative assistant. She worked at various places around DC, government and non-government. I started working for my dad when I was eleven.

'When I turned eleven, that summer they said "you're going to work for your father now", so I started taking buses downtown to my dad's place. For years I worked for him and I learned the business, so when he got sick in '75, during my first semester in college – he had a heart attack then he got cancer – I dropped out of college to run the business. When you ran a business back in the day you didn't have insurance, so I really had to do that.

'But really I didn't want to go back to college. In the end my father had to sell the business as a way of telling me it was time to go back. He ended up working at a succession of jobs in restaurants after that, till he got too sick to work.

'I went back to school, put myself through college selling women's shoes: from my teens on I'd worked a bunch of retail jobs. I continued to do that after college. I worked those kinds of jobs till I was thirty years old, and that's when I wrote my first book.'

So what provoked that? 'In college I took an elective class in hard-boiled detective fiction. This guy Charles Mish turned me to these books. I wasn't even a reader before that. Wasn't interested in books. The books they teach you in school definitely didn't have anything to do with my world, my world-view. They weren't about everyday people, working-class people, but crime fiction was. So I was like, "Wow, people are actually writing for a living about things I actually know a little about." I thought that's what I want to do, but it took me ten years till I felt like I had the chops to try.

'And the way I did that was by reading a lot for the next ten years, making up for lost time. While I was working these jobs, bartending and so on, I always had a book going. I got married when I was twenty-eight, we had a little house, more like a cottage, we didn't have any children. I felt like the time was then to try. And I did.

'I had a story to tell, which I'd had for years. It was about two guys on a sales floor. It was a punk-rock detective novel, which I felt nobody else was doing. When you're young you're full of piss and vinegar anyway, like I'm going to revolutionise this shit. I was just writing books for my generation which talk about the music and the popular culture. The punk thing was very inspirational to me; the whole movement was about you don't have to know how to play guitar, just pick it up and play. I certainly didn't know how to write a book. Punk gave me the inspiration to say at least I'll try.

'I sold it to the first publisher I sent it to. I didn't have an agent or anything. It took a year for him to pick it up from the slush pile. By then I'd gone ahead and started writing a second book. And I've written a book a year since. It's been a very workmanlike process. I was also working in the film business for a while. I wrote books at night or got up real early. I did that for ten years till I was self-sufficient enough to go out on my own.

'So I wrote *Nick's Trip*, the second Stefanos novel, then I wrote a pulp novel, *Shoedog*, just because I wanted to write a pulp novel, then I went back to Stefanos, and I knew when I was writing the third one that that was the end of it, writing first person about this guy. I've since brought him back in my books as a minor character. It's become a pattern of mine. Whether the books are successful or not, I tend to end a series after three or sometimes four books. Because I just feel like life's too short.'

The change from writing the Stefanos novels also, no doubt, reflected a desire to get away from writing a character very plainly modelled on himself: 'He definitely was autobiographical,' Pelecanos comments. 'The first book is all me. Then my life began to straighten out a little. I'm not going to detail everything I did, but I did everything that's in the books, certainly, and I was a harder drinker when I was younger. I mean, I was young, that's what you do, experiment with different things. Now I don't want to be getting like Jesus here, saying how I've found my way or anything, I'm just in a different phase of my life.'

It's a phase of life that revolves around work and family. George is nothing but friendly showing me around his Washington, but I'm in no doubt at all that really he'd rather be at home working. He's got that driven quality you often see in ex-alcoholics, but allied to a native steeliness that no doubt stopped him ever going all the way into alcoholism in the first place.

That and his family. Family is right at the root of Pelecanos's world-view. His books regularly pay tribute to the struggles of his father and grandfather to establish themselves in the USA. And while the male characters in his novels are generally faithless types, always tomcatting around the place, Pelecanos has been married to Emily – whom he met all the way back while working in the shoe shop – for two decades. They have three children, two boys and a girl, all adopted. His two sons were born in Brazil and his daughter in Guatemala. His older son is due to be playing his first high school football game this very afternoon; we'll be heading over to watch later on.

With that in mind it's time to get back to the DC tour. Next stop is south-east, over the river into Anacostia. This is serious ghetto territory. It's where perhaps the bleakest of Pelecanos's books, *Soul Circus*, takes place. I'm fearing the worst, something like the burned-out horror of the south Bronx, or westside Chicago, back in the '80s. Instead what I see is a more quotidian despair. The despair of housing projects that could maybe have been nice if enough people who lived in them had some kind of hope, but are instead the deceptively bland front line of the war against drugs, a war so futile it makes the Hundred Years War look positively well thought out.

Most depressing of all, however, are not the housing projects, which have a certain weary familiarity, but the schools. Each and very school in Anacostia, whether high school or elementary, looks like a prison, and is certainly fortified right up to maximum-security level. You look at places like these, and all those statistics about there being more black men in prison than in higher education start to make sense. These places, after all, resemble prisons a lot more closely than they do Howard University. To add insult to injury these schools are almost invariably named after major civil rights figures: one is even named after Malcolm X. It's hard to imagine Malcolm being too chuffed to see his name being franchised out to endless holding pens for the underclass. And, conversely, what does it teach children? That Martin Luther King and Malcolm X are the patron saints of failing schools?

Even in the bleakness of Anacostia, though, there are signs of life. There are stores and malls, albeit run-down, depressing ones; there is still a sense that this is a community that does at least function, unlike the anarchic badlands of the '80s.

And then I see something really weird. We pass a clothes store with a sign declaring that it sells 'nostalgia' clothes. I'm stunned. The cult of the retro is, it seems to me, profoundly un-American. I noticed its creeping rise in Los Angeles years ago, saw that for the first time America was becoming self-conscious about its history. But in general the lure of the retro is a lure that black communities have been immune to. Black street fashion has always been about the newest and the sharpest. The idea of wearing clothes that used to belong to someone else was shameful – as it generally is in communities for which poverty is too close for comfort.

I'm tempted to stop and have a look inside, find out what kind of nostalgia the people of Anacostia are in the market for, but the shop is closed and anyway we're on a tight schedule.

We've just about got time to have some lunch before we have to be at the high school out in the Maryland boondocks where George's son will be playing his first match. There's nowhere much to eat in Anacostia so George decides to head out towards our destination.

The part of Maryland we're travelling through seems to be mostly fairly low-rent suburbia. The regular shopping malls major on the lower-end stores and restaurants, plenty of McDonald's and Payless Shoe Source outlets. It's all utterly unremarkable until, after half an hour or so, I realise that all the people I can see going about their unremarkable suburban business are black. And then I realise that I'm in part of America I've not only never been to before, but have barely seen represented on the TV, or in the movies – black suburbia.

Once we're close to our destination we pull into one of the malls and forgo the charms of a takeaway calling itself 'steak in a sack' in favour of an anonymous but pleasant Thai joint.

And as we wait for our food to arrive we get back to the interview. Returning to the Nick Stefanos books, which finish up with *Down Where the Dead Men Go*, in which Stefanos is sinking into alcoholism, I wondered whether he hadn't been tempted to do a Lawrence Block and turn Stefanos into one of those popular AA detectives, make him a DC Matt Scudder.

Pelecanos smiles at the idea and says: 'It was a conscious decision on my part, not to do that. I felt like that sub-genre of detective fiction was getting really tired and there were so many reformed alcoholic 'tecs out there. There's one or two guys who make it worthwhile, James Lee Burke and Laurence Block. After that it's all parody.'

Instead Pelecanos embarked on writing his DC quartet. Except he didn't know when he started out that it would be a quartet. Rather he wanted to fulfil his long-held ambition of writing a book about his family history, in particular his father's and grandfather's lives. 'I wanted to write a bigger book, third person, and to write about the immigrant experience, so I had the idea to write Once Upon A Time in DC. That's *The Big Blowdown*. It was a big turning point for me. It blew up a whole lot of possibilities.'

In particular it gave him the notion that this was just the starting point for a historical series. The only question was which period to jump to next. 'I thought about a sequel and what interested me was that in the '40s people didn't leave the house without a Windsor knot and a fedora and an overcoat, but you go forward thirty years and you see this guy's son with long hair and ripped jeans selling marijuana on the street. So how did that happen?

'So *King Suckerman* came about. I was trying to do my version of an Elmore Leonard novel. And then, from there, I saw that I could go to the summer of '86 next, and show what happened when crack came to town. That was *The Sweet Forever*, then *Shame the Devil* would wrap it all up, show what happened to these characters. Especially with the race thing. In the '70s we'd thought we'd all walk forward together. By the '90s it was over, we were as far apart as ever. Because of economics, people were getting left behind.'

It's these four novels that provide perhaps the clearest, most comprehensive account of the Pelecanos vision to date, and are probably the best place for a new reader to start. For his next book, however, Pelecanos decided to do something at once more and less commercial. More commercial in that he started a series of novels with a private-detective protagonist, which is the kind of thing publishers like to hear. Less commercial, though, in that the PI in question was a middle-aged black guy with a fondness for massage parlours, a Marion Barry kind of detective, in fact.

'I felt I was ready to write a book from the perspective of a black man,' comments Pelecanos. 'I had gotten better as a writer and I knew more. I was in my forties and I knew more about life. They would be my books about race in America. You take a book like *Bonfire of the Vanities*, which is for me probably the most overrated piece of American fiction of the last twenty-five years. The reason that book is so popular is that it told people – white people, that is, black people didn't want anything to do with that book – that they didn't have a problem. The rich guy Sherman has a problem 'cause he doesn't understand black people, but you, the reader, do. I wanted to write a book that points a finger back at the reader and says, wait a minute, you do have a problem, and points back at myself too, for that matter.'

The character that is used to make a lot of these points is Terry Quinn, a white ex-cop who becomes Strange's quarrelsome sidekick: 'I didn't know Quinn was just going to be a part of the plot. I didn't expect him to become such a major character but he did,' comments Pelecanos, before pointing out that, unlike most salt'n'pepper detective team-ups, this one doesn't end in mutual understanding and shared laughter: 'With this guy Quinn, what I didn't want him ever to do was hold hands with Strange and say, "You know, deep down we really are the same inside, colour doesn't matter," and all this bullshit. Instead he never learns. Quinn doesn't learn. He's annoying, he's thick and by the third book I knew what was going to happen to him.

'And that was me pulling the pin on my career again too, just as things were starting to get successful, but it worked for the book. I gave my publisher the choice of an alternative ending, but my editor, Michael Pietsch, said the way you wrote it the first time works better. I'm very proud of those books, I think they got stronger as they went along. And they led me into *Hard Revolution*, a book I'd wanted to write my whole career but hadn't had the chops to do.'

Hard Revolution, his latest book at the time of the interview, is indeed an epic. It's a novel that takes a bunch of characters, among them a young Derek Strange, through the 1960s. But this isn't the '60s of peace, love and Woodstock, it's the '60s of civil rights, anger and riots. It's a big subject, but one that's filtered as ever through the personal.

'To go back to the beginning, when my parents sent me down to work with my dad, it was right after the riots in '68. The riots happened in April, they sent me down to work with him in June. I took the bus down Georgia Avenue every day and everything had gone, there was just rubble and smoke, the scene of the riots was still a mess.

'I had seen Dr King speak four days before his death. And you know, all my life I'd been wondering what really happened that weekend he was murdered. Because things changed after that – black people on the bus were standing pretty tall, they were wearing louder clothes than before. And down at my father's place – remember, this is the South we're talking about, and people had been very subservient up to that point – it was never going to be like that any more. There was a woman called Ida who worked for my dad. That summer, after the riots, a woman called her a dumb nigger. Ida told her off in front of everybody, the all-white customers. If that had happened before someone would have complained. Not any more. My father started to let the employees listen to whatever they wanted when they were working – soul stations. That gave me a lifetime love of that music. That book is a culmination of all that.'

Alongside the last few books, George has also been heavily involved in screenwriting, At first, and unsurprisingly given his background in movie production, he looked towards the big screen and wrote several movie scripts that haven't quite got off the blocks. Latterly, though, his involvement with the small screen has been rather more productive. In particular he has been writing and co-producing *The Wire*. This is a Baltimore-set cop show, developed by David Simon, of *Homicide* fame, and undoubtedly the most challenging series of its kind ever made. It has scores of characters and dialogue that's so street as to be unintelligible for the first several episodes. Then your ear tunes into what they're saying and the characters come into focus and – if you're me at least – you're hooked. I asked George how his involvement with the show came about.

'David Simon approached me after his girlfriend, the writer Laura Lippman, turned him on to my books. He saw the similarities in what we were doing and pitched the series to me as a social crime novel for television. I ended up as a producer and story editor. The experience was good, and I'm very proud to have been a part of the show, but the time devoted to it encroached on my novel-writing, so I have pulled back to being a writer without on-set responsibilities.'

Watching *The Wire* it has struck me that, whereas once upon a time novels were complex and TV shows for dummies, these days that was starting to be reversed. *The Wire* is far more psychologically subtle, and complex in its plotting, than any contemporary serial killer novel or by-the-numbers police procedural. I wondered what George thought about that, doing my best to make it clear that I was excepting him from any charge of dumbing down: 'In twelve hours of television you can veer off track in ways you cannot in a novel, which by definition has to be much tighter,' he told me. 'But I think my books are pretty broad in that way to begin with. I try to create a city of characters and give equal weight to all…a fictional world that reflects the real world, in varying perspectives. You're correct in pointing out that most bestselling fiction does not attempt to do this. The formula is usually to concentrate on a protagonist who faces challenges and then wins in the end. A murder is solved and the world is righted, put back in order, again. I tend to reject that notion in my books. *The Wire* walks the same kind of territory. It was a good fit for me.'

And on that note our food comes and we eat and get out of there and head over to the high school in the middle of nowhere much, where it turns out that the game has been postponed for four hours. So I don't get to see Pelecanos Jr play football. Instead we head back into the city, where George drops me at my hotel and we say our goodbyes.

I decide to head back up to Shaw, have another look around. Oh, OK, and another chilli dog from Ben's, but only the one this time. I had just eaten lunch.

And after that I feel in need of a cup of coffee, so I stop at a place a little way along U Street called the Love Café, which is a big smart boho café, with an array of fine-looking cakes baked on-site, and is clearly doing a decent job of taking on Starbucks at its own game, and is a black-owned and -operated concern with a racially mixed clientele.

It feels like progress, in a 'modern capitalism is the system we live in, so get with the programme' kind of way. It feels like a place where people are coming together. And it makes me think of something Pelecanos wrote me in an e-mail a while back and is worth bearing in mind alongside the justified bleakness of much of his fiction: 'Sometimes I look at the young folks in this country, who generally don't seem to have the hang-ups we adults have regarding race, and I think, maybe it's just time that this country needs. That when we die out and the new generations come up, this problem will just fade. It's sad, isn't it, that it can't seem to get fixed any other way.'

It seems like, just maybe, that the fixing is already under way. Let's hope so.

7   Hollywood Beach, Florida: body heat

SIXTEEN YEARS LATER and I'm back in Fort Lauderdale Airport, the place I started the original book. Has it changed? Probably a little, I'm sure there's a Starbucks around here somewhere, but basically it feels the same – airport-like, you know? No, what's really changed in the interim is me.

Last time I came here, I was twenty-seven years old and pretty damn sure I knew it all. I knew why I was here and what I wanted to do. I wanted to write a book about American crime fiction that was as fast and exciting as an American crime novel. I wanted to see everything, do everything. And I wanted the writers I was going to meet to be every bit as funny/drunk/whacked out/hard-living/ armed to the teeth as the characters they wrote about. And any time they failed to live up to my expectations I was pretty hard on them. Well, not hard exactly but unsparing – what I saw was what I wrote, with little consideration for how they might feel about it.

Now I'm forty-four years old, and I've done nothing but write for a living for the past sixteen years, and I have a lot more sympathy for the folks I met last time. The frustrations and disappointments I saw on their faces then are now right there any time I look in the mirror.

To give you an idea of just how long ago it was since I was here last, they were filming *Miami Vice* right around the corner from where I was staying, and the place I was staying in was an art deco hotel and it was cheap and mostly filled with old people, and James

Hall wanted to visit my room to use it as setting for nefarious drug-related activities. There was not a supermodel in sight. If you see *Miami Vice* now it looks like a relic from a bygone age.

Evidently I was just one of many visitors to South Beach who saw the potential in the place. The next time I visited, maybe five years later, the place was transformed. Gone were the retirees: in their place were implausibly good-looking young people on roller blades. The welfare hotels were all being refurbished and their prices quadrupled. It didn't even come as much of a surprise to me: during the intervening years you couldn't open a glossy magazine, of the kind I was making a living writing for, without coming upon a fashion shoot using South Beach as a backdrop. Sun, sea and art deco. Gianni Versace's mansion, Chris Blackwell's hotels.

Actually it was unsurprising in another way too. That's to say that at a certain point in my life I couldn't help realising that most of the things I liked, and felt as if I'd discovered for myself – whether the art deco hotels of South Beach or the novels of Elmore Leonard or the earlier recordings of Dolly Parton – were actually being picked up on simultaneously by thousands of other people. There's something weirdly collective about taste.

You can see it most clearly in the matters of names and houses. Names first: I remember when my first friends to have a kid called their son Max and I thought, hey, that's a weird name for a kid. But over the next few years it emerged that a sizeable percentage of all the other young educated types having kids had also somehow simultaneously alighted on the name Max. As for houses, well, almost everywhere I've ever lived, when I moved there it's been a run-down inner city neighbourhood with old-men's pubs and working-men's caffs. And by the time I've left it's become full of gastropubs and boutiques selling designer children's clothing. What's happened in the meantime is that loads more people like me have moved in.

And of course people like me end up spending our time complaining about how much better things used to be before people like me showed up and ruined them.

So, anyway, this time at Fort Lauderdale Airport the last thing on my mind is getting a cab to take me all the way down to South Beach. This time, I'll be heading to Hollywood Beach, just a couple of miles down the coast.

Hollywood Beach is old-school Florida, the kind of place people from the snowbird states come to spend their holidays, or come to live if their lives aren't working out farther north, and not to have their picture taken for European fashion magazines. And it's where Vicki Hendricks lives.

Vicki Hendricks is one of the very few women writing contemporary noir fiction. That's noir as opposed to hard-boiled or simply crime fiction. Crime fiction generally offers a crime and a solution: there is an underlying sense that the world is rough and tough but, if the right cop or PI walks down those mean streets, he may hold the badness at bay for a while. Noir allows no such thing. The protagonist of the noir novel knows that he or she is screwed from the off. They know the world is unfair and expect nothing more than what they get. Which is, of course, nothing.

The noir novel tends to be the most highly critically praised and least commercially successful of genres. It's also the most male dominated of genres. It's easy to speculate as to why. One might suggest that there's something particularly masculine and self-indulgent about the perception that the world is screwed, the dice loaded against you. For women this is, for starters, not news and, for seconds, something you just have to get on and live with. By the same token, though, it's actually rather mystifying. For, given the very real extent to which the dice are loaded against women, surely noir should be their natural habitat.

What I suspect it boils down to is the matter of escapism. For the most part people who really have things hard tend to prefer books that offer a measure of escapism. You're trying to get by in a world stacked against you, you most likely don't want to read a book that tells you you have no chance; what you want is science fiction or chick lit or Agatha Christie.

Anyway, whatever the reason, the simple fact is that there are precious few women writing noir fiction these days. And it's not that there were many writing back in noir's '50s heyday either – a Delores Hitchens book here and a Leigh Brackett there hardly add up to a movement. Otherwise the most truly noir female voice of the past century is that of Jean Rhys.

Jean Rhys specialised in writing about women who have spent their youth orbiting around men, but without ever settling into family life, and find themselves adrift, unsure what they want from life.

Pretty much the same goes for Vicki Hendricks's heroines. Well, except for the fact that they come from a rather more proactive generation and tend to look for answers in the world of extreme sports, and are possessed by the kind of full-on sexual obsession that is only hinted at in Jean Rhys.

Vicki's first book, *Miami Purity*, of which more later, was published in a big way around ten years ago. Her American editor, Sonny Mehta at Knopf, no less, clearly had it in mind that female noir might be the next big thing.

I first met her when the book came out in Britain. I wrote a piece about the book for *GQ* and was rewarded with a meet-the-author lunch which saw Vicki talking happily about the new boat she'd bought with her advance, and the new novel she was just about to finish. All looked set fair.

But sadly the publisher's big dreams for *Miami Purity* didn't work out. Knopf lost interest and so too did her American agent and British publisher. By then I'd started working part time as an editor myself, and was only too happy to have the chance to pick up Vicki's work, starting with that second novel, a flat-out classic called *Iguana Love*. And since then I've been involved in publishing each of her succeeding novels: *Voluntary Madness*, *Sky Blues* and the upcoming *Cruel Poetry*.

In the modern world, however, the fact that I have been Vicki's editor all this time doesn't actually translate into a lot of time spent hanging out. Rather it's been a matter of e-mails and phone calls, plus a rather jet-lagged dinner in Miami five or so years ago.

So, when I come down the stairs to baggage reclaim at the airport, and I see Vicki waiting there with her long blonde hair and strong, almost Native American bone structure, there's a look of relief on her face that we've managed to recognise each other.

Salutations over with and my bag rescued, we head out to the car park and into Vicki's brand-new SUV, which has neat faux leopard-skin seat covers but is not, she stresses, really her kind of vehicle. She was talked into buying it because she wanted a vehicle big enough to hold all her sky-jumping gear. Sky jumping has become a big part of Vicki's life over the past decade. She used the sky-jumping world as the backdrop for her fourth novel, *Sky Blues*, but the obsession has outlived the novel, and she's now racked up several hundred dives, diving almost every weekend.

Or, at least, she had been diving every weekend up till recently. That's when she got the bad news. Back in the summer, just when I was planning this trip, Vicki found out she had breast cancer.

When she'd first heard the news Vicki's reaction had been to keep it quiet. She was concerned, as she put it in an e-mail, about the impact of the news 'on my persona as a sex and murder writer!' A couple of months and a first dose of chemo later, combined with a positive prognosis, and Vicki's attitude has changed. The treatment's going well, she tells me as we head out of the airport, and it's kind of become her new interest now

– an internal battle to fight as a change from her sporting battles with the elements.

From the airport we swing around to Vicki's new condo, in a gated community a little way inland from the beach. All around there's evidence of Hurricane Katrina's recent visit. The apartment complex itself, however, has come through intact. Vicki's just bought the place to live in with her boyfriend Brian. They met through skydiving, and have been together for a few years, but Brian has only recently given up his place in Chicago, and moved down to Florida to be with Vicki full time. He's a nice guy, bearded fiftyish, does something with computers and is, of course, extremely partial to skydiving. Once we're sat down in the apartment he tells me they're thinking of going up to Lake Okeechobee the next day for him to do some diving. Maybe I'd like to come along? And perhaps I'd like to try doing a tandem dive with him?

Well, that's a tricky one. Not the first part – heading up to central Florida to see the skydiving scene up close sounds fine. The second part, though, where I jump out of a plane strapped to some guy who seems very pleasant but I have, let's face it, only just met, and hope he remembers which toggle to pull before we plunge to our deaths? Well, it takes me a good millisecond to say thanks, but no thanks.

By now it's lunchtime. Brian has work to do, so Vicki drives me back on to Federal Highway and up a little way north to a place called Ernie's Bar-B-Q and Lounge for some traditional Florida cooking.

Tradition in Florida is, of course, a relative term, and what it means is a mix of blue-collar staples – burgers and barbecue and beer – plus some local fish dishes, mostly based around the conch and all served with sweet Caribbean-style Bimini bread, which makes me oddly nostalgic for Kensal Rise, north-west London, where I lived when I wrote the original *Badlands*, and which was well supplied with West Indian eateries, unlike Cardiff, where I now live.

The real deal with Ernie's, so Vicki tells me, has to do with the eponymous owner, Ernie Seibert, one of those fellers who decided that being in Florida gave them carte blanche to impersonate Ernest Hemingway. Ernie was a self-styled anarchist, given to writing slogans along the lines of 'Eliminate International Bankers, Eliminate War' across the walls. Whether his anarchism extended to dishing out free food is another matter. Anyway, Ernie passed on a couple of years back and now his slogans have been turned into instant heritage set in frames on the wall. Which makes the funkiness a little faux, but still, the conch fritters are chewy, the beer is cold, the bread sweet and the company good, so what the hell.

After lunch Vicki drops me off at my hotel, which turns out to be an enormous pink-and-brown 1920s pile, right on the beach. The ground floor consists of a semi-derelict shopping mall and the corridors on the upper floors are long and dingy and the rooms have kitchen facilities and it's hard not to be put in mind of a Charles Willeford novel. It's the kind of place Willeford's cop Hoke Moseley generally lived in. But it's cheap and it's clean and it has a pool and, by the time Vicki and Brian call to take me out for dinner, I'm feeling well refreshed.

'You ever see *Body Heat*?' Vicki asks as I climb into the SUV. 'Long time ago,' I say, and then ask why, and she explains that it was partly filmed right out on the Broadwalk, just along from my hotel. Cool. Or, rather, steamy.

The weather's steamy now, all right, hot and humid and right in the middle of hurricane season. Katrina passed over a few weeks earlier. It was just a baby hurricane then, a level one or two, not the level-four behemoth it became by the time it hit New Orleans. And right now Hurricane Ophelia is parked just off the Florida coast, a little way to the north. Watching the weather forecasts in these parts seems just a little bit more urgent that it does back home.

Next stop is a bar called Le Tub, right on the intra-coastal, the canal that runs parallel to the sea in these parts. Le Tub's a classic south Florida kind of place. The decor consists of old bath tubs and toilet bowls filled with flowers; there's a pool table and a jukebox inside, but in this weather we opt for sitting by the water, feeding the fish, drinking beer and listening to the locals complain about the article in *GQ* that said this place has the best hamburgers in the USA, which means that you now have a waiting time of about an hour and a half before you can get your hands on one.

So, rather than stay out here with the no-see-'ums for that long, we head down the road to Padrino's, a Cuban joint with air conditioning where we all eat plenty of rice and black-eyed beans, and Brian and I drink beer, and before long it's hard to mistake the tiredness in Vicki's eyes. Chemo evidently takes it out of you. Plus, she tells me, your taste-buds are shot and nothing tastes of anything. Alcohol in particular has no appeal at all.

It does have a certain appeal for me, though, so after Vicki and Brian drop me off I take a walk along the Broadwalk. There's a band playing in the outdoor bandshell and the tune sounds familiar, some kind of rock'n'roll standard. Then it hits the chorus and I know what it is. It's 'Marie, Marie', a slice of retro rock'n'roll originally written and recorded by LA's the Blasters, but popularised by Cardiff's own rock'n'roll legend Shakin' Stevens. Shaky is a man with one of the oddest career trajectories in pop history. He spent the late '60s and '70s playing in a rockabilly band called Shakin' Stevens and the Sunsets, playing regular benefits for the Communist Party, before becoming a solo act and housewives' favourite across Europe for most of the '80s, then disappearing from view almost entirely.

Just along the Broadwalk from the band shell there's a bar

called Nick's, which is where William Hurt first claps eyes on Kathleen Turner in *Body Heat*. Nick's place is actually pretty cool. It's dark and a little edgy, and outside the lurking hurricane is whipping up some odd, unsettling weather. Too unsettling to stay in one place for long. There's a bunch of roadhouse-type places along the Broadwalk, all with standard-issue hard-rock bar bands pounding out Bad Company tunes. Apparently this little stretch is particularly popular with French Canadians. Finally I settle on to a bar stool at a place that has a girl playing Neil Young covers at a volume that makes it possible to think. After a couple of songs, though, she gives up her guitar to a guy from the audience, who's evidently told his buddies that he is a hot-shit kind of picker. Which he isn't. The girl who's been playing gives him a look that says, 'Asshole, if you damage my guitar I'll kill you,' and goes outside for a cigarette. Then the redneck on my left tells me I'm sitting on his stool, and the rain starts beating against the windows, and I get up and out of there before either I or the bar get flattened.

Next morning, the wind has dropped and Vicki and Brian come by bright and early to drive up to the skydiving place. Or rather the 'drop zone', as skydivers apparently refer to such places. On the way up Brian reiterates his offer to take me on a tandem dive. I'm just flickering with interest, some part of me recognising that it must be an extraordinary feeling leaping out of a plane 13,000 feet up in the air. Then, however, conversation turns to last month's World Freefall Convention in Illinois. This is the big annual skydiving get-together, and Vicki and Brian were mortified to have missed it, owing to the health troubles. Then Vicki mentions that she'd just received an e-mail, saying that a guy they know from the Florida Drop Zone had died at the convention. 'Parachute didn't open apparently.'

'Oh,' I say, 'his parachute didn't open? Don't they have backup?'

Well, they explain, yes, in theory you do, but it seems it's not as failsafe as all that. If a couple of other things go wrong you might already be too low to release the reserve parachute and then, well, you're dead. Simple as that. And with this news whatever flickering notion of flying through the sky with Brian I may have been nurturing is promptly snuffed out.

Heading inland, Florida changes character pretty fast. The Everglades cover most of the inland area of southern Florida, though the developers are doing their best to eat away at it year by year. Its sheer swampy inhospitality to man, and friendliness to alligators, however, give it a certain resistance to overdevelopment. Head north though, the way we are, towards Lake Obeechobee, and soon you're in a different Florida again. This is scrubby, ugly, agricultural land.

The main town of Clewiston is home to the US Sugar Corporation and its subsidiary Southern Gardens Citrus – big sugar and big OJ. It's agri-business on a spectacular scale – 196,000 acres of land producing 700,000 tonnes of sugar and a startling 42 million gallons of orange juice each year.

Clewiston itself is a flat and featureless place with a scattering of appliance stores and the odd motel, all of it kind of temporary looking. To the north of Clewiston, close by the lake, are the ramshackle towns where the agri-business workers, the fruit pickers and cane cutters, live. We're headed west out on Route 27. After a couple of miles we pass a bar called Judy's Place, with a sign saying 'BIKERS WELCOME' – we're clearly deep into Florida cracker country.

Another mile or so and there's a sign on the left advertising AIR ADVENTURES. We turn down a little farm road that dead-ends at a tiny rural airport. There's an airport office on the left but all the action appears to be in a hangar to our right. Vicki leads the way over and, once my eyes have adjusted to the light, I can see I'm in a large space full of people – well, men mostly –

busy performing intricate folding operations with large objects made out of brightly coloured fabric – parachutes, it seems reasonable to assume.

There's a guy selling hot dogs over by the main entrance where the hangar opens up on to the runway. And around the edges there are clusters of guys standing around talking. There's an amiable mix of biker types and regular guys. Some couples, the odd family. There's not much posing going on. Sky-jumping culture isn't about talking the talk or walking the walk, it's about jumping out of aeroplanes at 13,000 feet with nothing but some parachute silk and some Velcro straps between you and oblivion. If you're prepared to do that then you've got all the respect you need coming your way.

More than that, talking to these people, Vicki's friends – there's a tall, skinny guy called Sherm, looks like a disbarred lawyer, there's good old boy Carl, who tells me about the time he saw the Stones at Knebworth, and there's Tom, a tattooed biker all sinew and skin and bone, he's had the big C too and commiserates with Vicki about the vicissitudes of chemotherapy, before showing me the eye tattooed on to the crown of his bald head 'for looking at the girls in the tittie bars' – what is clear is that these are people not bound together by wanting to be cool or tough or any of that, but rather by addiction. These people, Vicki and Brian too, have jumped not once or twice or half a dozen times, but hundreds of times. There's a very clear sense that it's only here that life really goes into Technicolor. The daily grind, once you're a sky jumper, is just monochrome, vanilla.

While Vicki's introducing me to her friends, Brian has booked himself on to the next plane taking folks on a one-way journey straight up into the sky, and gets down to the business of preparing his gear. Before long the plane, which looks small and ancient enough that I would be scared to get into it, let alone jump out of it, taxies to a stop outside the hangar, loads up with eager skydivers, and trundles down the runway.

It's going to take fifteen minutes or so before Brian falls to earth, so Vicki and I walk over to the office, where a bunch of college kids are signing up for tandem dives. They'll all be strapped to instructors while another pro videos their descent. This kind of thing costs a couple of hundred dollars a head and provides the bread-and-butter income for skydiving outfits. For most people it's a once-in-a-lifetime thrill, a video memory to shelve next to the one of you bungee jumping off a bridge. There's only a few, like Vicki, who are immediately hooked on the feeling. Once you are hooked, though, and once you've spent several thousand dollars buying your own gear, the cost of a skydiving fix goes down to around $20 a time. Though that soon adds up if you make four or five jumps a day, as some do.

Then we head outside, and before long we catch sight of Brian's blue-and-yellow parachute gently heading down to earth, and for a little while I feel a certain regret at not being the kind of person who's prepared to take risks with their life in exchange for moments of weightlessness.

Brian lands about as smoothly as a person can, and we head back inside while he packs his parachute away ready for next time. This is a job that repays concentration. If you're lazy or inexperienced you can pay one of the pros to pack your parachute away for you but Brian reckons, and I can't say that I disagree, that when it's a matter of life and death he'd sooner check that all the straps are in the right place himself.

Half an hour later and we're pulling up outside Judy's Place, and while the sign outside still proudly says BIKERS WELCOME, right now, in the middle of a hot, slow Saturday afternoon, they're ready to welcome just about anybody. The jukebox is full of good rabble-rousing tunes from George Thorogood to Lynyrd Skynyrd, but the joint is scarcely rocking. The bar staff have tattoos and attitude, but frankly things could hardly be more peaceful. It's like the atmosphere in the classic Spaghetti Western bar, just before Clint or Lee Van Cleef walks in. Torpid.

This is clearly the art-house version of the movie, though, because Clint never does come in. The sun keeps shining and the geckos keep basking. A couple of Coronas only increase the lethargy, and Vicki takes one look at me and Brian ready to nod out and announces she'll be doing the driving.

Back at her place and revived by a liberal injection of caffeine, we get down to talking, starting at the very beginning. 'I was born in Covington, Kentucky,' Vicki says, 'but I don't remember that because we moved into Ohio when I was really young. I grew up there, in Cincinnati. We lived in the suburbs. We had a bomb shelter in our basement made out of sandbags…it was kind of a strange childhood. I went to all-Catholic schools all the time. My mother didn't work. My father, he started out as an insurance man but then he sort of sold things. I remember one time he had like a thousand wool blankets in our basement. People would call and say how many they wanted. I loved that, answering the phone, telling people what colours we had. Later on he had some apartment buildings in downtown Cincinnati. I think he sold to people who didn't have much money and just collected on it once a month. I'm not really sure what kind of business this was, I never heard much about it. Then, when I was seventeen, he died.

'I read all the time. I went to college in Mount Saint Joseph, on the Ohio, an all-Catholic girls' college, for two years, then transferred to Kentucky for one year and Ohio State for the final year. I did almost all my college reading in high school, which was probably a good thing as then I found other things that were more fun. Like drinking and running around. I graduated, got married, and moved to Florida, for the weather really. I'm the kind of person who freezes and I always wanted to live in a warm climate.

'I came down here on spring break with my boyfriend and we decided to get married and move down here to live and that was… OK for a while. I was married for ten or eleven years here, had my son, got my master's in English, then I got divorced and went back to college at Florida International University. Meanwhile I did a lot of scuba diving and, you know, other…fun things.

'I always wanted to write but didn't for years and years, apart from some non-fiction in the early '80s, on lobstering and manatees. I thought I was just being lazy, but then I did classes in creative writing and figured out how to do it. As a child I read Nancy Drew then Agatha Christie, but I really didn't read any crime fiction after that till I taught a class in mystery fiction. I did my thesis on Henry James. But when I got to Florida International University and was introduced to James M. Cain I went crazy on him.

'At FIU I had two crime novelists, James Hall and Les Standiford, for tutors. Lynne Barrett, though, was actually my mentor. She was the one who recommended James Cain to me. Then, in James Hall's class, he had us pick a model and write a third of a novel based on that model. I picked *The Postman Always Rings Twice*. Mainly because it was very confined and short and had a first-person narrator – it seemed a lot easier than *Lolita* or *Catch 22* which other people did. I only had fifty-two pages to write! You had to follow the original very closely, write the same number of pages, same number of characters, look at how much summary there was and how much dialogue, and use the same proportions. See how many locations there were, really just analyse it for that kind of stuff. So you learned how to structure.'

So when did she realise that this exercise was taking on a life of its own? 'Probably never. When I started to write I didn't have much time – I was working and looking after my son – I didn't like to waste things and I had a third of a novel written, so I thought OK, I'll use it for my thesis. I never had any expectations for it, it was just fun to write. Then someone suggested sending it to Nat Sobel, who was Jim's agent and Les's agent at the time. So I sent him a few chapters and a synopsis and he wrote back, said I should make it into an updated version of *The Postman Always Rings Twice*! He didn't ask to see the rest, though. But I sent it back to him anyway – which was really unlike me – and he read it and he called me. He didn't like some things about it, he thought it'd be better set in a coffee shop and I should make the man the murderer and don't kill the dog!

'I couldn't really do those things without writing a new book but I didn't want to say forget it because this was the first agent to ever pay any attention to me. So I told him I was going to a workshop over the next weekend and I would think about it. Then I was at the conference and I got a message that my agent called. I was like, "My agent! Who might that be!"

'But he left a message and he said that Sonny Mehta was interested in the book. It was Friday afternoon and too late to call back and I'd never heard of Sonny Mehta, so everyone else at the workshop was more excited than I was. Then when I got back I had less than a week before I was off on a trip to the Peruvian jungle. So he had to wait a month till I came back before we could finally meet.'

The deal was for what Vicki has described elsewhere as 'more money than I could have imagined, if I'd had sense enough to start imagining'. It was something of a mixed blessing, however. One immediate consequence was that she discovered she was all of a sudden a 'crime writer', something she had never aspired to be. 'It never occurred to me that once I'd written something that was in the crime category, everything I wrote would be crime after that.'

Part of the reason Knopf paid such a handsome sum for *Miami Purity*, Vicki believes, is the perceived shock value of having a female lead character who positively revels in sex and violence rather than shying away from it. I wondered whether she'd consciously set out to shock. 'I wish I had more purpose,' she says. 'It just appealed to me to make the woman the murderer. I wasn't thinking that I was making her a masculine character or anything but I got all kinds of people saying I was trying to make a woman like a man. One reviewer said I had the mind of a gay man because I objectify men and women don't do that! Another reviewer on the *NYT* said he checked to make sure I was a woman and not a fake.'

Inevitably, given the fact that the lead character was a stripper, and that the novel offered a convincing picture of the world of Miami low life, there was plenty of speculation that this new writer must have emerged from this same *demi-monde* herself. And such speculation was no doubt fuelled by a James Ellroy cover blurb that described the book as 'an instant redneck idiot savant classic'.

It's a somewhat backhanded accolade which initially had Vicki bridling. After all, the fact was she was a college teacher, not a semi-literate stripper. That said, Ellroy wasn't the only one to figure that the verisimilitude of the setting and the sureness of the character portraits were signs that Vicki herself must have lived the life. So, it seems reasonable to ask, how did she come by her knowledge of the low life? Did she really not have much direct experience of that world?

'Not a whole lot,' she replies, 'but you don't really need all that much. Know a few people, hear a few stories. My boyfriend at the time had dated a dancer for a while before me, so he told me stuff about that scene. That seems to work really well for me, to get something second hand about somebody else. So that's how I started on the stripper thing. I didn't hang out in strip clubs much, though. I went to more after I wrote the book because they always wanted to take my picture in them.'

The arrival of a fat cheque for a first novel can often paralyse writers, making it particularly hard to write the next one. Fortunately Vicki was already embarked on her second book, *Iguana Love*. To my mind it's her finest work to date, an utterly compelling study of sexual obsession and alienation. Its heroine, Ramona, is a woman who, as the book opens, doesn't quite have it all, but certainly has what most people might consider enough: a good-looking husband called Gary, an apartment with a pool in Miami, a job as a nurse, a cat called Snickers. But it's not enough for her. In particular, Gary is not enough. Ramona craves wildness and Gary is happy with domesticity. She start hanging out with the divers at a local bar, has a fling and eventually kicks Gary out and replaces him with a pet iguana.

Step by step her life loses its moorings. She becomes infatuated with a diver called Enzo who's clearly not making all his money from giving scuba lessons. And as she loses control of her emotional life, her physical being also starts to mutate. A fondness for going to the gym becomes an obsession that she feeds with steroids, which begin to have a startling effect on her sexuality.

Iguana Love is a book that doesn't so much challenge gender stereotypes about love and lust as beat them to a bloody pulp. It's also a book, it transpires, that did have its roots a little closer to home than her debut.

'The idea for it came because I had this relationship that was like that. And around that time I got an iguana. I get these cravings for pets and then I go out and get one. And when you get an iguana, all of a sudden you meet all these other women who have iguanas. It's a very strange thing. So I called this particular woman whose iguana had died – she was trying to sell this three-thousand-dollar cage that was like ceiling high, six foot in diameter, with a water fountain in the bottom. The iguana's name was Chupa and she had this kind of gravestone on the window sill where he used to sit. I didn't buy the cage but I got some books from her, and as I was looking through one of the books I saw that she'd decorated it with hearts and written "I love you, Chupa" and stuff like that. Anyway, I got to know her a little and she showed me videos of her dancing with Chupa round her neck. He had been dead a couple of months, I think, by this time, but she still had these sucker bites on her arms – iguana kisses. It was really a little bit scary. Plus she had some problems going on, some kind of boyfriend problems. She started calling me in the middle of the night…

'That's where it started. And the idea of iguana love – love as a kind of challenge – I came up with that from the relationship I was in, I guess. Some people just don't know how to love, like an iguana. There was a line in the book this woman lent me, "No matter how much you love an iguana, he will never love you back". You know, because they're reptiles! And I thought of this woman who was desperately trying to get this iguana to love her…

'I was doing some bodybuilding at the time, a lot of gym stuff, so that got in there too. I had this vision of Ramona as this really big, developed woman. I've always hated the idea that women aren't as strong as men. I can work out every day and some guy that's never done a push-up in his life is still stronger than I am. It's only if you really bodybuild and take steroids and all that you can get past that. And that's always been really irritating to me – so I had Ramona go for it and try to be stronger than a man.

'And the scuba diving came in because I had just gone through the whole business of getting a rescue diver certificate, so that seemed to work in well as part of her goal. I always wanted to scuba dive from the time I moved down here, I started when my son was a year old. But I didn't have the money to buy the equipment so I didn't get to do it that much the first ten years, I guess. Then when I got divorced the first guy I got as a boyfriend had a boat! And that helped a lot and I started to scuba dive all the time.

'I never saw it as anything extreme or scary. I've always loved swimming, loved water. Then when I got the money from *Miami Purity* I felt like I could buy anything I wanted and so I bought a sailboat. That was hard to keep up; it quickly became clear I wasn't going to be able to keep coasting on my writing. I had to go back to work. Though I did get to sail to the Bahamas several times, which was fine, and good research. It was fun while it lasted.'

So when did she realise that the promised fame and fortune weren't going to work out, at least not right away? 'Well, it took Sonny seven months to tell me whether he wanted *Iguana Love* or not, I think he was waiting to see how many copies of *Miami Purity* came back. So seven months and then he turned it down...'

Nevertheless the *Miami Purity* money had given Vicki time not only to finish *Iguana Love* but also to write her third novel, the quirky and rather less noir *Voluntary Madness*, in which a girl called Juliette goes to Key West with her much older boyfriend, Punch, a failed writer, whose only interest is in drinking himself to death. Juliette, meanwhile, spends her time trying to dream up plans to distract him from this aim.

'Once I got the *Miami Purity* money I decided, "I'm a writer now, I should go and live in Key West for a while". So I went down and rented a little cottage in a compound. Turned out various writers lived there. It was really fun and I used to go out to the bars virtually every night and I would ride my bicycle. Then one night I had it stolen and I had to walk back and I was walking down Caroline Street from Duval and it was dark and a little spooky, and this guy passed me exposing himself. And I thought, why don't women ever do that?'

So the book starts with Juliette flashing bemused passers-by, hoping her escapades will entertain Punch. This is no easy task, as Punch is a chronic alcoholic, little interested in anything that can't be ordered at a bar and drunk. 'The whole alcoholic writer thing I got from a past boyfriend,' Vicki explains. 'He also taught in the college where I did and was a really bad drunk and he died a few years after we broke up, from diabetes.

'Punch, in the book, was kind of that character, except when I got into it he was almost unrecognisable except for his drunkenness and his diabetes. And I put the much younger woman in there because, making him such an extreme drunk, she had to be pretty naive to fall for him. I started gathering drunk stories like the one about the guy whose friends bring him home from the bar – and the wife opens the door and says, "Thanks, but where's his wheelchair?" That's a true story. I had to put it in there.

'Then I went to this really weird place called Coral Castle. It was built by this little scrawny guy for this woman who wouldn't have anything to do with him. Everything made out of coral, even the tables and chairs. He did all this then invited her down and she wouldn't go for it. It kind of reflected the whole love thing I was trying to get across in the book, how hard she tried to get Punch to love her.'

With *Voluntary Madness* Vicki hoped to break out of the whole crime/noir pigeon-hole in which she'd been placed. Pigeon-holes are tricky to escape, however, and the fact that this was basically a picaresque love story with a dark heart probably only confused readers looking for more harsh erotic noir, without attracting any new audience worth speaking of.

For the next book, *Sky Blues*, Vicki decided to return to the kind of novel that had made her name. And so we meet Desi Donne, a woman whose life is devoted to caring for animals and keeping well away from dangerous men, until she meets a guy called Tom, who introduces her to skydiving. And one or two other things, but let's deal with the skydiving first.

'*Sky Blues*, well, that was inspired by the whole skydiving, of course, and that was the result of having extra money and just doing anything I thought would be fun. I met these two people in the hot tub at a nudist camp in Florida, Laurie and Chick. I was doing research into some guy who was meant to be using steroids at the nudist camp. It was a really strange place. It wasn't like a naturist thing, it was more like a sex thing. Laurie and Chick had been to other nudist camps and they said normally if you get near anyone else there's like someone saying "no touching" – but this place it wasn't really like that!

'So I got to know these two people. They'd been graphic designers for years, never taken a day off, and then they'd decided they were going to start doing crazy things. So the nudist thing was one thing but they'd also taken up skydiving. They also did broken glass walking, fire walking, metal bending as well, which is a whole other thing. They started hosting these nights where you would do one face-your-fear thing after another. Anyway, I went up to Clewiston to go skydiving with them. And after I did the one jump I really wanted to do more. I started taking classes and going regularly and I was really sucked in.

'At first I just thought I'd take a couple of classes and then I'd write about it. But I found there was so much more to it. After a couple of classes I realised I still didn't know what I was doing. I started the book then, anyway, so you get all her impressions as she starts skydiving. But it took a couple of years to finish, with me doing more skydiving and less writing, Actually, for a while there I had thoughts of just leaving my job and becoming a skydiver. I've seen people do that.' She pauses. 'But it generally doesn't turn out too well…'

Once again, though, despite the inherent drama of the setting, the public remained widely indifferent: 'A lot of people don't even want to hear about skydiving. You start talking about it, they say, "No, no, my stomach feels funny." And skydivers generally don't read a lot! So…'

So she decided to keep on keeping on. Her new book, *Cruel Poetry*, is due out in early 2007. It's longer than her other books and employs multiple narrators, including for the first time a man. 'In *Cruel Poetry* there are three narrators. And it was so much fun to get away from the whole voice through one book. I always enjoy writing men and I think I know men really well, but even so it's such a creative venture. The three protagonists are a poetry professor – of course, I know lots of those. A girl who wants to be a writer – I know lots of those. And Renata – I kind of modelled her on someone I met at the gym.'

Renata is the central figure. A close cousin to Ramona from *Iguana Love* and Sherise from *Miami Purity*, she is perhaps the least conflicted Hendricks heroine, yet when it comes to her sexual appetites Renata is very fond of fucking. She's especially fond of fucking her boyfriend Francisco, but she's got plenty left over for friends and acquaintances. And what's left after that she sells on the open market. Renata doesn't mind; as far as she's concerned pleasure is all there is. Life isn't quite that simple for the other two protagonists, though. Poetry Professor Richard (aka 'Dr Dick') is completely obsessed with Renata, wants to throw his life away for her. And then there's Jules. She lives in the room next to Renata in the run-down Miami Beach hotel they both call home. She's trying to write a novel, but mostly she just listens through the wall to Renata's non-stop sex life. Then one evening she hears something terrible through the wall and events are put in motion that turn all three lives upside down.

'The theme this time was really the evolution of sexuality,' Vicki comments, musing on Renata's total (if ultimately calamitous) ease with her sexuality. 'Things are so much looser now – men being with men, women being with women, and women and men just mixing it up – the younger people now have so much less gender orientation than they used to. I've seen it a lot at the drop zones, and my students will write essays about how they all went out and…to them it's like everyday stuff.'

She pauses here. Then she says: 'I'm only really interested in obsession as motivation. I think this is a problem, it makes the books too similar. They all have the same motivation – obsession. But it's hard for me to believe that people will kill each other for money. To me no other motive makes more sense than some obsession that takes you past sanity. To me obsession is the most interesting thing in human nature, and this book it was time to have a male obsessed. I really like Richard, he's kind of disgusting but I like him. He feels real to me.'

This, I think, gets right to the heart of what makes Vicki Hendricks such a powerful, even important, writer. Just as the great '50s noirists, the Jim Thompsons and Charles Williamses, got right to the heart of the dark obsessions of their time, Vicki Hendricks seems to me to plug into the dark sexual obsessions of our own time like no other contemporary writer, male or female.

It also seems like a pretty good note to end up on. Time to head on out to dinner.

We drive to downtown Hollywood Beach, through the kind of heritage section, which must date back all the way to those far-off 1950s days when Charles Williams and John D. MacDonald sold hundreds of thousand of books via the nation's drugstores.

We end up at a fairly generic American place, looks a bit like the one where William Hurt runs into Kathleen Turner, plus about-to-be-murdered hubby, in *Body Heat*. As we eat Vicki talks about her future plans. Disillusion with publishing is evidently weighing heavy on her.

She has another novel of contemporary Floridian obsession mapped out, but right now she's not sure whether that's what she wants to write: 'The next novel may be historical fiction which is a whole new area for me – and you seem to get a better shot when it's your first book in an area and they don't know what it's going to do. Plus historical fiction is more popular than noir...'

Once again Vicki's tired by the end of the meal and they drop me off, back on the Broadwalk. I stroll up to Nick's for a couple of drinks, but when I head back outside the weather is turning strange again. There's a wind, the likes of which I've never encountered before, whipping up. There's rain sleeting in from odd angles. I decide to head back towards the hotel and on arrival contemplate a nightcap at the beachfront bar, but now the wind and rain are really starting to lash so I head inside, where someone tells me that's an honest-to-God tornado outside.

I head upstairs, admiring the way Florida provides so many natural metaphors just made for noir writers – sun and sand, hurricanes and swamps. Light and shade all right.

Upstairs I try to get a bottle of water from the drinks machine, stuck away in a little laundry room. It takes my money and hands me a Diet Coke in return. Not ever having had a taste for Coke, I'm about to leave it there and stomp off when a tough-looking young Hispanic guy with plentiful tattoos shows up. I tell him to beware the machine's erratic dispensing technique and offer him the Diet Coke, and he looks at me as if I'm crazy – 'I would never give my little girls caffeine,' he tells me. And I head for bed, thinking about how easily we stereotype people, and listening to the tornado whirling its way west, same way I'll be headed in the morning.

8   SoCal: where the debris meets the sea

AS I FLY into southern California, after a cross-country flight that has taken me right over the Gulf Coast floods, the landscape goes through a series of contortions. First mountains, then desert, then the coastal plain with its great sprawling city. The plane flies over it all and keeps on going out into the Pacific Ocean, before making a reluctant turn and heading back into the smog to land at LAX. Those few moments of flying west into the Pacific blue are enough to give me a sense of just how much this city is on the edge. America has finally come to its end, and all that remains is thousands of miles of blue.

It's an extraordinary tribute to human ingenuity, of course, that Los Angeles should have succeeded in coming into existence on such an unpromising strip of land between desert and ocean. So successful has it been, though, in conquering the landscape, that it's easy to forget just what an elemental place this is, and how thoroughly shaped by its surroundings. The desert at the city's back serves as a potent metaphor for the extent to which those who come here have burned their bridges: there's no going back from LA, you succeed or die. The ocean, meanwhile, plays a more complex part in California life. On the one hand it's the idyllic backdrop to a million postcards, on the other it's every bit as much a barrier as the desert; just as the desert announces there's no going back, so the ocean says there's no way forward. It's immutable, unconquerable.

But while the desert is mostly respected in its fierceness and aridity, the Californians have long loved to tangle with the sea, to defy it. And above all they've done so by surfing it. Surfing is the emblematic Californian pastime. From the '50s onwards it's been less a sport than a culture. It inspired movies first and then a whole genre of music, which began with Dick Dale's 'Wipe Out' and reached its apotheosis with the Beach Boys.

Never before or since has a major musical act been so identified with a sport as the Beach Boys with surfing. It would have been unimaginable for the Beatles to pose in soccer gear, or Elvis to wield a baseball bat. In a world where rock'n'roll was cool, sport was the epitome of not cool. Except for surfing, and maybe that's because surfing was less a sport than an image of utopia, the American dream written on the waves.

Personally, I have to say that for a long time it failed to do much for me. The Beach Boys were OK – it's hard music to dislike, though I could never quite buy the 'Brian Wilson is God' stuff that leads rock critics to endlessly vote *Pet Sounds* the greatest record of all time (and why would rock critics, that nerdiest, most citified of tribes, so idolise this bronzed outdoor music anyway? Oh yeah, that's one of those questions that answers itself, isn't it?). Anyway, like I say, the Beach Boys didn't do much for me, and neither did Gidget movies. The culture of it seemed a million miles away from the freezing beaches of South Wales. No, the first time I actually felt the appeal of surfing and its culture was when I read a paperback called *Tapping the Source* by Kem Nunn.

Tapping the Source is a coming-of-age surfing noir novel telling the story of a kid named Ike Tucker, from way out in the desert, coming to Huntington Beach, California's self-proclaimed surf city, to find his missing sister. He's heard that she disappeared off to Mexico in the company of some bad-ass surfers and, despite his youth and inexperience, he's determined to find out what happened to her.

In an effort to get close up to the guys who may know the answers, Ike takes up surfing, and the pages devoted to his first attempts made it clear to me, for the first time, that the ease and grace and general golden sun-kissed fantasy enshrined in the classic surfing photos are the exception, not the rule. Surfing, it transpires, is difficult, dangerous and fiercely competitive. On his first try Ike is punched out by a fellow surfer for inadvertently getting in the way, and it's only when he falls under the ambivalent care of surfer-turned-biker Preston that Ike begins to get the hang, not just of surfing, but of how to survive out of the water as well.

The Huntington Beach Nunn portrayed was a place on the cusp of change, a once laid-back hippy surfer hangout that was, at the turn of the '80s, becoming increasingly commercialised: more and more people came to surf, college kids on the one hand, runaways and dropouts on the other. The soundtrack, meanwhile, was changing too. Punk rock was the new sound in town, and its harsh rejection of the hippy values reflected the extent to which Nunn revealed those values to have curdled.

Tapping the Source is one of those books that stays with you. It was one of the few novels of its time to note the arrival of punk, to portray an America that was moving on from the Vietnam era. There were long-standing rumours that it was to be filmed. Other surfing films did come out – *Surf Nazis Must Die*, which, if memory serves, punk entrepreneur Malcolm McLaren had something to do with, and *Point Break* – both of them indebted in varying degrees to *Tapping the Source*.

But neither the novel in particular, nor surfing in general, was something I thought all that much about until the summer of 1998. That was when the second part of Kem Nunn's surfing trilogy, *The Dogs of Winter*, came out, and it was also when I moved back to Wales and discovered that, with the introduction of the lightweight affordable wet suit, surf culture had come to South Wales.

I'd only been back a couple of weeks when a friend suggested we could go surfing one Sunday. I was still more than somewhat dubious, but thought why not, attracted by the incongruity of the idea as much as anything else. And so we made the drive out west from Cardiff, past Swansea and out on to the Gower Peninsula, an outcrop of the Welsh coastline that feels oddly locked in time, stuck somewhere around 1965. At the very end of the peninsula is the village of Llangennith and its attendant beach, a great sandy bay with a fair complement of surfers. I hired a wet suit and a body board and gave it a go, and the first time a wave picked me up and carried me to the shore I was converted. Since then I've had, if not quite a love for surfing, at least what we Brits might call a definite fondness for it. I even put it in one my books. There's a surfing theme in my novel *Cardiff Dead*, my own coming-of-age noir-ish novel, which was a conscious tribute to the influence of Kem Nunn.

Not, I hasten to add, that I'm any good at it. But still, heading south from LAX towards the surfing coast of southern California, I'm looking forward to seeing what I can't help thinking of as 'real surfers' up close.

The drive down from the airport begins by skirting the ghettos of south central LA (places now so familiar from films and, especially, video games like *Grand Theft Auto* that one of the first questions my thirteen-year-old son asked me when I told him I was going to California was 'Are you going to Compton?'), before heading through a light industrial wilderness inland from Long Beach. Next, a right turn takes me through the heavily Vietnamese suburbia around the town of Westminster and down on to the Pacific Coast Highway, in one of its less romantic stretches, as it heads south into Huntington Beach, Surf City itself.

It's getting dark now, so the first thing is to find a place to stay. In *Tapping The Source* Ike Tucker finds a room in the seediest motel in town, the Sea View. These days seediness is thin on the ground: there's a Hilton and a Hyatt and a Best Western, but after nosing around a little I wind up at the Surf Inn. It's a '50s establishment, built on stilts, which seems to hark back satisfyingly to a rougher and readier Huntington Beach. The motel, like so many other old-school American motels, is run these days by an Indian family. And it's cheapish and clean and affords a sea view if you find the right spot on the roof.

Night comes down fast in these parts, and by the time I've showered and headed out, the ocean is no more than a dark presence thudding repeatedly against the shore. If it stays like this there'll surely be good surf in the morning. Meanwhile I amble along the seafront till I come to Main Street and turn inland to see what shakes in Huntington Beach by night.

The answer to that seems to be not a lot. Whatever edginess Huntington Beach may once have had seems, at least on this evening at the back end of September, to have been replaced by a sedate mix of clothes stores and theme bars – the kinds of places you can find in any mall anywhere. I grab a hamburger in a vaguely Hawaiian-themed sports bar and watch some baseball and head back to the hotel.

As I arrive back I notice for the first time that the house next door to my hotel, a regular suburban-looking house, nothing remotely fancy, has a single oil well in its yard, calmly pumping away through the night. It's so prosaic that the weirdness of it doesn't hit me for a while. Sure, doesn't everyone have an oil well in the back yard of their beachfront property? The casual proximity of industry and recreation is a reminder of just how new this all is, how recent its taming. It's only when I get to bed that I remember that Ike Tucker's hotel in *Tapping the Source* also has an oil well next to it. Perhaps I'm a little closer to the source than I realised.

I'm up early next morning. By eight o'clock I'm out on the

beach surveying the scene. The waves are still coming in and already there's a whole lot of people in the water. Maybe that's why Huntington Beach was so quiet the night before. Energy conservation. And while on land Huntington Beach may be pretty tame these days, here in the surprisingly cold water things are as serious as ever. To get a closer view I take a walk down the pier, rebuilt after being destroyed by monster waves in the '80s. Ike Tucker soon learned to his cost that the ocean close to the pier is no place for beginners, and the same is evidently true today. All the guys I can see below me are very good indeed, as you'd need to be to surf this close to the pier's concrete pilings, which could easily make a wipe-out fatal.

I watch them for a while, contemplate hiring a board and going in myself and decide against it, feeling way too old to go through the certain humiliation awaiting me in the surf. Instead I head back into the town, looking for traces of the old surf culture. It looks to be long gone. Jack's Surfshop has been here since 1957 but these days it's a giant purpose-built surfing superstore, in which the boards and wet suits play second fiddle to the clothing ranges produced by the ubiquitous brand names – Quiksilver, Billabong, Rip Curl et al.

Just off Main Street there's a Surfing Museum which is featuring a rather tenuously surfing-linked exhibition of ukuleles. It's nice enough but rather adds to my sense that surfing is something that used to be a home-made activity but has now been subsumed by global commerce. Much the same goes for the 'Surfing Walk of Fame' which I find myself following as I head back up the Pacific Coast Highway. It consists of a series of plaques built into the pavement celebrating the deeds of assorted top surfers, in obvious tribute to the Hollywood Walk of Fame. It's all much too clearly part of Huntington Beach's attempt to brand itself as 'Surf City' after the Jan and Dean song.

Now Kem Nunn is evidently well aware that the surfing

world has moved on since he wrote *Tapping the Source*. His second surfing novel, *The Dogs of Winter*, starts in Huntington Beach, but its nominal hero, a washed up surf photographer named Jack Fletcher, wastes little time in leaving town and heading north to the California–Oregon border, in search of big cold-water waves that only the truly hardcore would ever consider surfing.

The third, and most probably the final, book in the sequence, *Tijuana Straits*, also forswears the commercial surf scene, but this time heads in the opposite direction. It's set at the very opposite end of California, right down south on the Mexican border, and it's in that direction that I'm headed next.

Driving south from Huntington Beach, the first place I come to is the moneyed, yachting-crowd town of Newport Beach, which once boasted the Rendezvous Ballroom, where surf music was more or less invented, and then there's Laguna Beach, where Kem Nunn lives. Laguna Beach is one of those cute beachside towns that, a long time ago, was known as something of an artists' colony, but these days you'd have to be a pretty successful artist to live here.

Kem Nunn lives just above the town in a pleasingly ramshackle neighbourhood. It's the kind of place where private detectives live in books and Hollywood films, but probably not in real life. I ring the bell and Kem Nunn comes down to the gate. He's a tall lean individual with a neat beard and a serious, rather grave manner. You can imagine him as various things – reverend, academic, cellist – but it would be a while before you figured him for a surfer.

We chat briefly in the living room, and it's quickly apparent that this isn't going to be one of those interviews where you can just switch off and let the interviewee roll out his patter. Nunn is friendly enough but definitely reserved, so rather than just pitch straight into an interview I suggest taking a drive along the coast, to visit a few surf spots. Nunn assures me that there's not much to see any more, but agrees nevertheless.

While he's getting himself together to head out, I take a look at his CD collection. Heavy on the jazz and the country, plenty of Lucinda Williams and Gillian Welch, overall a high preponderance of records I own myself, which seems like a good omen.

Nunn says he'll drive, so we head outside and climb into his Lexus. What with the house and the car it's clear that Kem Nunn isn't doing too badly. I suspect it's not the books, which are more cult favourites than bestsellers, that have made the money. And, though his manner might suggest it, he doesn't have an academic job, as so many American writers do. So where has the money come from?

Well, it turns out that it's Hollywood which has provided the bulk of his living over the last couple of decades. He's had one of those curious careers – James Crumley's is similar – in which a writer makes more money writing pictures that never get made, or doctoring pictures for which he gets no credit, than writing the books that got Hollywood interested in the first place.

His latest gig is his first venture into television – no ordinary television show, though. Nunn has been asked to join the writing team for *Deadwood*, probably the coolest show on American TV right now, and he's spent the last few weeks hanging out on-set, soaking up the atmosphere. As if to prove the point he refers to a motorist who gets in our way as a hooplehead, then laughs and says that *Deadwood*-speak is infectious.

From his house on the hill we drive almost straight down towards the sea, and pull up outside a Ritz Carlton resort, built on the cliff top above the beach. This, he tells me, used to be known as Salt Creek. It's here he used to come on holiday with his parents. They used to camp on the beach, and it's the first place he saw people surf.

From here we head on to Dana Point. Nunn asks me whether I have ever heard of 'killer Dana'. I shake my head. Turns out it's a legendary surf break. Legendary is the word, though, because it's gone. Dana Point had been reconfigured as a yachting marina and the break no longer exists. Though its name lives on in a range of surf gear.

Just along from Dana Point is Doheny, one of the beaches immortalised in the Beach Boys' 'Surfin' USA'. You can still surf here, more or less, but only at one end of the beach. There's wi-fi throughout, though. Kem Nunn is unimpressed.

The trip is in danger of becoming a parade of places that used to be great and are now gone or gentrified out of all recognition, so I ask Nunn whether there's anywhere he likes to surf these days. He looks tempted to say no for a moment, lost in the Eeyore-ish pleasure of rubbishing all the redevelopment – something I'm very sympathetic to, as I tend to do the same thing whenever showing people around Cardiff – but finally he nods and admits that there is a place that isn't too bad.

So we carry on south till we get to the State Park at San Onofre. There's a guy on the gate controlling access to the car park. Kem shows him an annual pass which suggests that the beach may after all be a little more than all right. And so it is. It's a perfect California beach backed by dunes, credible surfmobiles in the car park and credible surfers on the water. We sit in silence for a little while, contemplating the scene. I resolve to take lessons when I get back to Wales, learn to surf properly.

It's only driving back out of the State Park that I notice the reason for this piece of coast's relative lack of development. Two large nuclear reactors right next to the freeway might have something to do with it. It's a very Kem Nunn juxtaposition.

From here on Kem is notably more cheery. He drives me up to San Clemente next, another beachside town where he spent a lot of time in his twenties. We drive into a funky little neighbourhood that is apparently home to a lot of surfers and shapers – guys who make custom surfboards. We're looking for Commander John, one of the models for Nunn's fictional crew of surf outlaws. There's no sign of him today, though, so we decide to get some food.

Nunn suggests a Mexican place called Olamendi's right on the Pacific Coast Highway and we head on up there, taking a brief detour for him to show me the place he gets his surfboards from.

Olamendi's may take the well-contested prize for the Mexican restaurant with the loudest decor I've ever been in. The walls are covered with fantastically lurid religious scenes, generally featuring Christ on the cross, interspersed with photos of famous regulars. Pride of place goes to none other than the thirty-seventh president of the United States, Richard Milhous Nixon. Peering at a picture of Tricky Dicky shaking hands with the owner, it strikes me that the reason why the famous 'would you buy a used car from this man' jibe failed to hurt Nixon's electoral results was that he looked so blatantly like a used-car salesman that there was no need to point it out. Indeed, it's more than likely that people voted for him precisely because he did look like a used-car salesman – what's more American than that?

Then, over enchiladas and Pacifico beers, we get to talking about Kem Nunn's journey from the California desert to Hollywood. 'I grew up in Pomona, the Pomona Valley. I grew up in a tract home there,' he tells me. 'My dad was a plumber.' He seems happy enough to leave it there, but a couple more questions elicit the fact that his childhood was not as prosaically suburban as all that. 'I had a kind of religious upbringing. My parents became Jehovah's Witnesses when I was very young. So for a while I actually had a ministerial draft deferment right out of high school, but I reached a point at which I was becoming increasingly unhappy doing what I'd always thought I should be doing.'

It's an answer that takes a moment or two to resonate. And then I get it. The central character in Nunn's second novel, the generally overlooked (it's the only one of his books to be currently out of print, both in the US and the UK) *Unassigned Territory*, a freewheeling and fantastical tale set in the Mojave Desert, is a young man named Obadiah Wheeler. He's a youthful preacher brought up in a cultish religious organisation. He possesses grave doubts with regard to his calling, but is reluctant to leave the order, as his status as minister has given him a draft exemption keeping him out of Vietnam. Aha, I think. There's always a certain satisfaction, I find, in spotting where the author appears in their own fiction.

Once the real Kem Nunn, as opposed to the fictional Obadiah, had lost his belief in his calling, he left the Pomona Valley and headed for the coast, drawn initially at least by a lifelong love of beaches and their attendant culture, and it was there that he spent the next decade. 'I lived in Santa Barbara for a while, then, over the next ten years, lived up and down the coast, from Santa Barbara to Dana Point. I had always loved beaches and I discovered I could eke out a living doing work on boats, so basically that's what I did.'

All of which sounds pretty much like what used to be called dropping out. So was it the whole '60s things which had provoked his change of direction? I wondered. 'Well,' he says, 'part of what I was doing during those years was coming out from under the belief system I was raised with and trying to find my own way. So, with respect to the '60s, in a way I was set apart from it, though I was very much intrigued by the whole counter-cultural movement. But I was drawn to the spirit of questioning authority and the status quo, because that was something I was doing in my own life. Trying to find some authentic way of living instead of what you'd always been told.'

That authentic way of living, for Nunn, was very closely bound up with the ocean in general, and surfing in particular: 'Surfing was increasingly part of my life. I had become interested in it when I was young in junior high, but I lived inland so it was hard to learn. That was one of my reasons for coming to the coast. I started to surf more, really learning how to do it.'

Along with the surfing and the boating, Nunn was also involved in the arts. He played mandolin in a bluegrass band, and had a long-standing affinity with the visual arts: 'In high school I'd always loved to paint but I came from a family and a community in which that sort of thing wasn't really encouraged. You were encouraged to find something more practical, to make a living. So, I suppose, in some other life I might have gone to art school.'

In the end it was more poverty than anything else which persuaded him to turn his talents to fiction instead: 'During my mid-twenties, when I found myself nickel-and-dime-ing it, working on boats, living on the cheap, I didn't feel like I had money for painting supplies and a space to work, but it was easy to get a typewriter and some paper and start banging out some stories.'

At first, however, those stories were not about the beach world he was living in, but the Pomona Valley life he'd left behind: 'In my last stint of ministerial work there I spent a lot of time with these bums and derelicts in Pomona. So I started writing some short stories about those people. Then I started to wonder if you could put them all together and make a novel out of them. It was kind of my first run at some of the material that eventually became my third book, *Pomona Queen*.'

Once he had some stories written Nunn started taking night classes at a local community college. There he met a California writer called Oakley Hall, who ran the writing programme at UC Irvine, and he persuaded Nunn to go back to school. He also turned Nunn on to the work of Robert Stone, in particular Stone's Vietnam novel, *Dog Soldiers*. This was to have a profound influence on Nunn, all the more so when Hall told him that Stone would actually be coming to the college the following year: '*Dog Soldiers* made a huge impression on me. I thought I could do something like that, and then I thought that no one had written about the surfing milieu in a very interesting way, so it was along about that time I began to think about *Tapping the Source*. I really wanted to have a draft of that finished by the time Robert Stone came.'

This time Nunn had decided to write about the world he saw around him: 'I was working a couple of days a week with a friend of mine who had a furniture finishing shop. One day we found this guy living in a box in a lot behind the shop. The guy was a good surfer and he wound up working with us, and one day his younger brother, Brett, showed up. Brett was this kid who'd been living in Huntington Beach. He was a jailbird kind of a kid and he had these stories to tell about life there. He'd had this job working for this ageing biker and his job kind of consisted of hanging out by the pier picking up runaway girls and bringing them back to this guy's place to party, the idea being that the girls all got high and the guy would get laid. And if that didn't happen the guy developed a habit of taking it out on Brett by knocking him around.

'He was one of those guys who had a sweet innocent side but he was also had a street tough side. When I met Brett he had this big black eye and there was something in him that suggested a character to me. I liked the idea, it's kind of an archetypal idea, of the kid taking on the quest that he's not really prepared for. So it was a combination of this kid showing up and my desire to write something about surfing culture as I had seen it. What

I saw with this kid was a way into that – he would have to enter this world to solve a mystery.'

And that's just what Nunn did: constructed a novel that effortlessly melded a coming-of-age story with a noir tale of Californian idealism turned sour, all set against the pristine fictional backdrop of the surfing world. And he did indeed finish the draft in time for Stone's arrival. Not only that but Stone liked the book enough to recommend it to his agent and the agent succeeded in selling the rights. Next stop fame and fortune. Well, more or less.

'It never did well in terms of sales,' says Nunn, 'but it was nominated for a National Book Award, and it got a lot of attention in Hollywood. It had a fairly lucrative movie sale: they didn't just option the book, they purchased it. And given the people who were involved it looked like it was really going to happen.' He laughs. 'So far in my experience of Hollywood it amazes me that anything ever gets made. It's had a long and tortured history in Hollywood. People still talk about trying to make it, but it's owned by Universal. I don't know, I have a feeling that someday they will make it. Someone will show up who wants to do it and has the juice. It'd be nice to see it. At least, I think it'd be nice to see it...'

Surely that would be tricky given that the world depicted has largely vanished? Not really, says Nunn. 'You get a good location scout, you can patch things together and it winds up looking pretty good. There are places like Imperial Beach and Avila Beach. They shot most of *Lords of Dogtown* with Imperial Beach as Venice.'

Well, here's hoping that Hollywood will indeed one day get round to it, rather than just ripping it off, as happened with the Keanu Reeves vehicle *Point Break*. Anyway, as first novels go, *Tapping the Source* had done a pretty good job of establishing

Kem Nunn as a name to watch. All he needed to do was follow up with another tough noir tale of life on the edge on the California beaches.

Instead he came up with *Unassigned Territory*, a surreal jaunt through the Mojave Desert that most *Tapping the Source* fans, myself included, found baffling and frankly disappointing.

Re-reading it now, and taking it on its own merits, I have to say I was completely wrong. It's a terrific book, a funny and profound fable of the search for love and meaning amid a California where pulp sci-fi and religious cults were but a hair's breadth away from each other (as L. Ron Hubbard very profitably discovered).

As Nunn has already intimated, it has its roots in autobiography. 'Yes, that was me wanting to write something about my experiences growing up as a Witness. I should add that I have a lot of affection for the community I grew up in – I wanted to write about a guy who was conflicted about all of that. I chose this fairly crazy story: part science fiction, part coming of age, part mystery.'

The fairly crazy story involves the young minister Obadiah Wheeler ending up lost in a desert hamlet whose only claim to fame is that it's the home of a hopeless roadside attraction that professes to be the home of the 'Mystery of the Mojave'. In fact over the years it's been home to a series of Mysteries of the Mojave – home-made monsters constructed from papier mâché and chicken wire by one Sarge Hummer. Oddly enough, however, the current monster, which appears just before Sarge's untimely death, does not appear to have been made of any recognisable materials.

In fact it looks positively extra-terrestrial. A whole cast of eccentrics are interested in acquiring the monster, but before any of them can get their hands on it, it's stolen by Sarge's daughter, the lovely Delandra Hummer, and her accomplice, the mixed-up preacher boy Obadiah himself. Trouble, as one might suspect, ensues. Enlightenment, of a sort, also.

Not only was the book a disconcerting departure for his new-found fans, it was also quite a long time coming. 'It took me quite a while because I moved to New York and then came back to California,' recalls Nunn, 'where I had to make up for lost time surfing all the waves I'd missed, so it took a long time to write and when it came out it wasn't the book a lot of people expected. My editor and agent were happy but, if you look at it from a purely commercial angle, I had begun with this kind of mystery novel – I never thought of it as a mystery, but people saw it that way – and a lot of people expected me to carry on with the surfing and the noir kind of story. But I still get a kick out of the book, it makes me laugh. It has a small, somewhat demented group of followers.'

And while crime fiction aficionados may have been disappointed, Hollywood was rather more enthusiastic: '*Tapping the Source* had opened doors for me in Hollywood. But *Unassigned Territory* was the book that led to me writing my first script. A producer named John Solomon, who was working on the Disney lot, was a huge fan of *Unassigned Territory* and he said, "Look, none of the people I know are ever going to make this book, but do you have any script ideas?" So I went to him with my first script and managed to get it optioned and that was the beginning of all that.'

'All that' is a screenwriting career that has kept the wolf away from Nunn's door for the past couple of decades – even though none of his scripts has actually been made. The nearest he has come is probably 1981's *Wild Things*, a twisty piece of modern noir set in south Florida, and probably most popular with viewers on account of the unusually explicit lesbian scenes between teen queens Neve Campbell and Denise Richards.

Nunn doesn't actually receive a writing credit, but describes his work on the script – originally written by Stephen Peters – as a 'page one rewrite'.

And while the lack of tangible results from his screenwriting years is inevitably frustrating, Nunn is generally sanguine about the business: 'The nice thing about Hollywood is that I've made decent money writing scripts and doctoring scripts and it has enabled me to write the books I want to write. So if I don't want to write about surfing I won't. There was a point where someone might have suggested I write a series but I'm quite happy not to have done that. To get on that treadmill with your books, always chasing that carrot, well, I'd prefer not to. And writing scripts puts me in touch with the kind of stuff that I think feeds my work, puts me in touch with different worlds. I've been sent to New Orleans to hang out with vice cops, or to New York to hang out with homicide detectives. I'm now friends with a guy who spent twelve years in the Navy SEALS, because we worked together on a project. You come into contact with the kind of people that you don't meet ordinarily. You especially do not meet them if you're teaching.'

That said, it's actually the case that Nunn's work sticks pretty close to his own history and long-standing preoccupations. His third novel, *Pomona Queen*, for instance, returned him to his roots.

'*Pomona Queen* was once again me going through my various experiences. *Tapping* had to do with my interest in beach culture and surfing, *Unassigned Territory* was me tapping into my Witness past, *Pomona Queen* was my ode to growing up in the Pomona Valley. I wanted to write about my family and the Valley. I didn't know at the beginning that everything would be telescoped into one night.'

As odes go it's a pretty backhanded one. The Pomona Valley depicted in the book is not one you're going to go out of your way to visit. Unless you have really quite a lot of tattoos and the attitude to back them up.

Pomona Queen saw Nunn heading back towards the ballpark of noir, but it was only with his next book that the *Tapping the Source* fans really began to take notice of him again. This was, not at all coincidentally, because Nunn's fourth novel, *The Dogs of Winter*, saw him venturing back into the surf. So what provoked the return?

'The surfing world has been a part of my experience and I had always been intrigued, because I grew up surfing in southern California, by the kind of surfing that goes on in the Pacific north-west,' says Nunn. 'I was friends with a surf photographer who used to tell me these stories about going to the beaches up there. The surfers are very territorial and he would hide his camera because if these people saw a camera they were likely to punch him out and throw his camera in the water – they have these secret spots they want to protect. The funny thing about that is the idea that there would be a mass migration of SoCal surfers into these cold, shark-infested, incredibly rough, rugged conditions.

'So really the thing that began it was that milieu. I spent a lot of time up there on the Olympic Peninsula in Washington where there's only one surf shop and it's called *Tapping the Source*. I was talking to this kid who worked there and I said it's funny because I wrote this book called *Tapping the Source* and he said I'd better get the manager and he's this big biker kind of guy. Turns out *Tapping the Source* is his favourite book of all time, his brother-in-law had read it in prison so he had this old beat-up paperback. He wanted me to sign the shop so I signed the wall…That was pretty trippy. And then I began to hear stories about this Indian reservation where there had been clashes between surfers and the people living there. I was introduced to a guy who was part Indian named Larry Matthews who got me out into the reservations up there. That's when the book really began to take off for me.'

It is indeed the milieu which makes *The Dogs of Winter* memorable. The intervening decade and a half between the two books has seen surfing go overground in a very big way. Surf-theme clothing can be bought everywhere from Bangkok to a shopping mall somewhere near you. Towns like Huntington Beach have made surfing part of their economic base with shops and schools and regular competitions where young men and women with serious sponsorship deals can battle it out in front of the TV cameras.

For older hardcore surfers like the novel's focal character, Drew Harmon, it's a desecration of everything they loved in the sport. And so Harmon has been drawn to a place where the sea is cold and rough, the sharks hungry, the waves big and frankly dangerous, and even to get to the sea you have to battle across hostile terrain through an Indian reservation full of people who'd sooner you stayed off their land. Welcome to Oregon. This is real going-gets-tough, tough-get-going territory and Nunn brings it spectacularly to life. Especially when the two main characters, Harmon and a washed-out surf photographer called Jack Fletcher, come to the fore.

Jack Fletcher is something of a hard-boiled fiction fixture, the guy who's thrown away his career in a welter of bad habits and worse marriages, but gets one last chance. Drew Harmon is a more enigmatic figure. I wondered how Nunn came up with him.

'I was intrigued by the kind of individual who would surf in those places, so I went to visit Greg Knoll, a legendary big-wave rider who was living up in that area. And one of the surfing archetypes is the guy who's had the promising pro career but walks away from it, has this whole thing abut the bastardising of the sport. So I created the figure of Drew Harmon as this big-wave rider who's gone off and surfed these big lonesome waves in northern California.'

Before moving on, I wondered whether Nunn had ever surfed up there himself.

'I didn't surf then as at the time I'd messed up my back,' he told me. 'I did surf north of San Francisco later on, when I was living there, at a place called Shark Pits – a name which gives you something to think about!'

It had taken Nunn thirteen years to write another surfing novel after *Tapping the Source*. So when his next novel, *Tijuana Straits*, showed up, a leisurely seven years down the pike, it was quite a surprise to see surfing figuring prominently once again. 'I had not thought of writing about surfing again,' says Nunn. 'I'd imagined a book that would take place in the South-West, another desert book like *Unassigned Territory*, but I wasn't exactly finding the stuff I thought I was going to find, so the book wasn't really getting off the ground.

'Then I began to hear stories about all the factory women who'd been murdered in Juarez and I thought that was fascinating. One reason was the way this indigenous culture was being messed with by the intrusion of these foreign-owned factories. Women were being employed in the factories while the men were unemployed. It was turning the culture on its head and some of the violence at least seemed to be growing out of that cultural inversion. For a while I even thought of trying to take on that story but frankly found it a little daunting.

'Instead I decided to go down and have a look at what I think of as my border – between Tijuana and Imperial Beach. So I drove down to Imperial Beach one day, I hadn't been there since I was a kid, and I walked out on the dunes there, approaching the Sloughs, and I seemed to recall that this was a surf spot I'd read about. Also, when you're standing there and you look back inland, you're looking into a valley which is this kind of no man's land between the two countries – if you look to the right there's the Tijuana bullring, to the left there's the hills of Point Loma. You feel like you're between two worlds.

'Then I called a friend of mine and asked him, "What do you know about the Tijuana Sloughs?" and he said, "Oh, that's a real Kem Nunn kind of place!" He immediately faxed over an article and I realised there was all this great California surfing lore about this place, these figures like Dempsey Holder – who I renamed as Hoddy in the book. It was a big-wave spot back when California didn't really have big-wave spots.

'So then I'm thinking there's the border, there's the no man's land, and then there's this surf spot. It all seemed to fall together and I thought this is a place I could write about. And I realised I couldn't write about it without having some element of surfing in it – it's part of the landscape. And then I thought, well, I've written about surfing in Huntington Beach, and I've written about it in the northern end of the state, so if I write about it at the southern end, then I've covered the place, and this can be the third part of my Californian surfing trilogy.'

And so it is. This is the surf world come to the very end of the line. The hero Sam 'The Gull' Fahey is a sometime surf champ, now an ex-con drug dealer turned worm farmer, with a 300-pound gorilla of guilt and self-disgust on his back. It's years since he's been in the water and, anyway, the Tijuana Straits, the big-wave spot just a couple of miles from his home, is now too polluted to surf.

His life is going nowhere when, early one morning, he finds a young woman walking on the beach, having narrowly survived death by drowning. At first he takes her for one more Mexican refugee, prepared to risk life and limb for a shot at the Yanqui dream. But it soon turns out that she's part of something bigger than that. She's an environmental and feminist activist, who's been trying to help the factory workers protest against their working conditions and also volunteering in a women's refuge. These activities have brought her to the attention of some seriously bad guys who've tried to kill her.

Now it's up to Sam whether he helps her or tosses her back to the wolves. Anyone who's ever read a hard-boiled crime novel – or been to a movie, come to that – will hardly be surprised to discover that he does indeed help her, and it does indeed cost him dear.

But if the story occasionally follows predictable lines, and if Nunn's fondness for biblical cadence, though no doubt rooted in his own religious upbringing, is occasionally rather too reminiscent of Cormac McCarthy, once again what strikes the reader powerfully is the milieu. Nunn does a wonderful job of evoking this strange no man's land between the US and Mexico, First World and Third.

So good a job, in fact, that I resolve to spend the next day checking it out. Meanwhile our conversation winds down. We talk about the environment, which not surprisingly is a cause close to Nunn's heart. I wonder whether that's definitely it as far as surfing goes in his fiction, and he says, 'Never say never.' And then it's time to get the bill and head off.

Kem Nunn has his parents staying. I have time for a swim in the Motor Inn, before getting in an early night in preparation for an early start and a drive down Mexico way.

In the morning I stop for breakfast right in the middle of Laguna Beach. A little coffee shop – bagel, juice, sun shining outside. It's idyllic: you can see just why people would spend millions to live the simple life here. Over to my left a couple of ageing surf dudes, all leathered, skin-cancered faces and long blond hair going grey under their baseball caps, are talking to a bunch of youthful lifeguards, and I can see that the young guys are really into listening to the old-timers telling them about how things used to be, and the radio in the café is tuned to an oldies station pumping out the Ronettes and Sonny & Cher, ramming home the point that this is a culture whose innocence has been well and truly lost over the last four decades.

On to the freeway then, and before long I'm skirting San Diego and its beaches and its naval dockyards, and the Mexican border is looming up ahead. I'd been planning on visiting Imperial Beach first, that last town before the border, but the lure of the unknown is too strong. At the border I park my car in a lot and then, rather than catch the shuttle bus, I decide to do as Sam Fahey does in *Tijuana Straits*, and walk into Mexico. This involves me in a wrong turn that leads me over the freeway on a footbridge. Worth it, though, because sitting on the bridge, waiting for nothing, are two Mexican guys with guitars, singing something sad in Spanish; not busking, just singing.

Another overpass takes me back in the right direction and gives me a good view of the whole border crossing area. There's an elaborate system of fences and walls and barbed wire and guardhouses, and it reminds me, inevitably, of the only similar structure I've visited before: the Berlin Wall. And it can't help strike me as odd that we in the West were so outraged about the Berlin Wall but so complaisant at our own walls. Perhaps there is some superior morality in building a wall to keep people out, as opposed to building one to keep people in, but there's also a fair old dash of equivalence too.

Crossing from the USA into Mexico – once you've figured out where the pedestrian access walkway is – is no problem. It's only once I've passed through the gate and am actually in Mexico that it strikes me that this is – as the soccer player Ian Rush once said of Italy – a foreign country. And people speak Spanish, which I don't, and use different money.

I'm completely unprepared. My traveller's cheques are all back in the car and I have eight dollars on me. Damn. I change the eight bucks into pesos, anyway, and carry on out of the border complex and into a peculiar modern marketplace – looks like a shopping centre in some hard-done-by corner of London. There's a bunch of stalls and shops selling souvenirs – Mexican hats, Metallica T-shirts – just what you'd expect at any busy border crossing.

More unusual, though, is the presence of a considerable number of pharmacies. Well, perhaps not exactly pharmacies in the sense of a place presided over by a pharmacist. Rather what we have here is a bunch of white-painted shops with advertising boards outside listing the products on offer. These are the same names you see on a billion spam e-mails – Valium, Viagra, Cialis, Xanax, Ambien, Prozac, Propecia. Dollar prices marked beside the names – $20 for thirty blue pills, $30 for fifty white ones.

The shops are clearly doing good business. And look closely and you'll realise that it's not just the vanity products, the ones promising to restore your erection and your hair, that are selling here, but drugs for cancer and HIV and all manner of other ailments. Indeed, in *Tijuana Straits* Fahey comes here to buy the relatively workaday Betadine and Cipro to treat the ailing Magdalena.

And why? Because what this is is a place for the USA's poor, those unhappy souls without health insurance, to buy their medication courtesy of the free market. And they'd just better hope like hell that the young Hispanic guys in the white coats who don't exactly look like pharmacists are at least selling genuine merchandise. It's hard to imagine there's anywhere else where the economies of the First and Third Worlds, normally kept at arm's length, are shoved together so rudely.

Thanking my lucky stars that I'm not in need of urgent medication, I carry on through the marketplace to a busy dusty square full of buses and traffic and people everywhere. According to the map, which I've thoughtfully left in the car, the city centre, or at least the touristic part, is pretty close to the border, but there's no obvious sign of it here. In the end I follow a bunch of backpackers and jump on the same bus as them, hoping they'll be heading for the centre. The bus is full of locals, including two more guys playing guitars and singing. I had no idea this country was so full of music. And after a short while I see a big street looming up ahead and a sign saying Avenida de la Revolución. Time to get off.

Walking down the Avenida, I remember one of my favourite unlikely Welsh heroes. As a Welsh person, you see, what with Wales being a small country and much overshadowed by England, we have a tendency to celebrate each and every achievement by a Welsh person, no matter how odd.

One of the oddest of the lot was a feller called Caryl ap Rhys Pryce, aka 'the Man Who Captured Tijuana'. Pryce was a career soldier who had been serving as a Mountie in Canada when he read of the Mexican revolution and decided to offer his services. On arrival he turned out to be one of the few people around with serious military experience, so he ended up leading a motley band of two hundred or so men, most of them not Mexicans at all, but American anarchists, members of the IWW.

He advanced on Tijuana and managed to capture it after a day's bloody fighting, despite the fact that his troops were virtually out of ammunition. Their next target was the port of Ensenada, immediately to the south, but they were too broke to buy the weaponry needed to launch an attack, so Pryce set himself to the task of fund-raising. This he did by legalising gambling, and turning a blind eye to all other kinds of related vices.

So Tijuana's reputation as the vice den to end them all is actually the fault of a Welshman. Funny, huh? As is the fact that Pryce went on to appear in early Hollywood cowboy movies, fought in the trenches in the First World War, and then vanished for good in the mid-1920s.

Just the contemplation of such a life makes me feel tired, so I stroll down the Avenida de la Revolución, enjoying the fact that, after a week of being surrounded by super-sized Americans, I'm in a place where I feel average height going on tall, and looking for somewhere to sit down and drink a beer and get something to eat for less than however many pesos I've got left.

It takes a little while as the Avenida too is dominated by free-market pharmacies and souvenir shops, but eventually I find a nice quiet cafeteria where I eat a couple of tacos and drink a Tecate. As I do so a couple of the guys in white coats who are dispensing a hundred valium for $24.99 next door come in a for a drink. They're surely still in their teens, and if either of them knows their bipolar disorder from their erectile dysfunction I'd be a mite surprised.

Suitably revived, I head back out into the midday sun and stroll some more. There's a street full of kick-boxing academies off to one side, then I take a left and I'm in a street full of sex bars. These are probably the most depressing-looking places of their ilk I've ever seen, fly-blown and filthy. The women outside, notionally enticing the punters, are without exception aged, whether prematurely or not it's hard to say, and all seem to have prominent facial disfigurements. The whole effect is like a public information film designed to put you off sex tourism. Maybe there are people out there for whom this level of desolate seediness is just what they're looking for, but I'm sure as hell I wouldn't like to meet them.

Still, it would be a misrepresentation to say this place is in any way typical of modern-day Tijuana. Rather it seems like the last vestige of a dying industry. There really must be more money in drugs than sex.

Back on the Avenida the atmosphere is for the most part bustling. There are big music bars, there's a Hard Rock Café and a spectacular Jai Alai fronton. I know I'm just scratching the surface here and there's something dissatisfying about that. Time to get back over the border.

Sam Fahey has to queue up for an hour and half to get back into the USA, but I'm through the customs in five minutes. Back in the car I try to follow the line of the border to the sea.

Soon I'm in a valley, the Tijuana river valley. It's quiet scrubby land broken up by an almost dry river bed and a similarly parched area of swampland. The only sign of life is a horse ranch. Eventually the road peters out at the entrance to something called the Border State Park. This is where the climactic events of *Tijuana Straits* take place as Fahey and Magdalena try to escape a gang of Mexican killers. It feels less like a park than a no man's land, or one of these bleak bits of countryside the army use for training manoeuvres. There's absolutely no sign of anyone else here. I wander about a bit, trying to get my bearings and find the way to the ocean.

In the distance I can hear a car. Before long an ancient Chevy Impala with blacked-out windows comes into view. It pulls up next to my car and out get two young Hispanic guys in full street rig. They look me over, find me of no interest and walk off purposefully in the direction of the border fence.

I start along a path I hope will bring me to the sea. It's quiet and frankly rather eerie. Finally there's a rise in the path ahead of me and I climb up and suddenly I'm in a kind of picnic zone with heavily watered green grass, a couple of tables, plus a parking lot, even though there's no access road that I can see. Straight ahead I can see the ocean. It's flat today so there's no sign of the big-wave spot out in the Sloughs. And to my left I can see the border fence, and beyond it the Tijuana bullring. The juxtaposition is startling: all that life on the far side of the fence, and this deserted, surely purely for show, picnic spot on the other side, my side.

As I head back to the car a helicopter comes out of the sky and swoops low over my head. I've had enough of this. Maybe it's just the effect of reading too much Kem Nunn, but I can't imagine anything good happening in this place.

Once in the car, I drive the five miles or so to Imperial Beach, the southernmost outpost of California surf culture. And, as Nunn suggested, it feels a lot less developed, a lot less moneyed than places like Laguna Beach or San Clemente.

Instead it's a dilapidated blue-collar town that just happens to have a beach and, as a result, feels the need to have a couple of shops selling surfing gear, and a forlorn-looking café offering cappuccino. Just outside the café, and opposite the pier, there is an odd assortment of neon-coloured Plexiglas arches. I peer at them for a while, then find a plaque on the pavement announcing that this is SurfHenge, a monument to southern California surf culture. Next to the arches is a selection of surfboard-shaped benches; these too bear plaques, celebrating local surf legends, among them Dempsey Holder, the model for Hoddy Younger in Nunn's book.

It's all rather bizarrely and endearingly amateurish. At one point in *Tijuana Straits*, Fahey takes Magdalena to Imperial Beach, and she asks him what the plastic arches are all about. 'I believe they are meant to represent waves,' he says, before giving in and declaring that they 'look like a fast food restaurant, without the food'. Which is about the size of it. I take a walk out on to the beach. There are still no waves and thus no surfers. Behind me a bunch of local teenagers are idly skateboarding around SurfHenge.

Fine, I'm at the end of the line. Nothing to do but go back.

9   Austin, Texas: don't move here

THERE'S A SONG playing over the sound system at the airport. It has me confused at first because I've got the same song on one of the CDs I'm carrying around with me to listen to in the car. It's Mary Gauthier singing 'Empty Spaces'. Mary's a country-folk singer-songwriter from New Orleans. I've promoted a couple of shows for her in Cardiff, and while the shows were well attended, it's fair to say that's she's not exactly a household name. Not exactly the kind of thing you expect to hear on an airport sound system while you're waiting for your case to show up on the baggage carousel.

Except in Austin. Austin, more than any other American city with the possible exception of New Orleans, is about music. Well, it's also about computers and students, but music's at its heart. It's taken a while for this to happen. Austin doesn't have the history of a New Orleans or a Memphis or a Nashville. It's not the home of blues or country or rock'n'roll. In fact its rise to prominence as a music city really began only in the '60s.

It began with clubs like Threadgill's putting on singers like Janis Joplin. The counter-culture was going on and the student town of Austin, home of the University of Texas, was the one safe-ish place in the Lone Star state to be a longhair. There was psychedelic music around, those who like that kind of thing swear by the Thirteenth Floor Elevators – but gradually what Austin came to offer was a home for longhairs who still loved the folk traditions, blues and country in particular. Offbeat country singers like Jerry Jeff Walker made their home there. And the real breakthrough came when Willie Nelson moved to Austin in the early '70s, tired of the Nashville production line. A new club had just opened called the World Armadillo Headquarters, and Willie started playing there, and outlaw country was born.

Other acts with a country hippy vibe started gravitating to the Austin scene: Commander Cody and his Lost Planet Airmen, Kinky Friedman, Joe Ely, Jimmie Dale Gilmore, *et al*. On the blues side of the tracks Stevie Ray Vaughan and the Fabulous Thunderbirds did their thing. Gradually word started to get around that Austin was a place to check out. New York scenesters from Jerry Wexler to Lester Bangs spent time there.

In the '80s a festival called South by South West, or SXSW, got started. Initially this programmed lots of cool country and folk, and what was starting to be known as alt.country music. People like me were dead keen on it. Various friends of mine went over to the festival, told me how great it was. Finally, in 1995, I went over myself and it was indeed great. There was a moment where I walked out of one club on a warm March night, the sound of Lucinda Williams still ringing in my ears, and heard Robert Earl Keen chiming up in the back yard of a restaurant across the way, when I thought this place is really too good to be true.

Since then I've spent a lot of time boring people about what a great little town Austin is and plotting to go back there, and now, ten years on, I am back, and to be honest I'm a little apprehensive that maybe it was indeed too good to be true. Or that it'll have changed out of recognition. After all, SXSW has now, I'm told, mushroomed into a giant music-business jamboree with more emphasis on indie than alt.country.

An hour or so out of the airport and I'm definitely coming round to that point of view. I've been lost on ring roads and stuck in traffic, trying to find my way back to the freeway-side hotel I passed twenty minutes ago.

When I do get to my hotel room it smells like someone died in it, which may explain why it was very, very cheap indeed. A quick check around the room reveals that the body has at least been removed, though there are a few dubious-looking stains in the bathroom. Did I mention that an inordinate number of serial killers seem to have lived in Austin at one time or another? Anyway.

OK, so my hotel is right next to a freeway, only accessible by car, and then only if you take your life in your hands every time you drive in or out of it, but never mind. I should only be ten minutes away from the laid-back, lovable, cowboy hippy Austin that I'm convinced I remember.

Well, another half-hour drive through gridlocked traffic and I've sort of found some kind of fragment of what I was looking for. At least, I've found the street where Waterloo Records and the Whole Foods supermarket were last time I was here. Waterloo Records is still there but the Whole Foods store, this very impressive all-organic supermarket, seems to have been replaced by a multi-storey car park. Well, with all this traffic I suppose they have to park somewhere.

So I head over to Waterloo Records and try to relax by staring at loads of records. It always used to work and I do find something I've been looking for, a record called *Seven And Six* by Bellwether, a fine alt.country band out of Minneapolis. I'm pleased about this and Waterloo Records is a very good record shop, but it's still a record shop with record-shop guys working in it, which means it could be anywhere, or at least anywhere cool. Time to go out and get among things, people. Real people, ones who don't spend too much of their time living through books and records.

On my way to the checkout, though, I pause by the books

section, have a quick gander and spot a copy of Jesse Sublett's new memoir, *Never the Same Again*. I've heard about this book. Jesse Sublett is a guy who used to play in various Austin bands and he wrote a series of rock'n'roll detective novels around the turn of the '90s. He's one of a couple of writers I'm planning on meeting up with in Austin.

I pick up a copy of the book, pay for the stuff and head outside, where it hits me that a lot of the reason I'm not feeling at one with this place is that I haven't eaten all day.

It's a problem simply remedied. Next door to Waterloo Records is the Waterloo Ice House. It has food. It has beer. Actually it has too much beer. After the guy has spent ten minutes telling me the names of all the different things they have on draught I can't remember any of them, so point at random. And, exhausted by excess choice, plump for a burger to eat.

Replenished, I head out back to the payphone and call Jesse Sublett's number. We fix up to meet for lunch tomorrow, and meanwhile he suggests I check out his old compadre Jon Dee Graham, who's playing at the Continental Club later on.

So that's what I do. Ten o'clock sees me pulling up in a parking lot on South Congress and walking back down the street towards the Continental Club, perennial fixture of the south Austin scene. South Austin is famously the most laid-back part of this laid-back city. It certainly feels that way tonight; the traffic has gone, the daytime heat has subsided and the vibe inside the club is as relaxed as they come. Jon Dee Graham is actually playing the opening slot tonight. Headlining is James McMurtry, the singer songwriter son of the writer Larry McMurtry (unsurprisingly, given his pedigree, McMurtry Junior is one of those acts that tend to be talked about in terms of how great their lyrics are).

Jon Dee Graham is really good. Fortysomething guy in a thrift-shop suit, sings like Tom Waits, if Tom Waits could sing, and plays guitar with savage economy. You can see in his eyes that this is a guy who used to think he was going to make it big then realised he wasn't and now doesn't give much of a shit. He, as they say these days, rocks.

After he's finished I hang around a bit, drink a couple of Shiner Bocks and watch as a roadie brings no less than six different guitars onstage for James McMurtry to play. This does not bode well. Then Mr McMurtry makes it onstage, starts playing and leaves me cold. Not so much literate as wordy, if you ask me, but maybe I was just tired.

Back at the hotel I read the first few pages of Jesse Sublett's memoir, in preparation for meeting him. And, Jesus Christ, in the first twenty pages we see him battling with cancer, some time in the late '90s, then flash back to the early '70s, his first band and, uh oh, his girlfriend getting murdered. I put the book down, exhausted. The room's smell is really starting to get to me now.

In the morning I notice that in addition to the smell thing there are also a number of cockroaches clambering around the walls. Enough, I feel, is enough. So I head over to reception and tell them about the cockroaches. Oh, says the girl on the desk, you must be on the ground floor, right? Uh-huh, I say. Well, she says, let's sort you out with a room on the second floor.

So she does, and from what I can see she knows her cockroaches and they don't like to climb this high. Also, the room doesn't smell as if anything really bad has happened in it just lately. Not something I could say for the laundry room, but you can't have everything.

Later on, laundry done, it's downtown to meet Jesse Sublett. He's suggested meeting at Threadgill's Armadillo World Headquarters. This is the latest restaurant and club run by a guy called Eddie Wilson, who used to run the late, lamented Armadillo World HQ in the '70s, and then bought Threadgill's diner in the '80s. The new place is just south of the river and it's purpose-built and comfortable, and has good bands on and is still identifiably a local institution and not a Hard Rock Café, but it still rather lacks the rock'n'roll patina.

Which is not something you could say about Jesse Sublett. Jesse is tall and skinny with jet-black hair, wears black leather and shades and looks in pretty good shape for a guy who had stage-four throat cancer seven years back and was given a nine per cent chance of survival.

Sat down at a table we get talking, establish a little common ground – James Ellroy, Jake Riviera – and drink plenty of iced tea. I eat an authentically bland meat-loaf special, and Jesse tells me about the book he's working on now, the true story of a gang of long-haired, hell-raising armed robbers who hung out in Austin in the '60s.

Jesse's clearly got a major interest in his city – he's actually from a small town called Johnson City out in the Texas hill country, but Austin's been his home since he left school, give or take a stint in LA – so after lunch he volunteers to take me for a drive around in his PT Cruiser, see some landmarks.

As we drive we get to talking about the links between rock'n'roll and crime fiction. It's certainly struck me how much the appreciation of certain kinds of music tends to go with certain kinds of crime fiction. It's an Americana thing in a way, or at least an aesthetic that seems to be particularly American.

Over the past five years I've been putting on monthly shows in Cardiff, mostly featuring American alt.country types, people like Mark Olson or Richard Buckner or Richmond Fontaine, names that I suspect are a lot more likely to resonate with readers of a book like this than with the general public. And one thing I can almost guarantee these days is that each and every one of these people will have an affection for the works of Jim Thompson. For some that may be as far as if goes – noir kingpin Thompson is getting to be up there with the Hunter S. Thompsons as a ubiquitous cult figure – but the majority will also have an interest in Charles Willeford or Nelson Algren, etc. etc. I'd like to think it's about appreciating art that tells the truth, or, to be more precise, maybe art that at least tries to tell the truth while attempting to give it some romanticism in the process.

Jesse is down with most of that, I suspect. He tells me how he got into reading classic crime fiction back in the '80s, to alleviate the boredom of life on the road. He started with Hammett and Chandler, then got into the more obscure stuff, lost Black Mask writers like Richard Torrey and Raoul Whitfield. And then he got the idea of bringing his two big interests –music and crime fiction – together.

It's a fusion that has been attempted now and again in the other direction. Various musicians have had a go at rendering noir, whether Green On Red calling their album *The Killer Inside Me*, Gallon Drunk making a record with Derek Raymond, or Warren Zevon writing songs with Carl Hiaasen. But while several former musicians have written crime novels – Kinky Friedman and Rupert Holmes, for starters – Jesse Sublett, surprisingly enough, is the only one to set them firmly in the world of rock'n'roll.

'I'd spent a good part of the last ten years in dark clubs and studios, an environment that provided plenty of fodder for plots and characters,' he explains in the memoir. 'I had faith in my protagonist too. I saw him as a bass-playing Philip Marlowe/ Sam Spade, tough and world weary but principled, a romantic at heart. No one else was doing detective novels like these, and the established authors got the details wrong when they wrote about rock'n'roll.'

Well, the first part of Jesse's closing statement is open to argument. I'd suggest there were quite a few people out there writing detective novels in the Hammett/Chandler tradition. It's the second half of the sentence which is more to the point.

Rock'n'roll novels, and particularly thrillers, do indeed tend to be let down by the obvious ignorance of the writers. Just try struggling your way through the great Elmore Leonard's lamentable music-biz novel *Be Cool* if you don't believe me.

Jesse's three Martin Fender novels do indeed get the details right. The first book, *The Rock Critic Murders*, though burdened by a hysterically busy and complicated plot, is at heart a simple and affecting story of the rock'n'roll dream going sour. There's a real sense throughout the three books of the reality of the rock'n'roll life, the drudgery, the endless petty humiliations, and the occasional moments of transcendence.

The Rock Critic Murders was optioned by the movies and Jesse was paid to write the screenplay, which has led to other film and TV writing gigs. The music career chuntered on alongside, a story of bands that never quite made it or bands led by used-to-bes. He played with Kathy Valentine of the Go Gos, both before and after her hit band. He played with Mick Taylor of the Rolling Stones, some while after his hit band. It's a hard-knock life, the rock'n'roll one, with its own bitter gags (samples: What d'you call a guitarist without a girlfriend? Homeless. What's the difference between a large pizza and a guitarist? A large pizza can feed a family of four. And so on).

Then came the bout with cancer, which through some combination of mental fortitude, luck and the support of his wife and son, he made it through, to be the one in eleven to survive. And then the aftermath of this bout with mortality caused him, as it often seems to do, to reflect on his own life. And in particular to start to deal with the one terrible event that has overshadowed his adult life: the murder of his first serious girlfriend just as he was starting out in the business.

By now, as it happens, we're driving through south Austin heading towards the site of that murder. It wasn't quite the first place Jesse lived when he moved to Austin, that had been an apartment on Barton Springs, but after a little while there his girlfriend Dianne had found them this house on Glendale. Jesse parks outside it. It looks idyllic. The neighbourhood feels as if it's out in the country somewhere, not within walking distance of the centre of a major city. It looks, it has to be said, like the kind of place in which it would be easy to be happy.

Jesse and Dianne were happy when they moved there in late 1975. They'd both dropped out of college in San Marcos and come to Austin to make their way in the world. Jesse was going to be a rock'n'roll musician, Dianne was going to be a painter. Meanwhile Dianne temped and Jesse did odd jobs, house-painting and so on. Austin was the kind of place back then where you could get by like that, even have a nice house to live in. Well, near enough anyway; to meet the rent they had a lodger, Jesse's old friend and sometime drummer Dean.

Fast-forward nine months or so to August 1976 and Jesse's band was starting to come off. They had their first out-of-town gig coming up on Sunday 15th. Only thing that was a drag was that Dean had become an unreliable drunk. Jesse had asked him to move out and he had agreed, but as he was moving his stuff out he'd come by with a low-life friend called Lyle, who, Jesse later discovered, was out on parole for rape. When Jesse found that out he told Dean not to bring Lyle round again. Dean took no notice, though, and even got Lyle to help him climb in through the bedroom window when he came back to pick up a few last things.

The Sunday night gig went like a charm. The band had played till 3 a.m., an outdoor gig outside of San Antonio. They slept late and rolled back into Austin on the afternoon of Monday, 16 August. Fazz Eddie the guitar player dropped Jesse off outside the house. He went in, found Dianne lying face down and naked on the bed. For a moment he thought she was sleeping but then found her cold to the touch. He turned her over and saw that she was dead, strangled with a pillowcase.

Jesse called the cops and found himself the prime suspect. He was taken to the station completely out of it with shock. It was only once he'd calmed down that he realised he had a very good idea who the murderer might be. He told the police about Dean's friend, said his name was Lyle, and he was a rapist from Kerrville.

That night Lyle Brummet was arrested and taken into custody just as Jesse was being released. Brummet confessed to the murder, confessed to several other murders as well, and implicated others in his crimes in an attempt to make a plea bargain. Partially successful, he avoided the death penalty – a serious threat in Texas, of course – but according to Jesse he's unlikely ever to be released from prison. Which is something of a relief.

It's a hell of a story and one that rather overshadows the rest of our drive around Austin, so before long we stop at an outdoor coffee shop on South Congress just along from the rock'n'roll mecca that is the Austin Motel and move the subject back to Jesse's subsequent rock career.

Jesse was one of those guys who, though they may not have known it, had just been waiting for punk to come along. He'd been trying to play classic Stones-y rock'n'roll in the laid-back mid '70s and the adrenalin rush of punk provided him with a context. Jesse and his crew went along to the legendary Sex Pistols show at Randy's Rodeo in San Antonio (his band, the Violators, would have been the support act, but the promoter told them they could only have the gig 'if he could fuck Marilyn, the drummer' – oh those liberated 1970s).

The Pistols gig finally sent the punk scene overground and Jesse's subsequent band the Skunks, became the biggest thing on the Austin circuit for a while. In fact they were more of a Dr Feelgood-style high-octane R&B band than out-and-out punk, and that's maybe why they never really made it big outside of Texas, despite regular forays to New York.

At this point, and by fairly remarkable coincidence, I look up and see a familiar face walking down the street in front of me. After a moment in which my brain refuses to compute the sighting, I call out 'Hey, Jon' and the guy stops and does his own double-take before saying 'Hey, John' back to me. The Jon in question, you see, is none other than Jon Langford, linchpin of original punk survivors the Mekons. Jon's originally from Newport, Wales, just up the road from where I live, and I've known him for a few years now. I also know he lives in Chicago these days and that he's always on tour and Austin is a particular home from home for him, but still. Weird, huh?

I introduce Jon to Jesse. They know of each other but have failed to meet before on the great rock'n'roll highway. Turns out Jon's in town to present some kind of stage show based on his life and music. He'll be performing it the following night at a theatre in east Austin, the black side of town. Do I fancy coming along?

I certainly do, and prior to that I fancy a drink or two, so we arrange to meet up later that night. Now it's time to get moving: Jon's off to rehearse, Jesse's off to pick up his son from school, and I'm heading back to the hotel to cool off in the pool.

Did I mention the hotel had a pool? Well, it does, and a decent-size one at that. It's always been mysteriously empty up to now, and when I get up close I figure this might have something to do with its being a strangely vivid green colour, and too cloudy to see the bottom. What the hell: it's too hot for me to care, so I get in and swim and don't notice any immediate toxic reaction, and then I get out and dry off and watch the hotel parking lot, over by the bar, steadily fill up with bikers. By the time I've gone back to my room, got showered and changed, there must be two hundred serious motorbikes parked up in front.

And yet by the time I get back that night, after a few drinks and a Mexican meal with Jon, there's absolutely no one there at all. And no debris blood or broken glass either. Bikers clearly aren't what they used to be.

Next morning I head downtown to meet up with Jesse again. On the way I stop off at Whole Foods for breakfast. By now I've figured out that the multi-storey car park where Whole Foods used to be hasn't replaced it. It's just the parking for the new improved Whole Foods, which turns out to be a gigantic palace of vaguely right-on food consumerism. The nearest thing to it would be an eco-friendly organic version of the Harrods food hall: it's every bit as lavish, has half a dozen places to sit down and eat or drink. This is hippy capitalism *in excelsis*, and it's hard to know whether to be impressed or alarmed. It's got all the contradictions of modern America in one – terribly politically correct and concerned about the state of the planet and at the same time, quite terrifyingly over-abundant. Great cookies, though.

Today Jesse wants to show me something of the way Austin was. So we head out west along the town lake that bisects the city till we come to Zilker Park and Barton Springs Pool. This is a big dammed-up piece of river and, again, it's idyllic except, Jesse says, in midsummer, when it gets way crowded and regularly has to be temporarily closed owing to excess faecal contamination. Nice. For now, though, on a hot September day with the kids in school, you could just stretch and let the world go by.

But neither I nor, I suspect, Jesse, is quite that laid back, so before long we're back in the car and heading a little farther west till we come to Mount Bonnell. A short hike up to the top and you can see just how far the city is starting to sprawl. I'm reminded of a list I saw in an alternative guidebook to Austin published a few years back. It included three commands to live by. The first two of them were in-jokes, the third one was 'Don't move here', which you strongly suspect isn't a joke at all.

Driving back into the city we keep on past downtown and over to the east side. This is the black and Hispanic part of town. East 11th Street is the heart of the black section. Once a thriving entertainment area, it's long been run down, but moves are afoot to revive it, banners proclaim than we're now in HISTORIC EAST AUSTIN. Jesse points out the surviving landmarks like the Victory Grill, a long-time blues hangout, and the school that his son has just started attending here under a new scheme to improve the integration levels. Which, as far as I can see, aren't at their worst in Austin but, this being America, are still a long way less than perfect.

And then it's time for Jesse to get back home. He's taking his son to see the Foo Fighters. Do I like them? I don't know, I say, I haven't really heard them which is true enough, as far as it goes, but the reason for that is partly that I can't imagine that I would like them much, and partly because these days I try to leave rock music to young people. In general I still cleave to the idea that there should be an age gap in music. When I listened to the Clash or the Mekons or whoever I didn't really want to do it in the company of my parents.

I realise that such a vibe – and indeed the word vibe itself – is horribly outdated, that father and son now happily exchange the contents of their iPods, but I've done my best to maintain it. Once my stepson reached his teens, in the early '90s, I forswore listening to hip-hop and soul in favour of folk and country, and was duly rewarded by expressions of disgust and the defiant blasting of Cypress Hill from his bedroom. Way I see it is that music is to the generation gap as football is to international politics – a proxy for outright warfare.

Of course, I don't say all this to Jesse, mostly because you only think of all this stuff some time later when you're sitting down writing things up, and also because I understand the coded yearning implicit in taking your son to a gig, the urge to pass on what you know to your son, and if, like Jesse, what you know is rock'n'roll, well, there you go. Doubtless if there were cool literary things you could go to with your son, I'd be pretty happy if Owen wanted to attend one.

Anyway, towards seven o'clock, while Jesse and his son are at the Foo Fighters, I'm back in east Austin, looking for the theatre where Jon Langford will be doing his thing. It turns out to be a brand-new building just off 11th street. It sports a nice exhibition devoted to notable black musicians from Austin, but otherwise seems weirdly deserted. Eventually I wander into the auditorium and find Jon finishing off his sound check. Looks like he'll be a little while yet so I head back out in search of something to eat.

The search ends a couple of blocks away at Gene's, a friendly local soul food place that serves up some pretty good gumbo and corn bread. Its full name is Gene's New Orleans Style Po-Boys and Deli, and in the wake of Katrina it's about as close as you're going to come to eating authentic N'Awlins food right now.

Back at the theatre a crowd has assembled and there's barely time for a glass of warm white wine before we're ushered into the auditorium. The show, a mixture of songs, visual and spoken word pieces, is an absolute winner if you happen to be a South Walian who grew up in the '60s and '70s, got into punk then spent time in America, and embraced the cheating charms of country music, and includes a song called 'Pill Sailor' about the disappearing docklands of Newport and Cardiff that fair brings a tear to the eye.

After the show we head off to the nearest bar. This is a place called the Longbranch just along from Gene's, and across the road from the Victory Grill, in what was once the heart of Austin's black entertainment district. From the outside the Longbranch looks like a regular neighbourhood place for working men to drink Bud and play pool. Inside it looks pretty much like that too, but the working men turn out to be a mix of punk rockers and hepcats with interesting facial hair and just a few old-school – i.e. black and Hispanic – locals.

Turns out the bar was taken over by a guy who used to run one of the rock'n'roll hangouts on Sixth Street. Sixth Street, though, has become a victim of its own success and is full of corporate-tourist-packed bars, so the hipper locals have started driving over to the east side. It's the kind of situation that could cause a bit of rub, but east Austin feels pretty laid back and the atmosphere is generally convivial. At least it is until, several beers down the line, I decide I fancy a game of pool. A guy called Steve, who is the boyfriend of Jon Langford's bandmate Sally Timms, has been playing with a couple of diminutive Mexican guys.

Steve is a large black guy who, though a film-maker these days, has done stints as a bouncer, and he tries to indicate that maybe the Mexican guys would prefer to play by themselves, but I'm too drunk by now to pay attention. So I allow Mexican guy number one to engage me in a macho handshake ritual while number two puts my money in the pool table. I bend down and put the balls on the table and indicate that I'm ready to go. Mexican guy number one, still smiling fixedly at me, suddenly reaches out and sweeps all the balls back into the pockets. Uh-oh. I smile back and retreat slowly, realising I've badly misjudged the situation. The two guys stare at me a while longer, then start yelling at each other. I move speedily away and rejoin the others at the bar.

'Christ, man,' says Steve, 'I thought the little fuckers were going to stab you.' Not long after that the bartender calls time, and while there's talk of going on to a club I decide I've pushed my luck far enough for one night.

• • •

Next morning I've got a little time to kill before my first meeting of the day. And so I give into habit and do a little book and records shopping. Actually, secondhand-book-buying has lost a lot of its charm for me since I first came to America. When I wrote the original version of this book I came home with trunk-loads of books. This time I haven't bought a thing.

The reason why? Well, maybe there's a little jadedness, an awareness that I have hundreds of unread books on my shelves already. But that never stopped me in the past. The real reason is the Internet. It's just too damn efficient. Time was, I would walk into secondhand bookstores across America and case their collection of paperbacks in the vague hope of alighting on a Jim Thompson or Charles Willeford rarity.

These days I could assemble a complete collection of Jim Thompson paperbacks in an hour or so's browsing on abebooks. com (in fact it's just taken me fifteen minutes to find first editions of all twelve of Jim Thompson's preposterously hard-to-find paperback originals written for Lion Books – *The Killer Inside Me, Recoil, The Criminal, A Hell Of A Woman, The Kill-off, Roughneck, Croppers Cabin, Bad Boy, The Golden Gizmo, A Swell Looking Babe, The Alcoholics* and *Savage Night* – all I need is $800 to pay for them), which kind of takes the fun out of it.

Records are a bit of a different matter. There isn't a second-hand record and CD site that I know of that's half as efficient as abebooks, and there's always new stuff out there that you didn't quite know existed till you see it in the rack. So I check out a couple of secondhand places, buy some old Tom T. Hall albums on vinyl from Antone's (Tom T. Hall, by the way, is a totally underrated American genius and I only wish this book had a Nashville chapter so I could work him in there somehow) before I end up in a small and exceedingly hip new record store on South Main called End of an Ear (which I am anorak enough to know is the title of Robert Wyatt's little-heard debut solo album, which makes me think maybe I'll fit in here). So I browse around the Devendra Banhart and Ash Ra Temple records, wonder at the amount of space given over to old school boot-boy punk, and then I'm startled to alight on a whole section devoted to the works of Jandek.

Jandek, in case you don't know, is a guy from Houston, Texas, who has been putting out records on his own label since 1978 at a rate of rather more than one a year. These records generally consist of Jandek playing an acoustic guitar without any sign whatsoever that he has the faintest idea of how to tune it, let alone play it, while over the top he tends to intone rather than sing disturbing/depressing free-form lyrics. After a decade or so of Jandek making these records and sending them out to be ignored by college radio stations, the kind of obsessive who was starting to find Austin madman Daniel Johnston and his home-made cassettes a little too, you know, obvious, started to take an interest, and a Jandek cult started to grow. Jandek himself, it has to be said, has a wonderful feel for how to develop a cult. His album covers are all photos with no writing on them, blurry shots of anonymous houses or living rooms, occasional shots of a man one takes to be Jandek himself, generally taken years before the release of the record in question. The only contact information is for a company called Corwood Industries with a PO box number in Houston. This, of course, is the only indication anywhere that Corwood Industries exists. Perfect outsider art.

Gradually the influence of Jandek has spread, most obviously in the work of Will Oldham, aka Bonnie Prince Billy, who also favours the dark interior and out-of-focus snapshot approach to album cover design. Not to mention the creepy country blues as played by a madman thing. None of his imitators, however, is able to duplicate Jandek's utter lack of conventional musicality. A movie, *Jandek on Corwood,* appeared in 2004, in which various talking heads opined about the mystery wrapped in an enigma that is Jandek.

And then, to general befuddlement, one night in Glasgow, of all places, Jandek walked onstage (announced only as 'a representative of Corwood Industries') in the midst of an art music festival and proceeded to play a set of a rickety sort of blues (backed, weirdly enough, by someone I know, a remarkable folk jazz drummer called Alex Neilson). In the world of underground music obsession people could hardly have been more amazed if Captain Beefheart had showed up to duet with Albert Ayler.

Anyway, that's who Jandek is, and I've never seen his records before in a record shop and even though I'm well aware that they're unlistenable to, there is some atavistic record-geek impulse to buy one even so, just to have this thing that will mark me out from my friends (but mark me out as what?). Then I sort of remember that I've sort of moved on, and anyway I've places to go and someone to see.

The person I have to see is someone with pretty much the opposite approach to career-building to Jandek. He's the current front runner in the race to become the next governor of Texas, Mr Kinky Friedman.

Kinky Friedman is one of those characters that you have no need to invent because he's busy doing the job for you. Whether as a singer or a crime novelist or an essayist or a politician, his primary drive is towards personal myth-making.

I first heard the name Kinky Friedman some time back in the mid '70s when I was in school and given to reading all three music papers – *Sounds*, *New Musical Express* and *Melody Maker* – from cover to cover every week (no, I didn't have a life). Now and again there would be a mention of Kinky Friedman and his band the Texas Jewboys, particularly when Kinky supported Bob Dylan on his Rolling Thunder Revue. None of the coverage, however, seemed to go much beyond the novelty angle: Jewish guy in cowboy hat sings country songs with funny titles. Then there would be a list of the funny titles: 'Asshole From El Paso', 'Get Your Biscuits In The Oven (And Your Buns In The Bed)', 'They Ain't Making Jews Like Jesus', etc. etc. And that would be it.

To be honest, not being much interested in country music as a teenager, and never being that fussed on comedy songs, I didn't think much about him. I certainly never knowingly actually heard any of his songs. Then, some time in the late '80s, I picked up a crime novel by this same Kinky Friedman (boy, it shows you how useful it is to have a wacky first name – if he'd stayed with Richard Friedman, would anyone have remembered him?). The novel featured a private eye, also called Kinky Friedman, and a sometime Jewish country singer. Actually he wasn't so much a private eye as a guy who bumbled around Greenwich Village spouting one-liners and occasionally stumbling over a clue. It was a nice idea, I thought, but I didn't feel it was all that well executed, and I suppose I half expected his literary career to pass by as quickly as his musical career.

But the books kept on coming. They were picked up by a British publisher, who put them out in a series of omnibus editions that did pretty well, especially when Kinky started to come over to the UK to publicise them. I saw him at some crime fiction festival or other when he turned up with a woman he introduced as a former Miss Texas – something he wasn't about to let anyone go unaware of – and he ran through a crowd-pleasing routine, happily playing up to a very British stereotype of what a Jewish cowboy ought to be like. Still didn't do much for me.

A couple of years later, though, I was asked to interview Kinky onstage at a London arts centre. For reasons not unconnected with needing the money I said yes and, in the interests of not coming over as a complete idiot, I read the book he was currently promoting. This was called *Armadillos and Old Lace* and it was set in and around something called the Echo Hill Ranch in Texas, where Kinky appeared to have grown up, and I liked it a whole lot better than *Greenwich Killing Time*, partly because I was a deal more curious about the Texas hill country than Greenwich Village.

So I interviewed Kinky onstage, and had a few beers with him before and after and found that once you got past the schtick, here was an interesting and likeable feller. Turned out he did indeed grow up on the Echo Hill Ranch. It was and is a summer camp for, mostly, Jewish kids, and it was run by his parents, who were both educationists. Kinky clearly loved it there, so much so, in fact, that he had recently gone back to live there. Afterwards I went back to the earlier books and enjoyed them more, stopped worrying about the sketchiness of the plots and started to notice the grace notes of sadness and even wisdom lurking underneath the barrage of one-liners and intermittent PC-bating childishness.

A year or two later, when I wrote my first book set in Cardiff, *Five Pubs, Two Bars and a Nightclub*, and the American publisher asked me who to send it to for quotes, I gave her a list of names of people I'd met over the years, and put Kinky's name down there as a bit of an afterthought, and was considerably surprised when the first person to respond was Kinky himself, with a very generous quote. Inevitably my opinion went up a notch, and then a further notch when he did the same for my next book.

So enthused was I, in fact, that next time he came to Britain on a reading tour I made the trip over to Bristol to introduce myself. This was a little harder than I anticipated. Meeting Kinky is a bit like meeting minor cigar-smoking royalty. It takes some while to communicate that you are anything other than a regular eager supplicant wanting a quick handshake or photo opportunity.

'Hi,' you say, 'I'm John Williams.'

'John, great to meet you,' he says, and shakes your hand and delivers a one-liner. For a moment you think he knows who you are and that's why he's said it was great to meet you, but then, as he starts to look perplexed by the fact you are still standing in front on him, and starts swivelling his eyes to look for more flesh to press, you jump in with a little more info. 'From Cardiff, Wales. You read my book.'

'Cardiff, Wales, that's great,' he says, resolved to humour you a little longer. 'I knew a guy from Wales once, name of Sperm – Sperm Wales!' Or something like that. When you don't just chuckle and move along this time, he starts to look positively exasperated. He's given you two one-liners, for Christ's sake, what more do you want? Blood?

So dispensing with dignity you opt for shouting, enunciating each word extra clearly. 'I wrote a book called *Five Pubs, Two Bars and a Nightclub* and another one called *Cardiff Dead*. You gave quotes for both of them. My name is John Williams.'

Finally the message come through. 'Hey,' he says again, 'great to meet you,' and shakes my hand again then introduces me to his sidekick, Little Jewford, a friend since childhood and a former Texas Jewboy.

I still feel like I'm basically in the way, so I slope off to the bar before much longer, feeling like a bit of an idiot. Onstage, though, Kinky spends a couple of minutes telling the audience that I am among them and that they should surely check out my books. Which is nice of him. The show was good, too. Kinky mixed up readings from his books with songs from the Texas Jewboy years. This was the first time I'd heard any of them and it turned out that for each silly piece of cod chauvinism like 'Get Your Biscuits In the Oven' there's a thoughtful, socially aware ballad like 'Sold American'. And it strikes me that Kinky's blankness before the show is most likely a simple case of nerves. It's easy to assume that a guy all dressed up and ready with the one-liners the way Kinky is must be a confident individual. But thinking about it, it seems just as plausible that the reverse should be true.

Anyway, that's my history with Kinky Friedman. So when I heard about his decision to run for governor of Texas, I figured that I could hardly come to Austin and not see the Kinkster's election machine in action.

By way of preparation for the trip I read Kinky's latest book, a slim guide to Austin. Actually it's not so much slim as downright lazy, as if Kinky asked the publishers how short a freewheeling travel guide could be, and then halved it. Much of it is taken up with thoroughly anodyne lists of bars and restaurants, but just now and again, in the chapter on local history for one, and the chapter on local musicians for two, you feel Kinky getting interested despite himself.

There's a great story about promoting Billy Joe Shaver at a benefit concert. At the end of Billy Joe's set, he's just saying there's one more special person he has to thank. Kinky senses that this is him, about to receive props for being the organiser of the event, so he strides towards the front of the stage, ready to jump up and guest on the encore. Instead Billie Joe completes his sentence and announced that that special person is '...Jesus Christ'. Leaving Kinky looking ever so slightly foolish.

And as ever with the Kinkster there's a hit of sadness always lurking under the one-liners; often, in fact, lurking within them. Take this observation on his suitability as a candidate for political office. 'I can work a room better than anyone...When I meet a potential voter, I'm good for precisely three minutes of superficial charm. If I stay for five minutes, I can almost see the pity in the person's eyes.' It's a quote I'll be reminded of time and again in the course of the day, never more so than at its start.

I catch up with Kinky at the Lee Mannix Centre for Canine Behaviour, in the south-western outskirts of Austin. It's a dog training centre having an open day. There's a handful of stalls and a fair few people wandering about with their dogs. There's a tombola, lemonade and lots of small children. There is also a man in a black leather jacket and a Stetson looking uncomfortably hot in the baking sun.

'Hi,' I say, 'I'm John Williams.'

'Great to meet you, John.'

Yeah,' I say, 'Kinky, I'm John Williams from Cardiff, Wales.'

'Wales, that's a beautiful country. I had a friend called Wales once...'

'KINKY, it's John Williams. You've read my books, you've given quotes for them. We've met before. Someone should have told you I was going to be here.'

'John, OK, right,' he says, and I can see him making the effort to retrieve my data from the memory banks. Then I can see him wondering whether or not to keep going with the Kinky schtick and deciding he really can't be bothered, which, I have to say, is a considerable relief.

'Goddammit,' he says then, 'it's too damn hot.'

Then Little Jewford materialises and says hello, complains about the heat as well, and suggests the Kinkster does what he has to do, and we get the hell out of there. Kinky clearly thinks this is a solid plan. So he heads over to the table where they'll be giving out the prizes to the best-trained dogs later on.

Little Jewford finds the microphone and introduces Kinky. Kinky thanks Jewford ('He's a Jew and he drives a Ford' he says, as he does every time he introduces Jewford, real name Jeff Shelby, to anyone) and then he makes a short speech. The jokes fall flat and the little girls clearly have no idea who he is but he gets through it and at the end there is a round of applause and a few people come up to wish him luck and then Jewford suggests we all head back into Austin as Kinky has a TV interview to record.

Sitting in the lobby of the local Fox affiliate TV station, Kinky looks utterly exhausted. He and Jewford have been campaigning across the state for the last week and he just wants to get home and put his feet up. But once he's in the studio with the lights on, and a perky young interviewer asking him questions, he brightens up and comes out with fluent funny answers to all the questions and, for the first time, it strikes me that this candidacy is both serious and actually in with an outside chance of succeeding. This becomes particularly clear when the interviewer brings up the subject of education. Kinky points out that Texas, the richest state in the Union, is currently fiftieth out of fifty states in education, and you can see that he, the son of educators, is genuinely appalled by this state of affairs.

Once the interview has wrapped and a remarkable number of Fox employees have come up to give Kinky their support, we head out to the north-west Austin house where Kinky's campaign is based.

It's an unremarkable place in a newish suburban development, and when we head inside it's very hard to tell what's going on here. There's a living room full of middle-aged guys watching a ball game. There's an office where Kinky stashes his stuff and there's a guy painting the front room green. There's also a guy called Goat, who looks a bit like a clean-shaven Willie Nelson, wandering about. Jewford, as ever, takes charge of the situation.

Let's go get some food, he suggests. Kinky agrees, asks me whether I'd like to get some Texas bar-b-q. Fine by me, I say, and we head off down the street to a Texas bar-b-q pit, i.e. a basic barn of a place that serves assorted barbecued meats, a bit of corn and coleslaw and, uh, that's about it. Kinky orders for everyone and before long we've all got hunks of charred flesh in front of us, and very good it is too. There's no alcohol on offer, so the feller called Goat has headed over the road and brought back some beers. Life is sweet.

Goat's full name turns out to be the Reverend Goat Carson.

Kinky explains that he's a street preacher from New Orleans and 'my own personal evacuee. Some people think because they've adopted a large number of families they're doing more than I am. But this is an intense evacuee relationship and may last the rest of our lives so…there's a commitment on my part'.

Goat cracks up at this and elaborates a little. Turns out he's a Native American who's been around the music business for years, working with the Neville Brothers among others, before getting into the street preaching thing. And he has indeed been evacuated. He's angered and depressed by the aftermath of Katrina. As far as he can see there's no way his house, or even his neighbourhood, will survive. He's fully expecting it to be torn down and rebuilt as a theme-park New Orleans, courtesy of Halliburton. Katrina, as far as he's concerned, has been allowed to carry out a job of slum clearance and open the city up to development profiteering.

That's the conspiracy theory surrounding Katrina's aftermath, and quite a mild version of it too. Several people I spoke to while travelling volunteered the theory that the second levee breach, the one that led to black New Orleans being flooded, was caused deliberately. Thus, the government blew up the levee to relieve the possibility of white areas being badly flooded, and to move the black people out.

Anyway, whether or not one buys the conspiracy theories, what everyone agrees on is the incompetence that has marked the clean-up operation. This evident disorganisation does, if nothing else, play to Kinky's campaign. His slogan 'How Hard Can It Be?' is finding a lot of approval, as the people of Texas watch their neighbours' lives being destroyed by the incompetence of the authorities. How hard indeed to do better then that?

It's a theme Kinky develops when we head back to the house to do the interview. Kinky installs himself in the office and switches into homespun politician mode. He's actually very impressive. This whole Kinky for Governor thing may have started as a joke, but it's clearly not one any longer. Just as in the television interview he comes over as passionate about both education and the environment. And while his dependence on rehearsed one-liners can be a little wearing in the course of a serious literary type interview, it's par for the course for an aspiring politician. Indeed, after a while, I start to suspect that, rather than politics being a sidetrack for this writer/musician, it's really the other way round; writing and music have been lengthy sidetracks for this born politician.

Kinky comes close to acknowledging as much when he explains how the project began: 'Probably started in Ireland in this little fuckin' town that Jewford knows the name of. A guy came up and said, "You know, Kinky, you're not a musician, you're a politician." Because the intervals between the songs were stronger than the songs themselves. At least, I assume that's what he meant. And he wasn't quite right. I'm not a politician and nor do I wish to be one when I grow up. But I do think what Texas needs right now is to get rid of the politicians we do have and replace them. with musicians. That's my idea...' He pauses then hits me with the punch line. 'Unfortunately I'm not a very good musician either.'

Kinky simply can't resist the lure of the one-liner and in the era of sound-bite politics why should he? The interview is littered with them. Apologies to those of you who may have come across some of these several times before.

On his leather jacket: 'It was given to me by my old friend Waylon Jennings slightly more than thirty years ago in Colorado. One night I told Waylon I liked his vest and he took it off and said take it, it's yours. And that's what I'm telling the people of Texas about our campaign – take it, it's yours.'

On the day he declared his candidacy: 'February third in front of the Alamo, I was half serious, half not. I told people

I was running for governor because I needed the closet space. Which was not true as I only have two outfits.' (This last, by the way, does not appear to be a joke; in fact most people suspect it's an exaggeration. Oh God, I'm doing it now.)

On the current Texas governor, Rick Parry: 'He goes to church a lot, which is either political or religious but not spiritual.'

On where he grew up: 'Born in Chicago, lived there about six months, couldn't find work, moved to Texas where I haven't worked since.' Boom, boom.

On his previous venture into public life: 'Kerrville, Texas, is where I ran for Justice of the Peace in 1986, and my fellow Kerrverts returned me to the private sector.'

On the oil question: 'We're running out of dinosaur wine. We've got to stop the Saudis from playing the jukebox and the rest of us dancing to the tune.' (His policy, by the way, is summed up like this: 'As regards oil I've suggested the Trust for Texas Heroes which is a one per cent surcharge on oil and natural gas which we estimate would bring in 1.5 to 2 billion dollars a year to be spent exclusively on raising the salaries of teachers, cops and fire-fighters. And I'm also recommending the state government get behind biodiesel and help Willie Nelson and myself sell the state biodiesel. Willie's bus ruins on a hundred per cent vegetable oil.')

On fiscal policy: 'I'm not an economist, I follow my father's line. His accountant once asked him what his financial goals were. My father said his financial goal was for his last cheque to bounce.'

On open government: 'I want to be the first governor with a listed phone number which you can call several hours a day.'

On moral teaching: 'You won't find another candidate who supports both prayer in school and gay marriage.'

On the death penalty (a big issue in the state that executes more people, by far, than any other): 'I'm not anti-death-penalty, but I'm damn sure against the wrong guy getting executed.'

And so on. After a while Kinky seems satisfied that he's got the election message over and we move on to talking about his career to date.

He offers a little more detail on his childhood: 'I lived in Austin, Houston, and the hill country, Kerrville. My dad was a professor of educational psychology at the University of Texas. My mother was the first speech therapist in the Houston school district. They started a camp for boys and girls, the Echo Hill Ranch, where I spent many summers.'

So what was it like being a Jew in Texas at that time? Did he experience any prejudice? 'No, not at all, most people were busy picking on the Mexicans. Jews had an opportunity to pass if they wanted to. But a Jew should be an outsider, that's one of the nicest things about being a Jew, to be on the outside looking in. That's a good vantage point. Like Lieutenant Columbo.'

The Echo Hill camp has a strong Jewish cultural identity, but also a distinctly Texan one. It's a combination Kinky has no problem with. His affection for Texan culture, while sometimes self-parodic, is plainly rooted in deep affection. Nowhere more so than in his fondness for that iconic Texan figure, the cowboy: 'I want to defend the name of the cowboy. People use it to mean a bully. The cowboy's never been a bully. Anne Frank had pictures of American cowboy stars pinned up on the wall in her secret annexe.'

But didn't the Texas Jewboys cater to liberal anti-Texan prejudice by parodying cowboy culture? Not in Kinky's view: 'No, we didn't. I wasn't parodying anything. I'm the bastard child of two cultures. I'm a cowboy and a Jew. It's absurd to be both those things but that's the way it is. I see them as endangered species these days because cowboys and Jews – real cowboys and Jews – care about everybody in the world.'

Rather, Kinky sees his vision of the cowboy as a liberal icon as one that is increasingly vindicated: 'Texas has been Austinised. Austin and the Kerrville folk festival used to be my power bases, all I had; today you can go to the most redneck part of Texas and they're voting for Kinky.'

Kinky himself left Austin in the mid '70s. The Texas Jewboys looked like making it big for a while, touring with Bob Dylan and all. That opportunity disappeared in a cloud of cocaine, and by the late '70s Kinky had moved to New York, where he embarked on a seven-year residency at the Lone Star Café. It's these years that he draws on for most of his fiction. They saw him running around with the hard-living crowd that people his books, including the writers Larry Ratso Sloman and Bill McGovern. It was also a time that nearly killed him: 'I'm very lucky to have survived New York. My friend Tom Baker had died, a lot of people were dropping like flies, kind of a life-in-the-fast-lane experience and I'd burned out on New York anyway. I came to Texas to recover and it did heal me.'

His return to Texas coincided with his mother being gravely ill. She died of cancer in 1985. And Kinky moved back into the family ranch, helping his father Tom, brother Roger and sister Marcie to run it in the summertime, and living on his own there – give or take a small menagerie – through the rest of the year.

It was a time that brought him back into the family, and family is clearly enormously important to Kinky. The legacy of his father Tom, 'Uncle Tom' to generations of camp-goers, who died in 2002, overshadows everything Kinky does. 'He died three years ago but he's still my special consultant on these matters,' he says of his decision to run for office.

Just before Tom Friedman died, Kinky wrote movingly about him, and in particular about his career as a Second World War Two flying hero, in an essay called 'The Navigator', written for *Texas Monthly*. Among the readers moved by it was another war veteran, George Bush Sr. He's not the only Bush to have taken an interest in Kinky's career, though, which may explain why one easy target he's reluctant to take pot shots at is the current pres.

This is most likely because Kinky, perhaps uniquely among contemporary writers, has been invited to the White House by both the last two presidents. Bill Clinton, whose love of crime fiction is well known, invited Kinky to a dinner, and apparently spent much of the evening trying to persuade the head of a film studio that she should film Kinky's novels.

George Bush, however, being a former governor of Texas, has a rather more long-standing claim on the Kinkster. Or at least his wife does. Before becoming First Lady, Laura Bush was a librarian, and she later helped set up the Texas Book Festival as well as fronting various campaigns to get children reading. She's a long-time Kinky fan and he reciprocates the sentiment vigorously. 'If Laura had married me,' he's quoted as saying, 'I'd be president of the United States, and George would be…I don't know, managing a Wal-Mart in Midland or something.'

The friendship has continued even after the junior Bushes made it to the White House. Kinky has been their guest there, not just for dinner but staying the night and all, and generally being treated as part of the family. He evidently reckons it's churlish to run down someone who's shown you that level of hospitality, and you can see his point.

And it may be that having had such unusual access to the corridors of power helped to persuade Kinky to go for it himself. That and the death of his father, which, I can't help suspecting, may in some way have been a liberation. He's no longer under the shadow of the universally loved war hero, Uncle Tom Friedman.

As we wind up the interview Kinky tells me, in an unusually quiet and serious tone, that 'I think me being elected would be great for the people of Texas and great for the office of the governorship, and it would be great for the Kinkster.'

Then, as if afraid that he's revealed a little too much, he adds,

'I know that if I lose I'm going to retire in a petulant snit to a goat farm for the rest of my life and not speak to anybody.'

After the interview we head on out for the day's final campaigning opportunity. It's at another pet-centred event. Pet by Pet West is being held at a bar called Opal Divine's, and they've invited the Kinkster along.

From the start it's obvious that this isn't going to work too well. What people there are are drinking in the bar. There's a band playing, to general indifference, and barbecues going, to rather more enthusiasm. Kinky orders a Guinness, does his best to press the flesh, and then gets buttonholed by a journalist from Oregon, who proceeds to grill him in minute detail about his policies. Kinky does his best, but after half an hour or so he just snaps, tells the writer he needs to go outside and smoke a cigar.

I find him outside a little while later, standing on his own and clearly hoping to be left that way. I know that feeling, so I join him in not saying anything for a bit and then he starts to unwind a little and he tells me about the time he was in South Africa, where his books are rather bizarrely popular, and he heard something Nelson Mandela said to his daughter, explaining that the reason he's never home is because there's millions of little girls all over South Africa he has to look out for.

'I was very touched by that and as someone who's not married, never been married, married to Texas, no kids of my own, I think that the politicians, with respect, have not been taking care of the kids. I now feel that every kid is my kid and I will look after them.'

And I think I believe him. There's something curiously childlike about the Kinkster. It makes you feel oddly protective of him. I suspect that's how Little Jewford feels as just then he appears and tells Kinky not to worry, they'll be heading off any minute. And that's where I leave him, a tired sixtysomething Jewish cowboy with an ancient leather jacket and a good heart.

10 West Plains, Missouri: Ozark Mountain daredevil

MOST PLACES I'VE been in the States I know a fair few people who've been there too. It's easy enough, even in Wales, to find people who've spent time in Miami or Los Angeles or Chicago. Even with the more out-of-the-way places, like Louisiana's cajun country, I know one or two Brits, and plenty of Americans, who've been there.

The Ozarks are a different matter. No one goes there from Britain, and the only Americans I know who've been there are working musicians, who will grudgingly admit to having passed through, but clearly don't want to dwell on it.

Inasmuch as the Ozarks have any public profile or place in the national myth, it's as a *Deliverance*-style backwoods place, full of illiterate rednecks fishing and drinking moonshine and intermarrying. The simple fact is that the Ozark Mountains are a bit of America that the world at large has decided to pass by, a part yet to be Starbucked.

I flew into St Louis, gateway airport to the Ozarks, on a Sunday afternoon. The flight from Austin via Houston was unremarkable apart from providing the most egregious example yet of a disturbing new trend I've spotted over the past weeks. That trend is the rise of the comedy airline crew. Maybe it's because the new wave of low-cost airlines I've been travelling with feel they need to mark themselves out from the old-school Pan-Am tradition, but wackiness seems to be the order of the day.

No one seems able to give the safety instructions without inserting a joke or two. Today's stewardess, a thirtysomething black woman, decides to take it to the next level and sings the damn thing cabaret style. And when she's done with singing she inserts a line about 'what to do in the eventuality that our flight becomes a cruise'. Which is quite funny, I think, but seems liable to alarm the more nervous passenger.

Anyway, the flight didn't become a cruise and the airport is near deserted on a hot Sunday afternoon, and in short order I pick up a car and head west out of St Louis, following I-44, the freeway that has replaced the old Route 66. Occasional billboards advertise Route 66 museums. Another one, fifty miles or so out of St Louis, and in the middle of nowhere, advertises a sex shop. A mile or so later yet another billboard exhorts drivers to forswear sex shops in favour of the Lord. I'm definitely entering the heartlands now.

The drive flies by for a while as I tune into an AM station that plays a really excellent selection of '60s and '70s country music, all the Loretta Lynn and George Jones and Porter Wagoner you never hear on regular country radio any more.

Reception starts to fade out, however, as I reach Rolla and turn off the freeway to head south into the Ozarks.

The Ozark Mountain region is for the most part surprisingly unmountainous. Things get a bit steeper over the border into Arkansas, but so far it's the Ozark gentle hills which I'm driving through, passing small towns whose every store seems to sell agricultural hardware, trying to find something on the radio that isn't hair metal, and finally landing up in West Plains, Missouri, the small town where the Woodrell family have lived for generations.

I first came here seven or eight years ago. I was on a trip to Branson, Missouri, a peculiar resort town devoted to the music time forgot (Andy Williams has a theatre there, so does Bobby

'Blue Velvet' Vinton and Jim 'Spider and Snakes' Stafford, there's a whole resort devoted to the legacy of Lawrence Welk, etc. etc.) to write a travel piece. It's a bit of a travel-section staple, the story in which a snotty person from London or New York goes to Branson and is horrified by its kitschiness and Bible Belt values. I'm sure that sort of thing is what the commissioning editor was expecting when she gave me the gig. In the end, being a perverse sort of feller, I quite liked it. I even quite liked the Osmonds on Ice (though I was running a fair old fever at the time, so I may have been hallucinating).

Anyway, I had two ulterior motives for taking the gig. One was to go and see the great Merle Haggard being inducted into the Oklahoma Music Hall of Fame, over in Muskogee. The second was to go and visit the guy whose then current novel, *Tomato Red*, had established him, in my mind, as one of the very best writers, in or out of crime fiction, in America.

Back then, West Plains seemed like a place on the verge of closing down. Or at least, as with so many small American towns, in danger of completely losing its downtown. I stayed in a very basic motel called, imaginatively enough, the West Plains Motel, and was entertained to discover that it was on Porter Wagoner Boulevard, named after the town's most famous son. It was on the edge of the downtown area, which was centred around a charming square that looked like the setting for an old-time, folksy small town America movie, except for the fact that most of the shops seemed to be either out of business or going that way fast. There was a classic little lunch counter, the Ozark Café, which looked as if it hadn't been touched since the 1930s, an uninspiring second-hand bookstore and not a great deal else.

Woodrell lived on the south side of town, up the hill in a neighbourhood whose demographic tilted more towards the poor white crystal-meth consumer than the leading American novelist. Dan and his partner and fellow writer, Katie Estill, lived next door to a couple who spent much of their time trying to kill each other after sampling their own home-made crystal-meth, and were wondering whether the upside of living there – having a nice and cheap house surrounded by plenty of greenery – was outweighed by the neighbourhood going-to-hell factor. They took me out for dinner to a place called the Northfork Steakhouse, and were pretty adamant that we should leave well before closing time, or things could get seriously ugly.

Eight years on, things have changed. For starters, as I cruise down Porter Wagoner Boulevard looking for my West Plains home away from home, I find myself passing a shiny new Holiday Inn and an even newer and shinier Super 8 Motel, before arriving at the West Plains Motel. This place has not got any shinier since my last visit. The room may even smell slightly worse than the one in Austin. I can't be bothered to complain, though, as I've been travelling all day.

So I dump my bags, call Daniel Woodrell and head up to the house: turns out they haven't moved after all. On the way I pass through the central square. It's definitely looking shinier: there's even some kid of a wine bar/restaurant there. There's no sign of a Starbucks, though.

Dan Woodrell's place is just as green and charming as before, and when Dan comes out to meet the car he tells me that it's also a lot quieter, as the previous neighbours have moved out.

And it's not only outside that things have improved. Katie has heard this very day that her latest novel has been accepted by St Martin's Press. This is big news. Katie was at the esteemed writing school at Iowa with Dan in the early 1980s – that's where they met – and since then they've both been struggling to make their way as writers. Dan has had plenty of ups and downs but has, at least, been consistently published. Katie, by contrast, didn't get her first book published till 2000, and then by a small, though high-quality, imprint. So, to sell a book to a mainstream publisher, after twenty years of work, is no small deal.

We have a few drinks to celebrate, catch up on the last half dozen or so years, talk a bit about Welsh literature (bizarrely enough, a major current interest of Dan's) and indeed about Wales itself. And then it's ten o'clock and I'm flagging, two aeroplanes and a 200-mile drive having taken their toll, and it's back to the motel where I'm tired enough not to notice the smell till morning, when I decide that I can maybe stretch to the forty bucks a night the Super 8 across the road is charging, and check myself out.

I was planning on stopping for breakfast at the Ozark Café, so I park along the street from it. But when I get up close there's a sign in the window saying it's closed indefinitely. Darn. Across the street, though, where the not-very-good second-hand bookstore used to be, there's a place called Java Jabez, which looks to be attempting to bring a bit of Seattle's caffeine sophistication to the Ozarks.

This may be a little over-adventurous, as it's completely empty when I walk in. I suspect I can see why when I sit down, scan the menu and find such unpromising attempts at sophistication as eggs with a special sauce, the special sauce in question featuring both habanero peppers and raspberries. Dear God, what happened to you, middle America?

A very indifferent plate of waffles and bacon later, I'm back out on the street and heading round to Dan's, where he's ready and waiting to take me on a tour of his fictional world.

We start off by driving round Dan's own neighbourhood. He points out the run-down little houses where the characters from *Tomato Red* lived, the cemetery in which the characters from *The Death of Sweet Mister* lived, and so on. As we drive Dan talks about his own family, which had been here for generations, and the ancient feuds that are a feature of small-town life. This is a poor town, the average income is well below the national average, but it's clearly a well-ordered and sedate one. There are plenty of churches and very few bars. Indeed, for years the town was dry, and I'd been struck by the absolute lack of anywhere to get a drink when I'd driven back to the motel the night before. Even the Northfork Steakhouse, an infamous trouble spot when I'd been here last, has now closed down.

It's also a very white town. I ask Dan whether it was always that way, and he says not exactly, and points in the general direction of an area that used to be called, with exquisite racial sensitivity, 'Nigger Hill'. There had been a black community living there since Civil War times, tolerated, though most certainly not integrated. Dan's father, he tells me, was the only paper boy prepared to deliver to Nigger Hill. Then came the civil rights era and the spectre of compulsory integration.

This was something the white people of West Plains were never going to stand for. They were not prepared to share their lunch counters with black people or see their kids going to school with black kids. The might of the Supreme Court was ranged against them, however, so they needed to come up with a solution.

They decided Nigger Hill should be modernised, as befits a new era, and while the modernisation was taking place, why naturally all the black people would have to move somewhere else, to St Louis or Memphis ideally. 'Basically,' Dan says, 'they railroaded them out of town.' And those that stayed tended to meet darker fates yet.

This is not a complete surprise if you've read Woodrell's work. While his love of his home town is clear, so too is his awareness of the darkness and intolerance of small-town life, never more vividly than in the climax to *Tomato Red*. Woodrell's Ozarks are not a bolthole from the outside world, they're a microcosm of its hates and fears.

Next, we head out of town a few miles, down ever smaller country roads, till we're motoring through a valley lined with down-at-heel houses, mostly spaced well apart but occasionally clustering together. There's an air of the gypsy camp about the place. It's called Collinsville, Dan tells me, and it's the inspiration for the place where his new novel, *Winter's Bone*, is set.

Pretty much everyone who lives in Collinsville; a place you'd be hard pressed to find on any map, is part of the Collins clan. And it's been that way for generations. The origins of the Collinses are unclear. Dan offers the theory that they may originally be mixed race, like the Melungeons of Appalachia (a whole other story and one well worth Googling), but he wouldn't advise telling them that.

The Collinses are the model for the Dolly clan who first appeared in *Give Us a Kiss* and move to centre stage in *Winter's Bone*. They're a lawless bunch, or at least, the laws they answer to are not those of the land. Driving through on the one road in or out we're attracting our share of curious looks, even on a benign late summer morning. And before long Woodrell hits the gas and moves us along. He's uneasy with the notion of showing people around the deprivation he uses in his work. There's something uncomfortably exploitative about it. I know this myself from taking people around the Cardiff housing estate much of my work is set in. It makes me wonder whether I have any right to represent these people's lives, given that I don't actually live among them – no matter that, like Dan, I live pretty close by, in a neighbourhood that is itself hardly posh.

The answer, I suppose, has to be in the writing itself. Whether it does justice to the lives of the people concerned. And Dan's most certainly does. *Winter's Bone* is a wonderful book, as beautiful and harsh and as indelibly of its people as an Appalachian folk song.

And it's not all deprivation here either: among the run-down shacks and trailers there's the occasional smart house belonging to one of the Collins success stories. What strikes me most, though, is that with a lot of writers, crime writers in particular, the places they write about are obviously dramatic – inner city ghettos, border crossings, etc. – and their work does a more or less good job in representing them, but tends not to surpass the reality. With Dan Woodrell it's the other way round. Collinsville is apparently mundane; it's only in his fiction that it becomes mythical, elemental.

All in all it's too nice a day to be dwelling on deprivation anyway, so Dan decides to show me some of the places he loves. We head farther out into the countryside, follow tracks down to a river. He points out a patch of land he and Katie had nearly bought, thinking they wanted to really get away from it all. Now he's not so sure whether that's the right thing to do.

Seeing the river has given Dan an idea, so we carry on driving till we come to a place called Dawt Mill, where the river is dammed up to provide a swimming hole, and he suggests we jump in. Which seems like a good idea. After all, as Doyle Redmond, the narrator of *Give Us a Kiss*, says, 'every flow of water has a stone lining in the Ozarks and you never know when you'll have the urge to dive in someplace'. The water is every bit as cold as you expect river water to be, but the sun is hot and the setting as tranquil as all get-out.

By the time we've dried off and got back on the road it's time for something to eat. The Ozarks aren't exactly over-burdened with quality dining options – looking at a list of restaurants in West Plain is like reviewing a roll-call of America's family-friendly chain restaurants – so after a moment's consideration Dan decides to head for somewhere called TJ's Hickory House.

Along the way we stop off at a roadside graveyard with a significant Woodrell population, before pulling up outside TJ's. It's a pretty standard roadhouse: check tablecloths, domestic beer and burgers. But the waitress is friendly, and the dark and cool are welcome after the heat outside, and it's a good space to get to talking about Dan's career to date, starting with his upbringing.

'I was born here in West Plains,' he tells me. 'Well, the nearest hospital was Springfield, so that's actually where I was born. We lived here till I was one. Then my dad, like so many others round here, needed to get a job, so we moved to the St Louis area. I lived in St Charles till I was fifteen. It's been swallowed by the metropolis since then, but at the time it had its own distinctive character. The area that's all casinos now is where I learned to swim, in the Missouri river sloughs. Hundreds of bums lived in the thickets near there, they had a bum village, rigged up ceilings in the trees and so on. It was a French town originally, you can still see that in the main street. It was a blue-collar town, it had a reputation for being kind of handy, there were quite a few fistfights, a little rougher than some places. I know my mother had trouble with it, compared to here.

'My mom was mostly at home. When I was about five she started working in the hospital as a receptionist. My dad sold metal and went to night school at Washington University. Then, when he graduated, he suddenly became an executive and transferred us to Kansas City, where we had a moment of modest prosperity. Then it was over. He got into a political thing with his boss and he lost, lost his job as well. He was at an age when it wasn't easy to catch back on. He was bitter and he drank. And he never did recover.'

The move to Kansas City, then, full of promise though it had been at first, was not a happy one: 'I lived in Kansas City for two years and I hated it. So much so that I left high school and joined the Marines the week I turned seventeen. I said, I'll go to

Vietnam before I spend another week in the fucking suburb. By then I'd been in a little trouble, so my mom and dad said maybe it's for the best. And it's a kind of family tradition: my dad and his brother had the same general trajectory of life.'

But the Marines too failed to quell the young Woodrell's ornery spirit: 'I liked my fellow marines. In the main they were a rough-and-tumble but democratic bunch. I didn't like pointless orders. They'd do things like march you into a wall to show your fidelity and obedience. I sort of liked it at first but you get tired of it pretty quick. Then I got into a little trouble again. I was on the island of Guam working guard duty in the jungle. The last Japanese guy from World War Two was still running loose out there. He was discovered after I came home. He said there had been others but he hadn't seen them in a long time! Anyway, after eighteen months I got into some drug trouble. By then I'd turned eighteen and a lot of guys I knew were very salty guys who'd been in Vietnam. They were older, faster, more sophisticated in their vices than I could have hoped to have been at that age, at least without their guidance. But with their guidance I was rapidly in over my head on the recreational drug side of things.

'The authorities asked me if I'd like to be rehabilitated. I said OK. They said are you going to mess with this drug or that drug? I said, I'm not interested in those particularly. Then they said, "What about pot?" I said "I ain't stopping pot. That would be crazy." So they discharged me. Pronounced anti-social tendencies. I thought at the height of Vietnam to be labelled anti-social by the Marine Corps was kind of interesting.'

And, as with many veterans, it took Woodrell a while to settle down in civilian life: 'I turned nineteen shortly after I got out. Not many jobs around. When I came home to Kansas City everybody I knew was using heroin, which they hadn't been when I left. I said, I'm going to the college farthest from here that I can still get state tuition under the GI Bill, and that was Fort Hay, Kansas state about three hundred miles west. So I was out there for almost three years, but I wasn't serious about it. I went off on extended hitch-hiking tours a couple of times, missed all the finals. I was walking across the campus one time when a van pulled up with a bunch of people I knew. They said, "Where you going?" I said, "To take my finals." They said, "Well, we're going to Colorado and we've got a brick of Lebanese hash." And boom. Poor impulse control.'

Gradually, though, Woodrell started to settle down. He returned to Kansas City and went back to college, studying literature. While he was there he wrote some short stories: 'I won a competition with the first one I ever wrote. Which gave me an unnatural notion of how easy this was going to be. The next year I won a bigger competition and the same the next year and I thought I was on to something. I knew what I wanted to do now, though it still seemed ridiculous.'

Why ridiculous? Mostly because Woodrell had not grown up around literary culture: 'I had only by accident read what you'd call serious literature before I went to KU. My mother pushed me on Twain so I read Twain all my life. I stumbled on Nelson Algren by accident. His stuff was over my head but I liked it. So Algren and Twain were the first two writers that really resonated for me. It was only at KU that I read Hemingway and the rest.'

Convinced that he'd found a vocation, Woodrell applied to the Creative Writing School at Iowa, perhaps the most prestigious in the USA. Woodrell was accepted but he's less than convinced it deserves its exalted reputation: 'I really enjoyed most of my fellow students and I met Katie there. But I didn't think most of the teachers amounted to much as teachers, and I didn't like the administration at all. I was asked to leave at one point. I didn't come away with any letters of recommendation and I've never been invited back, unlike almost everyone else

I know. But I did get my master's. And what was crucial there was there were students from a lot of elite schools there, and you got to measure yourself against them. So if you had any provincial doubts about whether you could compete with them head on, well, I found that you could. But you weren't going to win a decision, it had to be a knockout or you'd lose. So that motivated me ever since.'

Dan and Katie graduated in 1983. Dan had written a short story called 'Woe to Live On' while he was at Iowa, set during the Civil War in Missouri and telling the story of Quantrill's Raiders. He knew it was a story he wanted to turn into a novel. But at that time he didn't feel quite ready to write it. Instead he embarked on a crime novel.

'I wrote *Under the Bright Lights* just to see if I could write a novel. I wasn't expecting to go down that route as a writer per se, but it interested me. I'd always liked Chandler. I liked Elmore Leonard a lot, those early ones. I really used to love William McIlvanney. I just really like the verve and muscle of good crime fiction, the narrative punch of it. Also the point of view, the attitude. The underlying principle of good crime fiction is an insistence on a kind of root democracy. I've always responded to that notion.'

Under the Bright Lights was a dark crime story revolving around the exploits of the Shade family, a rambunctious crew whose members include both criminals and police: 'I had an idea to do with cops and criminals: how they've often known each other since grade school. St Charles was that way. One of the top detectives there came from one of the most notorious criminal families. Once when I was a kid we were shopping and…well, somebody had taken a shot at one of this detective's brothers, while he was engaged in criminal activity, but so what! And there on the steps of the police station, in broad daylight, was the detective who had caught this guy, and he was now hitting him with his pistol. My mom pulled me along and I was going, "How could that happen? They're not supposed to do that." So I had the idea of a cop whose family and class entanglements sometimes made him less of a traditional cop.'

Rather than set the novel in St Charles itself, however, Woodrell took elements of the place and used them as the basis for the wholly fictional Louisiana town of St Bruno: 'St Charles is a river town, a Missouri river town. It was originally French and the north end was known as Frogtown. And I knew about some of the other French towns up and down the Mississippi, so I took all this in and invented my mythical town that sort of floated up and down the Mississippi between New Orleans and Cape Giradeau. It kind of moved if I needed it to move – so I made up my mythical town and had fun with it.'

Having written the novel, Woodrell took a while to find an agent, and the agent took a while to find a publisher. Meanwhile Dan and Katie were struggling to get by: 'It didn't look like the book would sell, to the point that I'd almost forgotten about it,' he recalls. 'And we moved a lot without leaving a forwarding address, to get the bill collectors off our tail. So we did two or three of those moves and managed to lose the agent. He eventually found me in Arkansas, living in the delta. I got a telegram saying, "You need to call me." He'd sold the book months before.'

In fact the agent had negotiated a two-book deal, with Dan due to deliver a sequel, in true detective-novel fashion. Dan, however, hadn't yet grasped the expectations of publishers and was already hard at work turning his short story 'Woe to Live On' into a novel.

Set right here in the Ozarks, *Woe to Live On* is a vivid and deliberately – but never gratuitously – shocking account of the random madness of war. And for all its historical setting it's no less personal a book than his contemporary work: 'All sides of my family were here in the Ozarks at the time of the war. This town was burned down two or three times by both sides. That's how I got interested in the border wars. And, having grown up in the Vietnam era, I wanted to write about why and how Americans go to war. And I came to the conclusion the politics of it aren't worth a damn. For instance, I was researching this black guy who fought for the Confederates, who was friends with a fellow called George Todd. He went to fight with Todd because he was his friend. Which was about the same way I enlisted in the Marines during the Vietnam War.'

It was a major step forward from the thoroughly enjoyable but comparatively lightweight *Under the Bright Lights*. Commercially, though, it struck out at the time, much to Dan's dismay: 'Having published *Under the Bright Lights* first, it never occurred to me you couldn't do a book of short stories next, then a novel then another gangster book. Well, turns out you can't. *Woe to Live On* was very lightly supported when it was published here. The reviews said "Mystery writer writes cowboy book. Woodrell best get back to his hard trade of writing crime novels".'

Beers and burgers finished, it's time to move on out of TJ's Hickory House. We head back to West Plains, stop off at the chi-chi new deli and wine store to buy classy Californian cabernets to go with dinner, and then head back to the house, where Dan puts some James McMurtry on the sound system and we get back to the interview.

Following the commercial failure of *Woe to Live On*, Woodrell did indeed get back to writing crime novels. Starting with the promised sequel to *Under the Bright Lights*, *Muscle for the Wing*.

'It was a two-book deal, but I was in the middle of *Woe to Live On* then and I didn't want to drop it. So I finished *Woe to Live On*, and then I had to write a second Shade novel to fulfil the first contract.'

'I enjoyed writing it,' says Woodrell now, but there's no sign of great lasting enthusiasm for the project and, in truth, it's the most forgettable of his novels. Nor did it bring any great commercial reward. The trouble was, having written two crime novels with the same characters, as far as the publishing world was concerned Woodrell was now a confirmed genre man. And he felt he had no option but to carry on digging himself deeper into the role. So he geared himself up to write a third Shade novel.

'I was broke. We were in Arkansas; no jobs, no prospects, we had sixty-five dollars or something left. I went to a payphone and called my editor and pitched a story. I needed a deal and I needed it Tuesday. And I sold it over the phone, basically. Which did not put me in a very strong negotiating position. But I got something and I wrote *The Ones You Do*. By then I was getting a little farther from the path I wanted to be on but…life's life. And for me it put an end to the trilogy, which really didn't leave room for any more.'

It didn't, to be honest, exactly leave the crime-fiction-buying audience baying for more either. *The Ones You Do* is an odd, rambling, existential kind of a crime story, with absolutely none of the slick plotting or high-concept McGuffins that were starting to spell commercial success for contemporaries like Robert Crais or Michael Connolly. 'People didn't know what to make of it,' says Woodrell now.

When *The Ones You Do* flopped commercially it left Woodrell in a bad place, both financially and mentally: 'I kind of fell into a pit for a few years there. I didn't want to write. All four books had disappeared without a ripple. I just fell into a hole. Leave it kind of vague. I guess some of it was chemical, some of it spiritual. I just didn't want to write for the first time ever. I'd done it for ten years for nothing. It's pretty hard when you're writing like that for peanuts. You kind of have to make your peace with what you see happening to others, with work you didn't even consider very good. We lived in Arkansas, then Cleveland, then here, then we went to San Francisco for a couple of years.'

It was in San Francisco that things began to turn around. Woodrell started a new book, *Give Us a Kiss*, and he began with what he knew. The hero, Doyle Redmond, is a failed novelist who heads back to the Ozarks one step ahead of the bailiffs, and soon gets involved with blood feuds between local drug dealers. It's a bitter, oddly lyrical novel which brings the Ozarks to vivid life.

'I wrote *Give Us a Kiss* on Nob Hill in San Francisco,' Woodrell tells me. 'I'd got far away to a totally different world, and I was out there long enough to see the Ozarks from a different vantage point. *Give Us a Kiss* was fun and high spirited, if a little bitter in places, and it was coming right at you. That was what I needed to bring me back into writing.

'But we were almost down to out last couple of bucks out there. We were going to have to get square jobs, a fate which I just couldn't accept at this stage of life. I've never really had one. I've never worked steadily for anybody, never held a job for more than six months. I did all kinds of things: tar roofing, loading trucks and all that, but nothing I thought I would be stuck with. I didn't want to try and get a teaching gig – even if I was able to.'

But while the novel saw Doyle Redmond trapped in a self-destructive nosedive, ironically enough, it succeeded in rejuvenating its author's career. He found a new agent who loved the book and his long-time publishers, Henry Holt, accepted it gladly, offering a considerably bigger advance than he'd had before. Enough money, in fact, to give Dan and Katie some kind of security – at Ozark property prices if not San Francisco ones: 'It was enough to get this house, so Katie just flew home and I said find us a place with what you got and she was walking around and this house was empty, they'd just hammered in the "For Sale" sign, and we got it for a peanut and we've been here ever since.'

The publishers called *Give Us a Kiss* 'a country noir,' which was petty apt. Annie Proulx, quite out of the blue, gave it a rave of a blurb – '*Woodrell…celebrates blood kin, home country, and hot sex in this rich, funky, head-shakingly original novel. Woodrell is a ladystinger of a writer*'. Which didn't hurt. *Give Us a Kiss* may still have been ignored by the mainstream crime audience, but all of a sudden Woodrell was a cult writer rather than simply an obscure one.

Good though *Give Us a Kiss* was, his next book, *Tomato Red*, was even better; a wonderfully funny and tragic tale of blighted white-trash dreams, a country noir every bit as sharp and twisted as the best of Jim Thompson or Charles Williams. There's none of the self-referential spot-the-author stuff here, just a beautifully wrought tale of the ordinary disasters that befall people who start life on the wrong end of a raw deal. The story of a failed petty criminal called Sammy Barlach, it grips from the very first line – 'You're no angel, you know how this stuff comes to happen' – and never lets go. New in town, Sammy takes a little too much crack with some low lifes out by the trailer park and ends up passing out in the mansion he's just broken into. When he wakes up he's in the company of West Plains' two most dissatisfied citizens, Jason and Jamalee Merridew, the outcast children of the town whore, lifetime residents of the town's worst neigbourhood, the place they call Venus Holler.

Woodrell tells me where the characters began for him: 'Couple of things fed into that,' he says. 'There was a girl whose boyfriend tried to run her down with her own car right out in front of our house. By the time the cops got here he'd run off through the woods. She was all shaky and scared and I was out trying to help her but by the time the police got there she was mad at me for still standing there. She was just a little kid, but she was going, "Why don't you take a fuckin' picture, man?" Well, I thought, what a tough little kid.

'Then there was a woman living in this house down by our garden. She was an ex-hooker, not supposed to be doing it any more, but I noticed a lot of guys going over there. Turned out she was selling crack. And she had a daughter who was about thirteen and she tried to have a little style. At the time, believe it or not, we had the main phone around here; a lot of people would come and use the phone. So this girl would come over and she seemed like a smart, decent kid, considering the circumstances, but I thought it won't be long…And that started me thinking and led to Jamalee and then to *Tomato Red*.'

Now, for many years it's been a truism to say that the great unmentioned gulf in American life is that based on race. But beyond even race, the one real unmentionable is class – America clings hard to its egalitarian dream. And *Tomato Red* is all about class. It's about being born to the pure redneck/hillbilly/white trash/trailer park existence that qualifies you in American life only to appear on the *Jerry Springer Show*.

'There are people so alienated from the mainstream of American culture,' says Woodrell, 'that it's like a parallel universe. They don't expect anything but trouble from the square world. Every time you interact with that world they want to give you a ticket, send you to jail, draft you. It's never good. So they live by a separate value system. I've felt that way myself. When I got to graduate school in Iowa, I didn't get it. People would say things, and where I was from you'd smack them; where they're from you're supposed to come back with a witty rejoinder.'

Sammy Barlach is resigned to his fate and so is Bev the hooker. They've been around some, they know how it goes, which end of the stick you can expect to get. But the nineteen-year-old redhead Jamalee and her beautiful gay seventeen-year-old brother Jason believe there's got to be something more. So Jason works in the hair salon where the girls all swoon over him, while Jamalee reads etiquette books and watches movies to plan their better life together. Now and then they break into rich folks' houses so they can accustom themselves to the better life. That's how they happen to run into Sammy and everything starts to fall apart.

From its farcical beginning to the awful stupid tragedy that is its denouement, this is a flat-out marvellous book. Rooted in the purest '50s noir tradition, this is nevertheless the purest of literary fictions. Like a murder ballad or a prison-yard blues, *Tomato Red* is written in the kind of vernacular poetry you want to read and re-read to learn by heart.

One major difference between *Give Us a Kiss* and *Tomato Red* is that while the former was written from the point of view of the outsider, or rather of the prodigal son returning after a long absence, and allows the place to be seen through the eyes of a writer, *Tomato Red* is much more a view from the inside. For while the main protagonist, Sammy Barlach, comes from out of town, the place he comes from is not much different. It's a world he knows all too well. With the third of his Ozark novels, though, Woodrell went all the way inside.

The Death of Sweet Mister is set entirely within the world of West Plains (or West Table, as Woodrell calls it in his books), and its narrator is a twelve-year-old boy.

'I was actually reluctant to do it,' says Woodrell. 'Kid narrators can be a little cutesy. He wasn't. I started getting a sense of him and his mother. The idea of being inside a personality, a culture or a family that's considered being transgressive is almost comfortable to me, I don't have to make a big leap. For some reason I can put myself in there pretty deeply.'

There's one obvious precedent for all American novels with twelve-year-old boys at their centre – the work of Mark Twain, a novelist whose influence is so big that it's easy to take it for granted: 'Definitely there's an influence of Twain,' agrees Woodrell, 'I forget to even mention it sometimes it seems so blatant to me. Every summer my mother insisted I read more Twain. Some of them, like *Tom Sawyer*, I read every summer. We'd make a little raft and float around on it.'

The childhood depicted in the *Death of Sweet Mister* is a long way less than idyllic. To call the twelve-year-old Shug's relationship with his alcoholic mother dysfunctional wouldn't be the half of it. Again, though, there's this constant tension between the actual beauty of the language and the quotidian darkness of the lives he writes about. A Mark Twain for the Jerry Springer age? Why not.

'To me that book is where I finally became a novelist on the path I wanted to be on. *Tomato Red* opened the door, and *Sweet Mister*, that's my favourite one, along with the one I've just completed. I'm not as rambunctious any more. It's still got crime elements in it, though, so you can embrace it on that level if you want to.'

The new book, imminent as we speak, has been some five years in the writing. It's called *Winter's Bone*: 'It's about a family called the Dollys who are mentioned in *Give Us a Kiss*,' Woodrell tells me. 'They're an extended criminal clan and the main character, Ree, is a sixteen-year-old girl whose father is out on bail. He disappears and he'd put their house up as his bond. She's got two little brothers and a mentally ill mother. She's got to save their house and then she can get out of there. It's about her quest to save her father. But it's not that simple, as she's also got to deal with being a sixteen-year-old girl.'

It's also, as I've mentioned already, somewhat more than good. It's a dense, short book made up of sentence after sentence of remarkable richness, a book that bears the hallmarks of having been crafted expertly over an extended period of time. That Woodrell has been able to spend a goodly length of time writing this book, and the one before it, is not so much because he's suddenly a bestseller, but because, seven or so years back, Woodrell's luck finally turned.

His least successful novel of all, *Woe to Live On*, was picked up by Ang Lee and turned into a film entitled *Ride with the Devil*. It's not, it has to be said, Ang Lee's most highly regarded effort, being notably slow to get going, but Woodrell's understandably not about to bad-mouth it.

'I'll never be unhappy about that experience because it was their payments that allowed me to experiment, to take my work in the way I wanted it to go. They took the wolf away from the door for a good three years. Which was not a position I'd ever been in before. Y'know, they made a movie. I wrote a book. For the most part I'm pretty happy with the movie, a lot of the dialogue comes straight from the book, so you got to see that. Not everyone likes the way the dialogue was utilised, but I did.'

Of course, this being Dan Woodrell's life, all did not go perfectly. The studio seemed reluctant to really get behind the film: 'It never got any kind of chance. Ang Lee continues to speak highly of it. Jeffrey Wright says it was his favourite part ever. I guess it was too confusing for people, the sensibility of it. My main tick with the movie is it starts a little slowly 'cause they put in an opening scene to explain what was happening.'

But, as he points out, hit film or not, it gave him the time to emerge as the writer he always promised to be. I wondered whether his steadily increasing literary standing made him think of getting out of the Ozarks, and moving to somewhere where it would be easier to bask in the warm glow of literary approbation.

'I don't think I need to move,' he says, after a significant pause that suggests he has at least entertained the idea. 'I think there are things about this place I wouldn't know if I didn't live here. But there's also a point at which you're not filling the reservoir with enough other things…It's a pretty limited way of life here. Very removed from the way the rest of the country looks. No literary scene or anything like that, though with Amazon and Netflix…And I do like having my privacy, so…'

He pauses again, then brightens and carries on. 'And I do have a relationship with this area. I don't want to live on the Upper West Side or something. There is something here for me…I'm just one generation from illiteracy; my grandmother was illiterate on one side of the family. Though oddly enough my grandmother on the other side was a bookworm, so go figure. In a way the problem with such regions as this is that everyone who can leave, leaves. It's not that I'm here on a mission to get young people to become writers, but I do think people knowing that there's a guy in town who's had a movie made from his book, and didn't leave, helps. Plus the longer I'm here, the more I can see what could be done with it as a writer.'

There's a pervasive notion in literary circles that for a writer to shun café society and base himself somewhere remote and working class must be a kind of affectation. And it's certainly the case that those writers, myself included, who live away from the literary hot spots tend to suspect that the dice are loaded against us, that metropolitan insiders are scooping all the big deals with their fey tales of medialand life. It's a paranoia that Woodrell freely admits to suffering from in spades. I wondered whether he thought there was a danger in becoming a professional outsider.

Woodrell weighs the question and comes up with this: 'I went through therapy at one point during the dark gap there. And a lot came out about my class resentments and so forth. When I was a little kid I was accelerated, jumped grades, they wanted me to represent the school in spelling bees and all that, but I was also from a certain kind of background that I recognised wasn't an exalted one. The therapist's notion was that I was still this little kid saying, "I can do anything, let me have a shot and I can win."'

And then he suddenly leaves the well-trodden matter of class resentments and the degree to which they're justified, and starts talking about his childhood again. Up to now, when he's spoken about it, it's always been in terms of his bad-boy attitude, but now he reveals a different side.

'I get a lot of my friendships and kinships out of books,' he says, by way of a preamble. 'I've always been that way. I was born sick and I was bed bound quite often. I couldn't eat or hold food down properly till I was operated on when I was eleven or twelve, so I spent a lot of my time reading. I was supposed to die two or three times. My intestines were knotted and they couldn't tell what the ailment was for a long time. I had pneumonia three times. The intestinal problem got so bad that at one point they reckoned they had twenty-four hours before I was going to die. So they actually split me all down my stomach for exploratory surgery and they found my appendix had knotted round the liver, and it was way up where it wasn't supposed to be, and it had corrupted and was rotting into the liver. They had to cut all my stomach muscles to get in there, so it was over a year before I was able to run again. It was good for my reading. I got into Robert Louis Stevenson. Things like that you hear so often with writers.'

And it's perhaps this instinctive understanding of vulnerability that these years bred into the bone, at least as much as his class empathy with the underdog, which makes Daniel Woodrell not just a regional writer or a blue-collar writer or whatever, but one whose subject, like that of all great writers, is simply the human condition.

Epilogue: a nightcap in the Dresden rooms

THE NIGHT BEFORE I flew back to the UK I was in Hollywood, having a few drinks at a place called the Dresden Rooms, with a writer called Terrill Lee Lankford. There was a sort of ironic, sort of not, cabaret band playing requests from the crowd of thirtysomething hipsters, at a volume too loud to make talking viable, and I started wondering how it had been on this journey: how American had changed, how crime writing had changed, how I had changed.

These questions had been thrown up repeatedly during the day. Once I'd realised I was going to have an extra day free in Los Angeles I'd got in touch with Terrill Lankford and he'd offered to show me around. I'd got in touch with him because I'd read and liked his last couple of books, *Earthquake Weather* and *Blonde Lightning*, two smart, dark thrillers set in the movie business, and also because it was easy to get hold of him as he subscribes to the same Internet mailing list I do. The list is called 'rara-avis', and it's devoted to the discussion of hard-boiled crime fiction. It's an interesting lively list with a higher than usual percentage of members who are also published writers. It's a good place – can an e-mail list ever be described as a place? – to discover both new writers and forgotten writers.

It's also symptomatic of how much things have changed. Back in 1989, to get hold of Terrill Lankford I would have had to call his American publisher, who would then have put me in touch with his agent, and a week or so later I would probably have ended up with a phone number. But I wouldn't have done that because I wouldn't have heard of him in the first place, as he's not yet published in Britain.

Instead, I saw Lankford's name crop up on rara-avis, I went on to Amazon and ordered the book. I read it, liked it and was able to e-mail the author. It's much simpler. The Internet has made everything much simpler. Thanks to the Internet everything is available. I discover a new writer, I can get their books from Amazon. If someone recommends a lost '50s noirist, I can get their stuff from abebooks.

On the downside this easiness does seem to lead to a certain devaluation. There is not the excitement I felt when, for example, on a trip to New York in 1988, I went into the Mysterious Bookstore and the guy on the counter recommended I buy a paperback of James Lee Burke's *The Neon Rain*. I took it home, read it, told my friends to check him out, and started to comb secondhand bookstores for the half-dozen books Burke had previously published, enjoying the spirit of the chase.

And it's not just books this applies to. Take the motels I've stayed in. By and large I booked most of them over the Internet before I left. It saves time and I got better rates than I would have done by just turning up. It does, however, rather lessen the surprise.

But then it's a lot harder to be surprised, full stop, at forty-four than it was when I was twenty-seven. I suppose what one hopes is that one's perceptions will make up in depth what they lack in newness. It's certainly what I look for these days, depth over novelty. I'd sooner listen to Mississippi John Hurt or Ralph Stanley any day, ahead of the Strokes or Kanye West or Jack Johnson or Sufjan Stevens or whatever. And if you ask me why, I'd say because these old guys have depth and breadth and they're singing out of life, while these other people are kids who know little of life. But maybe I'm just getting old.

Take the places I've been today with Terrill. We've been hitting the old school Hollywood landmarks; Larry Edmunds's cinema bookstore, Boardner's bar for drinks, Musso and Frank's for dinner. I like them all. The cinema bookstore is a good bookstore and Boardner's is as close to a real bar as you can get in Los Angeles. First time I went there I was with a very strange man called John Gilmore, who'd written a very strange book about the Black Dahlia. At the time it was a perfect '50s dive bar. Since then it's been tarted up a bit, and presumably it's got something of a hipster clientele, given that Ryan Adams goes on about hanging out there a lot, but this afternoon it was dark and quiet and cool. Musso and Frank's is, of course, legendary, like La Coupole or Elaine's. It's the place every Hollywood writer there's even been has hung out. Faulkner, Isherwood, Chandler, etc. etc. And, wisely, they haven't changed a thing since. It's a perfectly preserved American steakhouse from a bygone era. Writers still like it. Terrill comes here with his friend Michael Connolly.

As I say, I like all these places. I'd be tempted to say more about them, though, if I hadn't just checked and confirmed that they've all got websites, which will tell you all the guff about what famous people ate or drank there, and throw in some pictures for good measure. You know the old thing about pictures stealing the soul. Well, I suspect the net does much the same thing to writers.

At the very least it means that we have to work a bit harder. You've got to get up early to find a place that doesn't feature on the World Wide Web. And if it's hard for travel writers it's hard for crime writers too. In my original introduction I talked about the sense of place as being crucial to the writers I liked. But how long can that sense of place survive in a world that's been Gapped and Starbucked into submission?

And crime writing itself? Do I still believe it tells the truth in a way that mainstream literature fails to? Well, yes and no. I suspect what has happened is that I was not alone in feeling that mainstream fiction had become stuck in its ivory tower. Hard-boiled crime fiction has been taken increasingly seriously and its influence has started to be felt on the literary mainstream. The barriers have become blurred. Martin Amis has hailed Elmore Leonard as a master, James Ellroy talks about Don DeLillo as his main man. Daniel Woodrell has imperceptibly moved from being a crime novelist to a literary novelist while still keeping crimes of one sort or another as his subject. Myself, I've tried repeatedly to write crime novels and failed each time, unable to carry through with the essential bargain of a crime and a resolution, ending up in some sort of social realism. As a writer of fiction myself I'm a lot less inclined to lay down the law than when I was a critic.

And it has to be said that a lot of crime fiction, hard-boiled as well as cosy, is formulaic and really tells you very little about the world. More than a few of the crime writers I saw as beacons of hope two decades ago have happily settled into churning out series novels that conform entirely to the laws of diminishing returns.

That said, though, I still love crime fiction. I like the books, I like the world-view and I like the writers. I've enjoyed spending this day with Terrill, who's my age more or less, like me has had another career – film producer for him, journalist for me – has family responsibilities but likes to hang out and have a few drinks now and again. We've shared war stories of the publishing kind, both had ups and downs, both been frankly scared and exhilarated by not knowing what the future holds. There's a camaraderie between crime writers, however successful, or not, that you rarely see in the literary world – if there's a more hierarchical event than the Hay Literary Festival in Britain, I hope never to visit it.

In the end, I suppose what I was looking for then is what I'm looking for now, crime fiction that desires to tell the truth as well as to entertain. And if I'm not always looking for it in America these days – much of the best hard-boiled crime writing in recent years has seemed to me to come from outside the USA – that's perhaps in part a reflection of the extent to which the world is becoming Americanised. And I know people have much to say about the effects of globalisation, and I know that much of it I agree with, but it is also true than America has provided me with much of the culture that most sustains me. It's too easy to assume that the term Americanisation refers to a negative process.

And now the band has finished playing the last request. So here in the Dresden Rooms, a slightly too perfect slice of Americana (check its website to see what I mean), I'll buy one more round and then I'll call it a night.

Postscript to Part one

I WAS LUCKY with the timing of the original *Into the Badlands*, I interviewed a dozen or so writers, most of them more or less of the same generation, and I believe I caught the majority at their creative, if not commercial, peak. Here, very briefly, are updates on the work of those writers profiled in this first half of the book.

Carl Hiaasen

Carl Hiaasen, only three books into his career when I interviewed him, is now the enormously successful author of more than a dozen black-comedy thrillers which have become *sui generis*. No comic thriller writer who emerges now can avoid being compared to Hiaasen. Oddly there has been only one film made of his work. Maybe that's because the film in question was the spectacularly terrible *Striptease*. For a while I felt there was an off-putting tang of misanthropy to Hiaasen's work, a suggestion that the only thing wrong with the world is people, but he seems to have shaken this off with recent books, and while there's a certain amount of formula in his work, taken once in a while these are reliably funny entertainments.

James Lee Burke

James Lee Burke's third Dave Robicheaux novel was about to come out when I interviewed him. Since then he's written twelve more Robicheauxs, four Bill Bob Holland novels set in Texas, and a one-

off Civil War novel. The erstwhile drunk, who'd published half
a dozen books over twenty-five years, has turned into a book-
a-year man and gradually reaped the rewards of his industry.
The Robicheaux books are probably among the half-dozen best-
loved series in the genre. So it's churlish to suggest that fifteen
books is stretching it for one series character. With Burke,
though, the problem isn't that the quality dips, it's just that he's
written the same good book quite a lot of times. The other thing
that has struck me with increasing force over the years is that
these books, while ostensibly set in the present, are really taking
place in the 1950s.

James Ellroy

James Ellroy was well on the way to becoming the most
notorious figure in crime fiction when I interviewed him. He
was halfway through the LA quartet, the books on which his
reputation stands. His next book, *LA Confidential*, the third
part of the quartet, was, of course, filmed, and ensured its
author's commercial viability. The fourth novel, *White Jazz*,
saw Ellroy's style going into maxi-minimalist hyperdrive. Since
then, though, I've found it hard to love his work. The memoir
My Dark Places is, at least, interesting. The first two parts of
whatever he's calling his current series, *American Tabloid* and
The Cold Six Thousand, are, however, to my mind, respectively
boring and unreadable. Sorry.

Gar Anthony Haywood

Gar Anthony Haywood was probably the most obscure writer
at the time of the original book and, sad to say, not much has
changed since. Gar Haywood – despite having written several
more Aaron Gunner novels, two thoroughly charming mysteries
featuring a retired black couple, the Loudermilks, and a couple
of stand-alone thrillers under the name Ray Shannon – remains

relatively little read. This may have something to do with the emergence of Walter Mosley, another black writer writing crime novels set in LA. The fact that they're very, very different sorts of writers probably doesn't make much difference. There's generally only one slot for a black male crime writer at any given time, and Mosley currently has it.

James Crumley

James Crumley was in the latter stages of an epic period of writer's block when I interviewed him. He'd spent years trying to break out of the crime fiction ghetto with a work-in-progress, an epic Texas novel to be called *The Muddy Fork*. This never seemed to come off, so Crumley returned to writing crime novels. Somehow, though – and maybe it's just me – these subsequent books have a slight air of second best about them. The first of them, *The Mexican Tree Duck*, starts well and has a certain bravado. The second, *Bordersnakes*, is less successful; you can feel the writer willing the characters into life but not quite getting them there. The high point of late-period Crumley is probably *The Final Country*, which sees him in elegiac *Long Goodbye* mode.

Elmore Leonard

Elmore Leonard was probably the best known, and certainly the best established, of the authors I talked to in 1989. He'd been writing novels for thirty years, Westerns then crime, and was just coming off an epic fifteen-year hot streak during which almost every one of his annual novels had been a flat-out winner. Since 1989 Leonard has had perhaps his biggest hit with *Get Shorty*, an OK crowd-pleaser. He has had a whole heap of movies made out of his books, among the more notable being *Get Shorty* itself, *Out Of Sight* and *Jackie Brown* (from *Rum Punch*). His influence, meanwhile, has been incalculable, largely thanks to Tarantino's appropriation of Leonard's habit of having bad guys talk about popular culture and food while they go about their business. There's still a new Leonard every year, and if they're not as good as they once were, well, c'mon, the guy's in his eighties. And if there's a finer, more effortless stylist and storyteller than Leonard in the whole of crime fiction, do let me know.

Backtothebadlands.com

The original *Into The Badlands* featured a considerable amount of material that for reasons of space has not been reprinted in this volume. This included substantial interviews with James W. Hall, Tony Hillerman, Joe Gores, Josiah Thompson, Sara Paretsky, Eugene Izzi, George V. Higgins, Nick Tosches, Joseph Koenig and Andrew Vachss. All of these can now be read online at www.backtothebadlands.com, a site designed to complement this book. The site also features additional material (book reviews etc.) on many of the writers featured here, as well as interviews I have done over the years with other crime and noir writers.

Bibliography

A SELECTIVE LIST of works by the authors interviewed (most recent British and American editions)

James Lee Burke
Half of Paradise (Orion/Hyperion)
The Lost Get-back Boogie (Orion/Pocket)
The Convict and Other Stories (Orion/Hyperion)
The Neon Rain (Orion/Pocket)
Heaven's Prisoners (Orion/Pocket)
Black Cherry Blues (Orion/Avon)
Burning Angel (Orion/Hyperion)
Purple Cane Road (Orion/Dell)

James Crumley
One to Count Cadence (Picador/Vintage)
The Wrong Case (Picador/Vintage)
The Last Good Kiss (Picador/Vintage)
Dancing Bear (Picador/Vintage)
The Final Country (HarperCollins/Mysterious Press)

James Ellroy
Brown's Requiem (Arrow/Dark Alley)
Clandestine (Arrow/Dark Alley)
Blood on the Moon (Arrow/Vintage)
Silent Terror (Arrow/Dark Alley)
The Black Dahlia (Arrow/Warner)

The Big Nowhere (Arrow/Warner)
LA Confidential (Arrow/Warner)
White Jazz (Arrow/Vintage)
My Dark Places (Arrow/Vintage)

Gar Anthony Haywood
Fear of the Dark (o.p.)
Not Long For This World (o.p.)
You Can Die Trying (Serpent's Tail)

Elmore Leonard
The Big Bounce (Penguin/HarperTorch)
Swag (Penguin/HarperTorch)
Unknown Man Number 89 (Penguin/HarperTorch)
The Switch (Penguin/HarperTorch)
City Primeval (Penguin/HarperTorch)
Split Images (Penguin/HarperTorch)
Stick (Penguin/HarperTorch)
Glitz (Penguin/HarperTorch)
Freaky Deaky (Penguin/HarperTorch)

Kem Nunn
Tapping the Source (No Exit/Thunder's Mouth)
Unassigned Teritory (o.p.)
Pomona Queen (No Exit/Four Walls, Eight Windows)
The Dogs of Winter (No Exit/Scribner)
Tijuana Straits (No Exit/Scribner)

Daniel Woodrell
Under the Bright Lights (No Exit/Pocket)
Woe to Live On (No Exit/Pocket)
Muscle for the Wing (No Exit/Pocket)
The Ones You Do (No Exit/Pocket)

Give Us a Kiss (No Exit/Pocket)
Tomato Red (No Exit/Plume)
The Death of Sweet Mister (No Exit/Plume)
Winter's Bone (Sceptre/Little, Brown)

Vicki Hendricks
Miami Purity (o.p.)
Iguana Love (Serpent's Tail)
Voluntary Madness (Serpent's Tail)
Sky Blues (Serpent's Tail)
Cruel Poetry (Serpent's Tail)

Kinky Friedman
Greenwich Killing Time (Faber)
Elvis, Jesus and Coca-Cola (Faber/Bantam)
Armadillos and Old Lace (Faber/Bantam)
God Bless John Wayne (Faber/Bantam)
Roadkill (Faber/Ballantine)
Steppin' on a Rainbow (Faber/Pocket)
Meanwhile Back at the Ranch (Faber/Pocket)

George Pelecanos
A Firing Offense (Serpent's Tail)
Nick's Trip (Serpent's Tail)
Shoedog (Serpent's Tail/Warner)
Down by the River Where the Dead Men Go (Serpent's Tail)
The Big Blowdown (Serpent's Tail/St Martin's)
King Suckerman (Serpent's Tail/Dell)
The Sweet Forever (Serpent's Tail/Dell)
Shame the Devil (Orion/Dell)
Right As Rain (Orion/Warner)
Soul Circus (Orion/Warner)
Hard Revolution (Orion/Warner)